BEST STORIES OF O. HENRY

BEST STORIES OF
O. HENRY

SELECTED, AND WITH AN
INTRODUCTION BY
BENNETT CERF
AND
VAN H. CARTMELL

GARDEN CITY BOOKS
GARDEN CITY, NEW YORK

Contents

vi   *Contents*

Introduction

IN THE LATE FALL of 1944 the editor of a great metropolitan newspaper wrote a book about New York. It was a very good book; the reviewers liked it. The highest praise they could give it was to say that here, at last, was another author who knew and loved New York as well as O. Henry. Forty years after the O. Henry stories about "Bagdad on the Subway" first began to delight the reading public they still remain the standard by which all other literature on the subject is judged. The "four million" have become the "eight million," the slang that high lights his dialogue has been superseded by other passing catch phrases, restaurants and hotels that served as his locale were razed a generation ago, but O. Henry remains secure in the hearts of the public as the prose laureate of Manhattan Island.

Among the hundreds of stories O. Henry left behind him are many laid in Central America, and New Orleans, and the rolling plains of Texas. This volume, seeking to present the cream of his writings, includes a goodly representation of them all. The majority of the tales that you will find here, however, center about New York. That is the way the author would have wanted it. His heart belonged to that narrow strip of land that lies between the East River and the Hudson.

O. Henry, it is surely unnecessary to say, is a pseudonym. His real name was William Sydney Porter. He was born in Greensboro, North Carolina, in 1862, went to school there, and worked for five years in his uncle's drugstore. In 1882 he moved on to Texas, where he operated a short-lived hu-

morous weekly called the *Rolling Stone* and contributed a
column to the Houston *Daily Post*. He also served as teller in
an Austin bank, and that proved his temporary undoing. The
bank was mismanaged. There was a shortage of funds. Porter
was indicted.

Friendly biographers have hinted that Porter was innocent,
but his own actions belie that theory. He fled to New Orleans,
and then to Honduras, returning only when he heard that his
wife was desperately ill. Sentenced to five years' imprisonment
at the Ohio Federal Penitentiary, he actually served a little
over three. It was during this dark period in his life that he
developed into an author to be reckoned with. One of his
cellmates gave him the plot for "A Retrieved Reformation"
(reprinted in this volume), which Paul Armstrong later dram-
atized under the title of *Alias Jimmy Valentine*. It was a
smash success—the forerunner of a whole school of "cops-and-
robbers" dramaturgy—but Porter, unfortunately, got little of
the proceeds. It was in the penitentiary too that he met the
guard, Orrin Henry, from whom he borrowed a name.

In 1902 he first laid eyes on New York, and as "O. Henry"
soon began to flood the magazines with his stories. Words—
and plots—came easily to him—too easily perhaps. For eight
years he maintained a prodigious output, goaded continu-
ously by editors who had advanced him varying sums. He left
over six hundred complete stories behind when he died of
tuberculosis at forty-eight. "Pull up the shades so I can see
New York," were his last words. "I don't want to go home
in the dark."

O. Henry's first published book was *Cabbages and Kings*.
It appeared in 1904, and consisted principally of tales of adventure and revolution in Latin America. The stories "Shoes"
and "Ships" (really two parts of a single narrative) reprinted
here are from that volume. His next book, two years later,

really established his literary fame. This was *The Four Million*. It contained not only some of the best of his New York tales, but introduced to the public a relatively new device— the surprise or "twist" ending. To this day writers are striving to surpass him in this type of story, only to prove anew the truth of that old adage of the prize ring: you can't beat a champion at his own game. No fewer than eleven of the thirty-eight stories in this volume come from *The Four Million*.

The Trimmed Lamp, published in 1907, and *The Voice of the City*, a year later, proved even more popular than *The Four Million*. There are nine stories from the former in this collection; four from the latter. There were two O. Henry books in 1909: *Options* and *Roads of Destiny*, and two more in 1910, the year he died: *Whirligigs* and *Strictly Business*. Three other collections of his stories appeared after his death, and then all of them were assembled in one bumper volume that has enjoyed an enormous sale to this very day.

The bulk of O. Henry's written work, truth to tell, does not measure up too well against the exacting standards of the present day. Many of his stories were glib and superficial rather than profound, obviously hurried and cut closely to a pattern that had proven serviceable. His characters, like his plots, tended to repeat themselves, and sustained him only because he was a master at contriving every possible variation of a familiar theme. This volume of selected stories is conclusive evidence, in the editors' opinion, that O. Henry at his best, however, deserves rank with America's greatest masters of the short story. Such tales as "A Municipal Report," "An Unfinished Story," "A Blackjack Bargainer," "A Lickpenny Lover," "The Gift of the Magi," "Mammon and the Archer," and "Two Thanksgiving Day Gentlemen" (by actual count the O. Henry stories most often reprinted in anthologies) are

gems of their kind; mellow, humorous, ironic, ingenious, and
shot through with that eminently salable quality known as
"human interest." It is no accident that five of his seven most
famous stories are laid in the New York he loved so well.

BENNETT CERF and VAN CARTMELL

BEST STORIES OF O. HENRY

The Gift of the Magi

ONE DOLLAR AND EIGHTY-SEVEN CENTS. That was all. And sixty cents of it was in pennies. Pennies saved one and two at a time by bulldozing the grocer and the vegetable man and the butcher until one's cheeks burned with the silent imputation of parsimony that such close dealing implied. Three times Della counted it. One dollar and eighty-seven cents. And the next day would be Christmas.

There was clearly nothing to do but flop down on the shabby little couch and howl. So Della did it. Which instigates the moral reflection that life is made up of sobs, sniffles, and smiles, with sniffles predominating.

While the mistress of the home is gradually subsiding from the first stage to the second, take a look at the home. A furnished flat at $8 per week. It did not exactly beggar description, but it certainly had that word on the lookout for the mendicancy squad.

In the vestibule below was a letter-box into which no letter would go, and an electric button from which no mortal finger could coax a ring. Also appertaining thereunto was a card bearing the name "Mr. James Dillingham Young."

The "Dillingham" had been flung to the breeze during a former period of prosperity when its possessor was being paid $30 per week. Now, when the income was shrunk to $20, the letters of "Dillingham" looked blurred, as though they were thinking seriously of contracting to a modest and unassuming D. But whenever Mr. James Dillingham Young came home and reached his flat above he was called "Jim" and greatly hugged by Mrs. James Dillingham Young, already introduced to you as Della. Which is all very good.

Della finished her cry and attended to her cheeks with the powder rag. She stood by the window and looked out dully at a gray cat walking a gray fence in a gray backyard. Tomorrow would be Christmas Day and she had only $1.87 with which to buy Jim a present. She had been saving every penny she could for months, with this result. Twenty dollars a week doesn't go far. Expenses had been greater than she had calculated. They always are. Only $1.87 to buy a present for Jim. Her Jim. Many a happy hour she had spent planning for something nice for him. Something fine and rare and sterling—something just a little bit near to being worthy of the honor of being owned by Jim.

There was a pier-glass between the windows of the room. Perhaps you have seen a pier-glass in an $8 flat. A very thin and very agile person may, by observing his reflection in a rapid sequence of longitudinal strips, obtain a fairly accurate conception of his looks. Della, being slender, had mastered the art.

Suddenly she whirled from the window and stood before the glass. Her eyes were shining brilliantly, but her face had lost its color within twenty seconds. Rapidly she pulled down her hair and let it fall to its full length.

Now, there were two possessions of the James Dillingham Youngs in which they both took a mighty pride. One was Jim's gold watch that had been his father's and his grandfather's. The other was Della's hair. Had the Queen of Sheba lived in the flat across the airshaft, Della would have let her hair hang out the window some day to dry just to depreciate Her Majesty's jewels and gifts. Had King Solomon been the janitor, with all his treasures piled up in the basement, Jim would have pulled out his watch every time he passed, just to see him pluck at his beard from envy.

So now Della's beautiful hair fell about her rippling and shining like a cascade of brown waters. It reached below her knee and made itself almost a garment for her. And then she did it up again nervously and quickly. Once she faltered for a minute and stood still while a tear or two splashed on the worn red carpet.

On went her old brown jacket; on went her old brown hat. With a whirl of skirts and with the brilliant sparkle still in her eyes, she fluttered out the door and down the stairs to the street.

Where she stopped the sign read: "Mme. Sofronie. Hair Goods of All Kinds." One flight up Della ran, and collected herself, panting. Madame, large, too white, chilly, hardly looked the "Sofronie."

"Will you buy my hair?" asked Della.

"I buy hair," said Madame. "Take yer hat off and let's have a sight at the looks of it."

Down rippled the brown cascade.

"Twenty dollars," said Madame, lifting the mass with a practised hand.

"Give it to me quick," said Della.

Oh, and the next two hours tripped by on rosy wings. Forget the hashed metaphor. She was ransacking the stores for Jim's present.

She found it at last. It surely had been made for Jim and no one else. There was no other like it in any of the stores, and she had turned all of them inside out. It was a platinum fob chain simple and chaste in design, properly proclaiming its value by substance alone and not by meretricious ornamentation—as all good things should do. It was even worthy of The Watch. As soon as she saw it she knew that it must be Jim's. It was like him. Quietness and value—the description applied to both. Twenty-one dollars they took from her for it, and she hurried home with the 87 cents. With that chain on his watch Jim might be properly anxious about the time in any company. Grand as the watch was, he sometimes looked at it on the sly on account of the old leather strap that he used in place of a chain.

When Della reached home her intoxication gave way a little to prudence and reason. She got out her curling irons and lighted the gas and went to work repairing the ravages made by generosity added to love. Which is always a tremendous task, dear friends—a mammoth task.

Within forty minutes her head was covered with tiny, close-lying curls that made her look wonderfully like a truant schoolboy. She looked at her reflection in the mirror long, carefully, and critically.

"If Jim doesn't kill me," she said to herself, "before he takes a second look at me, he'll say I look like a Coney Island chorus girl. But what could I do—oh! what could I do with a dollar and eighty-seven cents?"

At 7 o'clock the coffee was made and the frying-pan was on the back of the stove hot and ready to cook the chops.

Jim was never late. Della doubled the fob chain in her hand and sat on the corner of the table near the door that he always entered. Then she heard his step on the stair away down on the first flight, and she turned white for just a moment. She had a habit of saying little silent prayers about the simplest everyday things, and now she whispered: "Please God, make him think I am still pretty."

The door opened and Jim stepped in and closed it. He looked thin and very serious. Poor fellow, he was only twenty-two—and to be burdened with a family! He needed a new overcoat and he was without gloves.

Jim stepped inside the door, as immovable as a setter at the scent of quail. His eyes were fixed upon Della, and there was an expression in them that she could not read, and it terrified her. It was not anger, nor surprise, nor disapproval,

nor horror, nor any of the sentiments that she had been prepared for. He simply stared at her fixedly with that peculiar
expression on his face.

Della wriggled off the table and went for him.

"Jim, darling," she cried, "don't look at me that way. I had
my hair cut off and sold it because I couldn't have lived
through Christmas without giving you a present. It'll grow out
again—you won't mind, will you? I just had to do it. My hair
grows awfully fast. Say 'Merry Christmas!' Jim, and let's be
happy. You don't know what a nice—what a beautiful, nice
gift I've got for you."

"You've cut off your hair?" asked Jim, laboriously, as if he
had not arrived at that patent fact yet even after the hardest
mental labor.

"Cut it off and sold it," said Della. "Don't you like me just
as well, anyhow? I'm me without my hair, ain't I?"

Jim looked about the room curiously.

"You say your hair is gone?" he said, with an air almost of
idiocy.

"You needn't look for it," said Della. "It's sold, I tell you
—sold and gone, too. It's Christmas Eve, boy. Be good to
me, for it went for you. Maybe the hairs on my head were
numbered," she went on with a sudden serious sweetness,
"but nobody could ever count my love for you. Shall I put
the chops on, Jim?"

Out of his trance Jim seemed quickly to wake. He enfolded
his Della. For ten seconds let us regard with discreet scrutiny
some inconsequential object in the other direction. Eight dollars a week or a million a year—what is the difference? A
mathematician or a wit would give you the wrong answer.
The magi brought valuable gifts, but that was not among
them. This dark assertion will be illuminated later on.

Jim drew a package from his overcoat pocket and threw it
upon the table.

"Don't make any mistake, Dell," he said, "about me. I don't think there's anything in the way of a haircut or a shave or a shampoo that could make me like my girl any less. But if you'll unwrap that package you may see why you had me going a while at first."

White fingers and nimble tore at the string and paper. And then an ecstatic scream of joy; and then, alas! a quick feminine change to hysterical tears and wails, necessitating the immediate employment of all the comforting powers of the lord of the flat.

For there lay The Combs—the set of combs, side and back, that Della had worshipped for long in a Broadway window. Beautiful combs, pure tortoise shell, with jewelled rims —just the shade to wear in the beautiful vanished hair. They were expensive combs, she knew, and her heart had simply craved and yearned over them without the least hope of possession. And now, they were hers, but the tresses that should have adorned the coveted adornments were gone.

But she hugged them to her bosom, and at length she was able to look up with dim eyes and a smile and say: "My hair grows so fast, Jim!"

And then Della leaped up like a little singed cat and cried, "Oh, oh!"

Jim had not yet seen his beautiful present. She held it out to him eagerly upon her open palm. The dull precious metal seemed to flash with a reflection of her bright and ardent spirit.

"Isn't it a dandy, Jim? I hunted all over town to find it. You'll have to look at the time a hundred times a day now. Give me your watch. I want to see how it looks on it."

Instead of obeying, Jim tumbled down on the couch and put his hands under the back of his head and smiled.

"Dell," said he, "let's put our Christmas presents away and keep 'em a while. They're too nice to use just at present. I sold the watch to get the money to buy your combs. And now suppose you put the chops on."

The magi, as you know, were wise men—wonderfully wise men—who brought gifts to the Babe in the manger. They invented the art of giving Christmas presents. Being wise, their gifts were no doubt wise ones, possibly bearing the privilege of exchange in case of duplication. And here I have lamely related to you the uneventful chronicle of two foolish children in a flat who most unwisely sacrificed for each other the greatest treasures of their house. But in a last word to the wise of these days let it be said that of all who give gifts these two were the wisest. Of all who give and receive gifts, such as they are wisest. Everywhere they are wisest. They are the magi.

A Cosmopolite in a Café

AT MIDNIGHT the café was crowded. By some chance the little table at which I sat had escaped the eye of incomers, and two vacant chairs at it extended their arms with venal hospitality to the influx of patrons.

And then a cosmopolite sat in one of them, and I was glad, for I held a theory that since Adam no true citizen of the world has existed. We hear of them, and we see foreign labels on much luggage, but we find travellers instead of cosmopolites.

I invoke your consideration of the scene—the marble-topped tables, the range of leather-upholstered wall seats, the gay company, the ladies dressed in demi-state toilets, speaking in an exquisite visible chorus of taste, economy, opulence or art; the sedulous and largess-loving *garçons*, the music wisely catering to all with its raids upon the composers; the *mélange* of talk and laughter—and, if you will, the Würzburger in the tall glass cones that bend to your lips as a ripe cherry sways on its branch to the beak of a robber jay. I was told by a sculptor from Mauch Chunk that the scene was truly Parisian.

My cosmopolite was named E. Rushmore Coglan, and he will be heard from next summer at Coney Island. He is to establish a new "attraction" there, he informed me, offering kingly diversion. And then his conversation ran along parallels of latitude and longitude. He took the great, round world in his hand, so to speak, familiarly, contemptuously, and it seemed no larger than the seed of a Maraschino cherry in a *table d'hôte* grapefruit. He spoke disrespectfully of the equator, he skipped from continent to continent, he derided the zones, he mopped up the high seas with his napkin. With a wave of his hand he would speak of a certain bazaar in Hyderabad. Whiff! He would have you on skis in Lapland. Zip! Now you rode the breakers with the Kanakas at Kealaikahiki. Presto! He dragged you through an Arkansas post-oak swamp, let you dry for a moment on the alkali plains of his Idaho ranch, then whirled you into the society of Viennese archdukes. Anon he would be telling you of a cold he acquired in a Chicago lake breeze and how old Escamila cured it in Buenos Ayres with a hot infusion of the *chuchula* weed. You would have addressed a letter to "E. Rushmore Coglan, Esq., the Earth, Solar System, the Universe," and mailed it, feeling confident that it would be delivered to him.

I was sure that I had found at last the one true cosmopolite since Adam, and I listened to his world-wide discourse fearful lest I should discover in it the local note of the mere globe-trotter. But his opinions never fluttered or drooped; he was as impartial to cities, countries, and continents as the winds or gravitation.

And as E. Rushmore Coglan prattled of this little planet I

thought with glee of a great almost-cosmopolite who wrote
for the whole world and dedicated himself to Bombay. In a
poem he has to say that there is pride and rivalry between
the cities of the earth, and that "the men that breed from
them, they traffic up and down, but cling to their cities' hem
as a child to the mother's gown." And whenever they walk
"by roaring streets unknown" they remember their native city
"most faithful, foolish, fond; making her mere-breathed name
their bond upon their bond." And my glee was roused because I had caught Mr. Kipling napping. Here I had found
a man not made from dust; one who had no narrow boasts
of birthplace or country, one who, if he bragged at all, would
brag of his whole round globe against the Martians and the
inhabitants of the Moon.

Expression on these subjects was precipitated from E.
Rushmore Coglan by the third corner to our table. While
Coglan was describing to me the topography along the Si-
berian Railway the orchestra glided into a medley. The con-
cluding air was "Dixie," and as the exhilarating notes tumbled
forth they were almost overpowered by a great clapping of
hands from almost every table.

It is worth a paragraph to say that this remarkable scene
can be witnessed every evening in numerous cafés in the City
of New York. Tons of brew have been consumed over theories
to account for it. Some have conjectured hastily that all
Southerners in town hie themselves to cafés at nightfall. This
applause of the "rebel" air in a Northern city does puzzle a
little; but it is not insolvable. The war with Spain, many years'
generous mint and watermelon crops, a few long-shot winners
at the New Orleans race track, and the brilliant banquets
given by the Indiana and Kansas citizens who compose the
North Carolina Society have made the South rather a "fad"
in Manhattan. Your manicure will lisp softly that your left
forefinger reminds her so much of a gentleman's in Rich-

mond, Va. Oh, certainly; but many a lady has to work now —the war, you know.

When "Dixie" was being played a dark-haired young man sprang up from somewhere with a Mosby guerrilla yell and waved frantically his soft-brimmed hat. Then he strayed through the smoke, dropped into the vacant chair at our table and pulled out cigarettes.

The evening was at the period when reserve is thawed. One of us mentioned three Würzburgers to the waiter; the dark-haired young man acknowledged his inclusion in the order by a smile and a nod. I hastened to ask him a question because I wanted to try out a theory I had.

"Would you mind telling me," I began, "whether you are from——"

The fist of E. Rushmore Coglan banged the table and I was jarred into silence.

"Excuse me," said he, "but that's a question I never like to hear asked. What does it matter where a man is from? Is it fair to judge a man by his post-office address? Why, I've seen Kentuckians who hated whiskey, Virginians who weren't descended from Pocahontas, Indianians who hadn't written a novel, Mexicans who didn't wear velvet trousers with silver dollars sewed along the seams, funny Englishmen, spendthrift Yankees, cold-blooded Southerners, narrow-minded Westerners, and New Yorkers who were too busy to stop for an hour on the street to watch a one-armed grocer's clerk do up cranberries in paper bags. Let a man be a man and don't handicap him with the label of any section."

"Pardon me," I said, "but my curiosity was not altogether an idle one. I know the South, and when the band plays 'Dixie' I like to observe. I have formed the belief that the man who applauds that air with special violence and ostensible sectional loyalty is invariably a native of either Secaucus, N. J., or the district between Murray Hill Lyceum and the

Harlem River, this city. I was about to put my opinion to the
test by inquiring of this gentleman when you interrupted with
your own—larger theory, I must confess."

And now the dark-haired young man spoke to me, and it
became evident that his mind also moved along its own set of
grooves.

"I should like to be a periwinkle," said he, mysteriously,
"on the top of a valley, and sing too-ralloo-ralloo."

This was clearly too obscure, so I turned again to Coglan.

"I've been around the world twelve times," said he. "I
know an Esquimau in Upernavik who sends to Cincinnati for
his neckties, and I saw a goat-herder in Uruguay who won a
prize in a Battle Creek breakfast food puzzle competition. I
pay rent on a room in Cairo, Egypt, and another in Yokohama
all the year around. I've got slippers waiting for me in a tea-
house in Shanghai, and I don't have to tell 'em how to cook
my eggs in Rio Janeiro or Seattle. It's a mighty little old
world. What's the use of bragging about being from the
North, or the South, or the old manor house in the dale, or
Euclid Avenue, Cleveland, or Pike's Peak, or Fairfax County,
Va., or Hooligan's Flats or any place? It'll be a better world
when we quit being fools about some mildewed town or ten
acres of swampland just because we happened to be born
there."

"You seem to be a genuine cosmopolite," I said, admiringly. "But it also seems that you would decry patriotism."

"A relic of the stone age," declared Coglan, warmly. "We
are all brothers—Chinamen, Englishmen, Zulus, Patagonians
and the people in the bend of the Kaw River. Some day all
this petty pride in one's city or state or section or country
will be wiped out, and we'll all be citizens of the world, as
we ought to be."

"But while you are wandering in foreign lands," I persisted, "do not your thoughts revert to some spot—some dear and——"

"Nary a spot," interrupted E. R. Coglan, flippantly. "The terrestrial, globular, planetary hunk of matter, slightly flattened at the poles, and known as the Earth, is my abode. I've met a good many object-bound citizens of this country abroad. I've seen men from Chicago sit in a gondola in Venice on a moonlight night and brag about their drainage canal. I've seen a Southerner on being introduced to the King of England hand that monarch, without batting his eyes, the information that his grand-aunt on his mother's side was related by marriage to the Perkinses, of Charleston. I knew a New Yorker who was kidnapped for ransom by some Afghanistan bandits. His people sent over the money and he came back to Kabul with the agent. 'Afghanistan?' the natives said to him through an interpreter. 'Well, not so slow, do you think?' 'Oh, I don't know,' says he, and he begins to tell them about a cab driver at Sixth Avenue and Broadway. Those ideas don't suit me. I'm not tied down to anything that isn't 8,000 miles in diameter. Just put me down as E. Rushmore Coglan, citizen of the terrestrial sphere."

My cosmopolite made a large adieu and left me, for he thought he saw some one through the chatter and smoke whom he knew. So I was left with the would-be periwinkle, who was reduced to Würzburger without further ability to voice his aspirations to perch, melodious, upon the summit of a valley.

I sat reflecting upon my evident cosmopolite and wondering how the poet had managed to miss him. He was my discovery and I believed in him. How was it? "The men that breed from them, they traffic up and down, but cling to their cities' hem as a child to the mother's gown."

Not so E. Rushmore Coglan. With the whole world for his——

My meditations were interrupted by a tremendous noise and conflict in another part of the café. I saw above the heads of the seated patrons E. Rushmore Coglan and a stranger to me engaged in terrific battle. They fought between the tables like Titans, and glasses crashed, and men caught their hats up and were knocked down, and a brunette screamed, and a blonde began to sing "Teasing."

My cosmopolite was sustaining the pride and reputation of the Earth when the waiters closed in on both combatants with their famous flying wedge formation and bore them outside, still resisting.

I called McCarthy, one of the French *garçons*, and asked him the cause of the conflict.

"The man with the red tie" (that was my cosmopolite), said he, "got hot on account of things said about the bum sidewalks and water supply of the place he come from by the other guy."

"Why," said I, bewildered, "that man is a citizen of the world—a cosmopolite. He——"

"Originally from Mattawamkeag, Maine, he said," continued McCarthy, "and he wouldn't stand for no knockin' the place."

Man About Town

THERE were two or three things that I wanted to know. I do not care about a mystery. So I began to inquire.

It took me two weeks to find out what women carry in dress suit cases. And then I began to ask why a mattress is made in two pieces. This serious query was at first received with suspicion because it sounded like a conundrum. I was at last assured that its double form of construction was designed to make lighter the burden of woman, who makes up beds. I was so foolish as to persist, begging to know why, then, they were not made in two equal pieces; whereupon I was shunned.

The third draught that I craved from the fount of knowledge was enlightenment concerning the character known as A Man About Town. He was more vague in my mind than a type should be. We must have a concrete idea of anything, even if it be an imaginary idea, before we can comprehend it. Now, I have a mental picture of John Doe that is as clear as a steel engraving. His eyes are weak blue; he wears a brown vest and a shiny black serge coat. He stands always in the sunshine chewing something; and he keeps half-shutting his pocket knife and opening it again with his thumb. And, if the Man Higher Up is ever found, take my assurance for it, he will be a large, pale man with blue wristlets showing under his cuffs, and he will be sitting to have his shoes polished within sound of a bowling alley, and there will be somewhere about him turquoises.

But the canvas of my imagination, when it came to limning the Man About Town, was blank. I fancied that he had a detachable sneer (like the smile of the Cheshire cat) and attached cuffs; and that was all. Whereupon I asked a newspaper reporter about him.

"Why," said he, "a 'Man About Town' is something between a 'rounder' and a 'clubman.' He isn't exactly—well, he fits in between Mrs. Fish's receptions and private boxing bouts. He doesn't—well, he doesn't belong either to the Lotos Club or to the Jerry McGeogheghan Galvanized Iron Workers' Apprentices' Left Hook Chowder Association. I don't exactly know how to describe him to you. You'll see him everywhere there's anything doing. Yes, I suppose he's a type. Dress clothes every evening; knows the ropes; calls every policeman and waiter in town by their first names. No; he never travels with the hydrogen derivatives. You generally see him alone or with another man."

My friend the reporter left me, and I wandered further afield. By this time the 3126 electric lights on the Rialto were alight. People passed, but they held me not. Paphian eyes rayed upon me, and left me unscathed. Diners, heimgangers, shop-girls, confidence men, panhandlers, actors, highwaymen, millionaires, and outlanders hurried, skipped, strolled, sneaked, swaggered, and scurried by me; but I took no note of them. I knew them all; I had read their hearts; they had served. I wanted my Man About Town. He was a type, and to drop him would be an error—a typograph—but no! let us continue.

Let us continue with a moral digression. To see a family reading the Sunday paper gratifies. The sections have been separated. Papa is earnestly scanning the page that pictures the young lady exercising before an open window, and bending—but there, there! Mamma is interested in trying to guess the missing letters in the word N—w Yo—k. The oldest girls are eagerly perusing the financial reports, for a certain young man remarked last Sunday night that he had taken a flyer in Q., X. & Z. Willie, the eighteen-year-old son, who attends the New York public school, is absorbed in the weekly article describing how to make over an old shirt, for he hopes to take a prize in sewing on graduation day.

Grandma is holding to the comic supplement with a two-hours' grip; and little Tottie, the baby, is rocking along the best she can with the real estate transfers. This view is intended to be reassuring, for it is desirable that a few lines of this story be skipped. For it introduces strong drink.

I went into a café to—and while it was being mixed I asked the man who grabs up your hot Scotch spoon as soon as you lay it down what he understood by the term, epithet, description, designation, characterization or appellation, viz.: a "Man About Town."

"Why," said he, carefully, "it means a fly guy that's wise to the all-night push—see? It's a hot sport that you can't bump to the rail anywhere between the Flatirons—see? I guess that's about what it means."

I thanked him and departed.

On the sidewalk a Salvation lassie shook her contribution receptacle gently against my waistcoat pocket.

"Would you mind telling me," I asked her, "if you ever meet with the character commonly denominated as 'A Man About Town' during your daily wanderings?"

"I think I know whom you mean," she answered, with a gentle smile. "We see them in the same places night after night. They are the devil's body guard, and if the soldiers of any army are as faithful as they are, their commanders are well served. We go among them, diverting a few pennies from their wickedness to the Lord's service."

She shook the box again and I dropped a dime into it.

In front of a glittering hotel a friend of mine, a critic, was climbing from a cab. He seemed at leisure; and I put my question to him. He answered me conscientiously, as I was sure he would.

"There is a type of 'Man About Town' in New York," he answered. "The term is quite familiar to me, but I don't think I was ever called upon to define the character before. It would be difficult to point you out an exact specimen. I would say, offhand, that it is a man who had a hopeless case of the peculiar New York disease of wanting to see and know. At 6 o'clock each day life begins with him. He follows rigidly the conventions of dress and manners; but in the business of poking his nose into places where he does not belong he could give pointers to a civet cat or a jackdaw. He is the man who has chased Bohemia about the town from rathskeller to roof

garden and from Hester Street to Harlem until you can't find
a place in the city where they don't cut their spaghetti with a
knife. Your 'Man About Town' has done that. He is always
on the scent of something new. He is curiosity, impudence,
and omnipresence. Hansoms were made for him, and gold-
banded cigars; and the curse of music at dinner. There are
not so many of him; but his minority report is adopted everywhere.

"I'm glad you brought up the subject; I've felt the influence
of this nocturnal blight upon our city, but I never thought
to analyze it before. I can see now that your 'Man About
Town' should have been classified long ago. In his wake
spring up wine agents and cloak models; and the orchestra
plays 'Let's All Go Up to Maud's' for him, by request, instead
of Händel. He makes his rounds every evening; while you and
I see the elephant once a week. When the cigar store is raided,
he winks at the officer, familiar with his ground, and walks
away immune, while you and I search among the Presidents
for names, and among the stars for addresses to give the desk
sergeant."

My friend, the critic, paused to acquire breath for fresh
eloquence. I seized my advantage.

"You have classified him," I cried with joy. "You have
painted his portrait in the gallery of city types. But I must
meet one face to face. I must study the Man About Town
at first hand. Where shall I find him? How shall I know him?"

Without seeming to hear me, the critic went on. And his
cab-driver was waiting for his fare, too.

"He is the sublimated essence of Butt-in; the refined, in-
trinsic extract of Rubber; the concentrated, purified, irrefuta-
ble, unavoidable spirit of Curiosity and Inquisitiveness. A
new sensation is the breath in his nostrils; when his experi-
ence is exhausted he explores new fields with the indefatiga-
bility of a——"

"Excuse me," I interrupted, "but can you produce one of this type? It is a new thing to me. I must study it. I will search the town over until I find one. Its habitat must be here on Broadway."

"I am about to dine here," said my friend. "Come inside, and if there is a Man About Town present I will point him out to you. I know most of the regular patrons here."

"I am not dining yet," I said to him. "You will excuse me. I am going to find my Man About Town this night if I have to rake New York from the Battery to Little Coney Island."

I left the hotel and walked down Broadway. The pursuit of my type gave a pleasant savor of life and interest to the air I breathed. I was glad to be in a city so great, so complex and diversified. Leisurely and with something of an air I strolled along with my heart expanding at the thought that I was a citizen of great Gotham, a sharer in its magnificence and pleasures, a partaker in its glory and prestige.

I turned to cross the street. I heard something buzz like a bee, and then I took a long, pleasant ride with Santos-Dumont.

When I opened my eyes I remembered a smell of gasoline, and I said aloud: "Hasn't it passed yet?"

A hospital nurse laid a hand that was not particularly soft upon my brow that was not at all fevered. A young doctor came along, grinned, and handed me a morning newspaper.

"Want to see how it happened?" he asked, cheerily. I read the article. Its headlines began where I heard the buzzing leave off the night before. It closed with these lines:

"——Bellevue Hospital, where it was said that his injuries were not serious. He appeared to be a typical Man About Town."

The Cop and the Anthem

ON HIS BENCH in Madison Square Soapy moved uneasily. When wild geese honk high of nights, and when women without sealskin coats grow kind to their husbands, and when Soapy moves uneasily on his bench in the park, you may know that winter is near at hand.

A dead leaf fell in Soapy's lap. That was Jack Frost's card. Jack is kind to the regular denizens of Madison Square, and gives fair warning of his annual call. At the corners of four streets he hands his pasteboard to the North Wind, footman of the mansion of All Outdoors, so that the inhabitants thereof may make ready.

Soapy's mind became cognizant of the fact that the time had come for him to resolve himself into a singular Committee of Ways and Means to provide against the coming rigor. And therefore he moved uneasily on his bench.

The hibernatorial ambitions of Soapy were not of the highest. In them were no considerations of Mediterranean cruises, of soporific Southern skies or drifting in the Vesuvian Bay. Three months on the Island was what his soul craved. Three months of assured board and bed and congenial company, safe from Boreas and bluecoats, seemed to Soapy the essence of things desirable.

For years the hospitable Blackwell's had been his winter quarters. Just as his more fortunate fellow New Yorkers had bought their tickets to Palm Beach and the Riviera each winter, so Soapy had made his humble arrangements for his annual hegira to the Island. And now the time was come. On the previous night three Sabbath newspapers, distributed beneath his coat, about his ankles and over his lap, had failed to repulse the cold as he slept on his bench near the spurting fountain in the ancient square. So the Island loomed big and timely in Soapy's mind. He scorned the provisions made in the name of charity for the city's dependents. In Soapy's opinion the Law was more benign than Philanthropy. There was an endless round of institutions, municipal and eleemosynary, on which he might set out and receive lodging and food accordant with the simple life. But to one of Soapy's proud spirit the gifts of charity are encumbered. If not in coin you must pay in humiliation of spirit for every benefit received at the hands of philanthropy. As Cæsar had his Brutus, every bed of charity must have its toll of a bath, every loaf of bread its compensation of a private and personal inquisition. Wherefore it is better to be a guest of the law, which, though conducted by rules, does not meddle unduly with a gentleman's private affairs.

Soapy, having decided to go to the Island, at once set about accomplishing his desire. There were many easy ways of doing this. The pleasantest was to dine luxuriously at some expensive restaurant; and then, after declaring insolvency, be handed over quietly and without uproar to a policeman. An accommodating magistrate would do the rest.

Soapy left his bench and strolled out of the square and across the level sea of asphalt, where Broadway and Fifth Avenue flow together. Up Broadway he turned, and halted at a glittering café, where are gathered together nightly the choicest products of the grape, the silkworm, and the protoplasm.

Soapy had confidence in himself from the lowest button of his vest upward. He was shaven, and his coat was decent and his neat black, ready-tied four-in-hand had been presented to him by a lady missionary on Thanksgiving Day. If he could reach a table in the restaurant unsuspected success would be his. The portion of him that would show above the table would raise no doubt in the waiter's mind. A roasted mallard duck, thought Soapy, would be about the thing— with a bottle of Chablis, and then Camembert, a demi-tasse and a cigar. One dollar for the cigar would be enough. The total would not be so high as to call forth any supreme manifestation of revenge from the café management; and yet the meat would leave him filled and happy for the journey to his winter refuge.

But as Soapy set foot inside the restaurant door the head waiter's eye fell upon his frayed trousers and decadent shoes. Strong and ready hands turned him about and conveyed him in silence and haste to the sidewalk and averted the ignoble fate of the menaced mallard.

Soapy turned off Broadway. It seemed that his route to the coveted Island was not to be an epicurean one. Some other way of entering limbo must be thought of.

At a corner of Sixth Avenue electric lights and cunningly displayed wares behind plate-glass made a shop window conspicuous. Soapy took a cobblestone and dashed it through the glass. People came running around the corner, a policeman in the lead. Soapy stood still, with his hands in his pockets, and smiled at the sight of brass buttons.

"Where's the man that done that?" inquired the officer, excitedly.

"Don't you figure out that I might have had something to do with it?" said Soapy, not without sarcasm, but friendly, as one greets good fortune.

The policeman's mind refused to accept Soapy even as a clue. Men who smash windows do not remain to parley with the law's minions. They take to their heels. The policeman saw a man halfway down the block running to catch a car. With drawn club he joined in the pursuit. Soapy, with disgust in his heart, loafed along, twice unsuccessful.

On the opposite side of the street was a restaurant of no

great pretensions. It catered to large appetites and modest purses. Its crockery and atmosphere were thick; its soup and napery thin. Into this place Soapy took his accusive shoes and telltale trousers without challenge. At a table he sat and consumed beefsteak, flapjacks, doughnuts and pie. And then to the waiter he betrayed the fact that the minutest coin and himself were strangers.

"Now, get busy and call a cop," said Soapy. "And don't keep a gentleman waiting."

"No cop for youse," said the waiter, with a voice like butter cakes and an eye like the cherry in a Manhattan cocktail. "Hey, Con!"

Neatly upon his left ear on the callous pavement two waiters pitched Soapy. He arose joint by joint, as a carpenter's rule opens, and beat the dust from his clothes. Arrest seemed but a rosy dream. The Island seemed very far away. A policeman who stood before a drug store two doors away laughed and walked down the street.

Five blocks Soapy travelled before his courage permitted him to woo capture again. This time the opportunity presented what he fatuously termed to himself a "cinch." A young woman of a modest and pleasing guise was standing before a show window gazing with sprightly interest at its display of shaving mugs and inkstands, and two yards from the window a large policeman of severe demeanor leaned against a water plug.

It was Soapy's design to assume the rôle of the despicable and execrated "masher." The refined and elegant appearance of his victim and the contiguity of the conscientious cop encouraged him to believe that he would soon feel the pleasant official clutch upon his arm that would insure his winter quarters on the right little, tight little isle.

Soapy straightened the lady missionary's ready-made tie, dragged his shrinking cuffs into the open, set his hat at a kill-

ing cant and sidled toward the young woman. He made eyes
at her, was taken with sudden coughs and "hems," smiled,
smirked and went brazenly through the impudent and contemptible litany of the "masher." With half an eye Soapy saw
that the policeman was watching him fixedly. The young
woman moved away a few steps, and again bestowed her
absorbed attention upon the shaving mugs. Soapy followed,
boldly stepping to her side, raised his hat and said:

"Ah there, Bedelia! Don't you want to come and play in
my yard?"

The policeman was still looking. The persecuted young
woman had but to beckon a finger and Soapy would be practically en route for his insular haven. Already he imagined he
could feel the cozy warmth of the station-house. The young
woman faced him and, stretching out a hand, caught Soapy's
coat sleeve.

"Sure, Mike," she said, joyfully, "if you'll blow me to a pail
of suds. I'd have spoke to you sooner, but the cop was
watching."

With the young woman playing the clinging ivy to his oak
Soapy walked past the policeman overcome with gloom. He
seemed doomed to liberty.

At the next corner he shook off his companion and ran. He
halted in the district where by night are found the lightest
streets, hearts, vows and librettos. Women in furs and men
in greatcoats moved gaily in the wintry air. A sudden fear
seized Soapy that some dreadful enchantment had rendered
him immune to arrest. The thought brought a little of panic
upon it, and when he came upon another policeman lounging
grandly in front of a transplendent theatre he caught at the
immediate straw of "disorderly conduct."

On the sidewalk Soapy began to yell drunken gibberish at
the top of his harsh voice. He danced, howled, raved, and
otherwise disturbed the welkin.

The policeman twirled his club, turned his back to Soapy and remarked to a citizen:

" 'Tis one of them Yale lads celebratin' the goose egg they give to the Hartford College. Noisy; but no harm. We've instructions to lave them be."

Disconsolate, Soapy ceased his unavailing racket. Would never a policeman lay hands on him? In his fancy the Island seemed an unattainable Arcadia. He buttoned his thin coat against the chilling wind.

In a cigar store he saw a well-dressed man lighting a cigar at a swinging light. His silk umbrella he had set by the door on entering. Soapy stepped inside, secured the umbrella and sauntered off with it slowly. The man at the cigar light followed hastily.

"My umbrella," he said, sternly.

"Oh, is it?" sneered Soapy, adding insult to petit larceny. "Well, why don't you call a policeman? I took it. Your umbrella! Why don't you call a cop? There stands one on the corner."

The umbrella owner slowed his steps. Soapy did likewise, with a presentiment that luck would again run against him. The policeman looked at the two curiously.

"Of course," said the umbrella man—"that is—well, you know how these mistakes occur—I—if it's your umbrella I hope you'll excuse me—I picked it up this morning in a restaurant—If you recognize it as yours, why—I hope you'll——"

"Of course it's mine," said Soapy, viciously.

The ex-umbrella man retreated. The policeman hurried to assist a tall blonde in an opera cloak across the street in front of a street car that was approaching two blocks away.

Soapy walked eastward through a street damaged by improvements. He hurled the umbrella wrathfully into an excavation. He muttered against the men who wear helmets and carry clubs. Because he wanted to fall into their clutches, they seemed to regard him as a king who could do no wrong.

At length Soapy reached one of the avenues to the east where the glitter and turmoil was but faint. He set his face down this toward Madison Square, for the homing instinct survives even when the home is a park bench.

But on an unusually quiet corner Soapy came to a standstill. Here was an old church, quaint and rambling and gabled. Through one violet-stained window a soft light glowed, where, no doubt, the organist loitered over the keys, making sure of his mastery of the coming Sabbath anthem. For there drifted out to Soapy's ears sweet music that caught and held him transfixed against the convolutions of the iron fence.

The moon was above, lustrous and serene; vehicles and pedestrians were few; sparrows twittered sleepily in the eaves—for a little while the scene might have been a country churchyard. And the anthem that the organist played cemented Soapy to the iron fence, for he had known it well in the days when his life contained such things as mothers and roses and ambitions and friends and immaculate thoughts and collars.

The conjunction of Soapy's receptive state of mind and the influences about the old church wrought a sudden and wonderful change in his soul. He viewed with swift horror the pit into which he had tumbled, the degraded days, unworthy desires, dead hopes, wrecked faculties and base motives that made up his existence.

And also in a moment his heart responded thrillingly to this novel mood. An instantaneous and strong impulse moved him to battle with his desperate fate. He would pull himself out of the mire; he would make a man of himself again; he would conquer the evil that had taken possession of him. There was time; he was comparatively young yet: he would resurrect his old eager ambitions and pursue them without faltering. Those solemn but sweet organ notes had set up a revolution in him. To-morrow he would go into the roaring downtown district and find work. A fur importer had once offered him a place as driver. He would find him to-morrow and ask for the position. He would be somebody in the world. He would——

Soapy felt a hand laid on his arm. He looked quickly around into the broad face of a policeman.

"What are you doin' here?" asked the officer.

"Nothin'," said Soapy.

"Then come along," said the policeman.

"Three months on the Island," said the Magistrate in the Police Court the next morning.

The Love-Philtre of Ikey Schoenstein

THE BLUE LIGHT DRUG STORE is downtown, between the Bowery and First Avenue, where the distance between the two streets is the shortest. The Blue Light does not consider that pharmacy is a thing of bric-à-brac, scent and ice-cream soda. If you ask it for pain-killer it will not give you a bonbon.

The Blue Light scorns the labor-saving arts of modern pharmacy. It macerates its opium and percolates its own laudanum and paregoric. To this day pills are made behind its tall prescription desk—pills rolled out on its own pill-tile, divided with a spatula, rolled with the finger and thumb, dusted with calcined magnesia and delivered in little round pasteboard pill-boxes. The store is on a corner about which coveys of ragged-plumed, hilarious children play and become candidates for the cough drops and soothing syrups that wait for them inside.

Ikey Schoenstein was the night clerk of the Blue Light and

the friend of his customers. Thus it is on the East Side, where the heart of pharmacy is not glacé. There, as it should be, the druggist is a counsellor, a confessor, an adviser, an able and willing missionary and mentor whose learning is respected, whose occult wisdom is venerated and whose medicine is often poured, untasted, into the gutter. Therefore Ikey's corniform, be-spectacled nose and narrow, knowledge-bowed figure was well known in the vicinity of the Blue Light, and his advice and notice were much desired.

Ikey roomed and breakfasted at Mrs. Riddle's two squares away. Mrs. Riddle had a daughter named Rosy. The circumlocution has been in vain—you must have guessed it—Ikey adored Rosy. She tinctured all his thoughts; she was the compound extract of all that was chemically pure and officinal—the dispensatory contained nothing equal to her. But Ikey was timid, and his hopes remained insoluble in the menstruum of his backwardness and fears. Behind his counter he was a superior being, calmly conscious of special knowledge and worth; outside he was a weak-kneed, purblind, motorman-cursed rambler, with ill-fitting clothes stained with chemicals and smelling of socotrine aloes and valerianate of ammonia.

The fly in Ikey's ointment (thrice welcome, pat trope!) was Chunk McGowan.

Mr. McGowan was also striving to catch the bright smiles tossed about by Rosy. But he was no out-fielder as Ikey was; he picked them off the bat. At the same time he was Ikey's friend and customer, and often dropped in at the Blue Light Drug Store to have a bruise painted with iodine or get a cut rubber-plastered after a pleasant evening spent along the Bowery.

One afternoon McGowan drifted in in his silent, easy way, and sat, comely, smooth-faced, hard, indomitable, good-natured, upon a stool.

"Ikey," said he, when his friend had fetched his mortar and

sat opposite, grinding gum benzoin to a powder, "get busy with your ear. It's drugs for me if you've got the line I need."

Ikey scanned the countenance of Mr. McGowan for the usual evidence of conflict, but found none.

"Take your coat off," he ordered. "I guess already that you have been stuck in the ribs with a knife. I have many times told you those Dagoes would do you up."

Mr. McGowan smiled. "Not them," he said. "Not any Dagoes. But you've located the diagnosis all right enough—it's under my coat, near the ribs. Say! Ikey—Rosy and me are goin' to run away and get married to-night."

Ikey's left forefinger was doubled over the edge of the mortar, holding it steady. He gave it a wild rap with the pestle, but felt it not. Meanwhile Mr. McGowan's smile faded to a look of perplexed gloom.

"That is," he continued, "if she keeps in the notion until the times comes. We've been layin' pipes for the getaway for two weeks. One day she says she will; the same evenin' she says nixy. We've agreed on to-night, and Rosy's stuck to the affirmative this time for two whole days. But it's five hours yet till the time, and I'm afraid she'll stand me up when it comes to the scratch."

"You said you wanted drugs," remarked Ikey.

Mr. McGowan looked ill at ease and harassed—a condition opposed to his usual line of demeanor. He made a patent-medicine almanac into a roll and fitted it with unprofitable carefulness about his finger.

"I wouldn't have this double handicap make a false start to-night for a million," he said. "I've got a little flat up in Harlem all ready, with chrysanthemums on the table and a kettle ready to boil. And I've engaged a pulpit pounder to be ready at his house for us at 9.30. It's got to come off. And if Rosy don't change her mind again!"—Mr. McGowan ceased, a prey to his doubts.

"I don't see then yet," said Ikey, shortly, "what makes it that you talk of drugs, or what I can be doing about it."

"Old man Riddle don't like me a little bit," went on the uneasy suitor, bent upon marshalling his arguments. "For a week he hasn't let Rosy step outside the door with me. If it wasn't for losin' a boarder they'd have bounced me long ago. I'm makin' $20 a week and she'll never regret flyin' the coop with Chunk McGowan."

"You will excuse me, Chunk," said Ikey. "I must make a prescription that is to be called for soon."

"Say," said McGowan, looking up suddenly, "say, Ikey, ain't there a drug of some kind—some kind of powders that'll make a girl like you better if you give 'em to her?"

Ikey's lip beneath his nose curled with the scorn of superior enlightenment; but before he could answer, McGowan continued:

"Tim Lacy told me he got some once from a croaker uptown and fed 'em to his girl in soda water. From the very first dose he was ace-high and everybody else looked like thirty cents to her. They was married in less than two weeks."

Strong and simple was Chunk McGowan. A better reader of men than Ikey was could have seen that his tough frame was strung upon fine wires. Like a good general who was about to invade the enemy's territory he was seeking to guard every point against possible failure.

"I thought," went on Chunk, hopefully, "that if I had one of them powders to give Rosy when I see her at supper tonight it might brace her up and keep her from reneging on the proposition to skip. I guess she don't need a mule team to drag her away, but women are better at coaching than they are at running bases. If the stuff'll work just for a couple of hours it'll do the trick."

"When is this foolishness of running away to be happening?" asked Ikey.

"Nine o'clock," said Mr. McGowan. "Supper's at seven. At eight Rosy goes to bed with a headache, at nine old Parvenzano lets me through to his backyard, where there's a board off Riddle's fence, next door. I go under her window and help her down the fire-escape. We've got to make it early on the preacher's account. It's all dead easy if Rosy don't balk when the flag drops. Can you fix me one of them powders, Ikey?"

Ikey Schoenstein rubbed his nose slowly.

"Chunk," said he, "it is of drugs of that nature that pharmaceutists must have much carefulness. To you alone of my acquaintance would I intrust a powder like that. But for you I shall make it, and you shall see how it makes Rosy to think of you."

Ikey went behind the prescription desk. There he crushed to a powder two soluble tablets, each containing a quarter of a grain of morphia. To them he added a little sugar of milk to increase the bulk, and folded the mixture neatly in a white paper. Taken by an adult this powder would insure several hours of heavy slumber without danger to the sleeper. This he handed to Chunk McGowan, telling him to administer it in a liquid if possible, and received the hearty thanks of the backyard Lochinvar.

The subtlety of Ikey's action becomes apparent upon recital of his subsequent move. He sent a messenger for Mr. Riddle and disclosed the plans of Mr. McGowan for eloping with Rosy. Mr. Riddle was a stout man, brick-dusty of complexion and sudden in action.

"Much obliged," he said, briefly, to Ikey. "The lazy Irish loafer! My own room's just above Rosy's. I'll just go up there myself after supper and load the shot-gun and wait. If he comes in my backyard he'll go away in a ambulance instead of a bridal chaise."

With Rosy held in the clutches of Morpheus for a many-hours deep slumber, and the blood-thirsty parent waiting, armed and forewarned, Ikey felt that his rival was close, indeed, upon discomfiture.

All night in the Blue Light Drug Store he waited at his duties for chance news of the tragedy, but none came.

At eight o'clock in the morning the day clerk arrived and Ikey started hurriedly for Mrs. Riddle's to learn the outcome. And, lo! as he stepped out of the store who but Chunk McGowan sprang from a passing street car and grasped his hand—Chunk McGowan with a victor's smile and flushed with joy.

"Pulled it off," said Chunk with Elysium in his grin. "Rosy hit the fire-escape on time to a second, and we was under the wire at the Reverend's at 9.30¼. She's up at the flat—she cooked eggs this mornin' in a blue kimono—Lord! how lucky I am! You must pace up some day, Ikey, and feed with us. I've got a job down near the bridge, and that's where I'm heading for now."

"The—the—powder?" stammered Ikey.

"Oh, that stuff you gave me!" said Chunk, broadening his grin; "well, it was this way. I sat down at the supper table last night at Riddle's, and I looked at Rosy, and I says to myself, 'Chunk, if you get the girl get her on the square—don't try any hocus-pocus with a thoroughbred like her.' And I keeps the paper you give me in my pocket. And then my lamps fall on another party present, who, I says to myself, is failin' in a proper affection toward his comin' son-in-law, so I watches my chance and dumps that powder in old man Riddle's coffee—see?"

Mammon and the Archer

OLD ANTHONY ROCKWALL, retired manufacturer and proprietor of Rockwall's Eureka Soap, looked out the library window of his Fifth Avenue mansion and grinned. His neighbor to the right—the aristocratic clubman, G. Van Schuylight Suffolk-Jones—came out to his waiting motorcar, wrinkling a contumelious nostril, as usual, at the Italian renaissance sculpture of the soap palace's front elevation.

"Stuck-up old statuette of nothing doing!" commented the ex-Soap King. "The Eden Musée'll get that old frozen Nesselrode yet if he don't watch out. I'll have this house painted red, white, and blue next summer and see if that'll make his Dutch nose turn up any higher."

And then Anthony Rockwall, who never cared for bells went to the door of his library and shouted "Mike!" in the same voice that had once chipped off pieces of the welkin on the Kansas prairies.

"Tell my son," said Anthony to the answering menial, "to come in here before he leaves the house."

When young Rockwall entered the library the old man laid aside his newspaper, looked at him with a kindly grimness on his big, smooth, ruddy countenance, rumpled his mop of white hair with one hand and rattled the keys in his pocket with the other.

"Richard," said Anthony Rockwall, "what do you pay for the soap that you use?"

Richard, only six months home from college, was startled a little. He had not yet taken the measure of this sire of his, who was as full of unexpectedness as a girl at her first party.

"Six dollars a dozen, I think, dad."

"And your clothes?"

"I suppose about sixty dollars, as a rule."

"You're a gentleman," said Anthony, decidedly. "I've heard of these young bloods spending $24 a dozen for soap, and going over the hundred mark for clothes. You've got as much money to waste as any of 'em, and yet you stick to what's decent and moderate. Now I use the old Eureka—not only for sentiment, but it's the purest soap made. Whenever you pay more than 10 cents a cake for soap you buy bad perfumes and labels. But 50 cents is doing very well for a young man in your generation, position and condition. As I said, you're a gentleman. They say it takes three generations to make one. They're off. Money'll do it as slick as soap grease. It's made you one. By hokey! it's almost made one of me. I'm nearly as impolite and disagreeable and ill-mannered as these two old knickerbocker gents on each side of me that can't sleep of nights because I bought in between 'em."

"There are some things that money can't accomplish," remarked young Rockwall, rather gloomily.

"Now, don't say that," said old Anthony, shocked. "I bet my money on money every time. I've been through the encyclopædia down to Y looking for something you can't buy with it; and I expect to have to take up the appendix next week. I'm for money against the field. Tell me something money won't buy."

"For one thing," answered Richard, rankling a little, "it won't buy one into the exclusive circles of society."

"Oho! won't it?" thundered the champion of the root of evil. "You tell me where your exclusive circles would be if the first Astor hadn't had the money to pay for his steerage passage over?"

Richard sighed.

"And that's what I was coming to," said the old man, less boisterously. "That's why I asked you to come in. There's something going wrong with you, boy. I've been noticing it for two weeks. Out with it. I guess I could lay my hands on eleven millions within twenty-four hours, besides the real estate. If it's your liver, there's the *Rambler* down in the bay, coaled, and ready to steam down to the Bahamas in two days."

"Not a bad guess, dad; you haven't missed it far."

"Ah," said Anthony, keenly; "what's her name?"

Richard began to walk up and down the library floor. There was enough comradeship and sympathy in this crude old father of his to draw his confidence.

"Why don't you ask her?" demanded old Anthony. "She'll jump at you. You've got the money and the looks, and you're a decent boy. Your hands are clean. You've got no Eureka soap on 'em. You've been to college, but she'll overlook that."

"I haven't had a chance," said Richard.

"Make one," said Anthony. "Take her for a walk in the park, or a straw ride, or walk home with her from church. Chance! Pshaw!"

"You don't know the social mill, dad. She's part of the stream that turns it. Every hour and minute of her time is arranged for days in advance. I must have that girl, dad, or this town is a blackjack swamp forevermore. And I can't write it—I can't do that."

"Tut!" said the old man. "Do you mean to tell me that with all the money I've got you can't get an hour or two of a girl's time for yourself?"

"I've put it off too late. She's going to sail for Europe at noon day after to-morrow for a two years' stay. I'm to see her alone to-morrow evening for a few minutes. She's at Larchmont now at her aunt's. I can't go there. But I'm allowed to meet her with a cab at the Grand Central Station to-morrow evening at the 8.30 train. We drive down Broadway to Wallack's at a gallop, where her mother and a box party will be waiting for us in the lobby. Do you think she would listen to a declaration from me during that six or eight minutes under those circumstances? No. And what chance would I have in the theatre or afterward? None. No, dad, this is one tangle that your money can't unravel. We can't buy one minute of time with cash; if we could, rich people would live longer. There's no hope of getting a talk with Miss Lantry before she sails."

"All right, Richard, my boy," said old Anthony, cheerfully. "You may run along down to your club now. I'm glad it ain't your liver. But don't forget to burn a few punk sticks in the joss house to the great god Mazuma from time to time. You say money won't buy time? Well, of course, you can't order eternity wrapped up and delivered at your residence for a price, but I've seen Father Time get pretty bad stone bruises on his heels when he walked through the gold diggings."

That night came Aunt Ellen, gentle, sentimental, wrinkled, sighing, oppressed by wealth, in to Brother Anthony at his evening paper, and began discourse on the subject of lovers' woes.

"He told me all about it," said Brother Anthony, yawning. "I told him my bank account was at his service. And then he began to knock money. Said money couldn't help. Said the rules of society couldn't be bucked for a yard by a team of ten millionaires."

"Oh, Anthony," sighed Aunt Ellen, "I wish you would not think so much of money. Wealth is nothing where a true affection is concerned. Love is all-powerful. If he only had spoken earlier! She could not have refused our Richard. But now I fear it is too late. He will have no opportunity to address her. All your gold cannot bring happiness to your son."

At eight o'clock the next evening Aunt Ellen took a quaint old gold ring from a moth-eaten case and gave it to Richard.

"Wear it to-night, nephew," she begged. "Your mother gave

it to me. Good luck in love she said it brought. She asked me to give it to you when you had found the one you loved."

Young Rockwall took the ring reverently and tried it on his smallest finger. It slipped as far as the second joint and stopped. He took it off and stuffed it into his vest pocket, after the manner of man. And then he 'phoned for his cab.

At the station he captured Miss Lantry out of the gabbing mob at eight thirty-two.

"We mustn't keep mamma and the others waiting," said she.

"To Wallack's Theatre as fast as you can drive!" said Richard, loyally.

They whirled up Forty-second to Broadway, and then down the white-starred lane that leads from the soft meadows of sunset to the rocky hills of morning.

At Thirty-fourth Street young Richard quickly thrust up the trap and ordered the cabman to stop.

"I've dropped a ring," he apologized, as he climbed out. "It was my mother's, and I'd hate to lose it. I won't detain you a minute—I saw where it fell."

In less than a minute he was back in the cab with the ring.

But within that minute a crosstown car had stopped directly in front of the cab. The cab-man tried to pass to the left, but a heavy express wagon cut him off. He tried the right and had to back away from a furniture van that had no business to be there. He tried to back out, but dropped his reins and swore dutifully. He was blockaded in a tangled mess of vehicles and horses.

One of those street blockades had occurred that sometimes tie up commerce and movement quite suddenly in the big city.

"Why don't you drive on?" said Miss Lantry, impatiently. "We'll be late."

Richard stood up in the cab and looked around. He saw a

congested flood of wagons, trucks, cabs, vans and street cars
filling the vast space where Broadway, Sixth Avenue, and
Thirty-fourth Street cross one another as a twenty-six inch
maiden fills her twenty-two inch girdle. And still from all the
cross streets they were hurrying and rattling toward the con-
verging point at full speed, and hurling themselves into the
straggling mass, locking wheels and adding their drivers' imprecations to the clamor. The entire traffic of Manhattan
seemed to have jammed itself around them. The oldest New
Yorker among the thousands of spectators that lined the
sidewalks had not witnessed a street blockade of the propor-
tions of this one.

"I'm very sorry," said Richard, as he resumed his seat, "but
it looks as if we are stuck. They won't get this jumble loosened up in an hour. It was my fault. If I hadn't dropped the
ring we——"

"Let me see the ring," said Miss Lantry. "Now that it can't
be helped, I don't care. I think theatres are stupid, anyway."

At 11 o'clock that night somebody tapped lightly on Anthony Rockwall's door.

"Come in," shouted Anthony, who was in a red dressing-
gown, reading a book of piratical adventures.

Somebody was Aunt Ellen, looking like a gray-haired
angel that had been left on earth by mistake.

"They're engaged, Anthony," she said, softly. "She has
promised to marry our Richard. On their way to the theatre
there was a street blockade, and it was two hours before their
cab could get out of it.

"And oh, Brother Anthony, don't ever boast of the power
of money again. A little emblem of true love—a little ring that
symbolized unending and unmercenary affection—was the
cause of our Richard finding his happiness. He dropped it
in the street, and got out to recover it. And before they could
continue the blockade occurred. He spoke to his love and won

her there while the cab was hemmed in. Money is dross compared with true love, Anthony."

"All right," said old Anthony. "I'm glad the boy has got what he wanted. I told him I wouldn't spare any expense in the matter if——"

"But, Brother Anthony, what good could your money have done?"

"Sister," said Anthony Rockwall, "I've got my pirate in a devil of a scrape. His ship has just been scuttled, and he's too good a judge of the value of money to let drown. I wish you would let me go on with this chapter."

The story should end here. I wish it would as heartily as you who read it wish it did. But we must go to the bottom of the well for truth.

The next day a person with red hands and a blue polka-dot necktie, who called himself Kelly, called at Anthony Rockwall's house, and was at once received in the library.

"Well," said Anthony, reaching for his check-book, "it was a good bilin' of soap. Let's see—you had $5,000 in cash."

"I paid out $300 more of my own," said Kelly. "I had to go a little above the estimate. I got the express wagons and cabs mostly for $5; but the trucks and two-horse teams mostly raised me to $10. The motormen wanted $10, and some of the loaded teams $20. The cops struck me hardest—$50 I paid two, and the rest $20 and $25. But didn't it work beautiful, Mr. Rockwall? I'm glad William A. Brady wasn't onto that little outdoor vehicle mob scene. I wouldn't want William to break his heart with jealousy. And never a rehearsal, either! The boys was on time to the fraction of a second. It was two hours before a snake could get below Greeley's statue."

"Thirteen hundred—there you are, Kelly," said Anthony, tearing off a check. "Your thousand, and the $300 you were out. You don't despise money, do you, Kelly?"

"Me?" said Kelly. "I can lick the man that invented poverty."

Anthony called Kelly when he was at the door.

"You didn't notice," said he, "anywhere in the tie-up, a kind of a fat boy without any clothes on shooting arrows around with a bow, did you?"

"Why, no," said Kelly, mystified. "I didn't. If he was like you say, maybe the cops pinched him before I got there."

"I thought the little rascal wouldn't be on hand," chuckled Anthony. "Good-by, Kelly."

Springtime à la Carte

IT WAS a day in March.

Never, never begin a story this way when you write one. No opening could possibly be worse. It is unimaginative, flat, dry, and likely to consist of mere wind. But in this instance it is allowable. For the following paragraph, which should have inaugurated the narrative, is too wildly extravagant and preposterous to be flaunted in the face of the reader without preparation.

Sarah was crying over her bill of fare.

Think of a New York girl shedding tears on the menu card!

To account for this you will be allowed to guess that the lobsters were all out, or that she had sworn ice-cream off during Lent, or that she had ordered onions, or that she had just come from a Hackett matinée. And then, all these theories being wrong, you will please let the story proceed.

The gentleman who announced that the world was an oyster which he with his sword would open made a larger hit than he deserved. It is not difficult to open an oyster with a sword. But did you ever notice any one try to open the terrestrial bivalve with a typewriter? Like to wait for a dozen raw opened that way?

Sarah had managed to pry apart the shells with her unhandy weapon far enough to nibble a wee bit at the cold and clammy world within. She knew no more shorthand than if she had been a graduate in stenography just let slip upon the world by a business college. So, not being able to stenog, she could not enter that bright galaxy of office talent. She was a free-lance typewriter and canvassed for odd jobs of copying.

The most brilliant and crowning feat of Sarah's battle with the world was the deal she made with Schulenberg's Home Restaurant. The restaurant was next door to the old red brick in which she hall-roomed. One evening after dining at Schulenberg's 40-cent, five-course *table d'hôte* (served as fast as you throw the five baseballs at the colored gentleman's head) Sarah took away with her the bill of fare. It was written in an almost unreadable script neither English nor German, and so arranged that if you were not careful you began with a toothpick and rice pudding and ended with soup and the day of the week.

The next day Sarah showed Schulenberg a neat card on which the menu was beautifully typewritten with the viands temptingly marshalled under their right and proper heads from "hors d'œuvre" to "not responsible for over-coats and umbrellas."

Schulenberg became a naturalized citizen on the spot. Before Sarah left him she had him willingly committed to an agreement. She was to furnish typewritten bills of fare for the twenty-one tables in the restaurant—a new bill for each day's dinner, and new ones for breakfast and lunch as often as changes occurred in the food or as neatness required.

In return for this Schulenberg was to send three meals per diem to Sarah's hall room by a waiter—an obsequious one if

possible—and furnish her each afternoon with a pencil draft
of what Fate had in store for Schulenberg's customers on the
morrow.

Mutual satisfaction resulted from the agreement. Schulenberg's patrons now knew what the food they ate was called
even if its nature sometimes puzzled them. And Sarah had
food during a cold, dull winter, which was the main thing
with her.

And then the almanac lied, and said that spring had come.
Spring comes when it comes. The frozen snows of January
still lay like adamant in the cross-town streets. The hand-
organs still played "In the Good Old Summertime," with their
December vivacity and expression. Men began to make thirty-
day notes to buy Easter dresses. Janitors shut off steam. And
when these things happen one may know that the city is still
in the clutches of winter.

One afternoon Sarah shivered in her elegant hall bedroom;
"house heated; scrupulously clean; conveniences; seen to be
appreciated." She had no work to do except Schulenberg's
menu cards. Sarah sat in her squeaky willow rocker, and
looked out the window. The calendar on the wall kept crying to her: "Springtime is here, Sarah—springtime is here, I
tell you. Look at me, Sarah, my figures show it. You've got a
neat figure yourself, Sarah—a—nice springtime figure—why
do you look out the window so sadly?"

Sarah's room was at the back of the house. Looking out the
window she could see the windowless rear brick wall of the
box factory on the next street. But the wall was clearest crystal; and Sarah was looking down a grassy lane shaded with
cherry trees and elms and bordered with raspberry bushes and
Cherokee roses.

Spring's real harbingers are too subtle for the eye and ear.
Some must have the flowering crocus, the wood-starring dog-
wood, the voice of bluebird—even so gross a reminder as the

farewell handshake of the retiring buckwheat and oyster before they can welcome the Lady in Green to their dull bosoms. But to old earth's choicest kind there come straight, sweet messages from his newest bride, telling them they shall be no stepchildren unless they choose to be.

On the previous summer Sarah had gone into the country and loved a farmer.

(In writing your story never hark back thus. It is bad art, and cripples interest. Let it march, march.)

Sarah stayed two weeks at Sunnybrook Farm. There she learned to love old Farmer Franklin's son Walter. Farmers have been loved and wedded and turned out to grass in less time. But young Walter Franklin was a modern agriculturist. He had a telephone in his cow house, and he could figure up exactly what effect next year's Canada wheat crop would have on potatoes planted in the dark of the moon.

It was in this shaded and raspberried lane that Walter had wooed and won her. And together they had sat and woven a crown of dandelions for her hair. He had immoderately praised the effect of the yellow blossoms against her brown tresses; and she had left the chaplet there, and walked back to the house swinging her straw sailor in her hands.

They were to marry in the spring—at the very first signs of spring, Walter said. And Sarah came back to the city to pound her typewriter.

A knock at the door dispelled Sarah's visions of that happy day. A waiter had brought the rough pencil draft of the Home Restaurant's next day fare in old Schulenberg's angular hand.

Sarah sat down to her typewriter and slipped a card between the rollers. She was a nimble worker. Generally in an hour and a half the twenty-one menu cards were written and ready.

To-day there were more changes on the bill of fare than usual. The soups were lighter; pork was eliminated from the entrées, figuring only with Russian turnips among the roasts. The gracious spirit of spring pervaded the entire menu. Lamb, that lately capered on the greening hillsides, was becoming exploited with the sauce that commemorated its gambols. The song of the oyster, though not silenced, was *dimuendo con amore*. The frying-pan seemed to be held, inactive, behind the beneficent bars of the broiler. The pie list swelled; the richer puddings had vanished; the sausage, with his drapery wrapped about him, barely lingered in a pleasant thanatopsis with the buckwheats and the sweet but doomed maple.

Sarah's fingers danced like midgets above a summer stream. Down through the courses she worked, giving each item its position according to its length with an accurate eye.

Just above the desserts came the list of vegetables. Carrots and peas, asparagus on toast, the perennial tomatoes and corn and succotash, lima beans, cabbage—and then——

Sarah was crying over her bill of fare. Tears from the depths of some divine despair rose in her heart and gathered to her eyes. Down went her head on the little typewriter stand; and the keyboard rattled a dry accompaniment to her moist sobs.

For she had received no letter from Walter in two weeks, and the next item on the bill of fare was dandelions—dandelions with some kind of egg—but bother the egg!—dandelions, with whose golden blooms Walter had crowned her his queen of love and future bride—dandelions, the harbingers of spring, her sorrow's crown of sorrow—reminder of her happiest days.

Madam, I dare you to smile until you suffer this test: Let the Marechal Niel roses that Percy brought you on the night you gave him your heart be served as a salad with French dressing before your eyes at a Schulenberg *table d'hôte*. Had Juliet so seen her love tokens dishonored the sooner would she have sought the lethean herbs of the good apothecary.

But what witch is Spring! Into the great cold city of stone and iron a message had to be sent. There was none to convey it but the little hardy courier of the fields with his rough green coat and modest air. He is a true soldier of fortune, this *dent-de-lion*—this lion's tooth, as the French chefs call him. Flowered, he will assist at love-making, wreathed in my lady's nut-brown hair; young and callow and unblossomed, he goes into the boiling pot and delivers the word of his sovereign mistress.

By and by Sarah forced back her tears. The cards must be written. But, still in a faint, golden glow from her dandelion dream, she fingered the typewriter keys absently for a little while, with her mind and heart in the meadow lane with her young farmer. But soon she came swiftly back to the rock-bound lanes of Manhattan, and the typewriter began to rattle and jump like a strike-breaker's motor car.

At 6 o'clock the waiter brought her dinner and carried away the typewritten bill of fare. When Sarah ate she set aside, with a sigh, the dish of dandelions with its crowning ovarious accompaniment. As this dark mass had been transformed from a bright and love-indorsed flower to be an ignominious vegetable, so had her summer hopes wilted and perished. Love may, as Shakespeare said, feed on itself: but Sarah could not bring herself to eat the dandelions that had graced, as ornaments, the first spiritual banquet of her heart's true affection.

At 7.30 the couple in the next room began to quarrel: the man in the room above sought for A on his flute; the gas went a little lower; three coal wagons started to unload—the only sound of which the phonograph is jealous; cats on the back fences slowly retreated toward Mukden. By these signs Sarah knew that it was time for her to read. She got out "The Cloister and the Hearth," the best non-selling book of the month, settled her feet on her trunk, and began to wander with Gerard.

The front door bell rang. The landlady answered it. Sarah left Gerard and Denys treed by a bear and listened. Oh, yes; you would, just as she did!

And then a strong voice was heard in the hall below, and Sarah jumped for her door, leaving the book on the floor and the first round easily the bear's.

You have guessed it. She reached the top of the stairs just as her farmer came up, three at a jump, and reaped and garnered her, with nothing left for the gleaners.

"Why haven't you written—oh, why?" cried Sarah.

"New York is a pretty large town," said Walter Franklin. "I came in a week ago to your old address. I found that you went away on a Thursday. That consoled some; it eliminated the possible Friday bad luck. But it didn't prevent my hunting for you with police and otherwise ever since!"

"I wrote!" said Sarah, vehemently.

"Never got it!"

"Then how did you find me?"

The young farmer smiled a springtime smile.

"I dropped into that Home Restaurant next door this evening," said he. "I don't care who knows it; I like a dish of some kind of greens at this time of the year. I ran my eye down that nice typewritten bill of fare looking for something in that line. When I got below cabbage I turned my chair over and hollered for the proprietor. He told me where you lived."

"I remember," sighed Sarah, happily. "That was dandelions below cabbage."

"I'd know that cranky capital W 'way above the line that your typewriter makes anywhere in the world," said Franklin.

"Why, there's no W in dandelions," said Sarah in surprise.

The young man drew the bill of fare from his pocket and pointed to a line.

Sarah recognized the first card she had typewritten that afternoon. There was still the rayed splotch in the upper right-hand corner where a tear had fallen. But over the spot where one should have read the name of the meadow plant, the clinging memory of their golden blossoms had allowed her fingers to strike strange keys.

Between the red cabbage and the stuffed green peppers was the item:

"DEAREST WALTER, WITH HARD-BOILED EGG."

From the Cabby's Seat

THE CABBY has his point of view. It is more single-minded, perhaps, than that of a follower of any other calling. From the high, swaying seat of his hansom he looks upon his fellow-men as nomadic particles, of no account except when possessed of migratory desires. He is Jehu, and you are goods in transit. Be you President or vagabond, to cabby you are only a Fare. He takes you up, cracks his whip, joggles your vertebræ and sets you down.

When time for payment arrives, if you exhibit a familiarity with legal rates you come to know what contempt is; if you find that you have left your pocketbook behind you are made to realize the mildness of Dante's imagination.

It is not an extravagant theory that the cabby's singleness of purpose and concentrated view of life are the results of the hansom's peculiar construction. The cock-of-the-roost sits aloft like Jupiter on an unsharable seat, holding your fate between two thongs of inconstant leather. Helpless, ridiculous, confined, bobbing like a toy mandarin, you sit like a rat in a trap—you, before whom butlers cringe on solid land—and must squeak upward through a slit in your peripatetic sarcophagus to make your feeble wishes known.

Then, in a cab, you are not even an occupant; you are contents. You are a cargo at sea, and the "cherub that sits up aloft" has Davy Jones's street and number by heart.

One night there were sounds of revelry in the big brick tenement house next door but one to McGary's Family Café. The sounds seemed to emanate from the apartments of the Walsh family. The sidewalk was obstructed by an assortment of interested neighbors, who opened a lane from time to time for a hurrying messenger bearing from McGary's goods pertinent to festivity and diversion. The sidewalk contingent was engaged in comment and discussion from which it made no effort to eliminate the news that Norah Walsh was being married.

In the fulness of time there was an eruption of the merrymakers to the sidewalk. The uninvited guests enveloped and permeated them, and upon the night air rose joyous cries, congratulations, laughter, and unclassified noises born of McGary's oblations to the hymeneal scene.

Close to the curb stood Jerry O'Donovan's cab. Nighthawk was Jerry called; but no more lustrous or cleaner hansom than his ever closed its doors upon point lace and November violets. And Jerry's horse! I am within bounds when I tell you that he was stuffed with oats until one of those old ladies who leave their dishes unwashed at home and go about having expressmen arrested, would have smiled—yes, smiled—to have seen him.

Among the shifting, sonorous, pulsing crowd glimpses could be had of Jerry's high hat, battered by the winds and rains of many years; of his nose like a carrot, battered by the frolicsome, athletic progeny of millionaires and by contumacious fares; of his brass-buttoned green coat, admired in the vicinity of McGary's. It was plain that Jerry had usurped the functions of his cab, and was carrying a "load." Indeed, the figure may be extended and he be likened to a bread-wagon if we admit the testimony of a youthful spectator, who was heard to remark "Jerry has got a bun."

From somewhere among the throng in the street or else out of the thin stream of pedestrians a young woman tripped and stood by the cab. The professional hawk's eye of Jerry caught the movement. He made a lurch for the cab, over-turning three or four onlookers and himself—no! he caught the cap of a water-plug and kept his feet. Like a sailor shinning up the ratlins during a squall Jerry mounted to his professional seat. Once he was there McGary's liquids were baffled. He seesawed on the mizzenmast of his craft as safe as a Steeple Jack rigged to the flagpole of a skyscraper.

"Step in, lady," said Jerry, gathering his lines.

The young woman stepped into the cab; the doors shut with a bang; Jerry's whip cracked in the air; the crowd in the gutter scattered, and the fine hansom dashed away 'cross town.

When the oat-spry horse had hedged a little his first spurt of speed Jerry broke the lid of his cab and called down through the aperture in the voice of a cracked megaphone, trying to please:

"Where, now, will ye be drivin' to?"

"Anywhere you please," came up the answer, musical and contented.

"'Tis drivin' for pleasure she is," thought Jerry. And then he suggested as a matter of course:

"Take a thrip around in the park, lady. 'Twill be ilegant cool and fine."

"Just as you like," answered the fare, pleasantly.

The cab headed for Fifth Avenue and sped up that perfect street. Jerry bounced and swayed in his seat. The potent fluids of McGary were disquieted and they sent new fumes to his head. He sang an ancient song of Killisnook and brandished his whip like a baton.

Inside the cab the fare sat up straight on the cushions, looking to right and left at the lights and houses. Even in the shadowed hansom her eyes shone like stars at twilight.

When they reached Fifty-ninth Street Jerry's head was bobbing and his reins were slack. But his horse turned in through the park gate and began the old familiar nocturnal round. And then the fare leaned back, entranced, and breathed deep the clean, wholesome odors of grass and leaf and bloom. And the wise beast in the shafts, knowing his ground, struck into his by-the-hour gait and kept to the right of the road.

Habit also struggled successfully against Jerry's increasing torpor. He raised the hatch of his storm-tossed vessel and made the inquiry that cabbies do make in the park.

"Like shtop at the Cas-sino, lady? Gezzer r'freshm's, 'n lish'n the music. Ev'body shtops."

"I think that would be nice," said the fare.

They reined up with a plunge at the Casino entrance. The cab doors flew open. The fare stepped directly upon the floor. At once she was caught in a web of ravishing music and dazzled by a panorama of lights and colors. Some one slipped a little square card into her hand on which was printed a number—34. She looked around and saw her cab twenty yards away already lining up in its place among the waiting mass of carriages, cabs, and motor cars. And then a man who seemed to be all shirt-front danced backward before her; and next she was seated at a little table by a railing over which climbed a jessamine vine.

There seemed to be a wordless invitation to purchase; she consulted a collection of small coins in a thin purse, and received from them license to order a glass of beer. There she sat, inhaling and absorbing it all—the new-colored, new-shaped life in a fairy palace in an enchanted wood.

At fifty tables sat princes and queens clad in all the silks and gems of the world. And now and then one of them would look curiously at Jerry's fare. They saw a plain figure dressed in a pink silk of the kind that is tempered by the word "foulard," and a plain face that wore a look of love of life that the queens envied.

Twice the long hands of the clocks went round. Royalties thinned from their *al fresco* thrones, and buzzed or clattered away in their vehicles of state. The music retired into cases of wood and bags of leather and baize. Waiters removed cloths pointedly near the plain figure sitting almost alone.

Jerry's fare rose, and held out her numbered card simply: "Is there anything coming on the ticket?" she asked.

A waiter told her it was her cab check, and that she should give it to the man at the entrance. This man took it, and called the number. Only three hansoms stood in line. The driver of one of them went and routed out Jerry asleep in his cab. He swore deeply, climbed to the captain's bridge and steered his craft to the pier. His fare entered, and the cab whirled into the cool fastnesses of the park along the shortest homeward cuts.

At the gate a glimmer of reason in the form of sudden suspicion seized upon Jerry's beclouded mind. One or two things occurred to him. He stopped his horse, raised the trap and dropped his phonographic voice, like a lead plummet, through the aperture:

"I want to see four dollars before goin' any further on th' thrip. Have ye got th' dough?"

"Four dollars!" laughed the fare, softly, "dear me, no. I've only got a few pennies and a dime or two."

Jerry shut down the trap and slashed his oat-fed horse. The clatter of hoofs strangled but could not drown the sound of his profanity. He shouted choking and gurgling curses at the starry heavens; he cut viciously with his whip at passing vehicles; he scattered fierce and everchanging oaths and imprecations along the streets, so that a late truck driver, crawling homeward, heard and was abashed. But he knew his recourse, and made for it at a gallop.

At the house with the green lights beside the steps he pulled up. He flung wide the cab doors and tumbled heavily to the ground.

"Come on, you," he said, roughly.

His fare came forth with the Casino dreamy smile still on her plain face. Jerry took her by the arm and led her into the police station. A gray-moustached sergeant looked keenly across the desk. He and the cabby were no strangers.

"Sargeant," began Jerry in his old raucous, martyred, thunderous tones of complaint, "I've got a fare here that——"

Jerry paused. He drew a knotted, red hand across his brow. The fog set up by McGary was beginning to clear away.

"A fare, sargeant," he continued, with a grin, "that I want to introduce to ye. It's me wife that I married at ould man Walsh's this evening. And a divil of a time we had, 'tis thrue. Shake hands wit th' sargeant, Norah, and we'll be off to home."

Before stepping into the cab Norah sighed profoundly.

"I've had such a nice time, Jerry," said she.

An Unfinished Story

WE NO LONGER GROAN and heap ashes upon our heads when the flames of Tophet are mentioned. For, even the preachers have begun to tell us that God is radium, or ether or some scientific compound, and that the worst we wicked ones may expect is a chemical reaction. This is a pleasing hypothesis;

but there lingers yet some of the old, goodly terror of ortho-
doxy.

There are but two subjects upon which one may discourse
with a free imagination, and without the possibility of being
controverted. You may talk of your dreams; and you may tell
what you heard a parrot say. Both Morpheus and the bird are
incompetent witnesses; and your listener dare not attack your
recital. The baseless fabric of a vision, then, shall furnish my
theme—chosen with apologies and regrets instead of the more
limited field of pretty Polly's small talk.

I had a dream that was so far removed from the higher
criticism that it had to do with the ancient, respectable, and
lamented bar-of-judgment theory.

Gabriel had played his trump; and those of us who could
not follow suit were arraigned for examination. I noticed at
one side a gathering of professional bondsmen in solemn
black and collars that buttoned behind; but it seemed there
was some trouble about their real estate titles; and they did
not appear to be getting any of us out.

A fly cop—an angel policeman—flew over to me and took
me by the left wing. Near at hand was a group of very
prosperous-looking spirits arraigned for judgment.

"Do you belong with that bunch?" the policeman asked.

"Who are they?" was my answer.

"Why," said he, "they are——"

But this irrelevant stuff is taking up space that the story
should occupy.

Dulcie worked in a department store. She sold Hamburg
edging, or stuffed peppers, or automobiles, or other little
trinkets such as they keep in department stores. Of what she
earned, Dulcie received six dollars per week. The remainder
was credited to her and debited to somebody else's account
in the ledger kept by G—— Oh, primal energy, you say, Reverend Doctor—— Well, then, in the Ledger of Primal Energy.

During her first year in the store, Dulcie was paid five dollars per week. It would be instructive to know how she lived on that amount. Don't care? Very well; probably you are interested in larger amounts. Six dollars is a larger amount. I will tell you how she lived on six dollars per week.

One afternoon at six, when Dulcie was sticking her hat pin within an eighth of an inch of her *medulla oblongata*, she said to her chum, Sadie—the girl that waits on you with her left side:

"Say, Sade, I made a date for dinner this evening with Piggy."

"You never did!" exclaimed Sadie, admiringly. "Well, ain't you the lucky one? Piggy's an awful swell; and he always takes a girl to swell places. He took Blanche up to the Hoffman House one evening, where they have swell music, and you see a lot of swells. You'll have a swell time, Dulce."

Dulcie hurried homeward. Her eyes were shining, and her cheeks showed the delicate pink of life's—real life's—approaching dawn. It was Friday; and she had fifty cents left of her last week's wages.

The streets were filled with the rush-hour floods of people. The electric lights of Broadway were glowing—calling moths from miles, from leagues, from hundreds of leagues out of darkness around to come in and attend the singeing school. Men in accurate clothes, with faces like those carved on cherry stones by the old salts in sailors' homes, turned and stared at Dulcie as she sped, unheeding, past them. Manhattan, the night-blooming cereus, was beginning to unfold its dead-white, heavy-odored petals.

Dulcie stopped in a store where goods were cheap and bought an imitation lace collar with her fifty cents. That money was to have been spent otherwise—fifteen cents for supper, ten cents for breakfast, ten cents for lunch. Another dime was to be added to her small store of savings; and five

cents was to be squandered for licorice drops—the kind
that made your cheek look like the toothache, and last as
long. The licorice was an extravagance—almost a carouse—
but what is life without pleasures?

Dulcie lived in a furnished room. There is this difference
between a furnished room and a boarding-house. In a furnished room, other people do not know it when you go
hungry.

Dulcie went up to her room—the third-floor-back in a West
Side brownstone-front. She lit the gas. Scientists tell us that
the diamond is the hardest substance known. Their mistake.
Landladies know of a compound beside which the diamond is
as putty. They pack it in the tips of gas-burners; and one may
stand on a chair and dig at it in vain until one's fingers are
pink and bruised. A hairpin will not remove it; therefore let
us call it immovable.

So Dulcie lit the gas. In its one-fourth-candle-power glow
we will observe the room.

Couch-bed, dresser, table, washstand, chair—of this much
the landlady was guilty. The rest was Dulcie's. On the dresser
were her treasures—a gilt china vase presented to her by Sadie,
a calendar issued by a pickle works, a book on the divination
of dreams, some rice powder in a glass dish, and a cluster of
artificial cherries tied with a pink ribbon.

Against the wrinkly mirror stood pictures of General Kitchener, William Muldoon, the Duchess of Marlborough, and
Benvenuto Cellini. Against one wall was a plaster of Paris
plaque of an O'Callahan in a Roman helmet. Near it was a
violent oleograph of a lemon-colored child assaulting an in-
flammatory butterfly. This was Dulcie's final judgment in art;
but it had never been upset. Her rest had never been disturbed by whispers of stolen copes; no critic had elevated his
eyebrows at her infantile entomologist.

Piggy was to call for her at seven. While she swiftly makes ready, let us discreetly face the other way and gossip.

For the room, Dulcie paid two dollars per week. On weekdays her breakfast cost ten cents; she made coffee and cooked an egg over the gaslight while she was dressing. On Sunday mornings she feasted royally on veal chops and pineapple fritters at "Billy's" restaurant, at a cost of twenty-five cents—and tipped the waitress ten cents. New York presents so many temptations for one to run into extravagance. She had her lunches in the department-store restaurant at a cost of sixty cents for the week; dinners were $1.05. The evening papers—show me a New Yorker going without his daily paper!—came to six cents; and two Sunday papers—one for the personal column and the other to read—were ten cents. The total amounts to $4.76. Now, one has to buy clothes, and——

I give it up. I hear of wonderful bargains in fabrics, and of miracles performed with needle and thread; but I am in doubt. I hold my pen poised in vain when I would add to Dulcie's life some of those joys that belong to woman by virtue of all the unwritten, sacred, natural, inactive ordinances of the equity of heaven. Twice she had been to Coney Island and had ridden the hobby-horses. 'Tis a weary thing to count your pleasures by summers instead of by hours.

Piggy needs but a word. When the girls named him, an undeserving stigma was cast upon the noble family of swine. The words-of-three-letters lesson in the old blue spelling book begins with Piggy's biography. He was fat; he had the soul of a rat, the habits of a bat, and the magnanimity of a cat. . . . He wore expensive clothes; and was a connoisseur in starvation. He could look at a shop-girl and tell you to an hour how long it had been since she had eaten anything more nourishing than marshmallows and tea. He hung about the shopping districts, and prowled around in department stores with his invitations to dinner. Men who escort dogs upon the streets at the end of a string look down upon him. He is a type; I can dwell upon him no longer; my pen is not the kind intended for him; I am no carpenter.

At ten minutes to seven Dulcie was ready. She looked at herself in the wrinkly mirror. The reflection was satisfactory. The dark blue dress, fitting without a wrinkle, the hat with its jaunty black feather, the but-slightly-soiled gloves—all representing self-denial, even of food itself—were vastly becoming.

Dulcie forgot everything else for a moment except that she was beautiful, and that life was about to lift a corner of its mysterious veil for her to observe its wonders. No gentleman had ever asked her out before. Now she was going for a brief moment into the glitter and exalted show.

The girls said that Piggy was a "spender." There would be a grand dinner, and music, and splendidly dressed ladies to look at and things to eat that strangely twisted the girls' jaws when they tried to tell about them. No doubt she would be asked out again.

There was a blue pongee suit in a window that she knew—by saving twenty cents a week instead of ten in—let's see—— Oh, it would run into years! But there was a second-hand store in Seventh Avenue where——

Somebody knocked at the door. Dulcie opened it. The landlady stood there with a spurious smile, sniffing for cooking by stolen gas.

"A gentleman's downstairs to see you," she said. "Name is Mr. Wiggins."

By such epithet was Piggy known to unfortunate ones who had to take him seriously.

Dulcie turned to the dresser to get her handkerchief; and then she stopped still, and bit her underlip hard. While looking in her mirror she had seen fairyland and herself, a princess, just awakening from a long slumber. She had forgotten

one that was watching her with sad, beautiful, stern eyes—
the only one there was to approve or condemn what she did.
Straight and slender and tall, with a look of sorrowful re-
proach on his handsome, melancholy face, General Kitchener
fixed his wonderful eyes on her out of his gilt photograph
frame on the dresser.

Dulcie turned like an automatic doll to the landlady.

"Tell him I can't go," she said, dully. "Tell him I'm sick,
or something. Tell him I'm not going out."

After the door was closed and locked, Dulcie fell upon her
bed, crushing her black tip, and cried for ten minutes. General
Kitchener was her only friend. He was Dulcie's ideal of a gallant knight. He looked as if he might have a secret sorrow,
and his wonderful moustache was a dream, and she was a
little afraid of that stern yet tender look in his eyes. She used
to have little fancies that he would call at the house sometime,
and ask for her, with his sword clanking against his high boots.
Once, when a boy was rattling a piece of chain against a lamp
post she had opened the window and looked out. But there
was no use. She knew that General Kitchener was away over
in Japan, leading his army against the savage Turks; and he
would never step out of his gilt frame for her. Yet one
look from him had vanquished Piggy that night. Yes, for that
night.

When her cry was over Dulcie got up and took off her best
dress, and put on her old blue kimono. She wanted no dinner.
She sang two verses of "Sammy." Then she became intensely
interested in a little red speck on the side of her nose. And
after that was attended to, she drew up a chair to the rickety
table, and told her fortune with an old deck of cards.

"The horrid, impudent thing!" she said aloud. "And I never
gave him a word or a look to make him think it!"

At nine o'clock Dulcie took a tin box of crackers and a little
pot of raspberry jam out of her trunk and had a feast. She

offered General Kitchener some jam on a cracker; but he only looked at her as the sphinx would have looked at a butterfly —if there are butterflies in the desert.

"Don't eat it if you don't want to," said Dulcie. "And don't put on so many airs and scold so with your eyes. I wonder if you'd be so superior and snippy if you had to live on six dollars a week."

It was not a good sign for Dulcie to be rude to General Kitchener. And then she turned Benvenuto Cellini face downward with a severe gesture. But that was not inexcusable; for she had always thought he was Henry VIII, and she did not approve of him.

At half-past nine Dulcie took a last look at the pictures on the dresser, turned out the light and skipped into bed. It's an awful thing to go to bed with a good-night look at General Kitchener, William Muldoon, the Duchess of Marlborough, and Benvenuto Cellini.

This story doesn't really get anywhere at all. The rest of it comes later—sometime when Piggy asks Dulcie again to dine with him, and she is feeling lonelier than usual, and General Kitchener happens to be looking the other way; and then——

As I said before, I dreamed that I was standing near a crowd of prosperous-looking angels, and a policeman took me by the wing and asked if I belonged with them.

"Who are they?" I asked.

"Why," said he, "they are the men who hired working-girls, and paid 'em five or six dollars a week to live on. Are you one of the bunch?"

"Not on your immortality," said I. "I'm only a fellow that set fire to an orphan asylum, and murdered a blind man for his pennies."

The Romance of a Busy Broker

PITCHER, confidential clerk in the office of Harvey Maxwell, broker, allowed a look of mild interest and surprise to visit his usually expressionless countenance when his employer briskly entered at half-past nine in company with his young lady stenographer. With a snappy "Good-morning, Pitcher," Maxwell dashed at his desk as though he were intending to leap over it, and then plunged into the great heap of letters and telegrams waiting there for him.

The young lady had been Maxwell's stenographer for a year. She was beautiful in a way that was decidedly unstenographic. She forewent the pomp of the alluring pompadour. She wore no chains, bracelets, or lockets. She had not the air of being about to accept an invitation to luncheon. Her dress was gray and plain, but it fitted her figure with fidelity and discretion. In her neat black turban hat was the gold-green wing of a macaw. On this morning she was softly and shyly radiant. Her eyes were dreamily bright, her cheeks genuine peach-blow, her expression a happy one, tinged with reminiscence.

Pitcher, still mildly curious, noticed a difference in her ways this morning. Instead of going straight into the adjoining room, where her desk was, she lingered, slightly irresolute, in the outer office. Once she moved over by Maxwell's desk, near enough for him to be aware of her presence.

The machine sitting at that desk was no longer a man; it was a busy New York broker, moved by buzzing wheels and uncoiling springs.

"Well—what is it? Anything?" asked Maxwell, sharply. His opened mail lay like a bank of stage snow on his crowded desk. His keen gray eye, impersonal and brusque, flashed upon her half impatiently.

"Nothing," answered the stenographer, moving away with a little smile.

"Mr. Pitcher," she said to the confidential clerk, "did Mr. Maxwell say anything yesterday about engaging another stenographer?"

"He did," answered Pitcher. "He told me to get another one. I notified the agency yesterday afternoon to send over a few samples this morning. It's 9.45 o'clock, and not a single picture hat or piece of pineapple chewing gum has showed up yet."

"I will do the work as usual, then," said the young lady, "until some one comes to fill the place." And she went to her desk at once and hung the black turban hat with the gold-green macaw wing in its accustomed place.

He who has been denied the spectacle of a busy Manhattan broker during a rush of business is handicapped for the profession of anthropology. The poet sings of the "crowded hour of glorious life." The broker's hour is not only crowded, but minutes and seconds are hanging to all the straps and packing both front and rear platforms.

And this day was Harvey Maxwell's busy day. The ticker began to reel out jerkily its fitful coils of tape, the desk telephone had a chronic attack of buzzing. Men began to throng into the office and call at him over the railing, jovially, sharply, viciously, excitedly. Messenger boys ran in and out with messages and telegrams. The clerks in the office jumped about like sailors during a storm. Even Pitcher's face relaxed into something resembling animation.

On the Exchange there were hurricanes and landslides and snowstorms and glaciers and volcanoes, and those elemental disturbances were reproduced in miniature in the broker's offices. Maxwell shoved his chair against the wall and transacted

business after the manner of a toe dancer. He jumped from
ticker to 'phone, from desk to door with the trained agility of
a harlequin.

In the midst of this growing and important stress the broker
became suddenly aware of a high-rolled fringe of golden hair
under a nodding canopy of velvet and ostrich tips, an imitation sealskin sacque and a string of beads as large as hickory
nuts, ending near the floor with a silver heart. There was a
self-possessed young lady connected with these accessories;
and Pitcher was there to construe her.

"Lady from the Stenographer's Agency to see about the
position," said Pitcher.

Maxwell turned half around, with his hands full of papers
and ticker tape.

"What position?" he asked, with a frown.

"Position of stenographer," said Pitcher. "You told me yesterday to call them up and have one sent over this morning."

"You are losing your mind, Pitcher," said Maxwell. "Why
should I have given you any such instructions? Miss Leslie
has given perfect satisfaction during the year she has been
here. The place is hers as long as she chooses to retain it.
There's no place open here, madam. Countermand that order
with the agency, Pitcher, and don't bring any more of 'em in
here."

The silver heart left the office, swinging and banging itself
independently against the office furniture as it indignantly departed. Pitcher seized a moment to remark to the bookkeeper
that the "old man" seemed to get more absent-minded and
forgetful every day of the world.

The rush and pace of business grew fiercer and faster. On
the floor they were pounding half a dozen stocks in which
Maxwell's customers were heavy investors. Orders to buy and
sell were coming and going as swift as the flight of swallows.
Some of his own holdings were imperilled, and the man was

working like some high-geared, delicate, strong machine—strung to full tension, going at full speed, accurate, never hesitating, with the proper word and decision and act ready and prompt as clockwork. Stocks and bonds, loans and mortgages, margins and securities—here was a world of finance, and there was no room in it for the human world or the world of nature.

When the luncheon hour drew near there came a slight lull in the uproar.

Maxwell stood by his desk with his hands full of telegrams and memoranda, with a fountain pen over his right ear and his hair hanging in disorderly strings over his forehead. His window was open, for the beloved janitress, Spring, had turned on a little warmth through the waking registers of the earth.

And through the window came a wandering—perhaps a lost —odor—a delicate, sweet odor of lilac that fixed the broker for a moment immovable. For this odor belonged to Miss Leslie; it was her own, and hers only.

The odor brought her vividly, almost tangibly before him. The world of finance dwindled suddenly to a speck. And she was in the next room—twenty steps away.

"By George, I'll do it now," said Maxwell, half aloud. "I'll ask her now. I wonder I didn't do it long ago."

He dashed into the inner office with the haste of a short trying to cover. He charged upon the desk of the stenographer.

She looked up at him with a smile. A soft pink crept over her cheek, and her eyes were kind and frank. Maxwell leaned one elbow on her desk. He still clutched fluttering papers with both hands and the pen was above his ear.

"Miss Leslie," he began, hurriedly, "I have but a moment to spare. I want to say something in that moment. Will you be my wife? I haven't had time to make love to you in the ordinary way, but I really do love you. Talk quick, please— those fellows are clubbing the stuffing out of Union Pacific."

"Oh, what are you talking about?" exclaimed the young lady. She rose to her feet and gazed upon him, round-eyed.

"Don't you understand?" said Maxwell, restively. "I want you to marry me. I love you, Miss Leslie. I wanted to tell you, and I snatched a minute when things had slackened up a bit. They're calling me for the 'phone now. Tell 'em to wait a minute, Pitcher. Won't you, Miss Leslie?"

The stenographer acted very queerly. At first she seemed overcome with amazement; then tears flowed from her wondering eyes; and then she smiled sunnily through them, and one of her arms slid tenderly about the broker's neck.

"I know now," she said, softly. "It's this old business that has driven everything else out of your head for the time. I was frightened at first. Don't you remember, Harvey? We were married last evening at 8 o'clock in the Little Church around the Corner."

The Furnished Room

RESTLESS, shifting, fugacious as time itself is a certain vast bulk of the population of the red brick district of the lower West Side. Homeless, they have a hundred homes. They flit from furnished room to furnished room, transients forever—transients in abode, transients in heart and mind. They sing "Home, Sweet Home" in ragtime; they carry their *lares et penates* in a bandbox; their vine is entwined about a picture hat; a rubber plant is their fig tree.

Hence the houses of this district, having had a thousand dwellers, should have a thousand tales to tell, mostly dull ones, no doubt; but it would be strange if there could not be found a ghost or two in the wake of all these vagrant guests.

One evening after dark a young man prowled among these crumbling red mansions, ringing their bells. At the twelfth he rested his lean hand-baggage upon the step and wiped the dust from his hatband and forehead. The bell sounded faint and far away in some remote, hollow depths.

To the door of this, the twelfth house whose bell he had rung, came a housekeeper who made him think of an unwholesome, surfeited worm that had eaten its nut to a hollow shell and now sought to fill the vacancy with edible lodgers.

He asked if there was a room to let.

"Come in," said the housekeeper. Her voice came from her throat; her throat seemed lined with fur. "I have the third-floor-back, vacant since a week back. Should you wish to look at it?"

The young man followed her up the stairs. A faint light from no particular source mitigated the shadows of the halls. They trod noiselessly upon a stair carpet that its own loom would have forsworn. It seemed to have become vegetable; to have degenerated in that rank, sunless air to lush lichen or spreading moss that grew in patches to the staircase and was viscid under the foot like organic matter. At each turn of the stairs were vacant niches in the wall. Perhaps plants had once been set within them. If so they had died in that foul and tainted air. It may be that statues of the saints had stood there, but it was not difficult to conceive that imps and devils had dragged them forth in the darkness and down to the unholy depths of some furnished pit below.

"This is the room," said the housekeeper, from her furry throat. "It's a nice room. It ain't often vacant. I had some most elegant people in it last summer—no trouble at all, and paid in advance to the minute. The water's at the end of the hall. Sprowls and Mooney kept it three months. They done a vaudeville sketch. Miss B'retta Sprowls—you may have heard of her—Oh, that was just the stage names—right there over the dresser is where the marriage certificate hung, framed. The gas is here, and you see there is plenty of closet room. It's a room everybody likes. It never stays idle long."

"Do you have many theatrical people rooming here?" asked the young man.

"They comes and goes. A good proportion of my lodgers is connected with the theatres. Yes, sir, this is the theatrical district. Actor people never stays long anywhere. I get my share. Yes, they comes and they goes."

He engaged the room, paying for a week in advance. He was tired, he said, and would take possession at once. He counted out the money. The room had been made ready, she said, even to towels and water. As the housekeeper moved away he put, for the thousandth time, the question that he carried at the end of his tongue.

"A young girl—Miss Vashner—Miss Eloise Vashner—do you remember such a one among your lodgers? She would be singing on the stage, most likely. A fair girl, of medium height and slender, with reddish, gold hair and dark mole near her left eyebrow."

"No, I don't remember the name. Them stage people has names they change as often as their rooms. They comes and they goes. No, I don't call that one to mind."

No. Always no. Five months of ceaseless interrogation and the inevitable negative. So much time spent by day in questioning managers, agents, schools and choruses; by night among the audiences of theatres from all-star casts down to music halls so low that he dreaded to find what he most hoped for. He who had loved her best had tried to find her. He was sure that since her disappearance from home this great, water-girt city held her somewhere, but it was like a monstrous quicksand, shifting its particles constantly, with no foundation, its upper granules of to-day buried to-morrow in ooze and slime.

The furnished room received its latest guest with a first glow of pseudo-hospitality, a hectic, haggard, perfunctory welcome like the specious smile of a demirep. The sophistical comfort came in reflected gleams from the decayed furniture, the ragged brocade upholstery of a couch and two chairs, a foot-wide cheap pier glass between the two windows, from one or two gilt picture frames and a brass bedstead in a corner.

The guest reclined, inert, upon a chair, while the room, confused in speech as though it were an apartment in Babel, tried to discourse to him of its divers tenantry.

A polychromatic rug like some brilliant-flowered, rectangular, tropical islet lay surrounded by a billowy sea of soiled matting. Upon the gay-papered wall were those pictures that pursue the homeless one from house to house—The Huguenot Lovers, The First Quarrel, The Wedding Breakfast, Psyche at the Fountain. The mantel's chastely severe outline was ingloriously veiled behind some pert drapery drawn rakishly askew like the sashes of the Amazonian ballet. Upon it was some desolate flotsam cast aside by the room's marooned when a lucky sail had borne them to a fresh port—a trifling vase or two, pictures of actresses, a medicine bottle, some stray cards out of a deck.

One by one, as the characters of a cryptograph became explicit, the little signs left by the furnished room's procession of guests developed a significance. The threadbare space in the rug in front of the dresser told that lovely women had marched in the throng. The tiny fingerprints on the wall spoke of little prisoners trying to feel their way to sun and air. A splattered stain, raying like the shadow of a bursting bomb, witnessed where a hurled glass or bottle had splintered with its contents against the wall. Across the pier glass had been scrawled with a diamond in staggering letters the name "Marie." It seemed that the succession of dwellers in the furnished room had turned in fury—perhaps tempted beyond forbearance by its garish coldness—and wreaked upon it their passions. The furniture was chipped and bruised; the couch, distorted by bursting springs, seemed a horrible monster that had been slain during the stress of some grotesque convulsion. Some more potent upheaval had cloven a great slice from the marble mantel. Each plank in the floor owned its particular cant and shriek as from a separate and individual agony. It seemed incredible that all this malice and injury had been wrought upon the room by those who had called it for a time their home; and yet it may have been the cheated home instinct surviving blindly, the resentful rage at false household gods that had kindled their wrath. A hut that is our own we can sweep and adorn and cherish.

The young tenant in the chair allowed these thoughts to file, soft-shod, through his mind, while there drifted into the room furnished sounds and furnished scents. He heard in one room a tittering and incontinent, slack laughter; in others the monologue of a scold, the rattling of dice, a lullaby, and one crying dully; above him a banjo tinkled with spirit. Doors banged somewhere; the elevated trains roared intermittently; a cat yowled miserably upon a back fence. And he breathed the breath of the house—a dank savor rather than a smell— a cold, musty effluvium as from underground vaults mingled with the reeking exhalations of linoleum and mildewed and rotten woodwork.

Then suddenly, as he rested there, the room was filled with the strong, sweet odor of mignonette. It came as upon a single buffet of wind with such sureness and fragrance and emphasis that it almost seemed a living visitant. And the man cried aloud: "What, dear?" as if he had been called, and sprang up and faced about. The rich odor clung to him and wrapped him around. He reached out his arms for it, all his senses for the time confused and commingled. How could one be peremptorily called by an odor? Surely it must have been a sound. But, was it not the sound that had touched, that had caressed him?

"She has been in this room," he cried, and he sprang to wrest from it a token, for he knew he would recognize the smallest thing that had belonged to her or that she had touched. This enveloping scent of mignonette, the odor that she had loved and made her own—whence came it?

The room had been but carelessly set in order. Scattered upon the flimsy dresser scarf were half a dozen hairpins—those discreet, indistinguishable friends of womankind, feminine of gender, infinite mood and uncommunicative of tense. These he ignored, conscious of their triumphant lack of identity. Ransacking the drawers of the dresser he came upon a discarded, tiny, ragged handkerchief. He pressed it to his face. It was racy and insolent with heliotrope; he hurled it to the floor. In another drawer he found odd buttons, a theatre programme, a pawnbroker's card, two lost marshmallows, a book on the divination of dreams. In the last was a woman's black satin hair bow, which halted him, poised between ice and fire. But the black satin hair bow also is femininity's demure, impersonal common ornament and tells no tales.

And then he traversed the room like a hound on the scent, skimming the walls, considering the corners of the bulging matting on his hands and knees, rummaging mantel and tables, the curtains and hangings, the drunken cabinet in the corner, for a visible sign, unable to perceive that she was there beside, around, against, within, above him, clinging to him, wooing him, calling him so poignantly through the finer senses that even his grosser ones became cognizant of the call. Once again he answered loudly: "Yes, dear!" and turned, wild-eyed, to gaze on vacancy, for he could not yet discern form and color and love and outstretched arms in the odor of mignonette. Oh, God! whence that odor, and since when have odors had a voice to call? Thus he groped.

He burrowed in crevices and corners, and found corks and cigarettes. These he passed in passive contempt. But once he found in a fold of the matting a half-smoked cigar, and this he ground beneath his heel with a green and trenchant oath. He sifted the room from end to end. He found dreary and ignoble small records of many a peripatetic tenant; but of her whom he sought, and who may have lodged there, and whose spirit seemed to hover there, he found no trace.

And then he thought of the housekeeper.

He ran from the haunted room downstairs and to a door that showed a crack of light. She came out to his knock. He smothered his excitement as best he could.

"Will you tell me, madam," he besought her, "who occupied the room I have before I came?"

"Yes, sir. I can tell you again. 'Twas Sprowls and Mooney, as I said. Miss B'retta Sprowls it was in the theatres, but Missis Mooney she was. My house is well known for respectability. The marriage certificate hung, framed, on a nail over——"

"What kind of a lady was Miss Sprowls—in looks, I mean?"

"Why, black-haired, sir, short, and stout, with a comical face. They left a week ago Tuesday."

"And before they occupied it?"

"Why, there was a single gentleman connected with the draying business. He left owing me a week. Before him was Missis Crowder and her two children, that stayed four months; and back of them was old Mr. Doyle, whose sons paid for him. He kept the room six months. That goes back a year, sir, and further I do not remember."

He thanked her and crept back to his room. The room was dead. The essence that had vivified it was gone. The perfume of mignonette had departed. In its place was the old, stale odor of mouldy house furniture, of atmosphere in storage.

The ebbing of his hope drained his faith. He sat staring

at the yellow, singing gaslight. Soon he walked to the bed and began to tear the sheets into strips. With the blade of his knife he drove them tightly into every crevice around windows and door. When all was snug and taut he turned out the light, turned the gas full on again and laid himself gratefully upon the bed.

.   .   .   .

It was Mrs. McCool's night to go with the can for beer. So she fetched it and sat with Mrs. Purdy in one of those subterranean retreats where housekeepers foregather and the worm dieth seldom.

"I rented out my third-floor-back this evening," said Mrs. Purdy, across a fine circle of foam. "A young man took it. He went up to bed two hours ago."

"Now, did ye, Mrs. Purdy, ma'am?" said Mrs. McCool, with intense admiration. "You do be a wonder for rentin' rooms of that kind. And did ye tell him, then?" she concluded in a husky whisper laden with mystery.

"Rooms," said Mrs. Purdy, in her furriest tones, "are furnished for to rent. I did not tell him, Mrs. McCool."

" 'Tis right ye are, ma'am; 'tis by renting rooms we kape alive. Ye have the rale sense for business, ma'am. There be many people will rayjict the rentin' of a room if they be tould a suicide has been after dyin' in the bed of it."

"As you say, we has our living to be making," remarked Mrs. Purdy.

"Yis, ma'am; 'tis true. 'Tis just one wake ago this day I helped ye lay out the third-floor-back. A pretty slip of a colleen she was to be killin' herself wid the gas—a swate little face she had, Mrs. Purdy, ma'am."

"She'd a-been called handsome, as you say," said Mrs. Purdy, assenting but critical, "but for that mole she had a-growin' by her left eyebrow. Do fill up your glass again, Mrs. McCool."

Roads of Destiny

I go to seek on many roads
  What is to be.
True heart and strong, with love to light—
Will they not bear me in the fight
To order, shun or wield or mould
  My Destiny?
        UNPUBLISHED POEMS OF DAVID MIGNOT.

THE song was over. The words were David's; the air, one of the countryside. The company about the inn table applauded heartily, for the young poet paid for the wine. Only the notary, M. Papineau, shook his head a little at the lines, for he was a man of books, and he had not drunk with the rest.

David went out into the village street, where the night air drove the wine vapor from his head. And then he remembered that he and Yvonne had quarrelled that day, and that he had resolved to leave his home that night to seek fame and honor in the great world outside.

"When my poems are on every man's tongue," he told himself, in a fine exhilaration, "she will, perhaps, think of the hard words she spoke this day."

Except the roysterers in the tavern, the village folk were abed. David crept softly into his room in the shed of his father's cottage and made a bundle of his small store of clothing. With this upon a staff, he set his face outward upon the road that ran from Vernoy.

He passed his father's herd of sheep huddled in their nightly pen—the sheep he herded daily, leaving them to scatter while he wrote verses on scraps of paper. He saw a light yet shining in Yvonne's window, and a weakness shook his purpose of a sudden. Perhaps that light meant that she rued, sleepless, her anger, and that morning might—— But, no! His decision was made. Vernoy was no place for him. Not one soul there could share his thoughts. Out along that road lay his fate and his future.

Three leagues across the dim, moonlit champaign ran the road, straight as a plowman's furrow. It was believed in the village that the road ran to Paris, at least; and this name the poet whispered often to himself as he walked. Never so far from Vernoy had David travelled before.

THE LEFT BRANCH

Three leagues, then, the road ran, and turned into a puzzle. It joined with another and a larger road at right angles. David stood, uncertain, for a while, and then took the road to the left.

Upon this more important highway were, imprinted in the dust, wheel tracks left by the recent passage of some vehicle. Some half an hour later these traces were verified by the sight of a ponderous carriage mired in a little brook at the bottom of a steep hill. The driver and postilions were shouting and tugging at the horses' bridles. On the road at one side stood a huge, black-clothed man and a slender lady wrapped in a long, light cloak.

David saw the lack of skill in the efforts of the servants. He quietly assumed control of the work. He directed the outriders to cease their clamor at the horses and to exercise their strength upon the wheels. The driver alone urged the animals with his familiar voice; David himself heaved a powerful shoulder at the rear of the carriage, and with one harmonious tug the great vehicle rolled up on solid ground. The outriders climbed to their places.

David stood for a moment upon one foot. The huge gentleman waved a hand. "You will enter the carriage," he said, in a voice large, like himself, but smoothed by art and habit. Obedience belonged in the path of such a voice. Brief as was the young poet's hesitation, it was cut shorter still by a renewal of the command. David's foot went to the step. In the darkness he perceived dimly the form of the lady upon the rear seat. He was about to seat himself opposite, when the voice again swayed him to its will. "You will sit at the lady's side."

The gentleman swung his great weight to the forward seat. The carriage proceeded up the hill. The lady was shrunk, silent, into her corner. David could not estimate whether she was old or young, but a delicate, mild perfume from her clothes stirred his poet's fancy to the belief that there was loveliness beneath the mystery. Here was an adventure such as he had often imagined. But as yet he held no key to it, for no word was spoken while he sat with his impenetrable companions.

In an hour's time David perceived through the window that the vehicle traversed the street of some town. Then it stopped in front of a closed and darkened house, and a postilion alighted to hammer impatiently upon the door. A latticed window above flew wide and a night-capped head popped out.

"Who are ye that disturb honest folk at this time of night? My house is closed. 'Tis too late for profitable travellers to be abroad. Cease knocking at my door, and be off."

"Open!" spluttered the postilion, loudly; "open for Monseigneur, the Marquis de Beaupertuys."

"Ah!" cried the voice above. "Ten thousand pardons, my lord. I did not know—the hour is so late—at once shall the door be opened, and the house placed at my lord's disposal."

Inside was heard the clink of chain and bar, and the door was flung open. Shivering with chill and apprehension, the landlord of the Silver Flagon stood, half clad, candle in hand, upon the threshold.

David followed the marquis out of the carriage. "Assist the lady," he was ordered. The poet obeyed. He felt her small hand tremble as he guided her descent. "Into the house," was the next command.

The room was the long dining-hall of the tavern. A great oak table ran down its length. The huge gentleman seated himself in a chair at the nearer end. The lady sank into another against the wall, with an air of great weariness. David stood, considering how best he might now take his leave and continue upon his way.

"My lord," said the landlord, bowing to the floor, "h-had I ex-expected this honor, entertainment would have been ready. T-t-there is wine and cold fowl and m-m-maybe——"

"Candles," said the marquis, spreading the fingers of one plump white hand in a gesture he had.

"Y-yes, my lord." He fetched half a dozen candles, lighted them, and set them upon the table.

"If monsieur would, perhaps, deign to taste a certain Burgundy—there is a cask——"

"Candles," said monsieur, spreading his fingers.

"Assuredly—quickly—I fly, my lord."

A dozen more lighted candles shone in the hall. The great bulk of the marquis overflowed his chair. He was dressed in fine black from head to foot save for the snowy ruffles at his wrist and throat. Even the hilt and scabbard of his sword were black. His expression was one of sneering pride. The ends of an upturned moustache reached nearly to his mocking eyes.

The lady sat motionless, and now David perceived that she was young, and possessed a pathetic and appealing beauty. He was startled from the contemplation of her forlorn loveliness by the booming voice of the marquis.

"What is your name and pursuit?"

"David Mignot. I am a poet."

The moustache of the marquis curled nearer to his eyes.

"How do you live?"

"I am also a shepherd; I guarded my father's flock," David answered, with his head high, but a flush upon his cheek.

"Then listen, master shepherd and poet, to the fortune you have blundered upon to-night. This lady is my niece, Mademoiselle Lucie de Varennes. She is of noble descent and is possessed of ten thousand francs a year in her own right. As to her charms, you have but to observe for yourself. If the inventory pleases your shepherd's heart, she becomes your wife at a word. Do not interrupt me. To-night I conveyed her to the château of the Comte de Villemaur, to whom her hand had been promised. Guests were present; the priest was waiting; her marriage to one eligible in rank and fortune was ready to be accomplished. At the altar this demoiselle, so meek and dutiful, turned upon me like a leopardess, charged me with cruelty and crimes, and broke, before the gaping priest, the troth I had plighted for her. I swore there and then, by ten thousand devils, that she should marry the first man we met after leaving the château, be he prince, charcoal-burner, or thief. You, shepherd, are the first. Mademoiselle must be wed this night. If not you, then another. You have ten minutes in which to make your decision. Do not vex me with words or questions. Ten minutes, shepherd; and they are speeding."

The marquis drummed loudly with his white fingers upon the table. He sank into a veiled attitude of waiting. It was as if some great house had shut its doors and windows against approach. David would have spoken, but the huge man's bearing stopped his tongue. Instead, he stood by the lady's chair and bowed.

"Mademoiselle," he said, and he marvelled to find his words

flowing easily before so much elegance and beauty. "You have heard me say I was a shepherd. I have also had the fancy, at times, that I am a poet. If it be the test of a poet to adore and cherish the beautiful, that fancy is now strengthened. Can I serve you in any way, mademoiselle?"

The young woman looked up at him with eyes dry and mournful. His frank, glowing face, made serious by the gravity of the adventure, his strong, straight figure and the liquid sympathy in his blue eyes, perhaps, also, her imminent need of long-denied help and kindness, thawed her to sudden tears.

"Monsieur," she said, in low tones, "you look to be true and kind. He is my uncle, the brother of my father, and my only relative. He loved my mother, and he hates me because I am like her. He has made my life one long terror. I am afraid of his very looks, and never before dared to disobey him. But to-night he would have married me to a man three times my age. You will forgive me for bringing this vexation upon you, monsieur. You will, of course, decline this mad act he tries to force upon you. But let me thank you for your generous words, at least. I have had none spoken to me in so long."

There was now something more than generosity in the poet's eyes. Poet he must have been, for Yvonne was forgotten; this fine, new loveliness held him with its freshness and grace. The subtle perfume from her filled him with strange emotions. His tender look fell warmly upon her. She leaned to it, thirstily.

"Ten minutes," said David, "is given me in which to do what I would devote years to achieve. I will not say I pity you, mademoiselle; it would not be true—I love you. I cannot ask love from you yet, but let me rescue you from this cruel man, and, in time, love may come. I think I have a future, I will not always be a shepherd. For the present I will cherish you with all my heart and make your life less sad. Will you trust your fate to me, mademoiselle?"

"Ah, you would sacrifice yourself from pity!"

"From love. The time is almost up, mademoiselle."

"You will regret it, and despise me."

"I will live only to make you happy, and myself worthy of you."

Her fine small hand crept into his from beneath her cloak.

"I will trust you," she breathed, "with my life. And—and love—may not be so far off as you think. Tell him. Once away from the power of his eyes I may forget."

David went and stood before the marquis. The black figure stirred, and the mocking eyes glanced at the great hall clock.

"Two minutes to spare. A shepherd requires eight minutes to decide whether he will accept a bride of beauty and income! Speak up, shepherd, do you consent to become mademoiselle's husband?"

"Mademoiselle," said David, standing proudly, "has done me the honor to yield to my request that she become my wife."

"Well said!" said the marquis. "You have yet the making of a courtier in you, master shepherd. Mademoiselle could have drawn a worse prize, after all. And now to be done with the affair as quick as the Church and the devil will allow!"

He struck the table soundly with his sword hilt. The landlord came, knee-shaking, bringing more candles in the hope of anticipating the great lord's whims. "Fetch a priest," said the marquis, "a priest; do you understand? In ten minutes have a priest here, or——"

The landlord dropped his candles and flew.

The priest came, heavy-eyed and ruffled. He made David Mignot and Lucie de Varennes man and wife, pocketed a gold piece that the marquis tossed him, and shuffled out again into the night.

"Wine," ordered the marquis, spreading his ominous fingers at the host.

"Fill glasses," he said, when it was brought. He stood up at the head of the table in the candlelight, a black mountain of venom and conceit, with something like the memory of an old love turned to poison in his eye, as it fell upon his niece.

"Monsieur Mignot," he said, raising his wine-glass, "drink after I say this to you: You have taken to be your wife one who will make your life a foul and wretched thing. The blood in her is an inheritance running black lies and red ruin. She will bring you shame and anxiety. The devil that descended to her is there in her eyes and skin and mouth that stoop even to beguile a peasant. There is your promise, monsieur poet, for a happy life. Drink your wine. At last, mademoiselle, I am rid of you."

The marquis drank. A little grievous cry, as if from a sudden wound, came from the girl's lips. David, with his glass in his hand, stepped forward three paces and faced the marquis. There was little of a shepherd in his bearing.

"Just now," he said calmly, "you did me the honor to call me 'monsieur.' May I hope, therefore, that my marriage to mademoiselle has placed me somewhat nearer to you in—let us say, reflected rank—has given me the right to stand more as an equal to monseigneur in a certain little piece of business I have in my mind?"

"You may hope, shepherd," sneered the marquis.

"Then," said David, dashing his glass of wine into the contemptuous eyes that mocked him, "perhaps you will condescend to fight me."

The fury of the great lord outbroke in one sudden curse like a blast from a horn. He tore his sword from its black sheath; he called to the hovering landlord: "A sword there, for this lout!" He turned to the lady, with a laugh that chilled her heart, and said: "You put much labor upon me, madame. It seems I must find you a husband and make you a widow in the same night."

"I know not sword-play," said David. He flushed to make the confession before his lady.

"'I know not sword-play,'" mimicked the marquis. "Shall we fight like peasants with oaken cudgels? *Hola!* François, my pistols!"

A postilion brought two shining great pistols ornamented with carven silver from the carriage holsters. The marquis tossed one upon the table near David's hand. "To the other end of the table," he cried; "even a shepherd may pull a trigger. Few of them attain the honor to die by the weapon of a De Beaupertuys."

The shepherd and the marquis faced each other from the ends of the long table. The landlord, in an ague of terror, clutched the air and stammered: "M-M-Monseigneur, for the love of Christ! not in my house!—do not spill blood—it will ruin my custom——" The look of the marquis, threatening him, paralyzed his tongue.

"Coward," cried the lord of Beaupertuys, "cease chattering your teeth long enough to give the word for us, if you can."

Mine host's knees smote the floor. He was without a vocabulary. Even sounds were beyond him. Still, by gestures he seemed to beseech peace in the name of his house and custom.

"I will give the word," said the lady, in a clear voice. She went up to David and kissed him sweetly. Her eyes were sparkling bright, and color had come to her cheek. She stood against the wall, and the two men levelled their pistols for her count.

"*Un—deux—trois!*"

The two reports came so nearly together that the candles flickered but once. The marquis stood, smiling, the fingers of his left hand resting, outspread, upon the end of the table. David remained erect, and turned his head very slowly, searching for his wife with his eyes. Then, as a garment falls from where it is hung, he sank, crumpled, upon the floor.

With a little cry of terror and despair, the widowed maid ran and stooped above him. She found his wound, and then looked up with her old look of pale melancholy. "Through his heart," she whispered. "Oh, his heart!"

"Come," boomed the great voice of the marquis, "out with you to the carriage! Daybreak shall not find you on my hands. Wed you shall be again, and to a living husband, this night. The next we come upon, my lady, highwayman or peasant. If the road yields no other, than the churl that opens my gates. Out with you to the carriage!"

The marquis, implacable and huge, the lady wrapped again in the mystery of her cloak, the postilion bearing the weapons —all moved out to the waiting carriage. The sound of its ponderous wheels rolling away echoed through the slumbering village. In the hall of the Silver Flagon the distracted landlord wrung his hands above the slain poet's body, while the flames of the four and twenty candles danced and flickered on the table.

The Right Branch

Three leagues, then, the road ran, and turned into a puzzle. It joined with another and a larger road at right angles. David stood, uncertain, for a while, and then took the road to the right.

Whither it led he knew not, but he was resolved to leave Vernoy far behind that night. He travelled a league and then passed a large château which showed testimony of recent entertainment. Lights shone from every window; from the great stone gateway ran a tracery of wheel tracks drawn in the dust by the vehicles of the guests.

Three leagues farther and David was weary. He rested and

slept for a while on a bed of pine boughs at the roadside.
Then up and on again along the unknown way.

Thus for five days he travelled the great road, sleeping upon
Nature's balsamic beds or in peasants' ricks, eating of their
black, hospitable bread, drinking from streams or the willing
cup of the goatherd.

At length he crossed a great bridge and set his foot within
the smiling city that has crushed or crowned more poets
than all the rest of the world. His breath came quickly as Paris
sang to him in a little undertone her vital chant of greeting—
the hum of voice and foot and wheel.

High up under the eaves of an old house in the Rue Conti,
David paid for lodging, and set himself, in a wooden chair, to
his poems. The street, once sheltering citizens of import and
consequence, was now given over to those who ever follow in
the wake of decline.

The houses were tall and still possessed of a ruined dignity,
but many of them were empty save for dust and the spider.
By night there was the clash of steel and the cries of brawlers
straying restlessly from inn to inn. Where once gentility abode
was now but a rancid and rude incontinence. But here David
found housing commensurate to his scant purse. Daylight and
candlelight found him at pen and paper.

One afternoon he was returning from a foraging trip to the
lower world, with bread and curds and a bottle of thin wine.
Halfway up his dark stairway he met—or rather came upon,
for she rested on the stair—a young woman of a beauty that
should balk even the justice of a poet's imagination. A loose,
dark cloak, flung open, showed a rich gown beneath. Her eyes
changed swiftly with every little shade of thought. Within one
moment they would be round and artless like a child's, and
long and cozening like a gypsy's. One hand raised her gown,
undraping a little shoe, high-heeled, with its ribbons dan-
gling, untied. So heavenly she was, so unfitted to stoop, so

qualified to charm and command! Perhaps she had seen
David coming, and had waited for his help there.

Ah, would monsieur pardon that she occupied the stairway, but the shoe!—the naughty shoe! Alas! it would not
remain tied. Ah! if monsieur *would* be so gracious!

The poet's fingers trembled as he tied the contrary ribbons.
Then he would have fled from the danger of her presence,
but the eyes grew long and cozening, like a gypsy's, and held
him. He leaned against the balustrade, clutching his bottle of
sour wine.

"You have been so good," she said, smiling. "Does monsieur, perhaps, live in the house?"

"Yes, madame. I—I think so, madame."

"Perhaps in the third story, then?"

"No, madame; higher up."

The lady fluttered her fingers with the least possible gesture
of impatience.

"Pardon. Certainly I am not discreet in asking. Monsieur
will forgive me? It is surely not becoming that I should inquire where he lodges."

"Madame, do not say so. I live in the——"

"No, no, no; do not tell me. Now I see that I erred. But I
cannot lose the interest I feel in this house and all that is in
it. Once it was my home. Often I come here but to dream of
those happy days again. Will you let that be my excuse?"

"Let me tell you, then, for you need no excuse," stammered
the poet. "I live in the top floor—the small room where the
stairs turn."

"In the front room?" asked the lady, turning her head side-
wise.

"The rear, madame."

The lady sighed, as if with relief.

"I will detain you no longer, then, monsieur," she said,
employing the round and artless eye. "Take good care of my

house. Alas! only the memories of it are mine now. Adieu, and accept my thanks for your courtesy."

She was gone, leaving but a smile and a trace of sweet perfume. David climbed the stairs as one in slumber. But he awoke from it, and the smile and the perfume lingered with him and never afterward did either seem quite to leave him. This lady of whom he knew nothing drove him to lyrics of eyes, chansons of swiftly conceived love, odes to curling hair, and sonnets to slippers on slender feet.

Poet he must have been, for Yvonne was forgotten; this fine, new loveliness held him with its freshness and grace. The subtle perfume about her filled him with strange emotions.

On a certain night three persons were gathered about a table in a room on the third floor of the same house. Three chairs and the table and a lighted candle upon it was all the furniture. One of the persons was a huge man, dressed in black. His expression was one of sneering pride. The ends of his upturned moustache reached nearly to his mocking eyes. Another was a lady, young and beautiful, with eyes that could be round and artless, like a child's, or long and cozening, like a gypsy's, but were now keen and ambitious, like any other conspirator's. The third was a man of action, a combatant, a bold and impatient executive, breathing fire and steel. He was addressed by the others as Captain Desrolles.

This man struck the table with his fist, and said, with controlled violence:

"To-night. To-night as he goes to midnight mass. I am tired of the plotting that gets nowhere. I am sick of signals and ciphers and secret meetings and such *baragouin*. Let us be honest traitors. If France is to be rid of him, let us kill in the open, and not hunt with snares and traps. To-night, I say. I back my words. My hand will do the deed. To-night, as he goes to mass."

The lady turned upon him a cordial look. Woman, however wedded to plots, must ever thus bow to rash courage. The big man stroked his upturned moustache.

"Dear captain," he said, in a great voice, softened by habit, "this time I agree with you. Nothing is to be gained by waiting. Enough of the palace guards belong to us to make the endeavor a safe one."

"To-night," repeated Captain Desrolles, again striking the table. "You have heard me, marquis; my hand will do the deed."

"But now," said the huge man, softly, "comes a question. Word must be sent to our partisans in the palace, and a signal agreed upon. Our stanchest men must accompany the royal carriage. At this hour what messenger can penetrate so far as the south doorway? Ribout is stationed there; once a message is placed in his hands, all will go well."

"I will send the message," said the lady.

"You, countess?" said the marquis, raising his eyebrows. "Your devotion is great, we know, but——"

"Listen!" exclaimed the lady, rising and resting her hands upon the table; "in a garret of this house lives a youth from the provinces as guileless and tender as the lambs he tended there. I have met him twice or thrice upon the stairs. I questioned him, fearing that he might dwell too near the room in which we are accustomed to meet. He is mine, if I will. He writes poems in his garret, and I think he dreams of me. He will do what I say. He shall take the message to the palace."

The marquis rose from his chair and bowed. "You did not permit me to finish my sentence, countess," he said. "I would have said: 'Your devotion is great, but your wit and charm are infinitely greater.'"

While the conspirators were thus engaged, David was polishing some lines addressed to his *amorette d'escalier*. He heard a timorous knock at his door, and opened it, with a great throb, to behold her there, panting as one in straits, with eyes wide open and artless, like a child's.

"Monsieur," she breathed, "I come to you in distress. I believe you to be good and true, and I know of no other help. How I flew through the streets among the swaggering men! Monsieur, my mother is dying. My uncle is a captain of guards in the palace of the king. Some one must fly to bring him. May I hope——"

"Mademoiselle," interrupted David, his eyes shining with the desire to do her service, "your hopes shall be my wings. Tell me how I may reach him."

The lady thrust a sealed paper into his hand.

"Go to the south gate—the south gate, mind—and say to the guards there, 'The falcon has left his nest.' They will pass you, and you will go to the south entrance to the palace. Repeat the words, and give this letter to the man who will reply, 'Let him strike when he will.' This is the password, monsieur, entrusted to me by my uncle, for now when the country is disturbed and men plot against the king's life, no one without it can gain entrance to the palace grounds after nightfall. If you will, monsieur, take him this letter so that my mother may see him before she closes her eyes."

"Give it me," said David, eagerly. "But shall I let you return home through the streets alone so late? I——"

"No, no—fly. Each moment is like a precious jewel. Some time," said the lady, with eyes long and cozening, like a gypsy's, "I will try to thank you for your goodness."

The poet thrust the letter into his breast, and bounded down the stairway. The lady, when he was gone, returned to the room below.

The eloquent eyebrows of the marquis interrogated her.

"He is gone," she said, "as fleet and stupid as one of his own sheep, to deliver it."

The table shook again from the batter of Captain Desrolles's fist.

"Sacred name!" he cried; "I have left my pistols behind! I can trust no others."

"Take this," said the marquis, drawing from beneath his cloak a shining, great weapon, ornamented with carven silver. "There are none truer. But guard it closely, for it bears my arms and crest, and already I am suspected. Me, I must put many leagues between myself and Paris this night. Tomorrow must find me in my château. After you, dear countess."

The marquis puffed out the candle. The lady, well cloaked, and the two gentlemen softly descended the stairway and flowed into the crowd that roamed along the narrow pavements of the Rue Conti.

David sped. At the south gate of the king's residence a halberd was laid to his breast, but he turned its point with the words: "The falcon has left his nest."

"Pass, brother," said the guard, "and go quickly."

On the south steps of the palace they moved to seize him, but again the *mot de passe* charmed the watchers. One among them stepped forward and began: "Let him strike——" But a flurry among the guards told of a surprise. A man of keen look and soldierly stride suddenly pressed through them and seized the letter which David held in his hand. "Come with me," he said, and led him inside the great hall. Then he tore open the letter and read it. He beckoned to a man uniformed as an officer of musketeers, who was passing. "Captain Tetreau, you will have the guards at the south entrance and the south gate arrested and confined. Place men known to be loyal in their places." To David he said: "Come with me."

He conducted him through a corridor and an anteroom into a spacious chamber, where a melancholy man, sombrely dressed, sat brooding in a great leather-covered chair. To that man he said:

"Sire, I have told you that the palace is as full of traitors and spies as a sewer is of rats. You have thought, sire, that it was my fancy. This man penetrated to your very door by their connivance. He bore a letter which I have intercepted. I have brought him here that your majesty may no longer think my zeal excessive."

"I will question him," said the king, stirring in his chair. He looked at David with heavy eyes dulled by an opaque film. The poet bent his knee.

"From where do you come?" asked the king.

"From the village of Vernoy, in the province of Eure-et-Loir, sire."

"What do you follow in Paris?"

"I—I would be a poet, sire."

"What did you in Vernoy?"

"I minded my father's flock of sheep."

The king stirred again, and the film lifted from his eyes.

"Ah! in the fields?"

"Yes, sire."

"You lived in the fields; you went out in the cool of the morning and lay among the hedges in the grass. The flock distributed itself upon the hillside; you drank of the living stream; you ate your sweet brown bread in the shade; and you listened, doubtless, to blackbirds piping in the grove. Is not that so, shepherd?"

"It is, sire," answered David, with a sigh; "and to the bees at the flowers, and, maybe, to the grape gatherers singing on the hill."

"Yes, yes," said the king, impatiently; "maybe to them; but surely to the blackbirds. They whistled often, in the grove, did they not?"

"Nowhere, sire, so sweetly as in Eure-et-Loir. I have endeavored to express their song in some verses that I have written."

"Can you repeat those verses?" asked the king, eagerly. "A long time ago I listened to the blackbirds. It would be something better than a kingdom if one could rightly construe their song. And at night you drove the sheep to the fold and then sat, in peace and tranquillity, to your pleasant bread. Can you repeat those verses, shepherd?"

"They run this way, sire," said David, with respectful ardor:

> *"Lazy shepherd, see your lambkins*
> *Skip, ecstatic, on the mead;*
> *See the firs dance in the breezes,*
> *Hear Pan blowing at his reed.*

> *"Hear us calling from the tree-tops,*
> *See us swoop upon your flock;*
> *Yield us wool to make our nests warm*
> *In the branches of the—"*

"If it please your majesty," interrupted a harsh voice, "I will ask a question or two of this rhymester. There is little time to spare. I crave pardon, sire, if my anxiety for your safety offends."

"The loyalty," said the king, "of the Duke d'Aumale is too well proven to give offence." He sank into his chair, and the film came again over his eyes.

"First," said the duke, "I will read you the letter he brought:

"To-night is the anniversary of the dauphin's death. If he goes, as is his custom, to midnight mass to pray for the soul of his son, the falcon will strike, at the corner of the Rue Esplanade. If this be his intention, set a red light in the upper room at the southwest corner of the palace, that the falcon may take heed.

"Peasant," said the duke, sternly, "you have heard these words. Who gave you this message to bring?"

"My lord duke," said David, sincerely, "I will tell you. A lady gave it me. She said her mother was ill, and that this writing would fetch her uncle to her bedside. I do not know the meaning of the letter, but I will swear that she is beautiful and good."

"Describe the woman," commanded the duke, "and how you came to be her dupe."

"Describe her!" said David with a tender smile. "You would command words to perform miracles. Well, she is made of sunshine and deep shade. She is slender, like the alders, and moves with their grace. Her eyes change while you gaze into them; now round, and then half shut as the sun peeps between two clouds. When she comes, heaven is all about her; when she leaves, there is chaos and a scent of hawthorn blossoms. She came to me in the Rue Conti, number twenty-nine."

"It is the house," said the duke, turning to the king, "that we have been watching. Thanks to the poet's tongue, we have a picture of the infamous Countess Quebedaux."

"Sire and my lord duke," said David, earnestly, "I hope my poor words have done no injustice. I have looked into that lady's eyes. I will stake my life that she is an angel, letter or no letter."

The duke looked at him steadily. "I will put you to the proof," he said, slowly. "Dressed as the king, you shall, yourself, attend mass in his carriage at midnight. Do you accept the test?"

David smiled. "I have looked into her eyes," he said. "I had my proof there. Take yours how you will."

Half an hour before twelve the Duke d'Aumale, with his own hands, set a red lamp in a southwest window of the palace. At ten minutes to the hour, David, leaning on his arm, dressed as the king, from top to toe, with his head bowed in his cloak, walked slowly from the royal apartments to the waiting carriage. The duke assisted him inside and closed the door. The carriage whirled away along its route to the cathedral.

On the *qui vive* in a house at the corner of the Rue Esplanade was Captain Tetreau with twenty men, ready to pounce upon the conspirators when they should appear.

But it seemed that, for some reason, the plotters had slightly altered their plans. When the royal carriage had reached the Rue Christopher, one square nearer than the Rue Esplanade, forth from it burst Captain Desrolles, with his band of would-be regicides, and assailed the equipage. The guards upon the carriage, though surprised at the premature attack, descended and fought valiantly. The noise of conflict attracted the force of Captain Tetreau, and they came pelting down the street to the rescue. But, in the meantime, the desperate Desrolles had torn open the door of the king's carriage, thrust his weapon against the body of the dark figure inside, and fired.

Now, with loyal reinforcements at hand, the street rang with cries and the rasp of steel, but the frightened horses had dashed away. Upon the cushions lay the dead body of the poor mock king and poet, slain by a ball from the pistol of Monseigneur, the Marquis de Beaupertuys.

THE MAIN ROAD

Three leagues, then, the road ran, and turned into a puzzle. It joined with another and a larger road at right angles. David stood, uncertain, for a while, and then sat himself to rest upon its side.

Whither those roads led he knew not. Either way there seemed to lie a great world full of chance and peril. And then, sitting there, his eye fell upon a bright star, one that he and Yvonne had named for theirs. That set him thinking of

Yvonne, and he wondered if he had not been too hasty. Why should he leave her and his home because a few hot words had come between them? Was love so brittle a thing that jealousy, the very proof of it, could break it? Mornings always brought a cure for the little heartaches of evening. There was yet time for him to return home without any one in the sweetly sleeping village of Vernoy being the wiser. His heart was Yvonne's; there where he had lived always he could write his poems and find his happiness.

David rose, and shook off his unrest and the wild mood that had tempted him. He set his face steadfastly back along the road he had come. By the time he had retravelled the road to Vernoy, his desire to rove was gone. He passed the sheepfold, and the sheep scurried, with a drumming flutter, at his late footsteps, warming his heart by the homely sound. He crept without noise into his little room and lay there, thankful that his feet had escaped the distress of new roads that night.

How well he knew woman's heart! The next evening Yvonne was at the well in the road where the young congregated in order that the *curé* might have business. The corner of her eye was engaged in a search for David, albeit her set mouth seemed unrelenting. He saw the look; braved the mouth, drew from it a recantation and, later, a kiss as they walked homeward together.

Three months afterward they were married. David's father was shrewd and prosperous. He gave them a wedding that was heard of three leagues away. Both the young people were favorites in the village. There was a procession in the streets, a dance on the green; they had the marionettes and a tumbler out from Dreux to delight the guests.

Then a year, and David's father died. The sheep and the cottage descended to him. He already had the seemliest wife in the village. Yvonne's milk pails and her brass kettles were bright—*ouf!* they blinded you in the sun when you passed that way. But you must keep your eyes upon her yard, for her flower beds were so neat and gay they restored to you your sight. And you might hear her sing, aye, as far as the double chestnut tree above Père Gruneau's blacksmith forge.

But a day came when David drew out paper from a long-shut drawer, and began to bite the end of a pencil. Spring had come again and touched his heart. Poet he must have been, for now Yvonne was well-nigh forgotten. This fine new loveliness of earth held him with its witchery and grace. The perfume from her woods and meadows stirred him strangely. Daily had he gone forth with his flock, and brought it safe at night. But now he stretched himself under the hedge and pieced words together on his bits of paper. The sheep strayed, and the wolves, perceiving that difficult poems make easy mutton, ventured from the woods and stole his lambs.

David's stock of poems grew larger and his flock smaller. Yvonne's nose and temper waxed sharp and her talk blunt. Her pans and kettles grew dull, but her eyes had caught their flash. She pointed out to the poet that his neglect was reducing the flock and bringing woe upon the household. David hired a boy to guard the sheep, locked himself in the little room in the top of the cottage, and wrote more poems. The boy, being a poet by nature, but not furnished with an outlet in the way of writing, spent his time in slumber. The wolves lost no time in discovering that poetry and sleep are practically the same; so the flock steadily grew smaller. Yvonne's ill temper increased at an equal rate. Sometimes she would stand in the yard and rail at David through his high window. Then you could hear her as far as the double chestnut tree above Père Gruneau's blacksmith forge.

M. Papineau, the kind, wise, meddling old notary, saw this, as he saw everything at which his nose pointed. He went to David, fortified himself with a great pinch of snuff, and said:

"Friend Mignot, I affixed the seal upon the marriage certificate of your father. It would distress me to be obliged to attest a paper signifying the bankruptcy of his son. But that is what you are coming to. I speak as an old friend. Now, listen to what I have to say. You have your heart set, I perceive, upon poetry. At Dreux, I have a friend, one Monsieur Bril—Georges Bril. He lives in a little cleared space in a houseful of books. He is a learned man; he visits Paris each year; he himself has written books. He will tell you when the catacombs were made, how they found out the names of the stars, and why the plover has a long bill. The meaning and the form of poetry is to him as intelligent as the baa of a sheep is to you. I will give you a letter to him, and you shall take him your poems and let him read them. Then you will know if you shall write more, or give your attention to your wife and business."

"Write the letter," said David. "I am sorry you did not speak of this sooner."

At sunrise the next morning he was on the road to Dreux with the precious roll of poems under his arm. At noon he wiped the dust from his feet at the door of Monsieur Bril. That learned man broke the seal of M. Papineau's letter, and sucked up its contents through his gleaming spectacles as the sun draws water. He took David inside to his study and sat him down upon a little island beat upon by a sea of books.

Monsieur Bril had a conscience. He flinched not even at a mass of manuscript the thickness of a finger length and rolled to an incorrigible curve. He broke the back of the roll against his knee and began to read. He slighted nothing; he bored into the lump as a worm into a nut, seeking for a kernel.

Meanwhile, David sat, marooned, trembling in the spray of so much literature. It roared in his ears. He held no chart or compass for voyaging in that sea. Half the world, he thought, must be writing books.

Monsieur Bril bored to the last page of the poems. Then he took off his spectacles and wiped them with his handkerchief.

"My old friend, Papineau, is well?" he asked.

"In the best of health," said David.

"How many sheep have you, Monsieur Mignot?"

"Three hundred and nine, when I counted them yesterday. The flock has had ill fortune. To that number it has decreased from eight hundred and fifty."

"You have a wife and a home, and lived in comfort. The sheep brought you plenty. You went into the fields with them and lived in the keen air and ate the sweet bread of contentment. You had but to be vigilant and recline there upon nature's breast, listening to the whistle of the blackbirds in the grove. Am I right thus far?"

"It was so," said David.

"I have read all your verses," continued Monsieur Bril, his eyes wandering about his sea of books as if he conned the horizon for a sail. "Look yonder, through that window, Monsieur Mignot; tell me what you see in that tree."

"I see a crow," said David, looking.

"There is a bird," said Monsieur Bril, "that shall assist me where I am disposed to shirk a duty. You know that bird, Monsieur Mignot; he is the philosopher of the air. He is happy through submission to his lot. None so merry or full-crawed as he with his whimsical eye and rollicking step. The fields yield him what he desires. He never grieves that his plumage is not gay, like the oriole's. And you have heard, Monsieur Mignot, the notes that nature has given him? Is the nightingale any happier, do you think?"

David rose to his feet. The crow cawed harshly from his tree.

"I thank you, Monsieur Bril," he said, slowly. "There was not, then, one nightingale note among all those croaks?"

"I could not have missed it," said Monsieur Bril, with a

sigh. "I read every word. Live your poetry, man; do not try to write it any more."

"I thank you," said David, again. "And now I will be going back to my sheep."

"If you would dine with me," said the man of books, "and overlook the smart of it, I will give you reasons at length."

"No," said the poet, "I must be back in the fields cawing at my sheep."

Back along the road to Vernoy he trudged with his poems under his arm. When he reached his village he turned into the shop of one Zeigler, a Jew out of Armenia, who sold anything that came to his hand.

"Friend," said David, "wolves from the forest harass my sheep on the hills. I must purchase firearms to protect them. What have you?"

"A bad day, this, for me, friend Mignot," said Zeigler, spreading his hands, "for I perceive that I must sell you a weapon that will not fetch a tenth of its value. Only last week I bought from a peddler a wagon full of goods that he procured at a sale by a *commissionaire* of the crown. The sale was of the château and belongings of a great lord—I know not his title—who has been banished for conspiracy against the king. There are some choice firearms in the lot. This pistol—oh, a weapon fit for a prince!—it shall be only forty francs to you, friend Mignot—if I lost ten by the sale. But perhaps an arquebus——"

"This will do," said David, throwing the money on the counter. "Is it charged?"

"I will charge it," said Zeigler. "And, for ten francs more, add a store of powder and ball."

David laid his pistol under his coat and walked to his cottage. Yvonne was not there. Of late she had taken to gadding much among the neighbors. But a fire was glowing in the kitchen stove. David opened the door of it and thrust his poems in upon the coals. As they blazed up they made a singing, harsh sound in the flue.

"The song of the crow!" said the poet.

He went up to his attic room and closed the door. So quiet was the village that a score of people heard the roar of the great pistol. They flocked thither, and up the stairs where the smoke, issuing, drew their notice.

The men laid the body of the poet upon his bed, awkwardly arranging it to conceal the torn plumage of the poor black crow. The women chattered in a luxury of zealous pity. Some of them ran to tell Yvonne.

M. Papineau, whose nose had brought him there among the first, picked up the weapon and ran his eye over its silver mountings with a mingled air of connoisseurship and grief.

"The arms," he explained, aside, to the *curé*, "and crest of Monseigneur, the Marquis de Beaupertuys."

The Enchanted Profile

THERE are few Caliphesses. Women are Scheherazades by birth, predilection, instinct, and arrangement of the vocal cords. The thousand and one stories are being told every day by hundreds of thousands of viziers' daughters to their respective sultans. But the bow-string will get some of 'em yet if they don't watch out.

I heard a story, though, of one Lady Caliph. It isn't precisely an Arabian Nights story, because it brings in Cinderella, who flourished her dishrag in another epoch and country. So, if you don't mind the mixed dates (which seem to give it an Eastern flavor, after all), we'll get along.

In New York there is an old, old hotel. You have seen

woodcuts of it in the magazines. It was built—let's see—at
a time when there was nothing above Fourteenth Street except the old Indian trail to Boston and Hammerstein's office.
Soon the old hostelry will be torn down. And, as the stout
walls are riven apart and the bricks go roaring down the
chutes, crowds of citizens will gather at the nearest corners
and weep over the destruction of a dear old landmark. Civic
pride is strong in New Bagdad; and the wettest weeper and
the loudest howler against the iconoclasts will be the man
(originally from Terre Haute) whose fond memories of the
old hotel are limited to his having been kicked out from its
free-lunch counter in 1873.

At this hotel always stopped Mrs. Maggie Brown. Mrs.
Brown was a bony woman of sixty, dressed in the rustiest
black, and carrying a handbag made, apparently, from the
hide of the original animal that Adam decided to call an
alligator. She always occupied a small parlor and bedroom
at the top of the hotel at a rental of two dollars per day. And
always, while she was there, each day came hurrying to see her
many men, sharp-faced, anxious-looking, with only seconds to
spare. For Maggie Brown was said to be the third richest
woman in the world; and these solicitous gentlemen were
only the city's wealthiest brokers and business men seeking
trifling loans of half a dozen millions or so from the dingy old
lady with the prehistoric handbag.

The stenographer and typewriter of the Acropolis Hotel
(there! I've let the name of it out!) was Miss Ida Bates. She
was a holdover from the Greek classics. There wasn't a flaw
in her looks. Some old-timer in paying his regards to a lady
said: "To have loved her was a liberal education." Well, even
to have looked over the black hair and neat white shirtwaist
of Miss Bates was equal to a full course in any correspondence school in the country. She sometimes did a little typewriting for me and, as she refused to take the money in

advance, she came to look upon me as something of a friend and protégé. She had unfailing kindliness and good nature; and not even a whitelead drummer or a fur importer had ever dared to cross the dead line of good behavior in her presence. The entire force of the Acropolis, from the owner, who lived in Vienna, down to the head porter, who had been bedridden for sixteen years, would have sprung to her defence in a moment.

One day I walked past Miss Bates's little sanctum Remingtorium, and saw in her place a black-haired unit—unmistakably a person—pounding with each of her forefingers upon the keys. Musing on the mutability of temporal affairs, I passed on. The next day I went on a two weeks' vacation. Returning, I strolled through the lobby of the Acropolis, and saw, with a little warm glow of auld lang syne, Miss Bates, as Grecian and kind and flawless as ever, just putting the cover on her machine. The hour for closing had come; but she asked me in to sit for a few minutes in the dictation chair. Miss Bates explained her absence and return to the Acropolis Hotel in words identical with or similar to these following:

"Well, Man, how are the stories coming?"

"Pretty regularly," said I. "About equal to their going."

"I'm sorry," said she. "Good typewriting is the main thing in a story. You've missed me, haven't you?"

"No one," said I, "whom I have ever known knows as well as you do how to space properly belt buckles, semicolons, hotel guests, and hairpins. But you've been away, too. I saw a package of peppermint-pepsin in your place the other day."

"I was going to tell you about it," said Miss Bates, "if you hadn't interrupted me.

"Of course, you know about Maggie Brown, who stops here. Well, she's worth $40,000,000. She lives in Jersey in a ten-dollar flat. She's always got more cash on hand than half a dozen business candidates for vice-president. I don't know whether she carries it in her stocking or not, but I know she's mighty popular down in the part of the town where they worship the golden calf.

"Well, about two weeks ago, Mrs. Brown stops at the door and rubbers at me for ten minutes. I'm sitting with my side to her, striking off some manifold copies of a copper-mine proposition for a nice old man from Tonopah. But I always see everything all around me. When I'm hard at work I can see things through my side-combs; and I can leave one button unbuttoned in the back of my shirtwaist and see who's behind me. I didn't look around, because I make from eighteen to twenty dollars a week, and I didn't have to.

"That evening at knocking-off time she sends for me to come up to her apartment. I expected to have to typewrite about two thousand words of notes-of-hand, liens, and contracts, with a ten-cent tip in sight; but I went. Well, Man, I was certainly surprised. Old Maggie Brown had turned human.

" 'Child,' says she, 'you're the most beautiful creature I ever saw in my life. I want you to quit your work and come and live with me. I've no kith or kin,' says she, 'except a husband and a son or two, and I hold no communication with any of 'em. They're extravagant burdens on a hard-working woman. I want you to be a daughter to me. They say I'm stingy and mean, and the papers print lies about my doing my own cooking and washing. It's a lie,' she goes on. 'I put my washing out, except the handkerchiefs and stockings and petticoats and collars, and light stuff like that. I've got forty million dollars in cash and stocks and bonds that are as negotiable as Standard Oil, preferred, at a church fair. I'm a lonely old woman and I need companionship. You're the most beautiful human being I ever saw,' says she. 'Will you come and live with me? I'll show 'em whether I can spend money or not,' she says.

"Well, Man, what would you have done? Of course, I fell
to it. And, to tell you the truth, I began to like old Maggie.
It wasn't all on account of the forty millions and what she
could do for me. I was kind of lonesome in the world, too.
Everybody's got to have somebody they can explain to about
the pain in their left shoulder and how fast patent-leather
shoes wear out when they begin to crack. And you can't talk
about such things to men you meet in hotels—they're looking
for just such openings.

"So I gave up my job in the hotel and went with Mrs.
Brown. I certainly seemed to have a mash on her. She'd look
at me for half an hour at a time when I was sitting, reading,
or looking at the magazines.

"One time I says to her: 'Do I remind you of some de-
ceased relative or friend of your childhood, Mrs. Brown? I've
noticed you give me a pretty good optical inspection from
time to time.'

" 'You have a face,' she says, 'exactly like a dear friend of
mine—the best friend I ever had. But I like you for yourself,
child, too,' she says.

"And say, Man, what do you suppose she did? Loosened
up like a Marcel wave in the surf at Coney. She took me to
a swell dressmaker and gave her *à la carte* to fit me out—
money no object. They were rush orders, and madame locked
the front door and put the whole force to work.

"Then we moved to—where do you think?—no; guess again
—that's right—the Hotel Bonton. We had a six-room apartment; and it cost $100 a day. I saw the bill. I began to love
that old lady.

"And then, Man, when my dresses began to come in—oh,
I won't tell you about 'em! you couldn't understand. And I
began to call her Aunt Maggie. You've read about Cinderella,
of course. Well, what Cinderella said when the prince fitted

that 3½ A on her foot was a hard-luck story compared to the things I told myself.

"Then Aunt Maggie says she is going to give me a coming-out banquet in the Bonton that'll make moving Vans of all the old Dutch families on Fifth Avenue.

"'I've been out before, Aunt Maggie,' says I. 'But I'll come out again. But you know,' says I, 'that this is one of the swellest hotels in the city. And you know—pardon me—that it's hard to get a bunch of notables together unless you've trained for it.'

"'Don't fret about that, child,' says Aunt Maggie. 'I don't send out invitations—I issue orders. I'll have fifty guests here that couldn't be brought together again at any reception unless it were given by King Edward or William Travers Jerome. They are men, of course, and all of 'em either owe me money or intend to. Some of their wives won't come, but a good many will.'

"Well, I wish you could have been at that banquet. The dinner service was all gold and cut glass. There were about forty men and ladies present besides Aunt Maggie and I. You'd never have known the third richest woman in the world. She had on a new black silk dress with so much passementerie on it that it sounded exactly like a hailstorm I heard once when I was staying all night with a girl that lived on a top-floor studio.

"And my dress!—say, Man, I can't waste the words on you. It was all hand-made lace—where there was any of it at all—and it cost $300. I saw the bill. The men were all baldheaded or white-side-whiskered, and they kept up a running fire of light repartee about 3-per cents, and Bryan and the cotton crop.

"On the left of me was something that talked like a banker, and on my right was a young fellow who said he was a newspaper artist. He was the only—well, I was going to tell you.

"After the dinner was over Mrs. Brown and I went up to the apartment. We had to squeeze our way through a mob of reporters all the way through the halls. That's one of the things money does for you. Say, do you happen to know a newspaper artist named Lathrop—a tall man with nice eyes and an easy way of talking? No, I don't remember what paper he works on. Well, all right.

"When we got upstairs Mrs. Brown telephones for the bill right away. It came, and it was $600. I saw the bill. Aunt Maggie fainted. I got her on a lounge and opened the beadwork.

" 'Child,' says she, when she got back to the world, 'what was it? A raise of rent or an income-tax?'

" 'Just a little dinner,' says I. 'Nothing to worry about— hardly a drop in the bucket-shop. Sit up and take notice—a dispossess notice, if there's no other kind.'

"But, say, Man, do you know what Aunt Maggie did? She got cold feet! She hustled me out of that Hotel Bonton at nine the next morning. We went to a rooming-house on the lower West Side. She rented one room that had water on the floor below and light on the floor above. After we got moved all you could see in the room was about $1,500 worth of new swell dresses and a one-burner gas-stove.

"Aunt Maggie had had a sudden attack of the hedges. I guess everybody has got to go on a spree once in their life. A man spends his on highballs, and a woman gets woozy on clothes. But with forty million dollars—say! I'd like to have a picture of—but, speaking of pictures, did you ever run across a newspaper artist named Lathrop—a tall—oh, I asked you that before, didn't I? He was mighty nice to me at the dinner. His voice just suited me. I guess he must have thought I was to inherit some of Aunt Maggie's money.

"Well, Mr. Man, three days of that light-housekeeping was plenty for me. Aunt Maggie was affectionate as ever. She'd hardly let me get out of her sight. But let me tell you. She was a hedger from Hedgersville, Hedger County. Seventy-five cents a day was the limit she set. We cooked our own meals in the room. There I was, with a thousand dollars' worth of the latest things in clothes, doing stunts over a one-burner gas-stove.

"As I say, on the third day I flew the coop. I couldn't stand for throwing together a fifteen-cent kidney stew while wearing, at the same time, a $150 house-dress, with Valenciennes lace insertion. So I goes into the closet and puts on the cheapest dress Mrs. Brown had bought for me—it's the one I've got on now—not so bad for $75, is it? I'd left all my own clothes in my sister's flat in Brooklyn.

" 'Mrs. Brown, formerly "Aunt Maggie," ' says I to her, 'I am going to extend my feet alternately, one after the other, in such a manner and direction that this tenement will recede from me in the quickest possible time. I am no worshipper of money,' says I, 'but there are some things I can't stand. I can stand the fabulous monster that I've read about that blows hot birds and cold bottles with the same breath. But I can't stand a quitter,' says I. 'They say you've got forty million dollars—well, you'll never have any less. And I was beginning to like you, too,' says I.

"Well, the late Aunt Maggie kicks till the tears flow. She offers to move into a swell room with a two-burner stove and running water.

" 'I've spent an awful lot of money, child,' says she. 'We'll have to economize for a while. You're the most beautiful creature I ever laid eyes on,' she says, 'and I don't want you to leave me.'

"Well, you see me, don't you? I walked straight to the Acropolis and asked for my job back, and I got it. How did you say your writings were getting along? I know you've lost out some by not having me to typewrite 'em. Do you ever have 'em illustrated? And, by the way, did you ever happen to know a newspaper artist—oh, shut up! I know I asked you before. I wonder what paper he works on? It's funny, but I couldn't help thinking that he wasn't thinking about the money he might have been thinking I was thinking I'd get from old Maggie Brown. If I only knew some of the newspaper editors I'd——"

The sound of an easy footstep came from the doorway. Ida Bates saw who it was with her back-hair comb. I saw her turn pink, perfect statue that she was—a miracle that I share with Pygmalion only.

"Am I excusable?" she said to me—adorable petitioner that she became. "It's—it's Mr. Lathrop. I wonder if it really wasn't the money—I wonder, if after all, he——"

Of course, I was invited to the wedding. After the ceremony I dragged Lathrop aside.

"You an artist," said I, "and haven't figured out why Maggie Brown conceived such a strong liking for Miss Bates—that was? Let me show you."

The bride wore a simple white dress as beautifully draped as the costumes of the ancient Greeks. I took some leaves from one of the decorative wreaths in the little parlor, and made a chaplet of them, and placed them on née Bates's shining chestnut hair, and made her turn her profile to her husband.

"By jingo!" said he. "Isn't Ida's head a dead ringer for the lady's head on the silver dollar?"

The Passing of Black Eagle

FOR SOME MONTHS of a certain year a grim bandit infested the Texas border along the Rio Grande. Peculiarly striking to the optic nerve was this notorious marauder. His personality secured him the title of "Black Eagle, the Terror of the Border." Many fearsome tales are on record concerning the doings of him and his followers. Suddenly, in the space of a single minute, Black Eagle vanished from earth. He was never heard of again. His own band never even guessed the mystery of his disappearance. The border ranches and settlements feared he would come again to ride and ravage the mesquite flats. He never will. It is to disclose the fate of Black Eagle that this narrative is written.

The initial movement of the story is furnished by the foot of a bartender in St. Louis. His discerning eye fell upon the form of Chicken Ruggles as he pecked with avidity at the free lunch. Chicken was a "hobo." He had a long nose like the bill of a fowl, an inordinate appetite for poultry, and a habit of gratifying it without expense, which accounts for the name given him by his fellow vagrants.

Physicians agree that the partaking of liquids at meal times is not a healthy practice. The hygiene of the saloon promulgates the opposite. Chicken had neglected to purchase a drink to accompany his meal. The bartender rounded the counter, caught the injudicious diner by the ear with a lemon squeezer, led him to the door and kicked him into the street.

Thus the mind of Chicken was brought to realize the signs of coming winter. The night was cold; the stars shone with unkindly brilliancy; people were hurrying along the streets in two egotistic, jostling streams. Men had donned their overcoats, and Chicken knew to an exact percentage the increased difficulty of coaxing dimes from those buttoned-in vest pockets. The time had come for his annual exodus to the South.

A little boy, five or six years old, stood looking with covetous eyes in a confectioner's window. In one small hand he held an empty two-ounce vial; in the other he grasped tightly something flat and round, with a shining milled edge. The scene presented a field of operations commensurate to Chicken's talents and daring. After sweeping the horizon to make sure that no official tug was cruising near, he insidiously accosted his prey. The boy, having been early taught by his household to regard altruistic advances with extreme suspicion, received the overtures coldly.

Then Chicken knew that he must make one of those desperate, nerve-shattering plunges into speculation that fortune sometimes requires of those who would win her favor. Five cents was his capital, and this he must risk against the chance of winning what lay within the close grasp of the youngster's chubby hand. It was a fearful lottery, Chicken knew. But he must accomplish his end by strategy, since he had a wholesome terror of plundering infants by force. Once, in a park, driven by hunger, he had committed an onslaught upon a bottle of peptonized infant's food in the possession of an occupant of a baby carriage. The outraged infant had so promptly opened its mouth and pressed the button that communicated with the welkin that help arrived, and Chicken did his thirty days in a snug coop. Wherefore he was, as he said, "leary of kids."

Beginning artfully to question the boy concerning his choice of sweets, he gradually drew out the information he wanted. Mamma said he was to ask the drug-store man for ten cents' worth of paregoric in the bottle; he was to keep his hand shut tight over the dollar; he must not stop to talk to any one in the street; he must ask the drug-store man to wrap up the change and put it in the pocket of his trousers. Indeed, they had pockets—two of them! And he liked chocolate creams best.

Chicken went into the store and turned plunger. He invested his entire capital in C. A. N. D. Y. stocks, simply to pave the way to the greater risk following.

He gave the sweets to the youngster, and had the satisfaction of perceiving that confidence was established. After that it was easy to obtain leadership of the expedition, to take the investment by the hand and lead it to a nice drug store he knew of in the same block. There Chicken, with a parental air, passed over the dollar and called for the medicine, while the boy crunched his candy, glad to be relieved of the responsibility of the purchase. And then the successful investor, searching his pockets, found an overcoat button—the extent of his winter trousseau—and, wrapping it carefully, placed the ostensible change in the pocket of confiding juvenility. Setting the youngster's face homeward, and patting him benevolently on the back—for Chicken's heart was as soft as those of his feathered namesakes—the speculator quit the market with a profit of 1,700 per cent. on his invested capital.

Two hours later an Iron Mountain freight engine pulled out of the railroad yards, Texas bound, with a string of empties. In one of the cattle cars, half buried in excelsior, Chicken lay at ease. Beside him in his nest was a quart bottle of very poor whisky and a paper bag of bread and cheese. Mr. Ruggles, in his private car, was on his trip south for the winter season.

For a week that car was trundled southward, shifted, laid over, and manipulated after the manner of rolling stock, but Chicken stuck to it, leaving it only at necessary times to satisfy his hunger and thirst. He knew it must go down to the cattle country, and San Antonio, in the heart of it, was his goal. There the air was salubrious and mild; the people indulgent and long-suffering. The bartenders there would not kick him. If he should eat too long or too often at one place they would swear at him as if by rote and without heat. They swore so drawlingly, and they rarely paused short of their full vocabulary, which was copious, so that Chicken had often gulped a good meal during the process of the vituperative prohibition. The season there was always spring-like; the plazas were pleasant at night, with music and gayety: except during the slight and infrequent cold snaps one could sleep comfortably out of doors in case the interiors should develop inhospitality.

At Texarkana his car was switched to the I. and G. N. Then still southward it trailed until, at length, it crawled across the Colorado bridge at Austin, and lined out, straight as an arrow, for the run to San Antonio.

When the freight halted at that town Chicken was fast asleep. In ten minutes the train was off again for Laredo, the end of the road. Those empty cattle cars were for distribution along the line at points from which the ranches shipped their stock.

When Chicken awoke his car was stationary. Looking out between the slats, he saw it was a bright, moonlit night. Scrambling out, he saw his car with three others abandoned on a little siding in a wild and lonesome country. A cattle pen and chute stood on one side of the track. The railroad bisected a vast, dim ocean of prairie, in the midst of which Chicken, with his futile rolling stock, was as completely stranded as was Robinson with his land-locked boat.

A white post stood near the rails. Going up to it, Chicken read the letters at the top, S. A. 90. Laredo was nearly as far to the south. He was almost a hundred miles from any town. Coyotes began to yelp in the mysterious sea around him. Chicken felt lonesome. He had lived in Boston without an education, in Chicago without nerve, in Philadelphia without a sleeping place, in New York without a pull, and in Pittsburgh sober, and yet he had never felt so lonely as now.

Suddenly through the intense silence, he heard the whicker of a horse. The sound came from the side of the track toward the east, and Chicken began to explore timorously in that direction. He stepped high along the mat of curly mesquite grass, for he was afraid of everything there might be in this

wilderness—snakes, rats, brigands, centipedes, mirages, cow-
boys, fandangoes, tarantulas, tamales—he had read of them in
the story papers. Rounding a clump of prickly pear that reared
high its fantastic and menacing array of rounded heads, he
was struck to shivering terror by a snort and a thunderous
plunge, as the horse, himself startled, bounded away some
fifty yards, and then resumed his grazing. But here was the
one thing in the desert that Chicken did not fear. He had
been reared on a farm; he had handled horses, understood
them, and could ride.

Approaching slowly and speaking soothingly, he followed
the animal, which, after its first flight, seemed gentle enough,
and secured the end of the twenty-foot lariat that dragged
after him in the grass. It required him but a few moments to
contrive the rope into an ingenious nose-bridle, after the style
of the Mexican *borsal*. In another he was upon the horse's
back and off at a splendid lope, giving the animal free choice
of direction. "He will take me somewhere," said Chicken to
himself.

It would have been a thing of joy, that untrammelled gallop over the moonlit prairie, even to Chicken, who loathed
exertion, but that his mood was not for it. His head ached;
a growing thirst was upon him; the "somewhere" whither his
lucky mount might convey him was full of dismal perad-
venture.

And now he noted that the horse moved to a definite goal.
Where the prairie lay smooth he kept his course straight as
an arrow's toward the east. Deflected by hill or arroyo or im-
practicable spinous brakes, he quickly flowed again into the
current, charted by his unerring instinct. At last, upon the
side of a gentle rise, he suddenly subsided to a complacent
walk. A stone's cast away stood a little mott of coma trees;
beneath it a *jacal* such as the Mexicans erect—a one-room
house of upright poles daubed with clay and roofed with

grass or tule reeds. An experienced eye would have estimated the spot as the headquarters of a small sheep ranch. In the moonlight the ground in the nearby corral showed pulverized to a level smoothness by the hoofs of the sheep. Everywhere was carelessly distributed the paraphernalia of the place— ropes, bridles, saddles, sheep pelts, wool sacks, feed troughs, and camp litter. The barrel of drinking water stood in the end of the two-horse wagon near the door. The harness was piled, promiscuous, upon the wagon tongue, soaking up the dew.

Chicken slipped to earth, and tied the horse to a tree. He halloed again and again, but the house remained quiet. The door stood open, and he entered cautiously. The light was sufficient for him to see that no one was at home. He struck a match and lighted a lamp that stood on a table. The room was that of a bachelor ranchman who was content with the necessaries of life. Chicken rummaged intelligently until he found what he had hardly dared hope for—a small brown jug that still contained something near a quart of his desire.

Half an hour later, Chicken—now a gamecock of hostile aspect—emerged from the house with unsteady steps. He had drawn upon the absent ranchman's equipment to replace his own ragged attire. He wore a suit of coarse brown ducking, the coat being a sort of rakish bolero, jaunty to a degree. Boots he had donned, and spurs that whirred with every lurching step. Buckled around him was a belt full of cartridges with a big six-shooter in each of its two holsters.

Prowling about, he found blankets, a saddle and bridle with which he caparisoned his steed. Again mounting, he rode swiftly away, singing a loud and tuneless song.

Bud King's band of desperadoes, outlaws and horse and cattle thieves were in camp at a secluded spot on the bank of the Frio. Their depredations in the Rio Grande country, while no bolder than usual, had been advertised more extensively, and Captain Kinney's company of rangers had been ordered down to look after them. Consequently, Bud King, who was a wise general, instead of cutting out a hot trail for the upholders of the law, as his men wished to do, retired for the time to the prickly fastnesses of the Frio valley.

Though the move was a prudent one, and not incompatible with Bud's well-known courage, it raised dissension among the members of the band. In fact, while they thus lay ingloriously *perdu* in the brush, the question of Bud King's fitness for the leadership was argued, with closed doors, as it were, by his followers. Never before had Bud's skill or efficiency been brought to criticism; but his glory was waning (and such is glory's fate) in the light of a newer star. The sentiment of the band was crystallizing into the opinion that Black Eagle could lead them with more luster, profit, and distinction.

This Black Eagle—sub-titled the "Terror of the Border"— had been a member of the gang about three months.

One night while they were in camp on the San Miguel water-hole a solitary horseman on the regulation fiery steed dashed in among them. The newcomer was of a portentous and devastating aspect. A beak-like nose with a predatory curve projected above a mass of bristling, blue-black whiskers. His eye was cavernous and fierce. He was spurred, sombre-roed, booted, garnished with revolvers, abundantly drunk, and very much unafraid. Few people in the country drained by the Rio Bravo would have cared thus to invade alone the camp of Bud King. But this fell bird swooped fearlessly upon them and demanded to be fed.

Hospitality in the prairie country is not limited. Even if your enemy pass your way you must feed him before you shoot him. You must empty your larder into him before you empty your lead. So the stranger of undeclared intentions was set down to a mighty feast.

A talkative bird he was, full of most marvellous loud tales

and exploits, and speaking a language at times obscure but
never colorless. He was a new sensation to Bud King's men,
who rarely encountered new types. They hung, delighted,
upon his vainglorious boasting, the spicy strangeness of his
lingo, his contemptuous familiarity with life, the world, and
remote places, and the extravagant frankness with which he
conveyed his sentiments.

To their guest the band of outlaws seemed to be nothing
more than a congregation of country bumpkins whom he was
"stringing for grub" just as he would have told his stories at
the back door of a farmhouse to wheedle a meal. And, indeed, his ignorance was not without excuse, for the "bad
man" of the Southwest does not run to extremes. Those
brigands might justly have been taken for a little party of
peaceable rustics assembled for a fish-fry or pecan gathering.
Gentle of manner, slouching of gait, soft-voiced, unpic-
turesquely clothed; not one of them presented to the eye any
witness of the desperate records they had earned.

For two days the glittering stranger within the camp was
feasted. Then, by common consent, he was invited to become
a member of the band. He consented, presenting for enroll-
ment the prodigious name of "Captain Montressor." This was
immediately overruled by the band, and "Piggy" substituted
as a compliment to the awful and insatiate appetite of its
owner.

Thus did the Texas border receive the most spectacular
brigand that ever rode its chaparral.

For the next three months Bud King conducted business
as usual, escaping encounters with law officers and being content with reasonable profits. The band ran off some very good
companies of horses from the ranges, and a few bunches of
fine cattle which they got safely across the Rio Grande and
disposed of to fair advantage. Often the band would ride into
the little villages and Mexican settlements, terrorizing the in-

habitants and plundering for the provisions and ammunition they needed. It was during these bloodless raids that Piggy's ferocious aspect and frightful voice gained him a renown more widespread and glorious than those other gentle-voiced and sad-faced desperadoes could have acquired in a lifetime.

The Mexicans, most apt in nomenclature, first called him The Black Eagle, and used to frighten the babes by threatening them with tales of the dreadful robber who carried off little children in his great beak. Soon the name extended, and Black Eagle, the Terror of the Border, became a recognized factor in exaggerated newspaper reports and ranch gossip.

The country from the Nueces to the Rio Grande was a wild but fertile stretch, given over to the sheep and cattle ranches. Range was free; the inhabitants were few; the law was mainly a letter, and the pirates met with little opposition until the flaunting and garish Piggy gave the band undue advertisement. Then Kinney's ranger company headed for those precincts, and Bud King knew that it meant grim and sudden war or else temporary retirement. Regarding the risk to be unnecessary, he drew off his band to an almost inaccessible spot on the bank of the Frio. Wherefore, as has been said, dissatisfaction arose among the members, and impeachment proceedings against Bud were premeditated, with Black Eagle in high favor for the succession. Bud King was not unaware of the sentiment, and he called aside Cactus Taylor, his trusted lieutenant, to discuss it.

"If the boys," said Bud, "ain't satisfied with me, I'm willin' to step out. They're buckin' against my way of handlin' 'em. And 'specially because I concludes to hit the brush while Sam Kinney is ridin' the line. I saves 'em from bein' shot or sent up on a state contract, and they up and says I'm no good."

"It ain't so much that," explained Cactus, "as it is they're plum locoed about Piggy. They want them whiskers and that nose of his to split the wind at the head of the column."

"There's somethin' mighty seldom about Piggy," declared Bud, musingly. "I never yet see anything on the hoof that he exactly grades up with. He can shore holler a plenty, and he straddles a hoss from where you laid the chunk. But he ain't never been smoked yet. You know, Cactus, we ain't had a row since he's been with us. Piggy's all right for skearin' the greaser kids and layin' waste a cross-roads store. I reckon he's the finest canned oyster buccaneer and cheese pirate that ever was, but how's his appetite for fightin'? I've knowed some citizens you'd think was starvin' for trouble get a bad case of dyspepsy the first dose of lead they had to take."

"He talks all spraddled out," said Cactus, "'bout the rookuses he's been in. He claims to have saw the elephant and hearn the owl."

"I know," replied Bud, using the cow-puncher's expressive phrase of skepticism, "but it sounds to me!"

This conversation was held one night in camp while the other members of the band—eight in number—were sprawling around the fire, lingering over their supper. When Bud and Cactus ceased talking they heard Piggy's formidable voice holding forth to the others as usual while he was engaged in checking, though never satisfying, his ravening appetite.

"Wat's de use," he was saying, "of chasin' little red cowses and hosses 'round for t'ousands of miles? Dere ain't nuttin' in it. Gallopin' t'rough dese bushes and briers, and gettin' a t'irst dat a brewery couldn't put out, and missin' meals! Say! You know what I'd do if I was main finger of dis bunch? I'd stick up a train. I'd blow de express car and make hard dollars where you guys get wind. Youse makes me tired. Dis sookcow kind of cheap sport gives me a pain."

Later on, a deputation waited on Bud. They stood on one leg, chewed mesquite twigs and circumlocuted, for they hated to hurt his feelings. Bud foresaw their business, and made it easy for them. Bigger risks and larger profits were what they wanted.

The suggestion of Piggy's about holding up a train had fired their imagination and increased their admiration for the dash and boldness of the instigator. They were such simple, artless, and custom-bound bush-rangers that they had never before thought of extending their habits beyond the running off of live-stock and the shooting of such of their acquaintances as ventured to interfere.

Bud acted "on the level," agreeing to take a subordinate place in the gang until Black Eagle should have been given a trial as leader.

After a great deal of consultation, studying of time-tables and discussion of the country's topography, the time and place for carrying out their new enterprise was decided upon. At that time there was a feedstuff famine in Mexico and a cattle famine in certain parts of the United States, and there was a brisk international trade. Much money was being shipped along the railroads that connected the two republics. It was agreed that the most promising place for the contemplated robbery was at Espina, a little station on the I. and G. N., about forty miles north of Laredo. The train stopped there one minute; the country around was wild and unsettled; the station consisted of but one house in which the agent lived.

Black Eagle's band set out, riding by night. Arriving in the vicinity of Espina, they rested their horses all day in a thicket a few miles distant.

The train was due at Espina at 10:30 P.M. They could rob the train and be well over the Mexican border with their booty by daylight the next morning.

To do Black Eagle justice, he exhibited no signs of flinching from the responsible honors that had been conferred upon him.

He assigned his men to their respective posts with discretion, and coached them carefully as to their duties. On each side of the track four of the band were to lie concealed in the chaparral. Gotch-Ear Rodgers was to stick up the station agent. Bronco Charlie was to remain with the horses, holding them in readiness. At a spot where it was calculated the engine would be when the train stopped, Bud King was to lie hidden on one side, and Black Eagle himself on the other. The two would get the drop on the engineer and fireman, force them to descend and proceed to the rear. Then the express car would be looted, and the escape made. No one was to move until Black Eagle gave the signal by firing his revolver. The plan was perfect.

At ten minutes to train time every man was at his post, effectually concealed by the thick chaparral that grew almost to the rails. The night was dark and lowering, with a fine drizzle falling from the flying gulf clouds. Black Eagle crouched behind a bush within five yards of the track. Two six-shooters were belted around him. Occasionally he drew a large black bottle from his pocket and raised it to his mouth.

A star appeared far down the track which soon waxed into the headlight of the approaching train. It came on with an increasing roar; the engine bore down upon the ambushing desperadoes with a glare and a shriek like some avenging monster come to deliver them to justice. Black Eagle flattened himself upon the ground. The engine, contrary to their calculations, instead of stopping between him and Bud King's place of concealment, passed fully forty yards farther before it came to a stand.

The bandit leader rose to his feet and peered around the bush. His men all lay quiet, awaiting the signal. Immediately opposite Black Eagle was a thing that drew his attention. Instead of being a regular passenger train it was a mixed one. Before him stood a box car, the door of which, by some means, had been left slightly open. Black Eagle went up to it and pushed the door farther open. An odor came forth—a damp, rancid, familiar, musty, intoxicating, beloved odor stirring strongly at old memories of happy days and travels. Black Eagle sniffed at the witching smell as the returned wanderer smells of the rose that twines his boyhood's cottage home. Nostalgia seized him. He put his hand inside. Excelsior—dry, springy, curly, soft, enticing, covered the floor. Outside the drizzle had turned to a chilling rain.

The train bell clanged. The bandit chief unbuckled his belt and cast it, with its revolvers, upon the ground. His spurs followed quickly, and his broad sombrero. Black Eagle was moulting. The train started with a rattling jerk. The ex-Terror of the Border scrambled into the box car and closed the door. Stretched luxuriously upon the excelsior, with the black bottle clasped closely to his breast, his eyes closed, and a foolish, happy smile upon his terrible features, Chicken Ruggles started upon his return trip.

Undisturbed, with the band of desperate bandits lying motionless, awaiting the signal to attack, the train pulled out from Espina. As its speed increased, and the black masses of chaparral went whizzing past on either side, the express messenger, lighting his pipe, looked through his window and remarked, feelingly:

"What a jim-dandy place for a hold-up!"

A *Retrieved Reformation*

A GUARD came to the prison shoe-shop, where Jimmy Valentine was assiduously stitching uppers, and escorted him to the front office. There the warden handed Jimmy his pardon, which had been signed that morning by the governor. Jimmy

took it in a tired kind of way. He had served nearly ten
months of a four-year sentence. He had expected to stay only
about three months, at the longest. When a man with as many
friends on the outside as Jimmy Valentine had is received in
the "stir" it is hardly worth while to cut his hair.

"Now, Valentine," said the warden, "you'll go out in the
morning. Brace up, and make a man of yourself. You're not
a bad fellow at heart. Stop cracking safes, and live straight."

"Me?" said Jimmy, in surprise. "Why, I never cracked a safe
in my life."

"Oh, no," laughed the warden. "Of course not. Let's see,
now. How was it you happened to get sent up on that Springfield job? Was it because you wouldn't prove an alibi for fear
of compromising somebody in extremely high-toned society?
Or was it simply a case of a mean old jury that had it in for
you? It's always one or the other with you innocent victims."

"Me?" said Jimmy, still blankly virtuous. "Why, warden, I
never was in Springfield in my life!"

"Take him back, Cronin," smiled the warden, "and fix him
up with outgoing clothes. Unlock him at seven in the morning, and let him come to the bull-pen. Better think over my
advice, Valentine."

At a quarter past seven on the next morning Jimmy stood
in the warden's outer office. He had on a suit of the villain-
ously fitting, ready-made clothes and a pair of the stiff,
squeaky shoes that the state furnishes to its discharged com-
pulsory guests.

The clerk handed him a railroad ticket and the five-dollar
bill with which the law expected him to rehabilitate himself
into good citizenship and prosperity. The warden gave him a
cigar, and shook hands. Valentine, 9762, was chronicled on
the books "Pardoned by Governor," and Mr. James Valentine
walked out into the sunshine.

Disregarding the song of the birds, the waving green trees,

and the smell of the flowers, Jimmy headed straight for a restaurant. There he tasted the first sweet joys of liberty in the shape of a broiled chicken and a bottle of white wine—followed by a cigar a grade better than the one the warden had given him. From there he proceeded leisurely to the depot. He tossed a quarter into the hat of a blind man sitting by the door, and boarded his train. Three hours set him down in a little town near the state line. He went to the café of one Mike Dolan and shook hands with Mike, who was alone behind the bar.

"Sorry we couldn't make it sooner, Jimmy, me boy," said Mike. "But we had that protest from Springfield to buck against, and the governor nearly balked. Feeling all right?"

"Fine," said Jimmy. "Got my key?"

He got his key and went upstairs, unlocking the door of a room at the rear. Everything was just as he had left it. There on the floor was still Ben Price's collar-button that had been torn from that eminent detective's shirt-band when they had overpowered Jimmy to arrest him.

Pulling out from the wall a folding-bed, Jimmy slid back a panel in the wall and dragged out a dust-covered suitcase. He opened this and gazed fondly at the finest set of burglar's tools in the East. It was a complete set, made of specially tempered steel, the latest designs in drills, punches, braces and bits, jimmies, clamps, and augers, with two or three novelties invented by Jimmy himself, in which he took pride. Over nine hundred dollars they had cost him to have made at ——, a place where they make such things for the profession.

In half an hour Jimmy went downstairs and through the café. He was now dressed in tasteful and well-fitting clothes, and carried his dusted and cleaned suitcase in his hand.

"Got anything on?" asked Mike Dolan, genially.

"Me?" said Jimmy, in a puzzled tone. "I don't understand.

I'm representing the New York Amalgamated Short Snap
Biscuit Cracker and Frazzled Wheat Company."

This statement delighted Mike to such an extent that
Jimmy had to take a seltzer-and-milk on the spot. He never
touched "hard" drinks.

A week after the release of Valentine, 9762, there was a
neat job of safe-burglary done in Richmond, Indiana, with no
clue to the author. A scant eight hundred dollars was all that
was secured. Two weeks after that a patented, improved,
burglar-proof safe in Logansport was opened like a cheese to
the tune of fifteen hundred dollars, currency; securities and
silver untouched. That began to interest the rogue-catchers.
Then an old-fashioned bank-safe in Jefferson City became
active and threw out of its crater an eruption of bank-notes
amounting to five thousand dollars. The losses were now high
enough to bring the matter up into Ben Price's class of work.
By comparing notes, a remarkable similarity in the methods
of the burglaries was noticed. Ben Price investigated the
scenes of the robberies, and was heard to remark:

"That's Dandy Jim Valentine's autograph. He's resumed
business. Look at that combination knob—jerked out as easy
as pulling up a radish in wet weather. He's got the only clamps
that can do it. And look how clean those tumblers were
punched out! Jimmy never has to drill but one hole. Yes, I
guess I want Mr. Valentine. He'll do his bit next time without
any short-time or clemency foolishness."

Ben Price knew Jimmy's habits. He had learned them while
working up the Springfield case. Long jumps, quick get-aways,
no confederates, and a taste for good society—these ways had
helped Mr. Valentine to become noted as a successful dodger
of retribution. It was given out that Ben Price had taken up
the trail of the elusive cracksman, and other people with
burglar-proof safes felt more at ease.

One afternoon Jimmy Valentine and his suitcase climbed

out of the mail-hack in Elmore, a little town five miles off
the railroad down in the black-jack country of Arkansas.
Jimmy, looking like an athletic young senior just home from
college, went down the board sidewalk toward the hotel.

A young lady crossed the street, passed him at the corner
and entered a door over which was the sign "The Elmore
Bank." Jimmy Valentine looked into her eyes, forgot what he
was, and became another man. She lowered her eyes and
colored slightly. Young men of Jimmy's style and looks were
scarce in Elmore.

Jimmy collared a boy that was loafing on the steps of the
bank as if he were one of the stock-holders, and began to ask
him questions about the town, feeding him dimes at intervals.
By and by the young lady came out, looking royally unconscious of the young man with the suitcase, and went her way.

"Isn't that young lady Miss Polly Simpson?" asked Jimmy,
with specious guile.

"Naw," said the boy. "She's Annabel Adams. Her pa owns
this bank. What'd you come to Elmore for? Is that a gold
watch-chain? I'm going to get a bulldog. Got any more
dimes?"

Jimmy went to the Planters' Hotel, registered as Ralph D.
Spencer, and engaged a room. He leaned on the desk and
declared his platform to the clerk. He said he had come to
Elmore to look for a location to go into business. How was the
shoe business, now, in the town? He had thought of the shoe
business. Was there an opening?

The clerk was impressed by the clothes and manner of
Jimmy. He, himself, was something of a pattern of fashion
to the thinly gilded youth of Elmore, but he now perceived
his shortcomings. While trying to figure out Jimmy's manner
of tying his four-in-hand, he cordially gave information.

Yes, there ought to be a good opening in the shoe line.
There wasn't an exclusive shoe-store in the place. The dry-

goods and general stores handled them. Business in all lines was fairly good. Hoped Mr. Spencer would decide to locate in Elmore. He would find it a pleasant town to live in, and the people very sociable.

Mr. Spencer thought he would stop over in the town a few days and look over the situation. No, the clerk needn't call the boy. He would carry up his suitcase, himself; it was rather heavy.

Mr. Ralph Spencer, the phœnix that arose from Jimmy Valentine's ashes—ashes left by the flame of a sudden and alternative attack of love—remained in Elmore, and prospered. He opened a shoe-store and secured a good run of trade.

Socially he was also a success, and made many friends. And he accomplished the wish of his heart. He met Miss Annabel Adams, and became more and more captivated by her charms.

At the end of a year the situation of Mr. Ralph Spencer was this: he had won the respect of the community, his shoe-store was flourishing, and he and Annabel were engaged to be married in two weeks. Mr. Adams, the typical, plodding, country banker, approved of Spencer. Annabel's pride in him almost equalled her affection. He was as much at home in the family of Mr. Adams and that of Annabel's married sister as if he were already a member.

One day Jimmy sat down in his room and wrote this letter, which he mailed to the safe address of one of his old friends in St. Louis:

Dear Old Pal:
I want you to be at Sullivan's place, in Little Rock, next Wednesday night at nine o'clock. I want you to wind up some little matters for me. And, also, I want to make you a present of my kit of tools. I know you'll be glad to get them—you couldn't duplicate the lot for a thousand dollars. Say, Billy, I've quit the old business—a year ago. I've got a nice store. I'm making

an honest living, and I'm going to marry the finest girl on earth two weeks from now. It's the only life, Billy—the straight one. I wouldn't touch a dollar of another man's money now for a million. After I get married I'm going to sell out and go West, where there won't be so much danger of having old scores brought up against me. I tell you, Billy, she's an angel. She believes in me; and I wouldn't do another crooked thing for the whole world. Be sure to be at Sully's, for I must see you. I'll bring along the tools with me.

Your old friend,
JIMMY.

On the Monday night after Jimmy wrote this letter, Ben Price jogged unobtrusively into Elmore in a livery buggy. He lounged about town in his quiet way until he found out what he wanted to know. From the drug-store across the street from Spencer's shoe-store he got a good look at Ralph D. Spencer.

"Going to marry the banker's daughter, are you, Jimmy?" said Ben to himself, softly. "Well, I don't know!"

The next morning Jimmy took breakfast at the Adamses. He was going to Little Rock that day to order his wedding-suit and buy something nice for Annabel. That would be the first time he had left town since he came to Elmore. It had been more than a year now since those last professional "jobs," and he thought he could safely venture out.

After breakfast quite a family party went down town to-gether—Mr. Adams, Annabel, Jimmy, and Annabel's married sister with her two little girls, aged five and nine. They came by the hotel where Jimmy still boarded, and he ran up to his room and brought along his suitcase. Then they went on to the bank. There stood Jimmy's horse and buggy and Dolph Gibson, who was going to drive him over to the railroad station.

All went inside the high, carved oak railings into the banking-room—Jimmy included, for Mr. Adams's future son-in-law was welcome anywhere. The clerks were pleased to be greeted by the good-looking, agreeable young man who was going to marry Miss Annabel. Jimmy set his suitcase down. Annabel, whose heart was bubbling with happiness and lively youth, put on Jimmy's hat and picked up the suitcase. "Wouldn't I make a nice drummer?" said Annabel. "My! Ralph, how heavy it is. Feels like it was full of gold bricks."

"Lot of nickel-plated shoe-horns in there," said Jimmy, coolly, "that I'm going to return. Thought I'd save express charges by taking them up. I'm getting awfully economical."

The Elmore Bank had just put in a new safe and vault. Mr. Adams was very proud of it, and insisted on an inspection by every one. The vault was a small one, but it had a new patented door. It fastened with three solid steel bolts thrown simultaneously with a single handle, and had a time-lock. Mr. Adams beamingly explained its workings to Mr. Spencer, who showed a courteous but not too intelligent interest. The two children, May and Agatha, were delighted by the shining metal and funny clock and knobs.

While they were thus engaged Ben Price sauntered in and leaned on his elbow, looking casually inside between the railings. He told the teller that he didn't want anything; he was just waiting for a man he knew.

Suddenly there was a scream or two from the women, and a commotion. Unperceived by the elders, May, the nine-year-old girl, in a spirit of play, had shut Agatha in the vault. She had then shot the bolts and turned the knob of the combination as she had seen Mr. Adams do.

The old banker sprang to the handle and tugged at it for a moment. "The door can't be opened," he groaned. "The clock hasn't been wound nor the combination set."

Agatha's mother screamed again, hysterically.

"Hush!" said Mr. Adams, raising his trembling hand. "All be quiet for a moment. Agatha!" he called as loudly as he could. "Listen to me." During the following silence they could just hear the faint sound of the child wildly shrieking in the dark vault in a panic of terror.

"My precious darling!" wailed the mother. "She will die of fright! Open the door! Oh, break it open! Can't you men do something?"

"There isn't a man nearer than Little Rock who can open that door," said Mr. Adams, in a shaky voice. "My God! Spencer, what shall we do? That child—she can't stand it long in there. There isn't enough air, and, besides, she'll go into convulsions from fright."

Agatha's mother, frantic now, beat the door of the vault with her hands. Somebody wildly suggested dynamite. Annabel turned to Jimmy, her large eyes full of anguish, but not yet despairing. To a woman nothing seems quite impossible to the powers of the man she worships.

"Can't you do something, Ralph—*try*, won't you?"

He looked at her with a queer, soft smile on his lips and in his keen eyes.

"Annabel," he said, "give me that rose you are wearing, will you?"

Hardly believing that she heard him aright, she unpinned the bud from the bosom of her dress, and placed it in his hand. Jimmy stuffed it into his vest-pocket, threw off his coat and pulled up his shirt-sleeves. With that act Ralph D. Spencer passed away and Jimmy Valentine took his place.

"Get away from the door, all of you," he commanded, shortly.

He set his suitcase on the table, and opened it out flat. From that time on he seemed to be unconscious of the presence of any one else. He laid out the shining, queer implements swiftly and orderly, whistling softly to himself as he always did when at work. In a deep silence and immovable, the others watched him as if under a spell.

In a minute Jimmy's pet drill was biting smoothly into the steel door. In ten minutes—breaking his own burglarious record—he threw back the bolts and opened the door.

Agatha, almost collapsed, but safe, was gathered into her mother's arms.

Jimmy Valentine put on his coat, and walked outside the railings toward the front door. As he went he thought he heard a far-away voice that he once knew call "Ralph!" But he never hesitated.

At the door a big man stood somewhat in his way.

"Hello, Ben!" said Jimmy, still with his strange smile. "Got around at last, have you? Well, let's go. I don't know that it makes much difference, now."

And then Ben Price acted rather strangely.

"Guess you're mistaken, Mr. Spencer," he said. "Don't believe I recognize you. Your buggy's waiting for you, ain't it?"

And Ben Price turned and strolled down the street.

The Renaissance at Charleroi

GRANDEMONT CHARLES was a little Creole gentleman, aged thirty-four, with a bald spot on the top of his head and the manners of a prince. By day he was a clerk in a cotton broker's office in one of those cold, rancid mountains of oozy brick, down near the levee in New Orleans. By night, in his three-story-high *chambre garnie* in the old French Quarter he was again the last male descendant of the Charles family, that noble house that had lorded it in France, and had pushed its way smiling, rapiered, and courtly into Louisiana's early and brilliant days. Of late years the Charleses had subsided into the more republican but scarcely less royally carried magnificence and ease of plantation life along the Mississippi. Perhaps Grandemont was even Marquis de Brassé. There was that title in the family. But a marquis on seventy-five dollars per month! *Vraiment!* Still, it has been done on less.

Grandemont had saved out of his salary the sum of six hundred dollars. Enough, you would say, for any man to marry on. So, after a silence of two years on that subject, he re-opened that most hazardous question to Mlle. Adèle Fauquier, riding down to Meade d'Or, her father's plantation. Her answer was the same that it had been any time during the last ten years: "First find my brother, Monsieur Charles."

This time he had stood before her, perhaps discouraged by a love so long and hopeless, being dependent upon a contingency so unreasonable, and demanded to be told in simple words whether she loved him or no.

Adèle looked at him steadily out of her gray eyes that betrayed no secrets and answered, a little more softly:

"Grandemont, you have no right to ask that question unless you can do what I ask of you. Either bring back brother Victor to us or the proof that he died."

Somehow, though five times thus rejected, his heart was not so heavy when he left. She had not denied that she loved. Upon what shallow waters can the bark of passion remain afloat! Or, shall we play the doctrinaire, and hint that at thirty-four the tides of life are calmer and cognizant of many sources instead of but one—as at four-and-twenty?

Victor Fauquier would never be found. In those early days of his disappearance there was money to the Charles name, and Grandemont had spent the dollars as if they were picayunes in trying to find the lost youth. Even then he had had small hope of success, for the Mississippi gives up a victim from its oily tangles only at the whim of its malign will.

A thousand times had Grandemont conned in his mind the scene of Victor's disappearance. And, at each time that Adèle had set her stubborn but pitiful alternative against his suit, still clearer it repeated itself in his brain.

The boy had been the family favorite: daring, winning, reckless. His unwise fancy had been captured by a girl on the plantation—the daughter of an overseer. Victor's family was in ignorance of the intrigue, as far as it had gone. To save them the inevitable pain that his course promised, Grandemont strove to prevent it. Omnipotent money smoothed the way. The overseer and his daughter left, between a sunset and dawn, for an undesignated bourne. Grandemont was confident that this stroke would bring the boy to reason. He rode over to Meade d'Or to talk with him. The two strolled out of the house and grounds, crossed the road, and, mounting the levee, walked its broad path while they conversed. A thundercloud was hanging, imminent, above, but, as yet, no rain fell. At Grandemont's disclosure of his interference in the clandestine romance, Victor attacked him, in a wild and sudden fury. Grandemont, though of slight frame, possessed muscles of iron. He caught the wrists amid a shower of blows descending upon him, bent the lad backward and stretched him upon the levee path. In a little while the gust of passion was spent, and he was allowed to rise. Calm now, but a powder mine where he had been but a whiff of the tantrums, Victor extended his hand toward the dwelling house of Meade d'Or.

"You and they," he cried, "have conspired to destroy my happiness. None of you shall ever look upon my face again."

Turning, he ran swiftly down the levee, disappearing in the darkness. Grandemont followed as well as he could, calling to him, but in vain. For longer than an hour he pursued the search. Descending the side of the levee, he penetrated the rank density of weeds and willows that undergrew the trees until the river's edge, shouting Victor's name. There was never an answer, though once he thought he heard a bubbling scream from the dun waters sliding past. Then the storm broke, and he returned to the house drenched and dejected.

There he explained the boy's absence sufficiently, he thought, not speaking of the tangle that had led to it, for he hoped that Victor would return as soon as his anger had cooled. Afterward, when the threat was made good and they saw his face no more, he found it difficult to alter his explanations of that night, and there clung a certain mystery to the boy's reasons for vanishing as well as to the manner of it.

It was on that night that Grandemont first perceived a new and singular expression in Adèle's eyes whenever she looked at him. And through the years following that expression was always there. He could not read it, for it was born of a thought she would never otherwise reveal.

Perhaps, if he had known that Adèle had stood at the gate on that unlucky night, where she had followed, lingering to await the return of her brother and lover, wondering why they had chosen so tempestuous an hour and so black a spot to hold converse—if he had known that a sudden flash of lightning had revealed to her sight that short, sharp struggle as Victor was sinking under his hands, he might have explained everything, and she——

I know not what she would have done. But one thing is clear—there was something besides her brother's disappearance between Grandemont's pleadings for her hand and Adèle's "yes." Ten years had passed, and what she had seen during the space of that lightning flash remained an indelible picture. She had loved her brother, but was she holding out for the solution of that mystery or for the "Truth"! Women have been known to reverence it, even as an abstract principle. It is said there have been a few who, in the matter of their affections, have considered a life to be a small thing as compared with a lie. That I do not know. But, I wonder, had Grandemont cast himself at her feet crying that his hand had sent Victor to the bottom of that inscrutable river, and that he could no longer sully his love with a lie, I wonder if—I wonder what she would have done!

But, Grandemont Charles, Arcadian little gentleman, never guessed the meaning of that look in Adèle's eyes; and from this last bootless payment of his devoirs he rode away as rich as ever in honor and love, but poor in hope.

That was in September. It was during the first winter month that Grandemont conceived his idea of the *renaissance*. Since Adèle would never be his, and wealth without her were useless trumpery, why need he add to that hoard of slowly harvested dollars? Why should he even retain that hoard?

Hundreds were the cigarettes he consumed over his claret, sitting at the little polished tables in the Royal Street cafés while thinking over his plan. By and by he had it perfect. It would cost, beyond doubt, all the money he had, but—*le jeu vaut la chandelle*—for some hours he would be once more a Charles of Charleroi. Once again should the nineteenth of January, that most significant day in the fortunes of the house of Charles, be fittingly observed. On that date the French king had seated a Charles by his side at table; on that date Armand Charles, Marquis de Brassé, landed, like a brilliant meteor, in New Orleans; it was the date of his mother's wedding; of Grandemont's birth. Since Grandemont could remember until the breaking up of the family that anniversary had been the synonym for feasting, hospitality, and proud commemoration.

Charleroi was the old family plantation, lying some twenty miles down the river. Years ago the estate had been sold to discharge the debts of its too-bountiful owners. Once again it had changed hands, and now the must and mildew of litigation had settled upon it. A question of heirship was in the courts, and the dwelling house of Charleroi, unless the tales

told of ghostly powdered and laced Charleses haunting its un-
echoing chambers were true, stood uninhabited.

Grandemont found the solicitor in chancery who held the
keys pending the decision. He proved to be an old friend of
the family. Grandemont explained briefly that he desired to
rent the house for two or three days. He wanted to give a
dinner at his old home to a few friends. That was all.

"Take it for a week—a month, if you will," said the solicitor; "but do not speak to me of rental." With a sigh he concluded: "The dinners I have eaten under that roof, *mon fils!*"

There came to many of the old-established dealers in furniture, china, silverware, decorations, and household fittings
at their stores on Canal, Chartres, St. Charles and Royal
streets, a quiet young man with a little bald spot on the top
of his head, distinguished manners, and the eye of a *connoisseur*, who explained what he wanted. To hire the complete
and elegant equipment of a dining-room, hall, reception-
room, and cloak-rooms. The goods were to be packed and
sent, by boat, to the Charleroi landing, and would be returned
within three or four days. All damage or loss to be promptly
paid for.

Many of those old merchants knew Grandemont by sight,
and the Charleses of old by association. Some of them were
of Creole stock and felt a thrill of responsive sympathy with
the magnificently indiscreet design of this impoverished clerk
who would revive but for a moment the ancient flame of glory
with the fuel of his savings.

"Choose what you want," they said to him. "Handle everything carefully. See that the damage bill is kept low, and the
charges for the loan will not oppress you."

To the wine merchants next; and here a doleful slice was
lopped from the six hundred. It was an exquisite pleasure to
Grandemont once more to pick among the precious vintages.
The champagne bins lured him like the abodes of sirens, but

these he was forced to pass. With his six hundred he stood before them as a child with a penny stands before a French doll. But he bought with taste and discretion of other wines —Chablis, Moselle, Château d'Or, Hochheimer, and port of right age and pedigree.

The matter of the cuisine gave him some studious hours until he suddenly recollected André—André, their old *chef*— the most sublime master of French Creole cookery in the Mississippi Valley. Perhaps he was yet somewhere about the plantation. The solicitor had told him that the place was still being cultivated, in accordance with a compromise agreement between the litigants.

On the next Sunday after the thought Grandemont rode, horseback, down to Charleroi. The big, square house with its two long ells looked blank and cheerless with its closed shutters and doors.

The shrubbery in the yard was ragged and riotous. Fallen leaves from the grove littered the walks and porches. Turning down the lane at the side of the house, Grandemont rode on to the quarters of the plantation hands. He found the workers streaming back from church, careless, happy, and bedecked in gay yellows, reds, and blues.

Yes, André was still there; his wool a little grayer; his mouth as wide; his laughter as ready as ever. Grandemont told him of his plan, and the old *chef* swayed with pride and delight. With a sigh of relief, knowing that he need have no further concern until the serving of that dinner was announced, he placed in André's hands a liberal sum for the cost of it, giving *carte blanche* for its creation.

Among the blacks were also a number of the old house servants. Absalom, the former major domo, and a half-dozen of the younger men, once waiters and attachés of the kitchen, pantry, and other domestic departments, crowded around to meet "*M'shi Grande.*" Absalom guaranteed to marshal, of these, a corps of assistants that would perform with credit the serving of the dinner.

After distributing a liberal largesse among the faithful, Grandemont rode back to town well pleased. There were many other smaller details to think of and provide for, but eventually the scheme was complete, and now there remained only the issuance of the invitations to his guests.

Along the river within the scope of a score of miles dwelt some half-dozen families with whose princely hospitality that of the Charleses had been contemporaneous. They were the proudest and most august of the old régime. Their small circle had been a brilliant one; their social relations close and warm; their houses full of rare welcome and discriminating bounty. Those friends, said Grandemont, should once more, if never again, sit at Charleroi on a nineteenth of January to celebrate the festal day of his house.

Grandemont had his cards of invitation engraved. They were expensive, but beautiful. In one particular their good taste might have been disputed; but the Creole allowed himself that one feather in the cap of his fugacious splendor. Might he not be allowed, for the one day of the *renaissance*, to be "Grandemont du Puy Charles, of Charleroi"? He sent the invitations out early in January so that the guests might not fail to receive due notice.

At eight o'clock in the morning of the nineteenth, the lower coast steamboat *River Belle* gingerly approached the long unused landing at Charleroi. The bridge was lowered, and a swarm of the plantation hands streamed along the rotting pier, bearing ashore a strange assortment of freight. Great shapeless bundles and bales and packets swathed in cloths and bound with ropes; tubs and urns of palms, evergreens, and tropical flowers; tables, mirrors, chairs, couches, carpets, and pictures—all carefully bound and padded against the dangers of transit.

Grandemont was among them, the busiest there. To the safe conveyance of certain large hampers eloquent with printed cautions to delicate handling he gave his superintendence, for they contained the fragile china and glassware. The dropping of one of those hampers would have cost him more than he could have saved in a year.

The last article unloaded, the *River Belle* backed off and continued her course down stream. In less than an hour everything had been conveyed to the house. And came then Absalom's task, directing the placing of the furniture and wares. There was plenty of help, for that day was always a holiday in Charleroi, and the Negroes did not suffer the old traditions to lapse. Almost the entire population of the quarters volunteered their aid. A score of piccaninnies were sweeping at the leaves in the yard. In the big kitchen at the rear André was lording it with his old-time magnificence over his numerous sub-cooks and scullions. Shutters were flung wide; dust spun in clouds; the house echoed to voices and the tread of busy feet. The prince had come again, and Charleroi woke from its long sleep.

The full moon, as she rose across the river that night and peeped above the levee, saw a sight that had been long missing from her orbit. The old plantation house shed a soft and alluring radiance from every window. Of its two-score rooms only four had been refurnished—the large reception chamber, the dining hall, and two smaller rooms for the convenience of the expected guests. But lighted wax candles were set in the windows of every room.

The dining hall was the *chef-d'œuvre*. The long table, set with twenty-five covers, sparkled like a winter landscape with its snowy napery and china and the icy gleam of crystal. The chaste beauty of the room had required small adornment. The polished floor burned to a glowing ruby with the reflection of candlelight. The rich wainscoting reached halfway to the ceiling. Along and above this had been set the relieving lightness of a few water-color sketches of fruit and flower.

The reception chamber was fitted in a simple but elegant style. Its arrangement suggested nothing of the fact that on the morrow the rooms would again be cleared and abandoned to the dust and the spider. The entrance hall was imposing with palms and ferns and the light of an immense candelabrum.

At seven o'clock Grandemont, in evening dress, with pearls —a family passion—in his spotless linen, emerged from somewhere. The invitations had specified eight as the dining hour. He drew an arm-chair upon the porch, and sat there, smoking cigarettes and half dreaming.

The moon was an hour high. Fifty yards back from the gate stood the house, under its noble grove. The road ran in front, and then came the grass-grown levee and the insatiate river beyond. Just above the levee top a tiny red light was creeping down and a tiny green one was creeping up. Then the passing steamers saluted, and the hoarse din startled the drowsy silence of the melancholy lowlands. The stillness returned, save for the little voices of the night—the owl's recitative, the capriccio of the crickets, the concerto of the frogs in the grass. The piccaninnies and the dawdlers from the quarters had been dismissed to their confines, and the mêlée of the day was reduced to an orderly and intelligent silence. The six colored waiters, in their white jackets, paced, cat-footed, about the table, pretending to arrange where all was beyond betterment. Absalom, in black and shining pumps, posed, superior, here and there where the lights set off his grandeur. And Grandemont rested in his chair, waiting for his guests.

He must have drifted into a dream—and an extravagant one —for he was master of Charleroi and Adèle was his wife. She was coming out to him now; he could hear her steps; he could feel her hand upon his shoulder——

"*Pardon moi, M'shi Grande*"—it was Absalom's hand touching him, it was Absalom's voice, speaking the *patois* of the blacks—"but it is eight o'clock."

Eight o'clock. Grandemont sprang up. In the moonlight he could see the row of hitching-posts outside the gate. Long ago the horses of the guests should have stood there. They were vacant.

A chanted roar of indignation, a just, waxing bellow of affront and dishonored genius came from André's kitchen, filling the house with rhythmic protest. The beautiful dinner, the pearl of a dinner, the little excellent superb jewel of a dinner! But one moment more of waiting and not even the thousand thunders of black pigs of the quarters would touch it!

"They are a little late," said Grandemont, calmly. "They will come soon. Tell André to hold back dinner. And ask him if, by some chance, a bull from the pastures has broken, roaring, into the house."

He seated himself again to his cigarettes. Though he had said it, he scarcely believed Charleroi would entertain company that night. For the first time in history the invitation of a Charles had been ignored. So simple in courtesy and honor was Grandemont and, perhaps, so serenely confident in the prestige of his name, that the most likely reasons for his vacant board did not occur to him.

Charleroi stood by a road traveled daily by people from those plantations whither his invitations had gone. No doubt even on the day before the sudden reanimation of the old house they had driven past and observed the evidences of long desertion and decay. They had looked at the corpse of Charleroi and then at Grandemont's invitations, and, though the puzzle or tasteless hoax or whatever the thing meant left them perplexed, they would not seek its solution by the folly of a visit to that deserted house.

The moon was now above the grove, and the yard was pied

with deep shadows save where they lightened in the tender glow of outpouring candlelight. A crisp breeze from the river hinted at the possibility of frost when the night should have become older. The grass at one side of the steps was specked with the white stubs of Grandemont's cigarettes. The cotton-broker's clerk sat in his chair with the smoke spiralling above him. I doubt that he once thought of the little fortune he had so impotently squandered. Perhaps it was compensation enough for him to sit thus at Charleroi for a few retrieved hours. Idly his mind wandered in and out many fanciful paths of memory. He smiled to himself as a paraphrased line of Scripture strayed into his mind: "A certain *poor* man made a feast."

He heard the sound of Absalom coughing a note of summons. Grandemont stirred. This time he had not been asleep —only drowsing.

"Nine o'clock, *M'shi Grande*," said Absalom in the uninflected voice of a good servant who states a fact unqualified by personal opinion.

Grandemont rose to his feet. In their time all the Charleses had been proven, and they were gallant losers.

"Serve dinner," he said, calmly. And then he checked Absalom's movement to obey, for something clicked the gate latch and was coming down the walk towards the house. Something that shuffled its feet and muttered to itself as it came. It stopped in the current of light at the foot of the steps and spake, in the universal whine of the gadding mendicant.

"Kind sir, could you spare a poor, hungry man, out of luck, a little to eat? And to sleep in the corner of a shed? For"— the thing concluded, irrelevantly—"I can sleep now. There are no mountains to dance reels in the night; and the copper kettles are all scoured bright. The iron band is still around my ankle, and a link, if it is your desire I should be chained."

It set a foot upon the step and drew up the rags that hung upon the limb. Above the distorted shoe, caked with the dust of a hundred leagues, they saw the link and the iron band. The clothes of the tramp were wrecked to piebald tatters by sun and rain and wear. A mat of brown, tangled hair and beard covered his head and face, out of which his eyes stared distractedly. Grandemont noticed that he carried in one hand a white, square card.

"What is that?" he asked.

"I picked it up, sir, at the side of the road." The vagabond handed the card to Grandemont. "Just a little to eat, sir. A little parched corn, a *tortilla*, or a handful of beans. Goat's meat I cannot eat. When I cut their throats they cry like children."

Grandemont held up the card. It was one of his own invitations to dinner. No doubt someone had cast it away from a passing carriage after comparing it with the tenantless house at Charleroi.

"From the hedges and highways bid them come," he said to himself, softly smiling. And then to Absalom: "Send Louis to me."

Louis, once his own body-servant, came promptly, in his white jacket.

"This gentleman," said Grandemont, "will dine with me. Furnish him with bath and clothes. In twenty minutes have him ready and dinner served."

Louis approached the disreputable guest with the suavity due to a visitor to Charleroi, and spirited him away to inner regions.

Promptly, in twenty minutes, Absalom announced dinner, and, a moment later, the guest was ushered into the dining hall where Grandemont waited, standing, at the head of the table. The attentions of Louis had transformed the stranger into something resembling the polite animal. Clean linen and an old evening suit that had been sent down from town to clothe a waiter had worked a miracle with his exterior. Brush and comb had partially subdued the wild disorder of his hair. Now he might have passed for no more extravagant a thing than one of those *poseurs* in art and music who affect such oddity of guise. The man's countenance and demeanor, as he approached the table, exhibited nothing of the awkwardness or confusion to be expected from his Arabian Nights change. He allowed Absalom to seat him at Grandemont's right hand with the manner of one thus accustomed to be waited upon.

"It grieves me," said Grandemont, "to be obliged to exchange names with a guest. My own name is Charles."

"In the mountains," said the wayfarer, "they call me Gringo. Along the roads they call me Jack."

"I prefer the latter," said Grandemont. "A glass of wine with you, Mr. Jack."

Course after course was served by the supernumerous waiters. Grandemont, inspired by the results of André's exquisite skill in cookery and his own in the selection of wines, became the model host, talkative, witty, and genial. The guest was fitful in conversation. His mind seemed to be sustaining a succession of waves of dementia followed by intervals of comparative lucidity. There was the glassy brightness of recent fever in his eyes. A long course of it must have been the cause of his emaciation and weakness, his distracted mind, and the dull pallor that showed even through the tan of wind and sun.

"Charles," he said to Grandemont—for thus he seemed to interpret his name—"you never saw the mountains dance, did you?"

"No, Mr. Jack," answered Grandemont, gravely, "the spectacle has been denied me. But, I assure you, I can understand it must be a diverting sight. The big ones, you know, white with snow on the tops, waltzing—*décolleté*, we may say."

"You first scour the kettles," said Mr. Jack, leaning toward him excitedly, "to cook the beans in in the morning, and you lie down on a blanket and keep quite still. Then they come out and dance for you. You would go out and dance with them but you are chained every night to the centre pole of the hut. You believe the mountains dance, don't you, Charlie?"

"I contradict no traveler's tales," said Grandemont, with a smile.

Mr. Jack laughed loudly. He dropped his voice to a confidential whisper.

"You are a fool to believe it," he went on. "They don't really dance. It's the fever in your head. It's the hard work and the bad water that does it. You are sick for weeks and there is no medicine. The fever comes on every evening, and then you are as strong as two men. One night the *compañia* are lying drunk with *mescal*. They have brought back sacks of silver dollars from a ride, and they drink to celebrate. In the night you file the chain in two and go down the mountain. You walk for miles—hundreds of them. By and by the mountains are all gone, and you come to the prairies. They do not dance at night; they are merciful, and you sleep. Then you come to the river, and it says things to you. You follow it down, down, but you can't find what you are looking for."

Mr. Jack leaned back in his chair, and his eyes slowly closed. The food and wine had steeped him in a deep calm. The tense strain had been smoothed from his face. The languor of repletion was claiming him. Drowsily he spoke again.

"It's bad manners—I know—to go to sleep—at table—but —that was—such a good dinner—Grande, old fellow."

Grande! The owner of the name started and set down his glass. How should this wretched tatterdemalion whom he had invited, Caliphlike, to sit at his feast know his name?

Not at first, but soon, little by little, the suspicion, wild and unreasonable as it was, stole into his brain. He drew out his watch with hands that almost balked him by their trembling, and opened the back case. There was a picture there —a photograph fixed to the inner side.

Rising, Grandemont shook Mr. Jack by the shoulder. The weary guest opened his eyes. Grandemont held the watch.

"Look at this picture, Mr. Jack. Have you ever——"

"*My sister Adèle!*"

The vagrant's voice rang loud and sudden through the room. He started to his feet, but Grandemont's arms were about him, and Grandemont was calling him "Victor!— Victor Fauquier! *Merci, merci, mon Dieu!*"

Too far overcome by sleep and fatigue was the lost one to talk that night. Days afterward, when the tropic *calentura* had cooled in his veins, the disordered fragments he had spoken were completed in shape and sequence. He told the story of his angry flight, of toils and calamities on sea and shore, of his ebbing and flowing fortune in southern lands, and of his latest peril when, held a captive, he served menially in a stronghold of bandits in the Sonora Mountains of Mexico. And of the fever that seized him there and his escape and delirium, during which he strayed, perhaps led by some marvelous instinct, back to the river on whose bank he had been born. And of the proud and stubborn thing in his blood that had kept him silent through all those years, clouding the honor of one, though he knew it not, and keeping apart two loving hearts. "What a thing is love!" you may say. And if I grant it, you shall say, with me: "What a thing is pride!"

On a couch in the reception chamber Victor lay, with a dawning understanding in his heavy eyes and peace in his softened countenance. Absalom was preparing a lounge for the transient master of Charleroi, who, to-morrow, would be again the clerk of a cotton broker, but also——

"To-morrow," Grandemont was saying, as he stood by the

couch of his guest, speaking the words with his face shining as must have shone the face of Elijah's charioteer when he announced the glories of that heavenly journey—"To-morrow I will take you to Her."

Shoes

JOHN DE GRAFFENREID ATWOOD ate of the lotus, root, stem, and flower. The tropics gobbled him up. He plunged enthusiastically into his work, which was to try to forget Rosine.

Now, they who dine on the lotus rarely consume it plain. There is a sauce *au diable* that goes with it; and the distillers are the chefs who prepare it. And on Johnny's menu card it read "brandy." With a bottle between them, he and Billy Keogh would sit on the porch of the little consulate at night and roar out great, indecorous songs, until the natives, slipping hastily past, would shrug a shoulder and mutter things to themselves about the "*Americanos diablos.*"

One day Johnny's *mozo* brought the mail and dumped it on the table. Johnny leaned from his hammock, and fingered the four or five letters dejectedly. Keogh was sitting on the edge of the table chopping lazily with a paper knife at the legs of a centipede that was crawling among the stationery. Johnny was in that phase of lotus-eating when all the world tastes bitter in one's mouth.

"Same old thing!" he complained. "Fool people writing for information about the country. They want to know all about raising fruit, and how to make a fortune without work. Half of 'em don't even send stamps for a reply. They think a consul hasn't anything to do but write letters. Slit those envelopes

for me, old man, and see what they want. I'm feeling too
rocky to move."

Keogh, acclimated beyond all possibility of ill-humor, drew
his chair to the table with smiling compliance on his rose-
pink countenance, and began to slit open the letters. Four
of them were from citizens in various parts of the United
States who seemed to regard the consul at Coralio as a
cyclopædia of information. They asked long lists of questions, numerically arranged, about the climate, products, possibilities, laws, business chances, and statistics of the country
in which the consul had the honor of representing his own
government.

"Write 'em, please, Billy," said that inert official, "just a
line, referring them to the latest consular report. Tell 'em the
State Department will be delighted to furnish the literary
gems. Sign my name. Don't let your pen scratch, Billy; it'll
keep me awake."

"Don't snore," said Keogh, amiably, "and I'll do your work
for you. You need a corps of assistants, anyhow. Don't see
how you ever get out a report. Wake up a minute!—here's
one more letter—it's from your own town, too—Dalesburg."

"That so?" murmured Johnny, showing a mild obligatory
interest. "What's it about?"

"Postmaster writes," explained Keogh. "Says a citizen of the
town wants some facts and advice from you. Says the citizen
has an idea in his head of coming down where you are and
opening a shoe store. Wants to know if you think the business
would pay. Says he's heard of the boom along this coast, and
wants to get in on the ground floor."

In spite of the heat and his bad temper, Johnny's hammock swayed with his laughter. Keogh laughed too; and the
pet monkey on the top shelf of the bookcase chattered in
shrill sympathy with the ironical reception of the letter from
Dalesburg.

"Great bunions!" exclaimed the consul. "Shoe store! What'll they ask about next, I wonder? Overcoat factory, I reckon. Say, Billy—of our 3,000 citizens, how many do you suppose ever had on a pair of shoes?"

Keogh reflected judicially.

"Let's see—there's you and me and——"

"Not me," said Johnny, promptly and incorrectly, holding up a foot encased in a disreputable deerskin *zapato*. "I haven't been a victim to shoes in months."

"But you've got 'em, though," went on Keogh. "And there's Goodwin and Blanchard and Geddie and old Lutz and Doc Gregg and that Italian that's agent for the banana company, and there's old Delgado—no; he wears sandals. And, oh, yes; there's Madama Ortiz, 'what kapes the hotel'—she had on a pair of red slippers at the *baile* the other night. And Miss Pasa, her daughter, that went to school in the States—she brought back some civilized notions in the way of footgear. And there's the *comandante's* sister that dresses up her feet on feast-days—and Mrs. Geddie, who wears a two with a Castilian instep—and that's about all the ladies. Let's see— don't some of the soldiers at the *cuartel*—no that's so; they're allowed shoes only when on the march. In barracks they turn their little toeses out to grass."

"'Bout right," agreed the consul. "Not over twenty out of the three thousand ever felt leather on their walking arrangements. Oh, yes; Coralio is just the town for an enterprising shoe store—that doesn't want to part with its goods. Wonder if old Patterson is trying to jolly me! He always was full of things he called jokes. Write him a letter, Billy. I'll dictate it. We'll jolly him back a few."

Keogh dipped his pen, and wrote at Johnny's dictation. With many pauses, filled in with smoke and sundry travellings of the bottle and glasses, the following reply to the

Dalesburg communication was perpetrated:

Mr. Obadiah Patterson,
    Dalesburg, Ala.

Dear Sir: In reply to your favor of July 2d, I have the honor to inform you that, according to my opinion, there is no place on the habitable globe that presents to the eye stronger evidence of the need of a first-class shoe store than does the town of Coralio. There are 3,000 inhabitants in the place, and not a single shoe store! The situation speaks for itself. This coast is rapidly becoming the goal of enterprising business men, but the shoe business is one that has been sadly overlooked or neglected. In fact, there are a considerable number of our citizens actually without shoes at present.

Besides the want above mentioned, there is also a crying need for a brewery, a college of higher mathematics, a coal yard, and a clean and intellectual Punch and Judy show. I have the honor to be, sir,

Your Obt. Servant,
John de Graffenreid Atwood,
U. S. Consul at Coralio.

P. S.—Hello! Uncle Obadiah. How's the old burg racking along? What would the government do without you and me? Look out for a green-headed parrot and a bunch of bananas soon, from your old friend

Johnny.

"I throw in that postscript," explained the consul, "so Uncle Obadiah won't take offence at the official tone of the letter! Now, Billy, you get that correspondence fixed up, and send Pancho to the post-office with it. The *Ariadne* takes the mail out to-morrow if they make up that load of fruit to-day."

The night programme in Coralio never varied. The recreations of the people were soporific and flat. They wandered about, barefoot and aimless, speaking lowly and smoking cigar or cigarette. Looking down on the dimly lighted ways one seemed to see a threading maze of brunette ghosts tangled with a procession of insane fire-flies. In some houses the thrumming of lugubrious guitars added to the depression of the *triste* night. Giant tree-frogs rattled in the foliage as loudly as the end man's "bones" in a minstrel troupe. By nine o'clock the streets were almost deserted.

Not at the consulate was there often a change of bill. Keogh would come there nightly, for Coralio's one cool place was the little seaward porch of that official residence.

The brandy would be kept moving; and before midnight sentiment would begin to stir in the heart of the self-exiled consul. Then he would relate to Keogh the story of his ended romance. Each night Keogh would listen patiently to the tale, and be ready with untiring sympathy.

"But don't you think for a minute"—thus Johnny would always conclude his woeful narrative—"that I'm grieving about that girl, Billy. I've forgotten her. She never enters my mind. If she were to enter that door right now, my pulse wouldn't gain a beat. That's all over long ago."

"Don't I know it?" Keogh would answer. "Of course you've forgotten her. Proper thing to do. Wasn't quite O. K. of her to listen to the knocks that—er—Dink Pawson kept giving you."

"Pink Dawson!"—a world of contempt would be in Johnny's tones—"Poor white trash! That's what he was. Had five hundred acres of farming land, though; and that counted. Maybe I'll have a chance to get back at him some day. The Dawsons weren't anybody. Everybody in Alabama knows the Atwoods. Say, Billy—did you know my mother was a De Graffenreid?"

"Why, no," Keogh would say; "is that so?" He had heard it some three hundred times.

"Fact. The De Graffenreids of Hancock County. But I never think of that girl any more, do I, Billy?"

"Not for a minute, my boy," would be the last sounds heard by the conqueror of Cupid.

At this point Johnny would fall into a gentle slumber, and Keogh would saunter out to his own shack under the calabash tree at the edge of the plaza.

In a day or two the letter from the Dalesburg postmaster and its answer had been forgotten by the Coralio exiles. But on the 26th day of July the fruit of the reply appeared upon the tree of events.

The *Andador,* a fruit steamer that visited Coralio regularly, drew into the offing and anchored. The beach was lined with spectators while the quarantine doctor and the custom-house crew rowed out to attend to their duties.

An hour later Billy Keogh lounged into the consulate, clean and cool in his linen clothes, and grinning like a pleased shark.

"Guess what?" he said to Johnny, lounging in his hammock.

"Too hot to guess," said Johnny, lazily.

"Your shoe-store man's come," said Keogh, rolling the sweet morsel on his tongue, "with a stock of goods big enough to supply the continent as far down as Tierra del Fuego. They're carting his cases over to the custom-house now. Six barges full they brought ashore and have paddled back for the rest. Oh, ye saints in glory! won't there be regalements in the air when he gets onto the joke and has an interview with Mr. Consul? It'll be worth nine years in the tropics just to witness that one joyful moment."

Keogh loved to take his mirth easily. He selected a clean place on the matting and lay upon the floor. The walls shook with his enjoyment. Johnny turned half over and blinked.

"Don't tell me," he said, "that anybody was fool enough to take that letter seriously."

"Four-thousand-dollar stock of goods!" gasped Keogh, in

ecstasy. "Talk about coals to Newcastle! Why didn't he take a ship-load of palm-leaf fans to Spitzbergen while he was about it? Saw the old codger on the beach. You ought to have been there when he put on his specs and squinted at the five hundred or so barefooted citizens standing around."

"Are you telling the truth, Billy?" asked the consul, weakly.

"Am I? You ought to see the buncoed gentleman's daughter he brought along. Looks! She makes the brick-dust señoritas here look like tar-babies."

"Go on," said Johnny, "if you can stop that asinine giggling. I hate to see a grown man make a laughing hyena of himself."

"Name is Hemstetter," went on Keogh. "He's a—— Hello! what's the matter now?"

Johnny's moccasined feet struck the floor with a thud as he wriggled out of his hammock.

"Get up, you idiot," he said, sternly, "or I'll brain you with this inkstand. That's Rosine and her father. Gad! what a drivelling idiot old Patterson is! Get up here, Billy Keogh, and help me. What the devil are we going to do? Has all the world gone crazy?"

Keogh rose and dusted himself. He managed to regain a decorous demeanor.

"Situation has got to be met, Johnny," he said, with some success at seriousness. "I didn't think about its being your girl until you spoke. First thing to do is to get them comfortable quarters. You go down and face the music, and I'll trot out to Goodwin's and see if Mrs. Goodwin won't take them in. They've got the decentest house in town."

"Bless you, Billy!" said the consul. "I knew you wouldn't desert me. The world's bound to come to an end, but maybe we can stave it off for a day or two."

Keogh hoisted his umbrella and set out for Goodwin's house. Johnny put on his coat and hat. He picked up the brandy bottle, but set it down again without drinking, and marched bravely down to the beach.

In the shade of the custom-house walls he found Mr. Hemstetter and Rosine surrounded by a mass of gaping citizens. The customs officers were ducking and scraping, while the captain of the *Andador* interpreted the business of the new arrivals. Rosine looked healthy and very much alive. She was gazing at the strange scenes around her with amused interest. There was a faint blush upon her round cheek as she greeted her old admirer. Mr. Hemstetter shook hands with Johnny in a very friendly way. He was an oldish, impractical man—one of that numerous class of erratic business men who are forever dissatisfied, and seeking a change.

"I am very glad to see you, John—may I call you John?" he said. "Let me thank you for your prompt answer to our postmaster's letter of inquiry. He volunteered to write to you on my behalf. I was looking about for something different in the way of a business in which the profits would be greater. I had noticed in the papers that this coast was receiving much attention from investors. I am extremely grateful for your advice to come. I sold out everything that I possess, and invested the proceeds in as fine a stock of shoes as could be bought in the North. You have a picturesque town here, John. I hope business will be as good as your letter justifies me in expecting."

Johnny's agony was abbreviated by the arrival of Keogh, who hurried up with the news that Mrs. Goodwin would be much pleased to place rooms at the disposal of Mr. Hemstetter and his daughter. So there Mr. Hemstetter and Rosine were at once conducted and left to recuperate from the fatigue of the voyage, while Johnny went down to see that the cases of shoes were safely stored in the customs warehouse pending their examination by the officials. Keogh, grinning like a shark, skirmished about to find Goodwin, to instruct him not to expose to Mr. Hemstetter the true state of Coralio as a shoe market until Johnny had been given a chance to redeem the situation, if such a thing were possible.

That night the consul and Keogh held a desperate consultation on the breezy porch of the consulate.

"Send 'em back home," began Keogh, reading Johnny's thoughts.

"I would," said Johnny, after a little silence; "but I've been lying to you, Billy."

"All right about that," said Keogh, affably.

"I've told you hundreds of times," said Johnny, slowly, "that I had forgotten that girl, haven't I?"

"About three hundred and seventy-five," admitted the monument of patience.

"I lied," repeated the consul, "every time. I never forgot her for one minute. I was an obstinate ass for running away just because she said 'No' once. And I was too proud a fool to go back. I talked with Rosine a few minutes this evening up at Goodwin's. I found out one thing. You remember that farmer fellow who was always after her?"

"Dink Pawson?" asked Keogh.

"Pink Dawson. Well, he wasn't a hill of beans to her. She says she didn't believe a word of the things he told her about me. But I'm sewed up now, Billy. That tomfool letter we sent ruined whatever chance I had left. She'll despise me when she finds out that her old father has been made the victim of a joke that a decent school boy wouldn't have been guilty of. Shoes! Why he couldn't sell twenty pairs of shoes in Coralio if he kept store here for twenty years. You put a pair of shoes on one of these Caribs or Spanish brown boys and what'd he do? Stand on his head and squeal until he'd kicked 'em off. None of 'em ever wore shoes and they never will. If I send 'em back home I'll have to tell the whole story, and what'll she think of me? I want that girl worse than ever, Billy, and now when she's in reach I've lost her forever because I tried to be funny when the thermometer was at 102."

"Keep cheerful," said the optimistic Keogh. "And let 'em open the store. I've been busy myself this afternoon. We can stir up a temporary boom in foot-gear anyhow. I'll buy six pairs when the doors open. I've been around and seen all the fellows and explained the catastrophe. They'll all buy shoes like they was centipedes. Frank Goodwin will take cases of 'em. The Geddies want about eleven pairs between 'em. Clancy is going to invest the savings of weeks, and even old Doc Gregg wants three pairs of alligator-hide slippers if they've got any tens. Blanchard got a look at Miss Hemstetter; and as he's a Frenchman, no less than a dozen pairs will do for him."

"A dozen customers," said Johnny, "for a $4,000 stock of shoes! It won't work. There's a big problem here to figure out. You go home, Billy, and leave me alone. I've got to work at it all by myself. Take that bottle of Three-star along with you —no, sir; not another ounce of booze for the United States consul. I'll sit here to-night and pull out the think stop. If there's a soft place on this proposition anywhere I'll land on it. If there isn't there'll be another wreck to the credit of the gorgeous tropics."

Keogh left, feeling that he could be of no use. Johnny laid a handful of cigars on a table and stretched himself in a steamer chair. When the sudden daylight broke, silvering the harbor ripples, he was still sitting there. Then he got up, whistling a little tune, and took his bath.

At nine o'clock he walked down to the dingy little cable office and hung for half an hour over a blank. The result of his application was the following message, which he signed and had transmitted at a cost of $33:

To PINKNEY DAWSON,
    Dalesburg, Ala.
  Draft for $100 comes to you next mail. Ship me immediately
500 pounds stiff, dry cockleburrs. New use here in arts. Market
price twenty cents pound. Further orders likely. Rush.

Ships

WITHIN A WEEK a suitable building had been secured in the
Calle Grande, and Mr. Hemstetter's stock of shoes arranged
upon their shelves. The rent of the store was moderate; and
the stock made a fine showing of neat white boxes, attractively
displayed.

Johnny's friends stood by him loyally. On the first day
Keogh strolled into the store in a casual kind of way about
once every hour, and bought shoes. After he had purchased
a pair each of extension soles, congress gaiters, button kids,
low-quartered calfs, dancing pumps, rubber boots, tans of
various hues, tennis shoes and flowered slippers, he sought
out Johnny to be prompted as to names of other kinds that
he might inquire for. The other English-speaking residents
also played their parts nobly by buying often and liberally.
Keogh was grand marshal, and made them distribute their pa-
tronage, thus keeping up a fair run of custom for several days.

Mr. Hemstetter was gratified by the amount of business
done thus far; but expressed surprise that the natives were so
backward with their custom.

"Oh, they're awfully shy," explained Johnny, as he wiped
his forehead nervously. "They'll get the habit pretty soon.
They'll come with a rush when they do come."

One afternoon Keogh dropped into the consul's office, chewing an unlighted cigar thoughtfully.

"Got anything up your sleeve?" he inquired of Johnny. "If you have it's about time to show it. If you can borrow some gent's hat in the audience, and make a lot of customers for an idle stock of shoes come out of it, you'd better spiel. The boys have all laid in enough foot-wear to last 'em ten years; and there's nothing doing in the shoe store but dolcy far nienty. I just came by there. Your venerable victim was standing in the door, gazing through his specs at the bare toes passing by his emporium. The natives here have got the true artistic temperament. Me and Clancy took eighteen tintypes this morning in two hours. There's been but one pair of shoes sold all day. Blanchard went in and bought a pair of fur-lined house-slippers because he thought he saw Miss Hemstetter go into the store. I saw him throw the slippers into the lagoon afterwards."

"There's a Mobile fruit steamer coming in to-morrow or next day," said Johnny. "We can't do anything until then."

"What are you going to do—try to create a demand?"

"Political economy isn't your strong point," said the consul, impudently. "You can't create a demand. But you can create a necessity for a demand. That's what I am going to do."

Two weeks after the consul sent his cable, a fruit steamer brought him a huge, mysterious brown bale of some unknown commodity. Johnny's influence with the custom-house people was sufficiently strong for him to get the goods turned over to him without the usual inspection. He had the bale taken to the consulate and snugly stowed in the back room.

That night he ripped open a corner of it and took out a handful of the cockleburrs. He examined them with the care with which a warrior examines his arms before he goes forth to battle for his lady-love and life. The burrs were the ripe August product, as hard as filberts, and bristling with spines

as tough and sharp as needles. Johnny whistled softly a little
tune, and went out to find Billy Keogh.

Later in the night, when Coralio was steeped in slumber,
he and Billy went forth into the deserted streets with their
coats bulging like balloons. All up and down the Calle
Grande they went, sowing the sharp burrs carefully in the
sand, along the narrow sidewalks, in every foot of grass between the silent houses. And then they took the side streets
and byways, missing none. No place where the foot of man,
woman or child might fall was slighted. Many trips they made
to and from the prickly hoard. And then, nearly at the dawn,
they laid themselves down to rest calmly, as great generals do
after planning a victory according to the revised tactics, and
slept, knowing that they had sowed with the accuracy of Satan
sowing tares and the perseverance of Paul planting.

With the rising sun came the purveyors of fruits and meats,
and arranged their wares in and around the little market-
house. At one end of the town near the seashore the market-
house stood; and the sowing of the burrs had not been
carried that far. The dealers waited long past the hour when
their sales usually began. None came to buy. "*Qué hay?*" they
began to exclaim, one to another.

At their accustomed time, from every 'dobe and palm hut
and grass-thatched shack and dim *patio* glided women—black
women, brown women, lemon-colored women, women dun
and yellow and tawny. They were the marketers starting to
purchase the family supply of cassava, plantains, meat, fowls,
and tortillas. Décolleté they were and bare-armed and barefooted, with a single skirt reaching below the knee. Stolid and
ox-eyed, they stepped from their doorways into the narrow
paths or upon the soft grass of the streets.

The first to emerge uttered ambiguous squeals, and raised
one foot quickly. Another step and they sat down, with shrill
cries of alarm, to pick at the new and painful insects that had

stung them upon the feet. "*Qué picadores diablos!*" they
screeched to one another across the narrow ways. Some tried
the grass instead of the paths, but there they were also stung
and bitten by the strange little prickly balls. They plumped
down in the grass, and added their lamentations to those of
their sisters in the sandy paths. All through the town was
heard the plaint of the feminine jabber. The venders in the
market still wondered why no customers came.

Then men, lords of the earth, came forth. They, too, began
to hop, to dance, to limp, and to curse. They stood stranded
and foolish, or stooped to pluck at the scourge that attacked
their feet and ankles. Some loudly proclaimed the pest to be
poisonous spiders of an unknown species.

And then the children ran out for their morning romp. And
now to the uproar was added the howls of limping infants
and cockleburred childhood. Every minute the advancing day
brought forth fresh victims.

Doña Maria Castillas y Buenventura de las Casas stepped
from her honored doorway, as was her daily custom, to pro-
cure fresh bread from the *panadería* across the street. She was
clad in a skirt of flowered yellow satin, a chemise of ruffled
linen, and wore a purple mantilla from the looms of Spain.
Her lemon-tinted feet, alas! were bare. Her progress was ma-
jestic, for were not her ancestors hidalgos of Aragon? Three
steps she made across the velvety grass, and set her aristocratic
sole upon a bunch of Johnny's burrs. Doña Maria Castillas y
Buenventura de las Casas emitted a yowl even as a wildcat.
Turning about, she fell upon hands and knees, and crawled
—ay, like a beast of the field she crawled back to her honorable
door-sill.

Don Señor Ildefonso Federico Valdazar, *Juez de la Paz*,
weighing twenty stone, attempted to convey his bulk to the
pulquería at the corner of the plaza in order to assuage his
matutinal thirst. The first plunge of his unshod foot into the

cool grass struck a concealed mine. Don Ildefonso fell like a
crumpled cathedral, crying out that he had been fatally bitten
by a deadly scorpion. Everywhere were the shoeless citizens
hopping, stumbling, limping, and picking from their feet the
venomous insects that had come in a single night to harass
them.

The first to perceive the remedy was Estebán Delgado, the
barber, a man of travel and education. Sitting upon a stone,
he plucked burrs from his toes, and made oration:

"Behold, my friend, these bugs of the devil! I know them
well. They soar through the skies in swarms like pigeons.
These are the dead ones that fell during the night. In Yucatan
I have seen them as large as oranges. Yes! There they hiss like
serpents, and have wings like bats. It is the shoes—the shoes
that one needs! *Zapatos—zapatos para mí!*"

Estebán hobbled to Mr. Hemstetter's store, and bought
shoes. Coming out, he swaggered down the street with im-
punity, reviling loudly the bugs of the devil. The suffering
ones sat up or stood upon one foot and beheld the immune
barber. Men, women, and children took up the cry: "*Zapatos!
zapatos!*"

The necessity for the demand had been created. The demand followed. That day Mr. Hemstetter sold three hundred
pairs of shoes.

"It is really surprising," he said to Johnny, who came up in
the evening to help him straighten out the stock, "how trade
is picking up. Yesterday I made but three sales."

"I told you they'd whoop things up when they got started,"
said the consul.

"I think I shall order a dozen more cases of goods, to keep
the stock up," said Mr. Hemstetter, beaming through his
spectacles.

"I wouldn't send in any orders yet," advised Johnny. "Wait
till you see how the trade holds up."

Each night Johnny and Keogh sowed the crop that grew dollars by day. At the end of ten days two-thirds of the stock of shoes had been sold; and the stock of cockleburrs was exhausted. Johnny cabled to Pink Dawson for another 500 pounds, paying twenty cents per pound as before. Mr. Hemstetter carefully made up an order for $1,500 worth of shoes from Northern firms. Johnny hung about the store until this order was ready for the mail, and succeeded in destroying it before it reached the post-office.

That night he took Rosine under the mango tree by Goodwin's porch, and confessed everything. She looked him in the eye, and said: "You are a very wicked man. Father and I will go back home. You say it was a joke? I think it is a very serious matter."

But at the end of half an hour's argument the conversation had been turned upon a different subject. The two were considering the respective merits of pale blue and pink wall paper with which the old colonial mansion of the Atwoods in Dalesburg was to be decorated after the wedding.

On the next morning Johnny confessed to Mr. Hemstetter. The shoe merchant put on his spectacles, and said through them: "You strike me as being a most extraordinary young scamp. If I had not managed this enterprise with good business judgment my entire stock of goods might have been a complete loss. Now, how do you propose to dispose of the rest of it?"

When the second invoice of cockleburrs arrived Johnny loaded them and the remainder of the shoes into a schooner, and sailed down the coast to Alazan.

There, in the same dark and diabolical manner, he repeated his success; and came back with a bag of money and not so much as a shoestring.

And then he besought his great uncle of the waving goatee and starred vest to accept his resignation, for the lotus no longer lured him. He hankered for the spinach and cress of Dalesburg.

The services of Mr. William Terence Keogh as acting consul, *pro tem.*, were suggested and accepted, and Johnny sailed with the Hemstetters back to his native shores.

Three days after Johnny's departure, two small schooners appeared off Coralio. After some delay a boat put off from one of them, and brought a sunburned young man ashore. This young man had a shrewd and calculating eye; and he gazed with amazement at the strange things that he saw. He found on the beach some one who directed him to the consul's office; and thither he made his way at a nervous gait.

Keogh was sprawled in the official chair, drawing caricatures of his uncle's head on an official pad of paper. He looked up at his visitor.

"Where's Johnny Atwood?" inquired the sunburned young man, in a business tone.

"Gone," said Keogh, working carefully at Uncle Sam's necktie.

"That's just like him," remarked the nut-brown one, leaning against the table. "He always was a fellow to gallivant around instead of 'tending to business. Will he be in soon?"

"Don't think so," said Keogh, after a fair amount of deliberation.

"I s'pose he's out at some of his tomfoolery," conjectured the visitor, in a tone of virtuous conviction. "Johnny never would stick to anything long enough to succeed. I wonder how he manages to run his business here, and never be 'round to look after it."

"I'm looking after the business just now," admitted the *pro tem.* consul.

"Are you—then, say!—where's the factory?"

"What factory?" asked Keogh, with a mildly polite interest.

"Why, the factory where they use them cockleburrs. Lord

knows what they use 'em for, anyway! I've got the basements
of both them ships out there loaded with 'em. I'll give you a
bargain in this lot. I've had every man, woman, and child
around Dalesburg that wasn't busy pickin' 'em for a month.
I hired these ships to bring 'em over. Everybody thought I
was crazy. Now, you can have this lot for fifteen cents a
pound, delivered on land. And if you want more I guess old
Alabam' can come up to the demand. Johnny told me when
he left home that if he struck anything down here that there
was any money in he'd let me in on it. Shall I drive the ships
in and hitch?"

A look of supreme, almost incredulous, delight dawned in
Keogh's ruddy countenance. He dropped his pencil. His eyes
turned upon the sunburned young man with joy in them mingled with fear lest his ecstasy should prove a dream.

"For God's sake, tell me," said Keogh, earnestly, "are you
Dink Pawson?"

"My name is Pinkney Dawson," said the cornerer of the
cockleburr market.

Billy Keogh slid rapturously and gently from his chair to
his favorite strip of matting on the floor.

There were not many sounds in Coralio on that sultry afternoon. Among those that were may be mentioned a noise of
enraptured and unrighteous laughter from a prostrate Irish-
American, while a sunburned young man, with a shrewd eye,
looked on him with wonder and amazement. Also the "tramp,
tramp, tramp" of many well-shod feet in the streets outside.
Also the lonesome wash of the waves that beat along the his-
toric shores of the Spanish Main.

The Hiding of Black Bill

A LANK, strong, red-faced man with a Wellington beak and small, fiery eyes tempered by flaxen lashes, sat on the station platform at Los Pinos swinging his legs to and fro. At his side sat another man, fat, melancholy, and seedy, who seemed to be his friend. They had the appearance of men to whom life had appeared as a reversible coat—seamy on both sides.

"Ain't seen you in about four years, Ham," said the seedy man. "Which way you been travelling?"

"Texas," said the red-faced man. "It was too cold in Alaska for me. And I found it warm in Texas. I'll tell you about one hot spell I went through there.

"One morning I steps off the International at a water-tank and lets it go on without me. 'Twas a ranch country, and fuller of spitehouses than New York City. Only out there they build 'em twenty miles away so you can't smell what they've got for dinner, instead of running 'em up two inches from their neighbors' windows.

"There wasn't any roads in sight, so I footed it 'cross country. The grass was shoe-top deep, and the mesquite timber looked just like a peach orchard. It was so much like a gentleman's private estate that every minute you expected a kennelful of bulldogs to run out and bite you. But I must have walked twenty miles before I came in sight of a ranch-house. It was a little one, about as big as an elevated railroad station.

"There was a little man in a white shirt and brown overalls and pink handkerchief around his neck rolling cigarettes under a tree in front of the door.

"'Greetings,' says I. 'Any refreshments, welcome, emoluments, or even work for a comparative stranger?'

"'Oh, come in,' says he, in a refined tone. 'Sit down on that stool, please. I didn't hear your horse coming.'

"'He isn't near enough yet,' says I. 'I walked. I don't want to be a burden, but I wonder if you have three or four gallons of water handy.'

"'You do look pretty dusty,' says he; 'but our bathing arrangements——'

"'It's a drink I want,' says I. 'Never mind the dust that's on the outside.'

"He gets me a dipper of water out of a red jar hanging up, and then goes on:

"'Do you want work?'

"'For a time,' says I. 'This is a rather quiet section of the country, isn't it?'

"'It is,' says he. 'Sometimes—so I have been told—one sees no human being pass for weeks at a time. I've been here only a month. I bought the ranch from an old settler who wanted to move farther west.'

"'It suits me,' says I. 'Quiet and retirement are good for a man sometimes. And I need a job. I can tend bar, salt mines, lecture, float stock, do a little middle-weight slugging, and play the piano.'

"'Can you herd sheep?' asks the little ranchman.

"'Do you mean *have* I heard sheep?' says I.

"'Can you herd 'em—take charge of a flock of 'em?' says he.

"'Oh,' says I, 'now I understand. You mean chase 'em around and bark at 'em like collie dogs. Well, I might,' says I. 'I've never exactly done any sheep-herding, but I've often seen 'em from car windows masticating daisies, and they don't look dangerous.'

"'I'm short a herder,' says the ranchman. 'You never can depend on the Mexicans. I've only got two flocks. You may take out my bunch of muttons—there are only eight hundred of 'em—in the morning, if you like. The pay is twelve dollars a month and your rations furnished. You camp in a tent on the prairie with your sheep. You do your own cooking, but wood and water are brought to your camp. It's an easy job.'

" 'I'm on,' says I. 'I'll take the job even if I have to garland my brow and hold on to a crook and wear a loose effect and play on a pipe like the shepherds do in pictures.'

"So the next morning the little ranchman helps me drive the flock of muttons from the corral to about two miles out and let 'em graze on a little hillside on the prairie. He gives me a lot of instructions about not letting bunches of them stray off from the herd, and driving 'em down to a water-hole to drink at noon.

" 'I'll bring out your tent and camping outfit and rations in the buckboard before night,' says he.

" 'Fine,' says I. 'And don't forget the rations. Nor the camping outfit. And be sure to bring the tent. Your name's Zollicoffer, ain't it?'

" 'My name,' says he, 'is Henry Ogden.'

" 'All right, Mr. Ogden,' says I. 'Mine is Mr. Percival Saint Clair.'

"I herded sheep for five days on the Rancho Chiquito; and then the wool entered my soul. That getting next to Nature certainly got next to me. I was lonesomer than Crusoe's goat. I've seen a lot of persons more entertaining as companions than those sheep were. I'd drive 'em to the corral and pen 'em every evening, and then cook my cornbread and mutton and coffee, and lie down in a tent the size of a tablecloth, and listen to the coyotes and whippoor-wills singing around the camp.

"The fifth evening, after I had coralled my costly but uncongenial muttons, I walked over to the ranch-house and stepped in the door.

" 'Mr. Ogden,' says I, 'you and me have got to get sociable. Sheep are all very well to dot the landscape and furnish eight-dollar cotton suitings for man, but for table-talk and fireside companions they rank along with five-o'clock teazers. If you've got a deck of cards, or a parcheesi outfit, or a game of authors, get 'em out, and let's get on a mental basis. I've got to do something in an intellectual line, if it's only to knock somebody's brains out.'

"This Henry Ogden was a peculiar kind of ranchman. He wore finger-rings and a big gold watch and careful neckties. And his face was calm, and his nose-spectacles was kept very shiny. I saw once, in Muscogee, an outlaw hung for murdering six men, who was a dead ringer for him. But I knew a preacher in Arkansas that you would have taken to be his brother. I didn't care much for him cither way; what I wanted was some fellowship and communion with holy saints or lost sinners—anything sheepless would do.

" 'Well, Saint Clair,' says he, laying down the book he was reading, 'I guess it must be pretty lonesome for you at first. And I don't deny that it's monotonous for me. Are you sure you corralled your sheep so they won't stray out?'

" 'They're shut up as tight as the jury of a millionaire murderer,' says I. 'And I'll be back with them long before they'll need their trained nurse.'

"So Ogden digs up a deck of cards, and we play casino. After five days and nights of my sheep-camp it was like a toot on Broadway. When I caught big casino I felt as excited as if I had made a million in Trinity. And when H. O. loosened up a little and told the story about the lady in the Pullman car I laughed for five minutes.

"That showed what a comparative thing life is. A man may see so much that he'd be bored to turn his head to look at a $3,000,000 fire or Joe Weber or the Adriatic Sea. But let him herd sheep for a spell, and you'll see him splitting his ribs laughing at 'Curfew Shall Not Ring To-night,' or really enjoying himself playing cards with ladies.

"By-and-by Ogden gets out a decanter of Bourbon, and there is a total eclipse of sheep.

" 'Do you remember reading in the papers about a month ago,' says he, 'about a train hold-up on the M. K. & T.? The express agent was shot through the shoulder and about $15,000 in currency taken. And it's said that only one man did the job.'

" 'Seems to me I do,' says I. 'But such things happen so often they don't linger long in the human Texas mind. Did they overtake, overhaul, seize, or lay hands upon the despoiler?'

" 'He escaped,' says Ogden. 'And I was just reading in a paper to-day that the officers have tracked him down into this part of the country. It seems the bills the robbers got were all the first issue of currency to the Second National Bank of Espinosa City. And so they've followed the trail where they've been spent, and it leads this way.'

"Ogden pours out some more Bourbon, and shoves me the bottle.

" 'I imagine,' says I, after ingurgitating another modicum of the royal booze, 'that it wouldn't be at all a disingenuous idea for a train-robber to run down into this part of the country to hide for a spell. A sheep-ranch, now,' says I, 'would be the finest kind of a place. Who'd ever expect to find such a desperate character among these song-birds and muttons and wild flowers? And, by the way,' says I, kind of looking H. Ogden over, 'was there any description mentioned to this single-handed terror? Was his lineaments or height and thickness or teeth fillings or style of habiliments set forth in print?"

" 'Why, no,' says Ogden; 'because they say nobody got a good sight of him because he wore a mask. But they know it was a train-robber called Black Bill, because he always works alone and because he dropped a handkerchief in the express-car that had his name on it.'

"'All right,' says I. 'I approve of Black Bill's retreat to the sheep-ranges. I guess they won't find him.'

"'There's one thousand dollars' reward for his capture,' says Ogden.

"'I don't need that kind of money,' says I, looking Mr. Sheepman straight in the eye. 'The twelve dollars a month you pay me is enough. I need a rest, and I can save up until I get enough to pay my fare to Texarkana, where my widowed mother lives. If Black Bill,' I goes on, looking significantly at Ogden, 'was to have come down this way—say, a month ago—and bought a little sheep-ranch and——'

"'Stop,' says Ogden, getting out of his chair and looking pretty vicious. 'Do you mean to insinuate——'

"'Nothing,' says I; 'no insinuations. I'm stating a hypodermical case. I say, if Black Bill had come down here and bought a sheep-ranch and hired me to Little-Boy-Blue 'em and treated me square and friendly, as you've done, he'd never have anything to fear from me. A man is a man, regardless of any complications he may have with sheep or railroad trains. Now you know where I stand.'

"Ogden looks black as camp-coffee for nine seconds, and then he laughs, amused.

"'You'll do, Saint Clair,' says he. 'If I *was* Black Bill I wouldn't be afraid to trust you. Let's have a game or two of seven-up to-night. That is, if you don't mind playing with a train-robber.'

"'I've told you,' says I, 'my oral sentiments, and there's no strings to 'em.'

"While I was shuffling after the first hand, I asks Ogden, as if the idea was a kind of a casualty, where he was from.

"'Oh,' says he, 'from the Mississippi Valley.'

"'That's a nice little place,' says I. 'I've often stopped over there. But didn't you find the sheets a little damp and the food poor? Now, I hail,' says I, 'from the Pacific Slope. Ever put up there?'

"'Too draughty,' says Ogden. 'But if you're ever in the Middle West just mention my name, and you'll get foot-warmers and dripped coffee.'

"'Well,' says I, 'I wasn't exactly fishing for your private tele-p'ione number and the middle name of your aunt that carried off that Cumberland Presbyterian minister. It don't matter. I just want you to know you are safe in the hands of your shepherd. Now, don't play hearts on spades, and don't get nervous.'

"'Still harping,' says Ogden, laughing again. 'Don't you suppose that if I was Black Bill and thought you suspected me, I'd put a Winchester bullet into you and stop my nervous-ness if I had any?'

"'Not any,' says I. 'A man who's got the nerve to hold up a train single-handed wouldn't do a trick like that. I've knocked about enough to know that them are the kind of men who put a value on a friend. Not that I can claim being a friend of yours, Mr. Ogden,' says I, 'being only your sheep-herder; but under more expeditious circumstances we might have been.'

"'Forget the sheep temporarily, I beg,' says Ogden, 'and cut for deal.'

"About four days afterwards, while my muttons was noon-ing on the water-hole and I deep in the interstices of making a pot of coffee, up rides softly on the grass a mysterious person in the garb of the being he wished to represent. He was dressed somewhere between a Kansas City detective, Buffalo Bill, and the town dog-catcher of Baton Rouge. His chin and eye wasn't moulded on fighting lines, so I knew he was only a scout.

"'Herdin' sheep?' he asks me.

"'Well,' says I, 'to a man of your evident gumptional endowments, I wouldn't have the nerve to state that I am engaged in decorating old bronzes or oiling bicycle sprockets.'

" 'You don't talk or look like a sheep-herder to me,' says he.

" 'But you talk like what you look like to me,' says I.

"And then he asks me who I was working for, and I shows him Rancho Chiquito, two miles away, in the shadow of a low hill, and he tells me he's a deputy sheriff.

" 'There's a train-robber called Black Bill supposed to be somewhere in these parts,' says the scout. 'He's been traced as far as San Antonio, and may be farther. Have you seen or heard of any strangers around here during the past month?'

" 'I have not,' says I, 'except a report of one over at the Mexican quarters of Loomis' ranch, on the Frio.'

" 'What do you know about him?' asks the deputy.

" 'He's three days old,' says I.

" 'What kind of a looking man is the man you work for?' he asks. 'Does old George Ramey own this place yet? He's run sheep here for the last ten years, but never had no success.'

" 'The old man has sold out and gone West,' I tells him. 'Another sheep-fancier bought him out about a month ago.'

" 'What kind of a looking man is he?' asks the deputy again.

" 'Oh,' says I, 'a big, fat kind of a Dutchman with long whiskers and blue specs. I don't think he knows a sheep from a ground-squirrel. I guess old George soaked him pretty well on the deal,' says I.

"After indulging himself in a lot more non-communicative information and two thirds of my dinner, the deputy rides away.

"That night I mentions the matter to Ogden.

" 'They're drawing the tendrils of the octopus around Black Bill,' says I. And then I told him about the deputy sheriff, and how I'd described him to the deputy, and what the deputy said about the matter.

" 'Oh, well,' says Ogden, 'let's don't borrow any of Black

Bill's troubles. We've a few of our own. Get the Bourbon out of the cupboard and we'll drink to his health—unless,' says he, with his little cackling laugh, 'you're prejudiced against train-robbers.'

" 'I'll drink,' says I, 'to any man who's a friend to a friend. And I believe that Black Bill,' I goes on, 'would be that. So here's to Black Bill, and may he have good luck.'

"And both of us drank.

"About two weeks later comes shearing-time. The sheep had to be driven up to the ranch, and a lot of frowzy-headed Mexicans would snip the fur off them with back-action scissors. So the afternoon before the barbers were to come I hustled my underdone muttons over the hill, across the dell, down by the winding brook, and up to the ranch-house, where I penned 'em in a corral and bade 'em my nightly adieus.

"I went from there to the ranch-house. I find H. Ogden, Esquire, lying asleep on his little cot bed. I guess he had been overcome by anti-insomnia or diswakefulness or some of the diseases peculiar to the sheep business. His mouth and vest were open, and he breathed like a second-hand bicycle pump. I looked at him and gave vent to just a few musings. 'Imperial Cæsar,' says I, 'asleep in such a way, might shut his mouth and keep the wind away.'

"A man asleep is certainly a sight to make angels weep. What good is all his brain, muscle, backing, nerve, influence, and family connections? He's at the mercy of his enemies, and more so of his friends. And he's about as beautiful as a cab-horse leaning against the Metropolitan Opera House at 12:30 A.M. dreaming of the plains of Arabia. Now, a woman asleep you regard as different. No matter how she looks, you know it's better for all hands for her to be that way.

"Well, I took a drink of Bourbon and one for Ogden, and started in to be comfortable while he was taking his nap. He had some books on his table on indigenous subjects, such as

Japan and drainage and physical culture—and some tobacco, which seemed more to the point.

"After I'd smoked a few, and listened to the sartorial breathing of H. O., I happened to look out the window toward the shearing-pens, where there was a kind of a road coming up from a kind of a road across a kind of a creek farther away.

"I saw five men riding up to the house. All of 'em carried guns across their saddles, and among 'em was the deputy that had talked to me at my camp.

"They rode up careful, in open formation, with their guns ready. I set apart with my eye the one I opinionated to be the boss muck-raker of this law-and-order cavalry.

"'Good-evening, gents,' says I. 'Won't you 'light and tie your horses?'

"The boss rides up close, and swings his gun over till the opening in it seems to cover my whole front elevation.

"'Don't you move your hands none,' says he, 'till you and me indulge in a adequate amount of necessary conversation.'

"'I will not,' says I. 'I am no deaf-mute, and therefore will not have to disobey your injunctions in replying.'

"'We are on the lookout,' says he, 'for Black Bill, the man that held up the Katy for $15,000 in May. We are searching the ranches and everybody on 'em. What is your name, and what do you do on this ranch?'

"'Captain,' says I, 'Percival Saint Clair is my occupation, and my name is sheep-herder. I've got my flock of veals—no, muttons—penned here to-night. The searchers are coming tomorrow to give them a haircut—with baa-a-rum, I suppose.'

"'Where's the boss of this ranch?' the captain of the gang asks me.

"'Wait just a minute, cap'n,' says I. 'Wasn't there a kind of a reward offered for the capture of this desperate character you have referred to in your preamble?'

" 'There's a thousand dollars' reward offered,' says the captain, 'but it's for his capture and conviction. There don't seem to be no provision made for an informer.'

" 'It looks like it might rain in a day or so,' says I, in a tired way, looking up at the cerulean blue sky.

" 'If you know anything about the locality, disposition, or secretiveness of this here Black Bill,' says he, in a severe dialect, 'you are amiable to the law in not reporting it.'

" 'I heard a fence-rider say,' says I, in a desultory kind of voice, 'that a Mexican told a cowboy named Jake over at Pidgin's store on the Nueces that he heard that Black Bill had been seen in Matamoras by a sheepman's cousin two weeks ago.'

" 'Tell you what I'll do, Tight Mouth,' says the captain after looking me over for bargains. 'If you put us on so we can scoop Black Bill, I'll pay you a hundred dollars out of my own —out of our own—pockets. That's liberal,' says he. 'You ain't entitled to anything. Now, what do you say?'

" 'Cash down now?' I ask.

"The captain has a sort of discussion with his helpmates, and they all produce the contents of their pockets for analysis. Out of the general results they figured up $102.30 in cash and $31 worth of plug tobacco.

" 'Come nearer, capitan meeo,' says I, 'and listen.' He so did.

" 'I am mighty poor and low down in the world,' says I. 'I am working for twelve dollars a month trying to keep a lot of animals together whose only thought seems to be to get asunder. Although,' says I, 'I regard myself as some better than the State of South Dakota, it's a come-down to a man who has heretofore regarded sheep only in the form of chops. I'm pretty far reduced in the world on account of foiled ambitions and rum and a kind of cocktail they make along the P. R. R. all the way from Scranton to Cincinnati—dry gin,

French vermouth, one squeeze of a lime, and a good dash of orange bitters. If you're ever up that way, don't fail to let one try you. And, again,' says I, 'I have never yet went back on a friend. I've stayed by 'em when they had plenty, and when adversity's overtaken me I've never forsook 'em.

" 'But,' I goes on, 'this is not exactly the case of a friend. Twelve dollars a month is only bowing-acquaintance money. And I do not consider brown beans and cornbread the food of friendship. I am a poor man,' says I, 'and I have a widowed mother in Texarkana. You will find Black Bill,' says I, 'lying asleep in this house on a cot in the room to your right. He's the man you want, as I know from his words and conversation. He was in a way a friend,' I explains, 'and if I was the man I once was the entire product of the mines of Gondola would not have tempted me to betray him. But,' says I, 'every week half of the beans was wormy, and not nigh enough wood in camp.

" 'Better go in careful, gentlemen,' says I. 'He seems impatient at times, and when you think of his late professional pursuits one would look for abrupt actions if he was come upon sudden.'

"So the whole posse unmounts and ties their horses, and unlimbers their ammunition and equipments, and tiptoes into the house. And I follows, like Delilah when she set the Philip Steins on to Samson.

"The leader of the posse shakes Ogden and wakes him up. And then he jumps up and two more of the reward-hunters grab him. Ogden was mighty tough with all his slimness, and gives 'em as neat a single-footed tussle against odds as I ever see.

" 'What does this mean?' he says, after they had him down.

" 'You're scooped in, Mr. Black Bill,' says the captain. 'That's all.'

" 'It's an outrage,' says H. Ogden, madder yet.

" 'It was,' says the peace-and-good-will man. 'The Katy wasn't bothering you, and there's a law against monkeying with express packages.'

"And he sits on H. Ogden's stomach and goes through his pockets symptomatically and careful.

" 'I'll make you perspire for this,' says Ogden, perspiring some himself. 'I can prove who I am.'

" 'So can I,' says the captain, as he draws from H. Ogden's inside coat-pocket a handful of new bills of the Second National Bank of Espinosa City. 'Your regular engraved Tuesdays-and-Fridays visiting-card wouldn't have a louder voice in proclaiming your indemnity than this here currency. You can get up now and prepare to go with us and expatriate your sins.'

"H. Ogden gets up and fixes his necktie. He says no more after they have taken the money off of him.

" 'A well-greased idea,' says the sheriff captain, admiring, 'to slip off down here and buy a little sheep-ranch where the hand of man is seldom heard. It was the slickest hide-out I ever see,' says the captain.

"So one of the men goes to the shearing-pen and hunts up the other herder, a Mexican they call John Sallies, and he saddles Ogden's horse, and the sheriffs all ride up close around him with their guns in hand, ready to take their prisoner to town.

"Before starting, Ogden puts the ranch in John Sallies' hands and gives him orders about the shearing and where to graze the sheep, just as if he intended to be back in a few days. And a couple of hours afterward one Percival Saint Clair, an ex-sheep-herder of the Rancho Chiquito, might have been seen, with a hundred and nine dollars—wages and blood money—in his pocket, riding south on another horse belonging to said ranch."

The red-faced man paused and listened. The whistle of a

coming freight-train sounded far away among the low hills.

The fat, seedy man at his side sniffed, and shook his frowzy head slowly and disparagingly.

"What is it, Snipy?" asked the other. "Got the blues again?"

"No, I ain't," said the seedy one, sniffing again. "But I don't like your talk. You and me have been friends, off and on, for fifteen year; and I never yet knew or heard of you giving anybody up to the law—not no one. And here was a man whose saleratus you had et and at whose table you had played games of cards—if casino can be so called. And yet you inform him to the law and take money for it. It never was like you, I say."

"This H. Ogden," resumed the red-faced man, "through a lawyer, proved himself free by alibis and other legal terminalities, as I so heard afterward. He never suffered no harm. He did me favors, and I hated to hand him over."

"How about the bills they found in his pocket?" asked the seedy man.

"I put 'em there," said the red-faced man, "while he was asleep, when I saw the posse riding up. I was Black Bill. Look out, Snipy, here she comes! We'll board her on the bumpers when she takes water."

The Duplicity of Hargraves

WHEN Major Pendleton Talbot, of Mobile, sir, and his daughter, Miss Lydia Talbot, came to Washington to reside, they selected for a boarding place a house that stood fifty yards back from one of the quietest avenues. It was an old-fashioned brick building, with a portico upheld by tall white pillars. The yard was shaded by stately locusts and elms, and a catalpa tree in season rained its pink and white blossoms upon the grass. Rows of high box bushes lined the fence and walks. It was the Southern style and aspect of the place that pleased the eyes of the Talbots.

In this pleasant, private boarding house they engaged rooms, including a study for Major Talbot, who was adding the finishing chapters to his book, "Anecdotes and Reminiscences of the Alabama Army, Bench, and Bar."

Major Talbot was of the old, old South. The present day had little interest or excellence in his eyes. His mind lived in that period before the Civil War, when the Talbots owned thousands of acres of fine cotton land and the slaves to till them; when the family mansion was the scene of princely hospitality, and drew its guests from the aristocracy of the South. Out of that period he had brought all of its old pride and scruples of honor, and antiquated and punctilious politeness, and (you would think) its wardrobe.

Such clothes were surely never made within fifty years. The major was tall, but whenever he made that wonderful, archaic genuflexion he called a bow, the corners of his frock coat swept the floor. That garment was a surprise even to Washington, which has long ago ceased to shy at the frocks and broad-brimmed hats of Southern congressmen. One of the boarders christened it a "Father Hubbard," and it certainly was high in the waist and full in the skirt.

But the major, with all his queer clothes, his immense area of plaited, ravelling shirt bosom, and the little black string tie with the bow always slipping on one side, both was smiled at and liked in Mrs. Vardeman's select boarding house. Some of the young department clerks would often "string him," as they called it, getting him started upon the subject dearest to him—the traditions and history of his beloved Southland. During his talks he would quote freely from the "Anecdotes and Reminiscences." But they were very careful not to let him see their designs, for in spite of his sixty-eight years, he could make the boldest of them uncomfortable under the steady regard of his piercing gray eyes.

Miss Lydia was a plump, little old maid of thirty-five, with smoothly drawn, tightly twisted hair that made her look still older. Old fashioned, too, she was; but ante-bellum glory did not radiate from her as it did from the major. She possessed a thrifty common sense; and it was she who handled the finances of the family, and met all comers when there were bills to pay. The major regarded board bills and wash bills as contemptible nuisances. They kept coming in so persistently and so often. Why, the major wanted to know, could they not be filed and paid in a lump sum at some convenient period—say when the "Anecdotes and Reminiscences" had been published and paid for? Miss Lydia would calmly go on with her sewing and say, "We'll pay as we go as long as the money lasts, and then perhaps they'll have to lump it."

Most of Mrs. Vardeman's boarders were away during the day, being nearly all department clerks and business men; but there was one of them who was about the house a great deal from morning to night. This was a young man named Henry Hopkins Hargraves—every one in the house addressed him by his full name—who was engaged at one of the popular vaudeville theatres. Vaudeville has risen to such a respectable plane in the last few years, and Mr. Hargraves was such a modest and well-mannered person, that Mrs. Vardeman could find no objection to enrolling him upon her list of boarders.

At the theatre Hargraves was known as an all-round dialect comedian, having a large repertoire of German, Irish, Swede, and black-face specialties. But Mr. Hargraves was ambitious, and often spoke of his great desire to succeed in legitimate comedy.

This young man appeared to conceive a strong fancy for Major Talbot. Whenever that gentleman would begin his Southern reminiscences, or repeat some of the liveliest of the anecdotes, Hargraves could always be found, the most attentive among his listeners.

For a time the major showed an inclination to discourage the advances of the "play actor," as he privately termed him; but soon the young man's agreeable manner and indubitable appreciation of the old gentleman's stories completely won him over.

It was not long before the two were like old chums. The major set apart each afternoon to read to him the manuscript of his book. During the anecdotes Hargraves never failed to laugh at exactly the right point. The major was moved to declare to Miss Lydia one day that young Hargraves possessed remarkable perception and a gratifying respect for the old régime. And when it came to talking of those old days—if Major Talbot liked to talk, Mr. Hargraves was entranced to listen.

Like almost all old people who talk of the past, the major loved to linger over details. In describing the splendid, almost royal, days of the old planters, he would hesitate until he had recalled the name of the Negro who held his horse, or the exact date of certain minor happenings, or the number of bales of cotton raised in such a year; but Hargraves never grew impatient or lost interest. On the contrary, he would advance questions on a variety of subjects connected with the life of that time, and he never failed to extract ready replies.

The fox hunts; the 'possum suppers; the hoe downs and jubilees in the Negro quarters; the banquets in the plantation-house hall, when invitations went for fifty miles around; the occasional feuds with the neighboring gentry; the major's duel with Rathbone Culbertson about Kitty Chalmers, who afterward married a Thwaite of South Carolina; and private yacht races for fabulous sums on Mobile Bay; the quaint beliefs, improvident habits, and loyal virtues of the old slaves—all these were subjects that held both the major and Hargraves absorbed for hours at a time.

Sometimes, at night, when the young man would be coming upstairs to his room after his turn at the theatre was over, the major would appear at the door of his study and beckon archly to him. Going in, Hargraves would find a little table set with a decanter, sugar bowl, fruit, and a big bunch of fresh green mint.

"It occurred to me," the major would begin—he was always ceremonious—"that perhaps you might have found your duties at the—at your place of occupation—sufficiently arduous to enable you, Mr. Hargraves, to appreciate what the poet might well have had in his mind when he wrote, 'tired Nature's sweet restorer,'—one of our Southern juleps."

It was a fascination to Hargraves to watch him make it. He took rank among artists when he began, and he never varied the process. With what delicacy he bruised the mint; with what exquisite nicety he estimated the ingredients; with what solicitous care he capped the compound with the scarlet fruit glowing against the dark green fringe! And then the hospitality and grace with which he offered it, after the selected oat straws had been plunged into its tinkling depths!

After about four months in Washington, Miss Lydia discovered one morning that they were almost without money. The "Anecdotes and Reminiscences" was completed, but publishers had not jumped at the collected gems of Alabama sense and wit. The rental of a small house which they still owned in Mobile was two months in arrears. Their board money for the month would be due in three days. Miss Lydia called her father to a consultation.

"No money?" said he with a surprised look. "It is quite annoying to be called on so frequently for these petty sums. Really, I——"

The major searched his pockets. He found only a two-dollar bill, which he returned to his vest pocket.

"I must attend to this at once, Lydia," he said. "Kindly get

me my umbrella and I will go down town immediately. The
congressman from our district, General Fulghum, assured me
some days ago that he would use his influence to get my book
published at an early date. I will go to his hotel at once and
see what arrangement has been made."

With a sad little smile Miss Lydia watched him button his
"Father Hubbard" and depart, pausing at the door, as he always did, to bow profoundly.

That evening, at dark, he returned. It seemed that Congressman Fulghum had seen the publisher who had the major's manuscript for reading. That person had said that if the
anecdotes, etc., were carefully pruned down about one half,
in order to eliminate the sectional and class prejudice with
which the book was dyed from end to end, he might consider
its publication.

The major was in a white heat of anger, but regained his
equanimity, according to his code of manners, as soon as he
was in Miss Lydia's presence.

"We must have money," said Miss Lydia, with a little wrinkle above her nose. "Give me the two dollars, and I will telegraph to Uncle Ralph for some to-night."

The major drew a small envelope from his upper vest
pocket and tossed it on the table.

"Perhaps it was injudicious," he said mildly, "but the sum
was so merely nominal that I bought tickets to the theatre
to-night. It's a new war drama, Lydia. I thought you would
be pleased to witness its first production in Washington. I
am told that the South has very fair treatment in the play. I
confess I should like to see the performance myself."

Miss Lydia threw up her hands in silent despair.

Still, as the tickets were bought, they might as well be used.
So that evening, as they sat in the theatre listening to the
lively overture, even Miss Lydia was minded to relegate their
troubles, for the hour, to second place. The major, in spotless

linen, with his extraordinary coat showing only where it was closely buttoned, and his white hair smoothly roached, looked really fine and distinguished. The curtain went up on the first act of "A Magnolia Flower," revealing a typical Southern plantation scene. Major Talbot betrayed some interest.

"Oh, see!" exclaimed Miss Lydia, nudging his arm, and pointing to her programme.

The major put on his glasses and read the line in the cast of characters that her finger indicated.

Col. Webster Calhoun. . . . H. Hopkins Hargraves.

"It's our Mr. Hargraves," said Miss Lydia. "It must be his first appearance in what he calls 'the legitimate.' I'm so glad for him."

Not until the second act did Col. Webster Calhoun appear upon the stage. When he made his entry Major Talbot gave an audible sniff, glared at him, and seemed to freeze solid. Miss Lydia uttered a little ambiguous squeak and crumpled her programme in her hand. For Colonel Calhoun was made up as nearly resembling Major Talbot as one pea does another. The long, thin, white hair, curly at the ends, the aristocratic beak of a nose, the crumpled, wide, ravelling shirt front, the string tie, with the bow nearly under one ear, were almost exactly duplicated. And then, to clinch the imitation, he wore the twin to the major's supposed to be unparalleled coat. High-collared, baggy, empire-waisted, ample-skirted, hanging a foot lower in front than behind, the garment could have been designed from no other pattern. From then on, the major and Miss Lydia sat bewitched, and saw the counterfeit presentment of a haughty Talbot "dragged," as the major afterward expressed it, "through the slanderous mire of a corrupt stage."

Mr. Hargraves had used his opportunities well. He had caught the major's little idiosyncrasies of speech, accent, and intonation and his pompous courtliness to perfection—exaggerating all to the purpose of the stage. When he performed that marvelous bow that the major fondly imagined to be the pink of all salutations, the audience sent forth a sudden round of hearty applause.

Miss Lydia sat immovable, not daring to glance toward her father. Sometimes her hand next to him would be laid against her cheek, as if to conceal the smile which, in spite of her disapproval, she could not entirely suppress.

The culmination of Hargraves's audacious imitation took place in the third act. The scene is where Colonel Calhoun entertains a few of the neighboring planters in his "den."

Standing at a table in the centre of the stage, with his friends grouped about him, he delivers that inimitable, rambling, character monologue so famous in "A Magnolia Flower," at the same time that he deftly makes juleps for the party.

Major Talbot, sitting quietly, but white with indignation, heard his best stories retold, his pet theories and hobbies advanced and expanded, and the dream of the "Anecdotes and Reminiscences" served, exaggerated and garbled. His favorite narrative—that of his duel with Rathbone Culbertson—was not omitted, and it was delivered with more fire, egotism, and gusto than the major himself put into it.

The monologue concluded with a quaint, delicious, witty little lecture on the art of concocting a julep, illustrated by the act. Here Major Talbot's delicate but showy science was reproduced to a hair's breadth—from his dainty handling of the fragrant weed—"the one-thousandth part of a grain too much pressure, gentlemen, and you extract the bitterness, instead of the aroma, of this heaven-bestowed plant"—to his solicitous selection of the oaten straws.

At the close of the scene the audience raised a tumultuous roar of appreciation. The portrayal of the type was so exact, so sure and thorough, that the leading characters in the play were forgotten. After repeated calls, Hargraves came before the curtain and bowed, his rather boyish face bright and flushed with the knowledge of success.

At last Miss Lydia turned and looked at the major. His thin nostrils were working like the gills of a fish. He laid both shaking hands upon the arms of his chair to rise.

"We will go, Lydia," he said, chokingly. "This is an abominable—desecration."

Before he could rise, she pulled him back into his seat.

"We will stay it out," she declared. "Do you want to advertise the copy by exhibiting the original coat?" So they remained to the end.

Hargraves's success must have kept him up late that night, for neither at the breakfast nor at the dinner table did he appear.

About three in the afternoon he tapped at the door of Major Talbot's study. The major opened it, and Hargraves walked in with his hands full of the morning papers—too full of his triumph to notice anything unusual in the major's demeanor.

"I put it all over 'em last night, major," he began, exultantly. "I had my inning, and, I think, scored. Here's what the *Post* says:

"His conception and portrayal of the old-time Southern colonel, with his absurd grandiloquence, his eccentric garb, his quaint idioms and phrases, his moth-eaten pride of family, and his really kind heart, fastidious sense of honor, and lovable simplicity, is the best delineation of a character rôle on the boards today. The coat worn by Colonel Calhoun is itself nothing less than an evolution of genius. Mr. Hargraves has captured his public.

"How does that sound, major, for a first nighter?"

"I had the honor"—the major's voice sounded ominously frigid—"of witnessing your very remarkable performance, sir, last night."

Hargraves looked disconcerted.

"You were there? I didn't know you ever—I didn't know you cared for the theatre. Oh, I say, Major Talbot," he exclaimed, frankly, "don't you be offended. I admit I did get a lot of pointers from you that helped me out wonderfully in the part. But it's a type, you know—not individual. The way the audience caught on shows that. Half the patrons of that theatre are Southerners. They recognized it."

"Mr. Hargraves," said the major, who had remained standing, "you have put upon me an unpardonable insult. You have burlesqued my person, grossly betrayed my confidence, and misused my hospitality. If I thought you possessed the faintest conception of what is the sign manual of a gentleman, or what is due one, I would call you out, sir, old as I am. I will ask you to leave the room, sir."

The actor appeared to be slightly bewildered, and seemed hardly to take in the full meaning of the old gentleman's words.

"I am truly sorry you took offence," he said, regretfully. "Up here we don't look at things just as you people do. I know men who would buy out half the house to have their personality put on the stage so the public would recognize it."

"They are not from Alabama, sir," said the major, haughtily.

"Perhaps not. I have a pretty good memory, major; let me quote a few lines from your book. In response to a toast at a banquet given in—Milledgeville, I believe—you uttered, and intend to have printed these words:

"The Northern man is utterly without sentiment or warmth except in so far as the feelings may be turned to his own commercial profit. He will suffer without resentment any imputation cast upon the honor of himself or his loved ones that does not bear with it the consequence of pecuniary loss. In his charity, he gives with a liberal hand; but it must be heralded with the trumpet and chronicled in brass.

"Do you think that picture is fairer than the one you saw of Colonel Calhoun last night?"

"The description," said the major, frowning, "is—not without grounds. Some exag—latitude must be allowed in public speaking."

"And in public acting," replied Hargraves.

"That is not the point," persisted the major, unrelenting. "It was a personal caricature. I positively decline to overlook it, sir."

"Major Talbot," said Hargraves, with a winning smile, "I wish you would understand me. I want you to know that I never dreamed of insulting you. In my profession, all life belongs to me. I take what I want, and what I can, and return it over the footlights. Now, if you will, let's let it go at that. I came in to see you about something else. We've been pretty good friends for some months, and I'm going to take the risk of offending you again. I know you are hard up for money—never mind how I found out; a boarding house is no place to keep such matters secret—and I want you to let me help you out of the pinch. I've been there often enough myself. I've been getting a fair salary all the season, and I've saved some money. You're welcome to a couple hundred—or even more—until you get——"

"Stop!" commanded the major, with his arm outstretched. "It seems that my book didn't lie, after all. You think your money salve will heal all the hurts of honor. Under no circumstances would I accept a loan from a casual acquaintance; and as to you, sir, I would starve before I would consider your insulting offer of a financial adjustment of the circumstances we have discussed. I beg to repeat my request relative to your quitting the apartment."

Hargraves took his departure without another word. He also left the house the same day, moving, as Mrs. Vardeman explained at the supper table, nearer the vicinity of the downtown theatre, where "A Magnolia Flower" was booked for a week's run.

Critical was the situation with Major Talbot and Miss Lydia. There was no one in Washington to whom the major's scruples allowed him to apply for a loan. Miss Lydia wrote a letter to Uncle Ralph, but it was doubtful whether that relative's constricted affairs would permit him to furnish help. The major was forced to make an apologetic address to Mrs. Vardeman regarding the delayed payment for board, referring to "delinquent rentals" and "delayed remittances" in a rather confused strain.

Deliverance came from an entirely unexpected source.

Late one afternoon the door maid came up and announced an old colored man who wanted to see Major Talbot. The major asked that he be sent up to his study. Soon an old darkey appeared in the doorway, with his hat in hand, bowing, and scraping with one clumsy foot. He was quite decently dressed in a baggy suit of black. His big, coarse shoes shone with a metallic lustre suggestive of stove polish. His bushy wool was gray—almost white. After middle life, it is difficult to estimate the age of a Negro. This one might have seen as many years as had Major Talbot.

"I be bound you don't know me, Mars' Pendleton," were his first words.

The major rose and came forward at the old, familiar style of address. It was one of the old plantation darkeys without a doubt; but they had been widely scattered, and he could not recall the voice or face.

"I don't believe I do," he said, kindly—"unless you will assist my memory."

"Don't you 'member Cindy's Mose, Mars' Pendleton, what 'migrated 'mediately after de war?"

"Wait a moment," said the major, rubbing his forehead with the tips of his fingers. He loved to recall everything connected with those beloved days. "Cindy's Mose," he reflected. "You worked among the horses—breaking the colts. Yes, I remember now. After the surrender, you took the name of— don't prompt me—Mitchell, and went to the West—to Nebraska."

"Yassir, yassir,"—the old man's face stretched with a delighted grin—"dat's him, dat's it. Newbraska. Dat's me— Mose Mitchell. Old Uncle Mose Mitchell, dey calls me now. Old mars', your pa, gimme a pah of dem mule colts when I lef' fur to staht me goin' with. You 'member dem colts, Mars' Pendleton?"

"I don't seem to recall the colts," said the major. "You know I was married the first year of the war and living at the old Follinsbee place. But sit down, sit down, Uncle Mose. I'm glad to see you. I hope you have prospered."

Uncle Mose took a chair and laid his hat carefully on the floor beside it.

"Yassir; of late I done mouty famous. When I first got to Newbraska, dey folks come all roun' me to see dem mule colts. Dey ain't see no mules like dem in Newbraska. I sold dem mules for three hundred dollars. Yassir—three hundred.

"Den I open a blacksmith shop, suh, and made some money and bought some lan'. Me and my old 'oman done raised up seb'm chillun, and all doin' well 'cept two of 'em what died. Fo' year ago a railroad come along and staht a town slam ag'inst my lan', and, suh, Mars' Pendleton, Uncle Mose am worth lem'm thousand dollars in money, property, and lan'."

"I'm glad to hear it," said the major, heartily. "Glad to hear it."

"And dat little baby of yo'n, Mars' Pendleton—one what you name Miss Lyddy—I be bound dat little tad done growed up tell nobody wouldn't know her."

The major stepped to the door and called: "Lydia, dear, will you come?"

Miss Lydia, looking quite grown up and a little worried, came in from her room.

"Dar, now! What'd I tell you? I knowed dat baby done be plum growed up. You don't 'member Uncle Mose, child?"

"This is Aunt Cindy's Mose, Lydia," explained the major. "He left Sunnymead for the West when you were two years old."

"Well," said Miss Lydia, "I can hardly be expected to remember you, Uncle Mose, at that age. And, as you say, I'm 'plum growed up,' and was a blessed long time ago. But I'm glad to see you, even if I can't remember you."

And she was. And so was the major. Something alive and tangible had come to link them with the happy past. The three sat and talked over the olden times, the major and Uncle Mose, correcting or prompting each other as they reviewed the plantation scenes and days.

The major inquired what the old man was doing so far from his home.

"Uncle Mose am a delicate," he explained, "to de grand Baptis' convention in dis city. I never preached none, but bein' a residin' elder in de church, and able fur to pay my own expenses, dey sent me along."

"And how did you know we were in Washington?" inquired Miss Lydia.

"Dey's a cullud man works in de hotel whar I stops, what comes from Mobile. He told me he seen Mars' Pendleton comin' outen dish here house one mawnin'.

"What I come fur," continued Uncle Mose, reaching into his pocket—"besides de sight of home folks—was to pay Mars' Pendleton what I owes him."

"Owe me?" said the major, in surprise.

"Yassir—three hundred dollars." He handed the major a

roll of bills. "When I lef' old mars' says: 'Take dem mule
colts, Mose, and, if it be so you gits able, pay fur 'em.' Yassir—dem was his words. De war had done lef' old mars' po'
hisself. Old mars' bein' long 'go dead, de debt descends to
Mars' Pendleton. Three hundred dollars. Uncle Mose is
plenty able to pay now. When dat railroad buy my lan' I laid
off to pay for dem mules. Count de money, Mars' Pendleton.
Dat's what I sold dem mules fur. Yassir."

Tears were in Major Talbot's eyes. He took Uncle Mose's
hand and laid his other upon his shoulder.

"Dear, faithful old servitor," he said in an unsteady voice,
"I don't mind saying to you that 'Mars' Pendleton' spent his
last dollar in the world a week ago. We will accept this money,
Uncle Mose, since, in a way, it is a sort of payment, as well
as a token of the loyalty and devotion of the old régime.
Lydia, my dear, take the money. You are better fitted than I
to manage its expenditure."

"Take it, honey," said Uncle Mose. "Hit belongs to you.
Hit's Talbot money."

After Uncle Mose had gone, Miss Lydia had a good cry
—for joy; and the major turned his face to a corner, and
smoked his clay pipe volcanically.

The succeeding days saw the Talbots restored to peace and
ease. Miss Lydia's face lost its worried look. The major appeared in a new frock coat, in which he looked like a wax
figure personifying the memory of his golden age. Another
publisher who read the manuscript of the "Anecdotes and
Reminiscences" thought that, with a little retouching and
toning down of the high lights, he could make a really bright
and salable volume of it. Altogether, the situation was comfortable, and not without the touch of hope that is often
sweeter than arrived blessings.

One day, about a week after their piece of good luck, a
maid brought a letter for Miss Lydia to her room. The post-

mark showed that it was from New York. Not knowing any one there, Miss Lydia, in a mild flutter of wonder, sat down by her table and opened the letter with her scissors. This was what she read:

DEAR MISS TALBOT:

I thought you might be glad to learn of my good fortune. I have received and accepted an offer of two hundred dollars per week by a New York stock company to play Colonel Calhoun in "A Magnolia Flower."

There is something else I wanted you to know. I guess you'd better not tell Major Talbot. I was anxious to make him some amends for the great help he was to me in studying the part, and for the bad humor he was in about it. He refused to let me, so I did it anyhow. I could easily spare the three hundred.

Sincerely yours,
H. HOPKINS HARGRAVES.

P. S. How did I play Uncle Mose?

Major Talbot, passing through the hall, saw Miss Lydia's door open and stopped.

"Any mail for us this morning, Lydia dear?" he asked.

Miss Lydia slid the letter beneath a fold of her dress.

"The *Mobile Chronicle* came," she said, promptly. "It's on the table in your study."

The Ransom of Red Chief

IT LOOKED like a good thing: but wait till I tell you. We were down South, in Alabama—Bill Driscoll and myself—when this kidnapping idea struck us. It was, as Bill afterward expressed it, "during a moment of temporary mental apparition"; but we didn't find that out till later.

There was a town down there, as flat as a flannel-cake, and called Summit, of course. It contained inhabitants of as un-deleterious and self-satisfied a class of peasantry as ever clustered around a Maypole.

Bill and me had a joint capital of about six hundred dollars, and we needed just two thousand dollars more to pull off a fraudulent town-lot scheme in Western Illinois with. We talked it over on the front steps of the Hotel. Philo-progenitiveness, says we, is strong in semi-rural communities; therefore, and for other reasons, a kidnapping project ought to do better there than in the radius of newspapers that send reporters out in plain clothes to stir up talk about such things. We knew that Summit couldn't get after us with anything stronger than constables and, maybe, some lackadaisical bloodhounds and a diatribe or two in the *Weekly Farmers' Budget*. So, it looked good.

We selected for our victim the only child of a prominent citizen named Ebenezer Dorset. The father was respectable and tight, a mortgage fancier and a stern, upright collection-plate passer and forecloser. The kid was a boy of ten, with bas-relief freckles, and hair the color of the cover of the magazine you buy at the news-stand when you want to catch a train. Bill and me figured that Ebenezer would melt down for a ransom of two thousand dollars to a cent. But wait till I tell you.

About two miles from Summit was a little mountain, covered with a dense cedar brake. On the rear elevation of this mountain was a cave. There we stored provisions.

One evening after sundown, we drove in a buggy past old Dorset's house. The kid was in the street, throwing rocks at a kitten on the opposite fence.

"Hey, little boy!" says Bill, "would you like to have a bag of candy and a nice ride?"

The boy catches Bill neatly in the eye with a piece of brick.

"That will cost the old man an extra five hundred dollars," says Bill, climbing over the wheel.

That boy put up a fight like a welter-weight cinnamon bear; but, at last, we got him down in the bottom of the buggy and drove away. We took him up to the cave, and I hitched the horse in the cedar brake. After dark I drove the buggy to the little village, three miles away, where we had hired it, and walked back to the mountain.

Bill was pasting court-plaster over the scratches and bruises on his features. There was a fire burning behind the big rock at the entrance of the cave, and the boy was watching a pot of boiling coffee, with two buzzard tail-feathers stuck in his red hair. He points a stick at me when I come up, and says:

"Ha! cursed paleface, do you dare to enter the camp of Red Chief, the terror of the plains?"

"He's all right now," says Bill, rolling up his trousers and examining some bruises on his shins. "We're playing Indian. We're making Buffalo Bill's show look like magic-lantern views of Palestine in the town hall. I'm Old Hank, the Trapper, Red Chief's captive, and I'm to be scalped at daybreak. By Geronimo! that kid can kick hard."

Yes, sir, that boy seemed to be having the time of his life. The fun of camping out in a cave had made him forget that he was a captive himself. He immediately christened me Snake-eye, the Spy, and announced that, when his braves returned from the warpath, I was to be broiled at the stake at the rising of the sun.

Then we had supper; and he filled his mouth full of bacon and bread and gravy, and began to talk. He made a during-dinner speech something like this:

"I like this fine. I never camped out before; but I had a pet 'possum once, and I was nine last birthday. I hate to go to school. Rats ate up sixteen of Jimmy Talbot's aunt's speckled hen's eggs. Are there any real Indians in these woods? I want some more gravy. Does the trees moving make the wind blow? We had five puppies. What makes your nose so red, Hank? My father has lots of money. Are the stars hot? I whipped Ed Walker twice, Saturday. I don't like girls. You dassent catch toads unless with a string. Do oxen make any noise? Why are oranges round? Have you got beds to sleep on in this cave? Amos Murray has got six toes. A parrot can talk, but a monkey or a fish can't. How many does it take to make twelve?"

Every few minutes he would remember that he was a pesky redskin, and pick up his stick rifle and tiptoe to the mouth of the cave to rubber for the scouts of the hated paleface. Now and then he would let out a war-whoop that made Old Hank the Trapper shiver. That boy had Bill terrorized from the start.

"Red Chief," says I to the kid, "would you like to go home?"

"Aw, what for?" says he. "I don't have any fun at home. I hate to go to school. I like to camp out. You won't take me back home again, Snake-eye, will you?"

"Not right away," says I. "We'll stay here in the cave awhile."

"All right!" says he. "That'll be fine. I never had such fun in all my life."

We went to bed about eleven o'clock. We spread down some wide blankets and quilts and put Red Chief between us. We weren't afraid he'd run away. He kept us awake for three hours, jumping up and reaching for his rifle and screeching: "Hist! pard," in mine and Bill's ears, as the fancied crackle of a twig or the rustle of a leaf revealed to his young imagination the stealthy approach of the outlaw band. At last, I fell into a troubled sleep, and dreamed that I had been kidnapped and chained to a tree by a ferocious pirate with red hair.

Just at daybreak, I was awakened by a series of awful

screams from Bill. They weren't yells, or howls, or shouts, or whoops, or yawps, such as you'd expect from a manly set of vocal organs—they were simply indecent, terrifying, humiliating screams, such as women emit when they see ghosts or caterpillars. It's an awful thing to hear a strong, desperate, fat man scream incontinently in a cave at daybreak.

I jumped up to see what the matter was. Red Chief was sitting on Bill's chest, with one hand twined in Bill's hair. In the other he had the sharp case-knife we used for slicing bacon; and he was industriously and realistically trying to take Bill's scalp, according to the sentence that had been pronounced upon him the evening before.

I got the knife away from the kid and made him lie down again. But, from that moment, Bill's spirit was broken. He laid down on his side of the bed, but he never closed an eye again in sleep as long as that boy was with us. I dozed off for a while, but along toward sun-up I remembered that Red Chief had said I was to be burned at the stake at the rising of the sun. I wasn't nervous or afraid; but I sat up and lit my pipe and leaned against a rock.

"What you getting up so soon for, Sam?" asked Bill.

"Me?" says I. "Oh, I got a kind of pain in my shoulder. I thought sitting up would rest it."

"You're a liar!" says Bill. "You're afraid. You was to be burned at sunrise, and you was afraid he'd do it. And he would, too, if he could find a match. Ain't it awful, Sam? Do you think anybody will pay out money to get a little imp like that back home?"

"Sure," said I. "A rowdy kid like that is just the kind that parents dote on. Now, you and the Chief get up and cook breakfast, while I go up on the top of this mountain and reconnoitre."

I went up on the peak of the little mountain and ran my eye over the contiguous vicinity. Over towards Summit I expected to see the sturdy yeomanry of the village armed with scythes and pitchforks beating the countryside for the dastardly kidnappers. But what I saw was a peaceful landscape dotted with one man ploughing with a dun mule. Nobody was dragging the creek; no couriers dashed hither and yon, bringing tidings of no news to the distracted parents. There was a sylvan attitude of somnolent sleepiness pervading that section of the external outward surface of Alabama that lay exposed to my view. "Perhaps," says I to myself, "it has not yet been discovered that the wolves have borne away the tender lambkin from the fold. Heaven help the wolves!" says I, and I went down the mountain to breakfast.

When I got to the cave I found Bill backed up against the side of it, breathing hard, and the boy threatening to smash him with a rock half as big as a cocoanut.

"He put a red-hot boiled potato down my back," explained Bill, "and then mashed it with his foot; and I boxed his ears. Have you got a gun about you, Sam?"

I took the rock away from the boy and kind of patched up the argument. "I'll fix you," says the kid to Bill. "No man ever yet struck the Red Chief but he got paid for it. You better beware!"

After breakfast the kid takes a piece of leather with strings wrapped around it out of his pocket and goes outside the cave unwinding it.

"What's he up to now?" says Bill, anxiously. "You don't think he'll run away, do you, Sam?"

"No fear of it," says I. "He don't seem to be much of a home body. But we've got to fix up some plan about the ransom. There don't seem to be much excitement around Summit on account of his disappearance; but maybe they haven't realized yet that he's gone. His folks may think he's spending the night with Aunt Jane or one of the neighbors. Anyhow, he'll be missed to-day. To-night we must get a message to his father demanding the two thousand dollars for his return."

Just then we heard a kind of war-whoop, such as David might have emitted when he knocked out the champion Goliath. It was a sling that Red Chief had pulled out of his pocket, and he was whirling it around his head.

I dodged, and heard a heavy thud and a kind of a sigh from Bill, like a horse gives out when you take his saddle off. A niggerhead rock the size of an egg had caught Bill just behind his left ear. He loosened himself all over and fell in the fire across the frying pan of hot water for washing the dishes. I dragged him out and poured cold water on his head for half an hour.

By and by, Bill sits up and feels behind his ear and says: "Sam, do you know who my favorite Biblical character is?"

"Take it easy," says I. "You'll come to your senses presently."

"King Herod," says he. "You won't go away and leave me here alone, will you, Sam?"

I went out and caught that boy and shook him until his freckles rattled.

"If you don't behave," says I, "I'll take you straight home. Now, are you going to be good, or not?"

"I was only funning," says he, sullenly. "I didn't mean to hurt Old Hank. But what did he hit me for? I'll behave, Snake-eye, if you won't send me home, and if you'll let me play the Black Scout to-day."

"I don't know the game," says I. "That's for you and Mr. Bill to decide. He's your playmate for the day. I'm going away for a while, on business. Now, you come in and make friends with him and say you are sorry for hurting him, or home you go, at once."

I made him and Bill shake hands, and then I took Bill aside and told him I was going to Poplar Grove, a little village three miles from the cave, and find out what I could about how the kidnapping had been regarded in Summit. Also, I thought it best to send a peremptory letter to old man Dorset that day, demanding the ransom and dictating how it should be paid.

"You know, Sam," says Bill, "I've stood by you without batting an eye in earthquakes, fire and flood—in poker games, dynamite outrages, police raids, train robberies, and cyclones. I never lost my nerve yet till we kidnapped that two-legged skyrocket of a kid. He's got me going. You won't leave me long with him, will you, Sam?"

"I'll be back some time this afternoon," says I. "You must keep the boy amused and quiet till I return. And now we'll write the letter to old Dorset."

Bill and I got paper and pencil and worked on the letter while Red Chief, with a blanket wrapped around him, strutted up and down, guarding the mouth of the cave. Bill begged me tearfully to make the ransom fifteen hundred dollars instead of two thousand. "I ain't attempting," says he, "to decry the celebrated moral aspect of parental affection, but we're dealing with humans, and it ain't human for anybody to give up two thousand dollars for that forty-pound chunk of freckled wildcat. I'm willing to take a chance at fifteen hundred dollars. You can charge the difference up to me."

So, to relieve Bill, I acceded, and we collaborated a letter that ran this way:

EBENEZER DORSET, ESQ.:

We have your boy concealed in a place far from Summit. It is useless for you or the most skilful detectives to attempt to find him. Absolutely, the only terms on which you can have him restored to you are these: We demand fifteen hundred dollars in large bills for his return; the money to be left at midnight to-night at the same spot and in the same box as your reply—

as hereinafter described. If you agree to these terms, send your answer in writing by a solitary messenger to-night at half-past eight o'clock. After crossing Owl Creek on the road to Poplar Grove, there are three large trees about a hundred yards apart, close to the fence of the wheat field on the right-hand side. At the bottom of the fence-post, opposite the third tree, will be found a small pasteboard box.

The messenger will place the answer in this box and return immediately to Summit.

If you attempt any treachery or fail to comply with our demand as stated, you will never see your boy again.

If you pay the money as demanded, he will be returned to you safe and well within three hours. These terms are final, and if you do not accede to them no further communication will be attempted.

Two Desperate Men.

I addressed this letter to Dorset, and put it in my pocket. As I was about to start, the kid comes up to me and says:

"Aw, Snake-eye, you said I could play the Black Scout while you was gone."

"Play it, of course," says I. "Mr. Bill will play with you. What kind of a game is it?"

"I'm the Black Scout," says Red Chief, "and I have to ride to the stockade to warn the settlers that the Indians are coming. I'm tired of playing Indian myself. I want to be the Black Scout."

"All right," says I. "It sounds harmless to me. I guess Mr. Bill will help you foil the pesky savages."

"What am I to do?" asks Bill, looking at the kid suspiciously.

"You are the hoss," says Black Scout. "Get down on your hands and knees. How can I ride to the stockade without a hoss?"

"You'd better keep him interested," said I, "till we get the scheme going. Loosen up."

Bill gets down on his all fours, and a look comes in his eye like a rabbit's when you catch it in a trap.

"How far is it to the stockade, kid?" he asks, in a husky manner of voice.

"Ninety miles," says the Black Scout. "And you have to hump yourself to get there on time. Whoa, now!"

The Black Scout jumps on Bill's back and digs his heels in his side.

"For Heaven's sake," says Bill, "hurry back, Sam, as soon as you can. I wish we hadn't made the ransom more than a thousand. Say, you quit kicking me or I'll get up and warm you good."

I walked over to Poplar Grove and sat around the post-office and store, talking with the chaw-bacons that came in to trade. One whiskerando says that he hears Summit is all upset on account of Elder Ebenezer Dorset's boy having been lost or stolen. That was all I wanted to know. I bought some smoking tobacco, referred casually to the price of black-eyed peas, posted my letter surreptitiously, and came away. The postmaster said the mail-carrier would come by in an hour to take the mail to Summit.

When I got back to the cave Bill and the boy were not to be found. I explored the vicinity of the cave, and risked a yodel or two, but there was no response.

So I lighted my pipe and sat down on a mossy bank to await developments.

In about half an hour I heard the bushes rustle, and Bill wabbled out into the little glade in front of the cave. Behind him was the kid, stepping softly like a scout, with a broad grin on his face. Bill stopped, took off his hat, and wiped his face with a red handkerchief. The kid stopped about eight feet behind him.

"Sam," says Bill, "I suppose you'll think I'm a renegade, but I couldn't help it. I'm a grown person with masculine proclivities and habits of self-defense, but there is a time when all systems of egotism and predominance fail. The boy is gone. I sent him home. All is off. There was martyrs in old times," goes on Bill, "that suffered death rather than give up the particular graft they enjoyed. None of 'em ever was subjugated to such supernatural tortures as I have been. I tried to be faithful to our articles of depredation; but there came a limit."

"What's the trouble, Bill?" I asks him.

"I was rode," says Bill, "the ninety miles to the stockade, not barring an inch. Then, when the settlers was rescued, I was given oats. Sand ain't a palatable substitute. And then, for an hour I had to try to explain to him why there was nothin' in holes, how a road can run both ways, and what makes the grass green. I tell you, Sam, a human can only stand so much. I takes him by the neck of his clothes and drags him down the mountain. On the way he kicks my legs black and blue from the knees down; and I've got to have two or three bites on my thumb and hand cauterized.

"But he's gone"—continues Bill—"gone home. I showed him the road to Summit and kicked him about eight feet nearer there at one kick. I'm sorry we lose the ransom; but it was either that or Bill Driscoll to the madhouse."

Bill is puffing and blowing, but there is a look of ineffable peace and growing content on his rose-pink features.

"Bill," says I, "there isn't any heart disease in your family, is there?"

"No," says Bill, "nothing chronic except malaria and accidents. Why?"

"Then you might turn around," says I, "and have a look behind you."

Bill turns and sees the boy, and loses his complexion and sits down plump on the ground and begins to pluck aimlessly at grass and little sticks. For an hour I was afraid of his mind.

And then I told him that my scheme was to put the whole job through immediately and that we would get the ransom and be off with it by midnight if old Dorset fell in with our proposition. So Bill braced up enough to give the kid a weak sort of a smile and a promise to play the Russian in a Japanese war with him as soon as he felt a little better.

I had a scheme for collecting that ransom without danger of being caught by counterplots that ought to commend itself to professional kidnappers. The tree under which the answer was to be left—and the money later on—was close to the road fence with big, bare fields on all sides. If a gang of constables should be watching for any one to come for the note, they could see him a long way off crossing the fields or in the road. But no, sirree! At half-past eight I was up in that tree as well hidden as a tree toad, waiting for the messenger to arrive.

Exactly on time, a half-grown boy rides up the road on a bicycle, locates the pasteboard box at the foot of the fence-post, slips a folded piece of paper into it, and pedals away again back toward Summit.

I waited an hour and then concluded the thing was square. I slid down the tree, got the note, slipped along the fence till I struck the woods, and was back at the cave in another half an hour. I opened the note, got near the lantern, and read it to Bill. It was written with a pen in a crabbed hand, and the sum and substance of it was this:

Two Desperate Men.

Gentlemen: I received your letter to-day by post, in regard to the ransom you ask for the return of my son. I think you are a little high in your demands, and I hereby make you a counter-proposition, which I am inclined to believe you will accept. You bring Johnny home and pay me two hundred and fifty dollars in cash, and I agree to take him off your hands. You had better come at night, for the neighbors believe he is lost, and I couldn't be responsible for what they would do to anybody they saw bringing him back. Very respectfully,

EBENEZER DORSET.

"Great Pirates of Penzance," says I; "of all the impudent——"

But I glanced at Bill, and hesitated. He had the most appealing look in his eyes I ever saw on the face of a dumb or a talking brute.

"Sam," says he, "what's two hundred and fifty dollars, after all? We've got the money. One more night of this kid will send me to a bed in Bedlam. Besides being a thorough gentleman, I think Mr. Dorset is a spendthrift for making us such a liberal offer. You ain't going to let the chance go, are you?"

"Tell you the truth, Bill," says I, "this little he ewe lamb has somewhat got on my nerves too. We'll take him home, pay the ransom, and make our getaway."

We took him home that night. We got him to go by telling him that his father had bought a silver-mounted rifle and a pair of moccasins for him, and we were to hunt bears the next day.

It was just twelve o'clock when we knocked at Ebenezer's front door. Just at the moment when I should have been abstracting the fifteen hundred dollars from the box under the tree, according to the original proposition, Bill was counting out two hundred and fifty dollars into Dorset's hand.

When the kid found out we were going to leave him at home he started up a howl like a calliope and fastened himself as tight as a leech to Bill's leg. His father peeled him away gradually, like a porous plaster.

"How long can you hold him?" asks Bill.

"I'm not as strong as I used to be," says old Dorset, "but I think I can promise you ten minutes."

"Enough," says Bill. "In ten minutes I shall cross the Central, Southern, and Middle Western States, and be legging it trippingly for the Canadian border."

And, as dark as it was, and as fat as Bill was, and as good a runner as I am, he was a good mile and a half out of Summit before I could catch up with him.

The Marry Month of May

Prithee, smite the poet in the eye when he would sing to you praises of the month of May. It is a month presided over by the spirits of mischief and madness. Pixies and flibbertigibbets haunt the budding woods; Puck and his train of midgets are busy in town and country.

In May Nature holds up at us a chiding finger, bidding us remember that we are not gods, but overconceited members of her own great family. She reminds us that we are brothers to the chowder-doomed clam and the donkey; lineal scions of the pansy and the chimpanzee, and but cousins-german to the cooing doves, the quacking ducks, and the housemaids and policemen in the parks.

In May Cupid shoots blindfolded—millionaires marry stenographers; wise professors woo white-aproned gum-chewers behind quick-lunch counters; schoolma'ams make big bad boys remain after school; lads with ladders steal lightly over lawns where Juliet waits in her trellised window with her telescope packed; young couples out for a walk come home married; old chaps put on white spats and promenade near the Normal School; even married men, grown unwontedly tender and sentimental, whack their spouses on the back and growl: "How goes it, old girl?"

This May, who is no goddess, but Circe, masquerading at the dance given in honor of the fair débutante, Summer, puts the kibosh on us all.

Old Mr. Coulson groaned a little, and then sat up straight in his invalid's chair. He had the gout very bad in one foot, a house near Gramercy Park, half a million dollars, and a daughter. And he had a housekeeper. Mrs. Widdup. The fact and the name deserve a sentence each. They have it.

When May poked Mr. Coulson he became elder brother to the turtle-dove. In the window near which he sat were boxes of jonquils, of hyacinths, geraniums, and pansies. The breeze brought their odor into the room. Immediately there was a well-contested round between the breath of the flowers and the able and active effluvium from gout liniment. The liniment won easily; but not before the flowers got an uppercut to old Mr. Coulson's nose. The deadly work of the implacable, false enchantress May was done.

Across the park to the olfactories of Mr. Coulson came other unmistakable, characteristic, copyrighted smells of spring that belong to the-big-city-above-the-Subway, alone. The smells of hot asphalt, underground caverns, gasoline, patchouli, orange peel, sewer gas, Albany grabs, Egyptian cigarettes, mortar and the undried ink on newspapers. The inblowing air was sweet and mild. Sparrows wrangled happily everywhere outdoors. Never trust May.

Mr. Coulson twisted the ends of his white mustache, cursed his foot, and pounded a bell on the table by his side.

In came Mrs. Widdup. She was comely to the eye, fair, flustered, forty, and foxy.

"Higgins is out, sir," she said, with a smile suggestive of vibratory massage. "He went to post a letter. Can I do anything for you, sir?"

"It's time for my aconite," said old Mr. Coulson. "Drop it for me. The bottle's there. Three drops. In water. D— that

is, confound Higgins! There's nobody in this house cares if
I die here in this chair for want of attention."

Mrs. Widdup sighed deeply.

"Don't be saying that, sir," she said. "There's them that
would care more than any one knows. Thirteen drops you
said, sir?"

"Three," said old man Coulson.

He took his dose and then Mrs. Widdup's hand. She
blushed. Oh, yes, it can be done. Just hold your breath and
compress the diaphragm.

"Mrs. Widdup," said Mr. Coulson, "the springtime's full
upon us."

"Ain't that right?" said Mrs. Widdup. "The air's real warm.
And there's bock-beer signs on every corner. And the park's
all yaller and pink and blue with flowers; and I have such
shooting pains up my legs and body."

"'In the spring,'" quoted Mr. Coulson, curling his mustache, "'a y— that is, a man's—fancy lightly turns to thoughts
of love.'"

"Lawsy, now!" exclaimed Mrs. Widdup; "ain't that right?
Seems like it's in the air."

"'In the spring,'" continued old Mr. Coulson, "'a livelier
iris shines upon the burnished dove.'"

"They do be lively, the Irish," sighed Mrs. Widdup, pensively.

"Mrs. Widdup," said Mr. Coulson, making a face at a
twinge of his gouty foot, "this would be a lonesome house
without you. I'm an—that is, I'm an elderly man—but I'm
worth a comfortable lot of money. If half a million dollars'
worth of Government bonds and the true affection of a heart
that, though no longer beating with the first ardor of youth,
can still throb with genuine——"

The loud noise of an overturned chair near the portières

of the adjoining room interrupted the venerable and scarcely suspecting victim of May.

In stalked Miss Van Meeker Constantia Coulson, bony, durable, tall, high-nosed, frigid, well-bred, thirty-five, in-the-neighborhood-of-Gramercy-Parkish. She put up a lorgnette. Mrs. Widdup hastily stooped and arranged the bandages on Mr. Coulson's gouty foot.

"I thought Higgins was with you," said Miss Van Meeker Constantia.

"Higgins went out," explained her father, "and Mrs. Widdup answered the bell. That is better now, Mrs. Widdup, thank you. No; there is nothing else I require."

The housekeeper retired, pink under the cool, inquiring stare of Miss Coulson.

"This spring weather is lovely, isn't it, daughter?" said the old man, consciously conscious.

"That's just it," replied Miss Van Meeker Constantia Coulson, somewhat obscurely. "When does Mrs. Widdup start on her vacation, papa?"

"I believe she said a week from to-day," said Mr. Coulson.

Miss Van Meeker Constantia stood for a minute at the window gazing toward the little park, flooded with the mellow afternoon sunlight. With the eye of a botanist she viewed the flowers—most potent weapons of insidious May. With the cool pulses of a virgin of Cologne she withstood the attack of the ethereal mildness. The arrows of the pleasant sunshine fell back, frostbitten, from the cold panoply of her unthrilled bosom. The odor of the flowers waked no soft sentiments in the unexplored recesses of her dormant heart. The chirp of the sparrows gave her a pain. She mocked at May.

But although Miss Coulson was proof against the season, she was keen enough to estimate its power. She knew that elderly men and thick-waisted women jumped as educated fleas in the ridiculous train of May, the merry mocker of the months. She had heard of foolish old gentlemen marrying their housekeepers before. What a humiliating thing, after all, was this feeling called love!

The next morning at 8 o'clock, when the iceman called, the cook told him that Miss Coulson wanted to see him in the basement.

"Well, ain't I the Olcott and Depew; not mentioning the first name at all?" said the iceman, admiringly, of himself.

As a concession he rolled his sleeves down, dropped his icehooks on a syringa and went back. When Miss Van Meeker Constantia Coulson addressed him he took off his hat.

"There is a rear entrance to this basement," said Miss Coulson, "which can be reached by driving into the vacant lot next door, where they are excavating for a building. I want you to bring in that way within two hours 1,000 pounds of ice. You may have to bring another man or two to help you. I will show you where I want it placed. I also want 1,000 pounds a day delivered the same way for the next four days. Your company may charge the ice on our regular bill. This is for your extra trouble."

Miss Coulson tendered a ten-dollar bill. The iceman bowed, and held his hat in his two hands behind him.

"Now if you'll excuse me, lady. It'll be a pleasure to fix things up for you any way you please."

Alas for May!

About noon Mr. Coulson knocked two glasses off his table, broke the spring of his bell, and yelled for Higgins at the same time.

"Bring an axe," commanded Mr. Coulson, sardonically, "or send out for a quart of prussic acid, or have a policeman come in and shoot me. I'd rather that than be frozen to death."

"It does seem to be getting cold, sir," said Higgins. "I hadn't noticed it before. I'll close the window, sir."

"Do," said Mr. Coulson. "They call this spring, do they? If it keeps up long I'll go back to Palm Beach. House feels like a morgue."

Later Miss Coulson dutifully came in to inquire how the gout was progressing.

"'Stantia," said the old man, "how is the weather outdoors?"

"Bright," answered Miss Coulson, "but chilly."

"Feels like the dead of winter to me," said Mr. Coulson.

"An instance," said Constantia, gazing abstractedly out of the window, "of 'winter lingering in the lap of spring,' though the metaphor is not in the most refined taste."

A little later she walked down by the side of the little park and on westward to Broadway to accomplish a little shopping.

A little later than that Mrs. Widdup entered the invalid's room.

"Did you ring, sir?" she asked, dimpling in many places. "I asked Higgins to go to the drug store, and I thought I heard your bell."

"I did not," said Mr. Coulson.

"I'm afraid," said Mrs. Widdup, "I interrupted you, sir, yesterday when you were about to say something."

"How comes it, Mrs. Widdup," said old man Coulson, sternly, "that I find it so cold in this house?"

"Cold, sir?" said the housekeeper, "why, now, since you speak of it it do seem cold in this room. But outdoors it's as warm and fine as June, sir. And how this weather do seem to make one's heart jump out of one's shirt waist, sir. And the ivy all leaved out on the side of the house, and the hand-organs playing, and the children dancing on the sidewalk— 'tis a great time for speaking out what's in the heart. You were saying yesterday, sir——"

"Woman!" roared Mr. Coulson, "you are a fool. I pay you to take care of this house. I am freezing to death in my own room, and you come in and drivel to me about ivy and hand-organs. Get me an overcoat at once. See that all doors and windows are closed below. An old, fat, irresponsible, one-sided object like you pratting about springtime and flowers in the middle of winter! When Higgins comes back, tell him to bring me a hot rum punch. And now get out!"

But who shall shame the bright face of May? Rogue though she be and disturber of sane men's peace, no wise virgin's cunning nor cold storage shall make her bow her head in the bright galaxy of months.

Oh, yes, the story was not quite finished.

A night passed, and Higgins helped old man Coulson in the morning to his chair by the window. The cold of the room was gone. Heavenly odors and fragrant mildness entered.

In hurried Mrs. Widdup, and stood by his chair. Mr. Coulson reached his bony hand and grasped her plump one.

"Mrs. Widdup," he said, "this house would be no home without you. I have half a million dollars. If that and the true affection of a heart no longer in its youthful prime, but still not cold could——"

"I found out what made it cold," said Mrs. Widdup, leaning against his chair. " 'Twas ice—tons of it—in the basement and in the furnace room, everywhere. I shut off the registers that it was coming through into your room, Mr. Coulson, poor soul! And now it's May-time again."

"A true heart," went on old man Coulson, a little wanderingly, "that the springtime has brought to life again, and—but what will my daughter say, Mrs. Widdup?"

"Never fear, sir," said Mrs. Widdup, cheerfully, "Miss Coulson, she ran away with the iceman last night, sir!"

The Whirligig of Life

JUSTICE-OF-THE-PEACE Benaja Widdup sat in the door of his office smoking his elder-stem pipe. Halfway to the Zenith the Cumberland range rose blue-gray in the afternoon haze. A speckled hen swaggered down the main street of the "settlement," cackling foolishly.

Up the road came a sound of creaking axles, and then a slow cloud of dust, and then a bull-cart bearing Ransie Bilbro and his wife. The cart stopped at the Justice's door, and the two climbed down. Ransie was a narrow six feet of sallow brown skin and yellow hair. The imperturbability of the mountains hung upon him like a suit of armor. The woman was calicoed, angled, snuff-brushed, and weary with unknown desires. Through it all gleamed a faint protest of cheated youth unconscious of its loss.

The Justice of the Peace slipped his feet into his shoes, for the sake of dignity, and moved to let them enter.

"We-all," said the woman, in a voice like the wind blowing through pine boughs, "wants a divo'ce." She looked at Ransie to see if he noted any flaw or ambiguity or evasion or partiality or self-partisanship in her statement of their business.

"A divo'ce," repeated Ransie, with a solemn nod. "We-all can't git along together nohow. It's lonesome enough fur to live in the mount'ins when a man and a woman keers fur one another. But when she's a-spittin' like a wildcat or a-sullenin' like a hoot-owl in the cabin, a man ain't got no call to live with her."

"When he's a no-'count varmint," said the woman, without any especial warmth, "a-traipsin' along of scalawags and moonshiners and a-layin' on his back pizen 'ith co'n whiskey, and a-pesterin' folks with a pack o' hungry, triflin' houn's to feed!"

"When she keeps a-throwin' skillet lids," came Ransie's antiphony, "and slings b'ilin' water on the best coon-dog in the Cumberlands, and sets herself again' cookin' a man's victuals, and keeps him awake o' nights accusin' him of a sight of doin's!"

"When he's al'ays a-fightin' the revenues, and gits a hard name in the mount'ins fur a mean man, who's gwine to be able fur to sleep o' nights?"

The Justice of the Peace stirred deliberately to his duties. He placed his one chair and a wooden stool for his petitioners. He opened his book of statutes on the table and scanned the index. Presently he wiped his spectacles and shifted his inkstand.

"The law and the statutes," said he, "air silent on the subjeck of divo'ce as fur as the jurisdiction of this co't air concerned. But, accordin' to equity and the Constitution and the golden rule, it's a bad barg'in that can't run both ways. If a justice of the peace can marry a couple, it's plain that he is bound to be able to divo'ce 'em. This here office will issue a decree of divo'ce and abide by the decision of the Supreme Co't to hold it good."

Ransie Bilbro drew a small tobacco-bag from his trousers pocket. Out of this he shook upon the table a five-dollar note. "Sold a b'arskin and two foxes fur that," he remarked. "It's all the money we got."

"The regular price of a divo'ce in this co't," said the Justice, "air five dollars." He stuffed the bill into the pocket of his homespun vest with a deceptive air of indifference. With much bodily toil and mental travail he wrote the decree upon half a sheet of foolscap, and then copied it upon the other. Ransie Bilbro and his wife listened to his reading of the document that was to give them freedom:

Know all men by these presents that Ransie Bilbro and his wife, Ariela Bilbro, this day personally appeared before me and promises that hereinafter they will neither love, honor, nor obey each other, neither for better nor worse, being of sound mind and body, and accept summons for divorce according to the peace and dignity of the State. Herein fail not, so help you God. Benaja Widdup, justice of the peace in and for the county of Piedmont, State of Tennessee.

The Justice was about to hand one of the documents to Ransie. The voice of Ariela delayed the transfer. Both men looked at her. Their dull masculinity was confronted by something sudden and unexpected in the woman.

"Judge, don't you give him that air paper yit. 'Tain't all settled, nohow. I got to have my rights first. I got to have my ali-money. 'Tain't no kind of a way to do fur a man to divo'ce his wife 'thout her havin' a cent fur to do with. I'm a-layin' off to be a-goin' up to brother Ed's up on Hogback Mount'in. I'm bound fur to hev a pa'r of shoes and some snuff and things besides. Ef Ranse kin affo'd a divo'ce, let him pay me ali-money."

Ransie Bilbro was stricken to dumb perplexity. There had been no previous hint of alimony. Women were always bringing up startling and unlooked-for issues.

Justice Benaja Widdup felt that the point demanded judicial decision. The authorities were also silent on the subject of alimony. But the woman's feet were bare. The trail to Hogback Mountain was steep and flinty.

"Ariela Bilbro," he asked, in official tones, "how much did you 'low would be good and sufficient ali-money in the case befo' the co't?"

"I 'lowed," she answered, "fur the shoes and all, to say five dollars. That ain't much fur ali-money, but I reckon that'll git me up to brother Ed's."

"The amount," said the Justice, "air not onreasonable. Ransie Bilbro, you air ordered by the co't to pay the plaintiff the sum of five dollars befo' the decree of divo'ce air issued."

"I hain't no mo' money," breathed Ransie, heavily. "I done paid you all I had."

"Otherwise," said the Justice, looking severely over his spectacles, "you air in contempt of co't."

"I reckon if you gimme till to-morrow," pleaded the husband, "I mout be able to rake or scrape it up somewhars. I never looked for to be a-payin' no ali-money."

"The case air adjourned," said Benaja Widdup, "till to-morrow, when you-all will present yo'selves and obey the order of the co't. Followin' of which the decrees of divo'ce will be delivered." He sat down in the door and began to loosen a shoestring.

"We mout as well go down to Uncle Ziah's," decided Ransie, "and spend the night." He climbed into the cart on one side, and Ariela climbed in on the other. Obeying the flap of his rope, the little red bull slowly came around on a tack, and the cart crawled away in the nimbus arising from its wheels.

Justice-of-the-peace Benaja Widdup smoked his elder-stem pipe. Late in the afternoon he got his weekly paper, and read it until the twilight dimmed its lines. Then he lit the tallow candle on his table, and read until the moon rose, marking the time for supper. He lived in the double log cabin on the slope near the girdled poplar. Going home to supper he crossed a little branch darkened by a laurel thicket. The dark figure of a man stepped from the laurels and pointed a rifle at his breast. His hat was pulled down low, and something covered most of his face.

"I want yo' money," said the figure, "'thout any talk. I'm

gettin' nervous, and my finger's a-wabblin' on this here trigger."

"I've only got f-f-five dollars," said the Justice, producing it from his vest pocket.

"Roll it up," came the order, "and stick it in the end of this here gun-bar'l."

The bill was crisp and new. Even fingers that were clumsy and trembling found little difficulty in making a spill of it and inserting it (this with less ease) into the muzzle of the rifle.

"Now I reckon you kin be goin' along," said the robber.

The Justice lingered not on his way.

The next day came the little red bull, drawing the cart to the office door. Justice Benaja Widdup had his shoes on, for he was expecting the visit. In his presence Ransie Bilbro handed to his wife a five-dollar bill. The official's eye sharply viewed it. It seemed to curl up as though it had been rolled and inserted into the end of a gun-barrel. But the Justice refrained from comment. It is true that other bills might be inclined to curl. He handed each one a decree of divorce. Each stood awkwardly silent, slowly folding the guarantee of freedom. The woman cast a shy glance full of constraint at Ransie.

"I reckon you'll be goin' back up to the cabin," she said, "along 'ith the bull-cart. There's bread in the tin box settin' on the shelf. I put the bacon in the b'ilin'-pot to keep the hounds from gettin' it. Don't forget to wind the clock to-night."

"You air a-goin' to your brother Ed's?" asked Ransie, with fine unconcern.

"I was 'lowin' to get along up thar afore night. I ain't sayin' as they'll pester theyselves any to make me welcome, but I hain't nowhar else fur to go. It's a right smart ways, and I reckon I better be goin'. I'll be a-sayin' good-bye, Ranse—that is, if you keer fur to say so."

"I don't know as anybody's a hound dog," said Ransie, in a martyr's voice, "fur to not want to say good-bye—'less you air so anxious to git away that you don't want me to say it."

Ariela was silent. She folded the five-dollar bill and her decree carefully, and placed them in the bosom of her dress. Benaja Widdup watched the money disappear with mournful eyes behind his spectacles.

And then with his next words he achieved rank (as his thoughts ran) with either the great crowd of the world's sympathizers or the little crowd of its great financiers.

"Be kind o' lonesome in the old cabin to-night, Ransie," he said.

Ransie Bilbro stared out at the Cumberlands, clear blue now in the sunlight. He did not look at Ariela.

"I 'low it might be lonesome," he said, "but when folks gits mad and wants a divo'ce, you can't make folks stay."

"There's others wanted a divo'ce," said Ariela, speaking to the wooden stool. "Besides, nobody don't want nobody to stay."

"Nobody never said they didn't."

"Nobody never said they did. I reckon I better start on now to brother Ed's."

"Nobody can't wind that old clock."

"Want me to go along 'ith you in the cart and wind it fur you, Ranse?"

The mountaineer's countenance was proof against emotion. But he reached out a big hand and enclosed Ariela's thin brown one. Her soul peeped out once through her impassive face, hallowing it.

"Them hounds sha'n't pester you no more," said Ransie. "I reckon I been mean and low down. You wind that clock, Ariela."

"My heart hit's in that cabin, Ranse," she whispered, "along 'ith you. I ain't a-goin' to git mad no more. Le's be startin', Ranse, so's we kin git home by sundown."

Justice-of-the-peace Benaja Widdup interposed as they started for the door, forgetting his presence.

"In the name of the State of Tennessee," he said, "I forbid you-all to be a-defyin' of its laws and statutes. This co't is mo' than willin' and full of joy to see the clouds of discord and misunderstandin' rollin' away from two lovin' hearts, but it air the duty of the co't to p'eserve the morals and integrity of the State. The co't reminds you that you air no longer man and wife, but air divo'ced by regular decree, and as such air not entitled to the benefits and 'purtenances of the matter-monal estate."

Ariela caught Ransie's arm. Did those words mean that she must lose him now when they had just learned the lesson of life?

"But the co't air prepared," went on the Justice, "fur to remove the disabilities set up by the decree of divo'ce. The co't air on hand to perform the solemn ceremony of marri'ge, thus fixin' things up and enablin' the parties in the case to resume the honor'ble and elevatin' state of mattermony which they desires. The fee fur performin' said ceremony will be, in this case, to wit, five dollars."

Ariela caught the gleam of promise in his words. Swiftly her hand went to her bosom. Freely as an alighting dove the bill fluttered to the Justice's table. Her sallow cheek colored as she stood hand in hand with Ransie and listened to the reuniting words.

Ransie helped her into the cart, and climbed in beside her. The little red bull turned once more, and they set out, hand-clasped, for the mountains.

Justice-of-the-peace Benaja Widdup sat in his door and took off his shoes. Once again he fingered the bill tucked down in his vest pocket. Once again he smoked his elder-stem pipe. Once again the speckled hen swaggered down the main street of the "settlement," cackling foolishly.

A Blackjack Bargainer

THE MOST DISREPUTABLE THING in Yancey Goree's law office was Goree himself, sprawled in his creaky old armchair. The rickety little office, built of red brick, was set flush with the street—the main street of the town of Bethel.

Bethel rested upon the foot-hills of the Blue Ridge. Above it the mountains were piled to the sky. Far below it the tur-bid Catawba gleamed yellow along its disconsolate valley.

The June day was at its sultriest hour. Bethel dozed in the tepid shade. Trade was not. It was so still that Goree, reclin-ing in his chair, distinctly heard the clicking of the chips in the grand-jury room, where the "court-house gang" was play-ing poker. From the open back door of the office a well-worn path meandered across the grassy lot to the court-house. The treading out of that path had cost Goree all he ever had—first inheritance of a few thousand dollars, next the old family home, and, latterly, the last shreds of his self-respect and man-hood. The "gang" had cleaned him out. The broken gambler had turned drunkard and parasite; he had lived to see this day come when the men who had stripped him denied him a seat at the game. His word was no longer to be taken. The daily bout at cards had arranged itself accordingly, and to him was assigned the ignoble part of the onlooker. The sheriff, the county clerk, a sportive deputy, a gay attorney, and a chalk-faced man hailing "from the valley," sat at table, and the sheared one was thus tacitly advised to go and grow more wool.

Soon wearying of his ostracism, Goree had departed for his office, muttering to himself as he unsteadily traversed the unlucky pathway. After a drink of corn whiskey from a demijohn under the table, he had flung himself into the chair, staring, in a sort of maudlin apathy, out at the mountains immersed in the summer haze. The little white patch he saw away up on the side of Blackjack was Laurel, the village near which he had been born and bred. There, also, was the birthplace of the feud between the Gorees and the Coltranes. Now no direct heir of the Gorees survived except this plucked and singed bird of misfortune. To the Coltranes, also, but one male supporter was left—Colonel Abner Coltrane, a man of substance and standing, a member of the State Legislature, and a contemporary with Goree's father. The feud had been a typical one of the region; it had left a red record of hate, wrong, and slaughter.

But Yancey Goree was not thinking of feuds. His befuddled brain was hopelessly attacking the problem of the future maintenance of himself and his favorite follies. Of late, old friends of the family had seen to it that he had whereof to eat and a place to sleep, but whiskey they would not buy for him, and he must have whiskey. His law business was extinct; no case had been intrusted to him in two years. He had been a borrower and a sponge, and it seemed that if he fell no lower it would be from lack of opportunity. One more chance —he was saying to himself—if he had one more stake at the game, he thought he could win; but he had nothing left to sell, and his credit was more than exhausted.

He could not help smiling, even in his misery, as he thought of the man to whom, six months before, he had sold the old Goree homestead. There had come from "back yan'" in the mountains two of the strangest creatures, a man named Pike

Garvey and his wife. "Back yan'," with a wave of the hand
toward the hills, was understood among the mountaineers to
designate the remotest fastnesses, the unplumbed gorges, the
haunts of lawbreakers, the wolf's den, and the boudoir of the
bear. In the cabin far up on Blackjack's shoulder, in the wild-
est part of these retreats, this odd couple had lived for twenty
years. They had neither dog nor children to mitigate the
heavy silence of the hills. Pike Garvey was little known in the
settlements, but all who had dealt with him pronounced him
"crazy as a loon." He acknowledged no occupation save that
of a squirrel hunter, but he "moonshined" occasionally by way
of diversion. Once the "revenues" had dragged him from his
lair, fighting silently and desperately like a terrier, and he had
been sent to state's prison for two years. Released, he popped
back into his hole like an angry weasel.

Fortune, passing over many anxious wooers, made a freak-
ish flight into Blackjack's bosky pockets to smile upon Pike
and his faithful partner.

One day a party of spectacled, knickerbockered, and altogether absurd prospectors invaded the vicinity of the Garveys'
cabin. Pike lifted his squirrel rifle off the hook and took a
shot at them at long range on the chance of their being revenues. Happily he missed, and the unconscious agents of good
luck drew nearer, disclosing their innocence of anything resembling law or justice. Later on, they offered the Garveys
an enormous quantity of ready, green, crisp money for their
thirty-acre patch of cleared land, mentioning, as an excuse for
such a mad action, some irrelevant and inadequate nonsense
about a bed of mica underlying the said property.

When the Garveys became possessed of so many dollars
that they faltered in computing them, the deficiencies of life
on Blackjack began to grow prominent. Pike began to talk
of new shoes, a hogshead of tobacco to set in the corner, a
new lock to his rifle; and, leading Martella to a certain spot

on the mountainside, he pointed out to her how a small can-
non—doubtless a thing not beyond the scope of their fortune
in price—might be planted so as to command and defend the
sole accessible trail to the cabin, to the confusion of revenues
and meddling strangers forever.

But Adam reckoned without his Eve. These things rep-
resented to him the applied power of wealth, but there slum-
bered in his dingy cabin an ambition that soared far above
his primitive wants. Somewhere in Mrs. Garvey's bosom still
survived a spot of femininity unstarved by twenty years of
Blackjack. For so long a time the sounds in her ears had been
the scaly-barks dropping in the woods at noon, and the wolves
singing among the rocks at night, and it was enough to have
purged her vanities. She had grown fat and sad and yellow
and dull. But when the means came, she felt a rekindled desire to assume the perquisites of her sex—to sit at tea tables;
to buy inutile things; to whitewash the hideous veracity of
life with a little form and ceremony. So she coldly vetoed
Pike's proposed system of fortifications, and announced that
they would descend upon the world, and gyrate socially.

And thus, at length, it was decided, and the thing done.
The village of Laurel was their compromise between Mrs.
Garvey's preference for one of the large valley towns and
Pike's hankering for primeval solitudes. Laurel yielded a halt-
ing round of feeble social distractions comportable with
Martella's ambitions, and was not entirely without recom-
mendation to Pike, its contiguity to the mountains presenting advantages for sudden retreat in case fashionable society
should make it advisable.

Their descent upon Laurel had been coincident with Yancey Goree's feverish desire to convert property into cash, and
they bought the old Goree homestead, paying four thousand
dollars ready money into the spendthrift's shaking hand.

Thus it happened that while the disreputable last of the

Gorees sprawled in his disreputable office, at the end of his
row, spurned by the cronies whom he had gorged, strangers
dwelt in the halls of his fathers.

A cloud of dust was rolling slowly up the parched street,
with something traveling in the midst of it. A little breeze
wafted the cloud to one side, and a new, brightly painted
carryall, drawn by a slothful gray horse, became visible. The
vehicle deflected from the middle of the street as it neared
Goree's office, and stopped in the gutter directly in front of
his door.

On the front seat sat a gaunt, tall man, dressed in black
broadcloth, his rigid hands incarcerated in yellow kid gloves.
On the back seat was a lady who triumphed over the June
heat. Her stout form was armored in a skin-tight silk dress
of the description known as "changeable," being a gorgeous
combination of shifting hues. She sat erect, waving a much-
ornamented fan, with her eyes fixed stonily far down the
street. However Martella Garvey's heart might be rejoicing at
the pleasures of her new life, Blackjack had done his work
with her exterior. He had carved her countenance to the im-
age of emptiness and inanity; had imbued her with the
stolidity of his crags and the reserve of his hushed interiors.
She always seemed to hear, whatever her surroundings were,
the scaly-barks falling and pattering down the mountainside.
She could always hear the awful silence of Blackjack sound-
ing through the stillest of nights.

Goree watched this solemn equipage, as it drove to his
door, with only faint interest but when the lank driver wrapped
the reins about his whip, and awkwardly descended, and
stepped into the office, he rose unsteadily to receive him,
recognizing Pike Garvey, the new, the transformed, the recently civilized.

The mountaineer took the chair Goree offered him. They
who cast doubts upon Garvey's soundness of mind had a

strong witness in the man's countenance. His face was too long, a dull saffron in hue, and immobile as a statue's. Pale-blue, unwinking round eyes without lashes added to the singularity of his gruesome visage. Goree was at a loss to account for the visit.

"Everything all right at Laurel, Mr. Garvey?" he inquired.

"Everything all right, sir, and mighty pleased is Missis Garvey and me with the property. Missis Garvey likes yo' old place, and she likes the neighborhood. Society is what she 'lows she wants, and she is gettin' of it. The Rogerses, the Hapgoods, the Pratts, and the Troys hev been to see Missis Garvey, and she hev et meals to most of thar houses. The best folks hev axed her to differ'nt kinds of doin's. I cyan't say, Mr. Goree, that sech things suits me—fur me, give me them thar." Garvey's huge yellow-gloved hand flourished in the direction of the mountains. "That's whar I b'long, 'mongst the wild honey bees and the b'ars. But that ain't what I come fur to say, Mr. Goree. Thar's somethin' you got what me and Missis Garvey wants to buy."

"Buy!" echoed Goree. "From me?" Then he laughed harshly. "I reckon you are mistaken about that. I sold out to you, as you yourself expressed it, 'lock, stock, and barrel.' There isn't even a ramrod left to sell."

"You've got it; and we 'uns want it. 'Take the money,' says Missis Garvey, 'and buy it fa'r and squar'.'"

Goree shook his head. "The cupboard's bare," he said.

"We've riz," pursued the mountaineer, undeflected from his object, "a heap. We was pore as possums, and now we could hev folks to dinner every day. We been reco'nized, Missis Garvey says, by the best society. But there's somethin' we need we ain't got. She says it ought to been put in the 'ventory ov the sale, but it 'tain't thar. 'Take the money, then,' she says, 'and buy it fa'r and squar'.'"

"Out with it," said Goree, his racked nerves growing impatient.

Garvey threw his slouch hat upon the table, and leaned forward, fixing his unblinking eyes upon Goree's.

"Thar's a old feud," he said, distinctly and slowly, "'tween you 'uns and the Coltranes."

Goree frowned ominously. To speak of his feud to a feudist is a serious breach of the mountain etiquette. The man from "back yan'" knew it as well as the lawyer did.

"Na offense," he went on, "but purely in the way of business. Missis Garvey hev studied all about feuds. Most of the quality folks in the mountains hev 'em. The Settles and the Goforths, the Rankins and the Boyds, the Silers and the Galloways, hev all been cyarin' on feuds f'om twenty to a hundred year. The last man to drap was when yo' uncle, Jedge Paisley Goree, 'journed co't and shot Len Coltrane f'om the bench. Missis Garvey and me, we come f'om the po' white trash. Nobody wouldn't pick a feud with we'uns, no mo'n with a fam'ly of treetoads. Quality people everywhar, says Missis Garvey, has feuds. We 'uns ain't quality, but we're buyin' into it as fur as we can. 'Take the money, then,' says Missis Garvey, 'and buy Mr. Goree's feud, fa'r and squar'.'"

The squirrel hunter straightened a leg half across the room, drew a roll of bills from his pocket, and threw them on the table.

"Thar's two hundred dollars, Mr. Goree, what you would call a fa'r price for a feud that's been 'lowed to run down like yourn hev. Thar's only you left to cyar' on yo' side of it, and you'd make mighty po' killin'. I'll take it off yo' hands, and it'll set me and Missis Garvey up among the quality. Thar's the money."

The little roll of currency on the table slowly untwisted itself, writhing and jumping as its folds relaxed. In the silence that followed Garvey's last speech the rattling of the poker chips in the court-house could be plainly heard. Goree knew that the sheriff had just won a pot, for the subdued whoop with which he always greeted a victory floated across the square upon the crinkly heat waves. Beads of moisture stood on Goree's brow. Stooping, he drew the wicker-covered demijohn from under the table, and filled a tumbler from it.

"A little corn liquor, Mr. Garvey? Of course you are joking about—what you spoke of? Opens quite a new market, doesn't it? Feuds, prime, two-fifty to three. Feuds, slightly damaged—two hundred, I believe you said, Mr. Garvey?"

Goree laughed self-consciously.

The mountaineer took the glass Goree handed him, and drank the whiskey without a tremor of the lids of his staring eyes. The lawyer applauded the feat by a look of envious admiration. He poured his own drink, and took it like a drunkard, by gulps, and with shudders at the smell and taste.

"Two hundred," repeated Garvey. "Thar's the money."

A sudden passion flared up in Goree's brain. He struck the table with his fist. One of the bills flipped over and touched his hand. He flinched as if something had stung him.

"Do you come to me," he shouted, "seriously with such a ridiculous, insulting, darn-fool proposition?"

"It's fa'r and squar'," said the squirrel hunter, but he reached out his hand as if to take back the money; and then Goree knew that his own flurry of rage had not been from pride or resentment, but from anger at himself, knowing that he would set foot in the deeper depths that were being opened to him. He turned in an instant from an outraged gentleman to an anxious chafferer recommending his goods.

"Don't be in a hurry, Garvey," he said, his face crimson and his speech thick. "I accept your p-p-proposition, though it's dirt cheap at two hundred. A t-trade's all right when both p-purchaser and b-buyer are s-satisfied. Shall I w-wrap it up for you, Mr. Garvey?"

Garvey rose, and shook out his broadcloth. "Missis Garvey will be pleased. You air out of it, and it stands Coltrane and Garvey. Just a scrap ov writin', Mr. Goree, you bein' a lawyer, to show we traded."

Goree seized a sheet of paper and a pen. The money was clutched in his moist hand. Everything else suddenly seemed to grow trivial and light.

"Bill of sale, by all means. 'Right, title, and interest in and to' . . . 'forever warrant and——' No, Garvey, we'll have to leave out that 'defend,'" said Goree with a loud laugh. "You'll have to defend this title yourself."

The mountaineer received the amazing screed that the lawyer handed him, folded it with immense labor, and placed it carefully in his pocket.

Goree was standing near the window. "Step here," he said, raising his finger, "and I'll show you your recently purchased enemy. There he goes, down the other side of the street."

The mountaineer crooked his long frame to look through the window in the direction indicated by the other. Colonel Abner Coltrane, an erect, portly gentleman of about fifty wearing the inevitable long, double-breasted frock coat of the Southern lawmaker, and an old high silk hat, was passing on the opposite sidewalk. As Garvey looked, Goree glanced at his face. If there be such a thing as a yellow wolf, here was its counterpart. Garvey snarled as his unhuman eyes followed the moving figure, disclosing long amber-colored fangs.

"Is that him? Why, that's the man who sent me to the pen'tentiary once!"

"He used to be district attorney," said Goree, carelessly. "And, by the way, he's a first-class shot."

"I kin hit a squirrel's eye at a hundred yard," said Garvey. "So that thar's Coltrane! I made a better trade than I was thinkin'. I'll take keer ov this feud, Mr. Goree, better'n you ever did!"

He moved toward the door, but lingered there, betraying a slight perplexity.

"Anything else to-day?" inquired Goree with frothy sarcasm. "Any family traditions, ancestral ghosts, or skeletons in the closet? Prices as low as the lowest."

"Thar was another thing," replied the unmoved squirrel hunter, "that Missis Garvey was thinkin' of. 'Tain't so much in my line as t'other, but she wanted partic'lar that I should inquire, and ef you was willin', 'pay fur it,' she says, 'fa'r and squar'.' Thar's a buryin' groun', as you know, Mr. Goree, in the yard of yo' old place, under the cedars. Them that lies thar is yo' folks what was killed by the Coltranes. The monyments has the names on 'em. Missis Garvey says a fam'ly buryin' groun' is a sho' sign of quality. She says ef we git the feud, thar's somethin' else ought to go with it. The names on them monyments is 'Goree,' but they can be changed to ourn by——"

"Go! Go!" screamed Goree, his face turning purple. He stretched out both hands toward the mountaineer, his fingers hooked and shaking. "Go, you ghoul! Even a Ch-Chinaman protects the g-graves of his ancestors—go!"

The squirrel hunter slouched out of the door to his carry-all. While he was climbing over the wheel Goree was collecting, with feverish celerity, the money that had fallen from his hand to the floor. As the vehicle slowly turned about, the sheep with a coat of newly grown wool, was hurrying, in indecent haste, along the path to the court-house.

At three o'clock in the morning they brought him back to his office, shorn and unconscious. The sheriff, the sportive deputy, the county clerk, and the gay attorney carried him, the chalk-faced man "from the valley" acting as escort.

"On the table," said one of them, and they deposited him there among the litter of his unprofitable books and papers.

"Yance thinks a lot of a pair of deuces when he's liquored up," sighed the sheriff, reflectively.

"Too much," said the gay attorney. "A man has no business to play poker who drinks as much as he does. I wonder how much he dropped to-night."

"Close to two hundred. What I wonder is whar he got it. Yance ain't had a cent fur over a month, I know."

"Struck a client, maybe. Well, let's get home before daylight. He'll be all right when he wakes up, except for a sort of beehive about the cranium."

The gang slipped away through the early morning twilight. The next eye to gaze upon the miserable Goree was the orb of day. He peered through the uncurtained window, first deluging the sleeper in a flood of faint gold, but soon pouring upon the mottled red of his flesh a searching, white, summer heat. Goree stirred, half unconsciously, among the table's débris, and turned his face from the window. His movement dislodged a heavy law book, which crashed upon the floor. Opening his eyes, he saw, bending over him, a man in a black frock coat. Looking higher, he discovered a well-worn silk hat, and beneath it the kindly, smooth face of Colonel Abner Coltrane.

A little uncertain of the outcome, the colonel waited for the other to make some sign of recognition. Not in twenty years had male members of these two families faced each other in peace. Goree's eyelids puckered as he strained his blurred sight toward this visitor, and then he smiled serenely.

"Have you brought Stella and Lucy over to play?" he said, calmly.

"Do you know me, Yancey?" asked Coltrane.

"Of course I do. You brought me a whip with a whistle in the end."

So he had—twenty-four years ago; when Yancey's father was his best friend.

Goree's eyes wandered about the room. The colonel understood. "Lie still, and I'll bring you some," said he. There was a pump in the yard at the rear, and Goree closed his eyes, listening with rapture to the click of its handle and the bubbling of the falling stream. Coltrane brought a pitcher of the cool water, and held it for him to drink. Presently Goree sat up—a most forlorn object, his summer suit of flax soiled and crumpled, his discreditable head tousled and unsteady. He tried to wave one of his hands toward the colonel.

"Ex-excuse—everything, will you?" he said. "I must have drunk too much whiskey last night, and gone to bed on the table." His brows knitted into a puzzled frown.

"Out with the boys a while?" asked Coltrane, kindly.

"No, I went nowhere. I haven't had a dollar to spend in the last two months. Struck the demijohn too often, I reckon, as usual."

Colonel Coltrane touched him on the shoulder.

"A little while ago, Yancey," he began, "you asked me if I had brought Stella and Lucy over to play. You weren't quite awake then, and must have been dreaming you were a boy again. You are awake now, and I want you to listen to me. I have come from Stella and Lucy to their old playmate, and to my old friend's son. They know that I am going to bring you home with me, and you will find them as ready with a welcome as they were in the old days. I want you to come to my house and stay until you are yourself again, and as much longer as you will. We heard of your being down in the world, and in the midst of temptation, and we agreed that you should come over and play at our house once more. Will you come, my boy? Will you drop our old family trouble and come with me?"

"Trouble!" said Goree, opening his eyes wide. "There was never any trouble between us that I know of. I'm sure we've always been the best of friends. But, good Lord, Colonel, how could I go to your home as I am—a drunken wretch, a miserable, degraded spendthrift and gambler——"

He lurched from the table to his armchair, and began to weep maudlin tears, mingled with genuine drops of remorse and shame. Coltrane talked to him persistently and reasonably, reminding him of the simple mountain pleasures of which he had once been so fond, and insisting upon the genuineness of the invitation.

Finally he landed Goree by telling him he was counting upon his help in the engineering and transportation of a large amount of felled timber from a high mountainside to a waterway. He knew that Goree had once invented a device for this purpose—a series of slides and chutes—upon which he had justly prided himself. In an instant the poor fellow, delighted at the idea of his being of use to any one, had paper spread upon the table, and was drawing rapid but pitifully shaky lines in demonstration of what he could and would do.

The man was sickened of the husks; his prodigal heart was turning again toward the mountains. His mind was yet strangely clogged, and his thoughts and memories were returning to his brain one by one, like carrier pigeons over a stormy sea. But Coltrane was satisfied with the progress he had made.

Bethel received the surprise of its existence that afternoon when a Coltrane and a Goree rode amicably together through the town. Side by side they rode, out from the dusty streets and gaping townspeople, down across the creek bridge, and up toward the mountain. The prodigal had brushed and washed and combed himself to a more decent figure, but he was unsteady in the saddle, and he seemed to be deep in the contemplation of some vexing problem. Coltrane left him in his mood, relying upon the influence of changed surroundings to restore his equilibrium.

Once Goree was seized with a shaking fit, and almost came

to a collapse. He had to dismount and rest at the side of the road. The colonel, foreseeing such a condition, had provided a small flask of whiskey for the journey but when it was offered to him Goree refused it almost with violence, declaring he would never touch it again. By and by he was recovered, and went quietly enough for a mile or two. Then he pulled up his horse suddenly, and said:

"I lost two hundred dollars last night, playing poker. Now, where did I get that money?"

"Take it easy, Yancey. The mountain air will soon clear it up. We'll go fishing, first thing, at the Pinnacle Falls. The trout are jumping there like bullfrogs. We'll take Stella and Lucy along, and have a picnic on Eagle Rock. Have you forgotten how a hickory-cured-ham sandwich tastes, Yancey, to a hungry fisherman?"

Evidently the colonel did not believe the story of his lost wealth; so Goree retired again into brooding silence.

By late afternoon they had traveled ten of the twelve miles between Bethel and Laurel. Half a mile this side of Laurel lay the old Goree place; a mile or two beyond the village lived the Coltranes. The road was now steep and laborious, but the compensations were many. The tilted aisles of the forest were opulent with leaf and bird and bloom. The tonic air put to shame the pharmacopæia. The glades were dark with mossy shade, and bright with shy rivulets winking from the ferns and laurels. On the lower side they viewed, framed in the near foliage, exquisite sketches of the far valley swooning in its opal haze.

Coltrane was pleased to see that his companion was yielding to the spell of the hills and woods. For now they had but to skirt the base of Painter's Cliff; to cross Elder Branch and mount the hill beyond, and Goree would have to face the squandered home of his fathers. Every rock he passed, every tree, every foot of the roadway, was familiar to him. Though he had forgotten the woods, they thrilled him like the music of *"Home, Sweet Home."*

They rounded the cliff, descended into Elder Branch, and paused there to let the horses drink and splash in the swift water. On the right was a rail fence that cornered there, and followed the road and stream. Inclosed by it was the old apple orchard of the home place; the house was yet concealed by the brow of the steep hill. Inside and along the fence, pokeberries, elders, sassafras, and sumac grew high and dense. At a rustle of their branches, both Goree and Coltrane glanced up, and saw a long, yellow, wolfish face above the fence, staring at them with pale, unwinking eyes. The head quickly disappeared; there was a violent swaying of the bushes, and an ungainly figure ran up through the apple orchard in the direction of the house zig-zagging among the trees.

"That's Garvey," said Coltrane; "the man you sold out to. There's no doubt but he's considerably cracked. I had to send him up for moonshining once, several years ago, in spite of the fact that I believed him irresponsible. Why, what's the matter, Yancey?"

Goree was wiping his forehead, and his face had lost its color. "Do I look queer, too?" he asked, trying to smile. "I'm just remembering a few more things." Some of the alcohol had evaporated from his brain. "I recollect now where I got that two hundred dollars."

"Don't think of it," said Coltrane, cheerfully. "Later on we'll figure it all out together."

They rode out of the branch, and when they reached the foot of the hill Goree stopped again.

"Did you ever suspect I was a very vain kind of fellow, Colonel?" he asked. "Sort of foolish proud about appearances?"

The colonel's eyes refused to wander to the soiled, sagging suit of flax and the faded slouch hat.

"It seems to me," he replied, mystified, but humoring him,

"I remember a young buck about twenty, with the tightest coat, the sleekest hair, and the prancingest saddle horse in the Blue Ridge."

"Right you are," said Goree, eagerly. "And it's in me yet, though it don't show. Oh, I'm as vain as a turkey gobbler, and as proud as Lucifer. I'm going to ask you to indulge this weakness of mine in a little matter."

"Speak out, Yancey. We'll create you Duke of Laurel and Baron of Blue Ridge, if you choose; and you shall have a feather out of Stella's peacock's tail to wear in your hat."

"I'm in earnest. In a few minutes we'll pass the house up there on the hill where I was born, and where my people have lived for nearly a century. Strangers live there now—and look at me! I am about to show myself to them ragged and poverty-stricken, a wastrel and a beggar. Colonel Coltrane, I'm ashamed to do it. I want you to let me wear your coat and hat until we are out of sight beyond. I know you think it a foolish pride, but I want to make as good a showing as I can when I pass the old place."

"Now, what does this mean?" said Coltrane to himself, as he compared his companion's sane looks and quiet demeanor with his strange request. But he was already unbuttoning the coat, assenting readily, as if the fancy were in no wise to be considered strange.

The coat and hat fitted Goree well. He buttoned the former about him with a look of satisfaction and dignity. He and Coltrane were nearly the same size—rather tall, portly, and erect. Twenty-five years were between them, but in appearance they might have been brothers. Goree looked older than his age; his face was puffy and lined; the colonel had the smooth, fresh complexion of a temperate liver. He put on Goree's disreputable old flax coat and faded slouch hat.

"Now," said Goree, taking up the reins, "I'm all right. I want you to ride about ten feet in the rear as we go by, Colo-

nel, so that they can get a good look at me. They'll see I'm
no back number yet, by any means. I guess I'll show up pretty
well to them once more, anyhow. Let's ride on."

He set out up the hill at a smart trot, the colonel following,
as he had been requested.

Goree sat straight in the saddle, with head erect, but his
eyes were turned to the right, sharply scanning every shrub
and fence and hiding-place in the old homestead yard. Once
he muttered to himself, "Will the crazy fool try it, or did I
dream half of it?"

It was when he came opposite the little family burying
ground that he saw what he had been looking for—a puff of
white smoke, coming from the thick cedars in one corner. He
toppled so slowly to the left that Coltrane had time to urge
his horse to that side, and catch him with one arm.

The squirrel hunter had not overpraised his aim. He had
sent the bullet where he intended, and where Goree had expected that it would pass—through the breast of Colonel Abner Coltrane's black frock coat.

Goree leaned heavily against Coltrane, but he did not fall.
The horses kept pace, side by side, and the colonel's arm kept
him steady. The little white houses of Laurel shone through
the trees, half a mile away. Goree reached out one hand and
groped until it rested upon Coltrane's fingers, which held his
bridle.

"Good friend," he said, and that was all.

Thus did Yancey Goree, as he rode past his old home,
make, considering all things, the best showing that was in his
power.

A Lickpenny Lover

THERE were 3,000 girls in the Biggest Store. Masie was one of them. She was eighteen and a saleslady in the gents' gloves. Here she became versed in two varieties of human beings— the kind of gents who buy their gloves in department stores and the kind of women who buy gloves for unfortunate gents. Besides this wide knowledge of the human species, Masie had acquired other information. She had listened to the promulgated wisdom of the 2,999 other girls and had stored it in a brain that was as secretive and wary as that of a Maltese cat. Perhaps nature, foreseeing that she would lack wise counsellors, had mingled the saving ingredient of shrewdness along with her beauty, as she has endowed the silver fox of the priceless fur above the other animals with cunning.

For Masie was beautiful. She was a deep-tinted blonde, with the calm poise of a lady who cooks butter cakes in a window. She stood behind her counter in the Biggest Store; and as you closed your hand over the tape-line for your glove measure you thought of Hebe; and as you looked again you wondered how she had come by Minerva's eyes.

When the floorwalker was not looking Masie chewed tutti frutti; when he was looking she gazed up as if at the clouds and smiled wistfully.

That is the shopgirl smile, and I enjoin you to shun it unless you are well fortified with callosity of the heart, caramels, and a congeniality for the capers of Cupid. This smile belonged to Masie's recreation hours and not to the store; but the floorwalker must have his own. He is the Shylock of the stores. When he comes nosing around the bridge of his nose is a toll-bridge. It is goo-goo eyes or "git" when he looks toward a pretty girl. Of course not all floorwalkers are thus. Only a few days ago the papers printed news of one over eighty years of age.

One day Irving Carter, painter, millionaire, traveller, poet, automobilist, happened to enter the Biggest Store. It is due to him to add that his visit was not voluntary. Filial duty took him by the collar and dragged him inside, while his mother philandered among the bronze and terra-cotta statuettes.

Carter strolled across to the glove counter in order to shoot a few minutes on the wing. His need for gloves was genuine; he had forgotten to bring a pair with him. But his action hardly calls for apology, because he had never heard of glove-counter flirtations.

As he neared the vicinity of his fate he hesitated, suddenly conscious of this unknown phase of Cupid's less worthy profession.

Three or four cheap fellows, sonorously garbed, were leaning over the counters, wrestling with the mediatorial hand-coverings, while giggling girls played vivacious seconds to their lead upon the strident string of coquetry. Carter would have retreated, but he had gone too far. Masie confronted him behind her counter with a questioning look in eyes as coldly, beautifully, warmly blue as the glint of summer sunshine on an iceberg drifting in Southern seas.

And then Irving Carter, painter, millionaire, etc., felt a warm flush rise to his aristocratically pale face. But not from diffidence. The blush was intellectual in origin. He knew in a moment that he stood in the ranks of the ready-made youths who wooed the giggling girls at other counters. Himself leaned against the oaken trysting place of a cockney Cupid with a desire in his heart for the favor of a glove salesgirl. He was no more than Bill and Jack and Mickey. And then he felt a sudden tolerance for them, and an elating, courageous contempt for the conventions upon which he had fed,

and an unhesitating determination to have this perfect creature for his own.

When the gloves were paid for and wrapped Carter lingered
for a moment. The dimples at the corners of Masie's damask
mouth deepened. All gentlemen who bought gloves lingered
in just that way. She curved an arm, showing like Psyche's
through her shirt-waist sleeve, and rested an elbow upon the
show-case edge.

Carter had never before encountered a situation of which
he had not been perfect master. But now he stood far more
awkward than Bill or Jack or Mickey. He had no chance of
meeting this beautiful girl socially. His mind struggled to recall the nature and habits of shopgirls as he had read or heard
of them. Somehow he had received the idea that they sometimes did not insist too strictly upon the regular channels of
introduction. His heart beat loudly at the thought of propos-
ing an unconventional meeting with this lovely and virginal
being. But the tumult in his heart gave him courage.

After a few friendly and well-received remarks on general
subjects, he laid his card by her hand on the counter.

"Will you please pardon me," he said, "if I seem too bold;
but I earnestly hope you will allow me the pleasure of seeing
you again. There is my name; I assure you that it is with the
greatest respect that I ask the favor of becoming one of your
fr—— acquaintances. May I not hope for the privilege?"

Masie knew men—especially men who buy gloves. Without
hesitation she looked him frankly and smilingly in the eyes,
and said:

"Sure. I guess you're all right. I don't usually go out with
strange gentlemen, though. It ain't quite ladylike. When
should you want to see me again?"

"As soon as I may," said Carter. "If you would allow me to
call at your home, I——"

Masie laughed musically. "Oh, gee, no!" she said, emphat-

ically. "If you could see our flat once! There's five of us in
three rooms. I'd just like to see ma's face if I was to bring a
gentleman friend there!"

"Anywhere, then," said the enamored Carter, "that will be
convenient to you."

"Say," suggested Masie, with a bright-idea look in her
peach-blow face; "I guess Thursday night will about suit me.
Suppose you come to the corner of Eighth Avenue and Forty-
eighth Street at 7:30. I live right near the corner. But I've got
to be back home by eleven. Ma never lets me stay out after
eleven."

Carter promised gratefully to keep the tryst, and then hastened to his mother, who was looking about for him to ratify
her purchase of a bronze Diana.

A salesgirl, with small eyes and an obtuse nose, strolled near
Masie, with a friendly leer.

"Did you make a hit with his nobs, Masie?" she asked,
familiarly.

"The gentleman asked permission to call," answered Masie,
with the grand air, as she slipped Carter's card into the bosom
of her waist.

"Permission to call!" echoed small eyes, with a snigger. "Did
he say anything about dinner in the Waldorf and a spin in
his auto afterward?"

"Oh, cheese it!" said Masie, wearily. "You've been used to
swell things, I don't think. You've had a swelled head ever
since that hose-cart driver took you out to a chop suey joint.
No, he never mentioned the Waldorf; but there's a Fifth Avenue address on his card, and if he buys the supper you can
bet your life there won't be no pigtail on the waiter what
takes the order."

As Carter glided away from the Biggest Store with his
mother in his electric runabout, he bit his lip with a dull pain
at his heart. He knew that love had come to him for the first

time in all the twenty-nine years of his life. And that the object of it should make so readily an appointment with him at a street corner, though it was a step toward his desires, tortured him with misgivings.

Carter did not know the shopgirl. He did not know that her home is often either a scarcely habitable tiny room or a domicile filled to overflowing with kith and kin. The street corner is her parlor, the park is her drawing room; the avenue is her garden walk; yet for the most part she is as inviolate mistress of herself in them as is my lady inside her tapestried chamber.

One evening at dusk, two weeks after their first meeting, Carter and Masie strolled arm-in-arm into a little, dimly-lit park. They found a bench, tree-shadowed and secluded, and sat there.

For the first time his arm stole gently around her. Her golden-bronze head slid restfully against his shoulder.

"Gee!" sighed Masie, thankfully. "Why didn't you ever think of that before?"

"Masie," said Carter, earnestly, "you surely know that I love you. I ask you sincerely to marry me. You know me well enough by this time to have no doubts of me. I want you, and I must have you. I care nothing for the difference in our stations."

"What is the difference?" asked Masie, curiously.

"Well, there isn't any," said Carter, quickly, "except in the minds of foolish people. It is in my power to give you a life of luxury. My social position is beyond dispute, and my means are ample."

"They all say that," remarked Masie. "It's the kid they all give you. I suppose you really work in a delicatessen or follow the races. I ain't as green as I look."

"I can furnish you all the proofs you want," said Carter,

gently. "And I want you, Masie. I loved you the first day I saw you."

"They all do," said Masie, with an amused laugh, "to hear 'em talk. If I could meet a man that got stuck on me the third time he'd seen me I think I'd get mashed on him."

"Please don't say such things," pleaded Carter. "Listen to me, dear. Ever since I first looked into your eyes you have been the only woman in the world for me."

"Oh, ain't you the kidder!" smiled Masie. "How many other girls did you ever tell that?"

But Carter persisted. And at length he reached the flimsy, fluttering little soul of the shopgirl that existed somewhere deep down in her lovely bosom. His words penetrated the heart whose very lightness was its safest armor. She looked up at him with eyes that saw. And a warm glow visited her cool cheeks. Tremblingly, awfully, her moth wings closed, and she seemed about to settle upon the flower of love. Some faint glimmer of life and its possibilities on the other side of her glove counter dawned upon her. Carter felt the change and crowded the opportunity.

"Marry me, Masie," he whispered, softly, "and we will go away from this ugly city to beautiful ones. We will forget work and business, and life will be one long holiday. I know where I should take you—I have been there often. Just think of a shore where summer is eternal, where the waves are always rippling on the lovely beach and the people are happy and free as children. We will sail to those shores and remain there as long as you please. In one of those far-away cities there are grand and lovely palaces and towers full of beautiful pictures and statues. The streets of the city are water, and one travels about in——"

"I know," said Masie, sitting up suddenly. "Gondolas."

"Yes," smiled Carter.

"I thought so," said Masie.

"And then," continued Carter, "we will travel on and see whatever we wish in the world. After the European cities we will visit India and the ancient cities there, and ride on elephants and see the wonderful temples of the Hindoos and the Brahmins and the Japanese gardens and the camel trains and chariot races in Persia, and all the queer sights of foreign countries. Don't you think you would like it, Masie?"

Masie rose to her feet.

"I think we had better be going home," she said, coolly. "It's getting late."

Carter humored her. He had come to know her varying, thistle-down moods, and that it was useless to combat them. But he felt a certain happy triumph. He had held for a moment, though but by a silken thread, the soul of his wild Psyche, and hope was stronger within him. Once she had folded her wings and her cool hand had closed about his own.

At the Biggest Store the next day Masie's chum, Lulu, waylaid her in an angle of the counter.

"How are you and your swell friend making it?" she asked.

"Oh, him?" said Masie, patting her side curls. "He ain't in it any more. Say, Lu, what do you think that fellow wanted me to do?"

"Go on the stage?" guessed Lulu, breathlessly.

"Nit; he's too cheap a guy for that. He wanted me to marry him and go down to Coney Island for a wedding tour!"

The Defeat of the City

ROBERT WALMSLEY's descent upon the city resulted in a Kilkenny struggle. He came out of the fight victor by a fortune and a reputation. On the other hand, he was swallowed up by the city. The city gave him what he demanded and then branded him with its brand. It remodelled, cut, trimmed, and stamped him to the pattern it approves. It opened its social gates to him and shut him in on a close-cropped, formal lawn with the select herd of ruminants. In dress, habits, manners, provincialism, routine, and narrowness he acquired that charming insolence, that irritating completeness, that sophisticated crassness, that over-balanced poise that makes the Manhattan gentleman so delightfully small in his greatness.

One of the up-state rural counties pointed with pride to the successful young metropolitan lawyer as a product of its soil. Six years earlier this country had removed the wheat straw from between its huckleberry-stained teeth and emitted a derisive and bucolic laugh as old man Walmsley's freckle-faced "Bob" abandoned the certain three-per-diem meals of the one-horse farm for the discontinuous quick lunch counters of the three-ringed metropolis. At the end of the six years no murder trial, coaching party, automobile accident or cotillion was complete in which the name of Robert Walmsley did not figure. Tailors waylaid him in the street to get a new wrinkle from the cut of his unwrinkled trousers. Hyphenated fellows in the clubs and members of the oldest subpœnaed families were glad to clap him on the back and allow him three letters of his name.

But the Matterhorn of Robert Walmsley's success was not scaled until he married Alicia Van Der Pool. I cite the Matterhorn, for just so high and cool and white and inaccessible was this daughter of the old burghers. The social Alps that ranged about her—over whose bleak passes a thousand climbers struggled—reached only to her knees. She towered in her own atmosphere, serene, chaste, prideful, wading in no fountains, dining no monkeys, breeding no dogs for bench shows. She was a Van Der Pool. Fountains were made to play for her; monkeys were made for other people's ancestors; dogs, she understood, were created to be companions of blind persons and objectionable characters who smoked pipes.

This was the Matterhorn that Robert Walmsley accomplished. If he found, with the good poet with the game foot and artificially curled hair, that he who ascends to mountain tops will find the loftiest peaks most wrapped in clouds and snow, he concealed his chilblains beneath a brave and smiling exterior. He was a lucky man and knew it, even though he were imitating the Spartan boy with an ice-cream freezer beneath his doublet frappéing the region of his heart.

After a brief wedding tour abroad, the couple returned to create a decided ripple in the calm cistern (so placid and cool and sunless it is) of the best society. They entertained at their red brick mausoleum of ancient greatness in an old square that is a cemetery of crumbled glory. And Robert Walmsley was proud of his wife; although while one of his hands shook his guests' the other held tightly to his alpenstock and thermometer.

One day Alicia found a letter written to Robert by his mother. It was an unerudite letter, full of crops and motherly love and farm notes. It chronicled the health of the pig and the recent red calf, and asked concerning Robert's in return. It was a letter direct from the soil, straight from home, full of biographies of bees, tales of turnips, pæans of new-laid eggs, neglected parents and the slump in dried apples.

"Why have I not been shown your mother's letters?" asked Alicia. There was always something in her voice that made you think of lorgnettes, of accounts at Tiffany's, of sledges smoothly gliding on the trail from Dawson to Forty Mile, of the tinkling of pendent prisms on your grandmothers' chandeliers, of snow lying on a convent roof, of a police sergeant refusing bail. "Your mother," continued Alicia, "invites us to make a visit to the farm. I have never seen a farm. We will go there for a week or two, Robert."

"We will," said Robert, with the grand air of an associate Supreme Justice concurring in an opinion. "I did not lay the invitation before you because I thought you would not care to go. I am much pleased at your decision."

"I will write to her myself," answered Alicia, with a faint foreshadowing of enthusiasm. "Félice shall pack my trunks at once. Seven, I think, will be enough. I do not suppose that your mother entertains a great deal. Does she give many house parties?"

Robert arose, and as attorney for rural places filed a demurrer against six of the seven trunks. He endeavored to define, picture, elucidate, set forth and describe a farm. His own words sounded strange in his ears. He had not realized how thoroughly urbsidized he had become.

A week passed and found them landed at the little country station five hours out from the city. A grinning, stentorian, sarcastic youth driving a mule to a spring wagon hailed Robert savagely.

"Hallo, Mr. Walmsley. Found your way back at last, have you? Sorry I couldn't bring in the automobile for you, but dad's bull-tonguing the ten-acre clover patch with it to-day. Guess you'll excuse my not wearing a dress suit over to meet you—it ain't six o'clock yet, you know."

"I'm glad to see you, Tom," said Robert, grasping his brother's hand. "Yes, I've found my way at last. You've a right to say 'at last.' It's been over two years since the last time. But it will be oftener after this, my boy."

Alicia, cool in the summer heat as an Arctic wraith, white as a Norse snow maiden in her flimsy muslin and fluttering lace parasol, came round the corner of the station; and Tom was stripped of his assurance. He became chiefly eyesight clothed in blue jeans, and on the homeward drive to the mule alone did he confide in language the inwardness of his thoughts.

They drove homeward. The low sun dropped a spend-thrift flood of gold upon the fortunate fields of wheat. The cities were far away. The road lay curling around wood and dale and hill like a ribbon lost from the robe of careless summer. The wind followed like a whinnying colt in the track of Phœbus's steeds.

By and by the farmhouse peeped gray out of its faithful grove; they saw the long lane with its convoy of walnut trees running from the road to the house; they smelled the wild rose and the breath of cool, damp willows in the creek's bed. And then in unison all the voices of the soil began a chant addressed to the soul of Robert Walmsley. Out of the tilted aisles of the dim wood they came hollowly; they chirped and buzzed from the parched grass; they trilled from the ripples of the creek ford; they floated up in clear Pan's pipe notes from the dimming meadows; the whippoorwills joined in as they pursued midges in the upper air, slow-going cow-bells struck out a homely accompaniment—and this was what each one said: "You've found your way back at last, have you?"

The old voices of the soil spoke to him. Leaf and bud and blossom conversed with him in the old vocabulary of his careless youth—the inanimate things, the familiar stones and rails, the gates and furrows and roofs and turns of road had an eloquence, too, and a power in the transformation. The country had smiled and he had felt the breath of it, and his heart was drawn as if in a moment back to his old love. The city was far away.

This rural atavism, then, seized Robert Walmsley and possessed him. A queer thing he noticed in connection with it was that Alicia, sitting at his side, suddenly seemed to him a stranger. She did not belong to this recurrent phase. Never before had she seemed so remote, so colorless and high—so intangible and unreal. And yet he had never admired her more than when she sat there by him in the rickety spring wagon, chiming no more with his mood and with her environment than the Matterhorn chimes with a peasant's cabbage garden.

That night when the greetings and the supper were over, the entire family, including Buff, the yellow dog, bestrewed itself upon the front porch. Alicia, not haughty but silent, sat in the shadow dressed in an exquisite pale-gray tea gown. Robert's mother discoursed to her happily concerning marmalade and lumbago. Tom sat on the top step; Sisters Millie and Pam on the lowest step to catch the lightning bugs. Mother had the willow rocker. Father sat in the big armchair with one of its arms gone. Buff sprawled in the middle of the porch in everybody's way. The twilight pixies and pucks stole forth unseen and plunged other poignant shafts of memory into the heart of Robert. A rural madness entered his soul. The city was far away.

Father sat without his pipe, writhing in his heavy boots, a sacrifice to rigid courtesy. Robert shouted: "No, you don't!" He fetched the pipe and lit it; he seized the old gentleman's boots and tore them off. The last one slipped suddenly, and Mr. Robert Walmsley, of Washington Square, tumbled off the porch backward with Buff on top of him, howling fearfully. Tom laughed sarcastically.

Robert tore off his coat and vest and hurled them into a lilac bush.

"Come out here, you landlubber," he cried to Tom, "and I'll put grass seed on your back. I think you called me a 'dude' a while ago. Come along and cut your capers."

Tom understood the invitation and accepted it with delight. Three times they wrestled on the grass, "side holds," even as the giants of the mat. And twice was Tom forced to bite grass at the hands of the distinguished lawyer. Dishevelled, panting, each still boasting of his own prowess, they stumbled back to the porch. Millie cast a pert reflection upon the qualities of a city brother. In an instant Robert had secured a horrid katydid in his fingers and bore down upon her. Screaming wildly, she fled up the lane pursued by the avenging glass of form. A quarter of a mile and they returned, she full of apology to the victorious "dude." The rustic mania possessed him unabatedly.

"I can do up a cowpenful of you slow hayseeds," he proclaimed, vaingloriously. "Bring on your bulldogs, your hired men, and your log-rollers."

He turned handsprings on the grass that prodded Tom to envious sarcasm. And then, with a whoop, he clattered to the rear and brought back Uncle Ike, a battered colored retainer of the family, with his banjo, and strewed sand on the porch and danced "Chicken in the Bread Tray" and did buck-and-wing wonders for half an hour longer. Incredibly wild and boisterous things he did. He sang, he told stories that set all but one shrieking, he played the yokel, the humorous clod-hopper; he was mad, mad with the revival of the old life in his blood.

He became so extravagant that once his mother sought gently to reprove him. Then Alicia moved as though she were about to speak, but she did not. Through it all she sat immovable, a slim, white spirit in the dusk that no man might question or read.

By and by she asked permission to ascend to her room, saying that she was tired. On her way she passed Robert. He was standing in the door, the figure of vulgar comedy, with ruffled hair, reddened face and unpardonable confusion of attire—no trace there of the immaculate Robert Walmsley, the courted clubman and ornament of select circles. He was doing a conjuring trick with some household utensils, and the family, now won over to him without exception, was beholding him with worshipful admiration.

As Alicia passed in Robert started suddenly. He had forgotten for the moment that she was present. Without a glance at him she went on upstairs.

After that the fun grew quiet. An hour passed in talk, and then Robert went up himself.

She was standing by the window when he entered their room. She was still clothed as when they were on the porch. Outside and crowding against the window was a giant apple tree, full blossomed.

Robert sighed and went near the window. He was ready to meet his fate. A confessed vulgarian, he foresaw the verdict of justice in the shape of that still, whiteclad form. He knew the rigid lines that a Van Der Pool would draw. He was a peasant gambolling indecorously in the valley, and the pure, cold, white, unthawed summit of the Matterhorn could not but frown on him. He had been unmasked by his own actions. All the polish, the poise, the form that the city had given him had fallen from him like an ill-fitting mantle at the first breath of a country breeze. Dully he awaited the approaching condemnation.

"Robert," said the calm, cool voice of his judge, "I thought I married a gentleman."

Yes, it was coming. And yet, in the face of it, Robert Walmsley was eagerly regarding a certain branch of the apple tree upon which he used to climb out of that very window. He believed he could do it now. He wondered how many blossoms there were on the tree—ten millions? But here was someone speaking again:

"I thought I married a gentleman," the voice went on, "but——"

Why had she come and was standing so close by his side?

"But I find that I have married"—was this Alicia talking?—"something better—a man—Bob, dear, kiss me, won't you?"

The city was far away.

Squaring the Circle

AT THE HAZARD of wearying youth this tale of vehement emotions must be prefaced by a discourse on geometry.

Nature moves in circles; Art in straight lines. The natural is rounded; the artificial is made up of angles. A man lost in the snow wanders, in spite of himself, in perfect circles; the city man's feet, denaturalized by rectangular streets and floors, carry him ever away from himself.

The round eyes of childhood typify innocence; the narrow line of the flirt's optic proves the invasion of art. The horizontal mouth is the mark of determined cunning; who has not read Nature's most spontaneous lyric in lips rounded for the candid kiss?

Beauty is Nature in perfection; circularity is its chief attribute. Behold the full moon, the enchanting gold ball, the domes of splendid temples, the huckleberry pie, the wedding ring, the circus ring, the ring for the waiter, and the "round" of drinks.

On the other hand, straight lines show that Nature has been deflected. Imagine Venus's girdle transformed into a "straight front"!

When we begin to move in straight lines and turn sharp corners our natures begin to change. The consequence is that Nature, being more adaptive than Art, tries to conform to its sterner regulations. The result is often a rather curious product—for instance: A prize chrysanthemum, wood alcohol whiskey, a Republican Missouri, cauliflower *au gratin*, and a New Yorker.

Nature is lost quickest in a big city. The cause is geometrical, not moral. The straight lines of its streets and architecture, the rectangularity of its laws and social customs, the undeviating pavements, the hard, severe, depressing, uncompromising rules of all its ways—even of its recreation and sports—coldly exhibit a sneering defiance of the curved line of Nature.

Wherefore, it may be said that the big city has demonstrated the problem of squaring the circle. And it may be added that this mathematical introduction precedes an account of the fate of a Kentucky feud that was imported to the city that has a habit of making its importations conform to its angles.

The feud began in the Cumberland Mountains between the Folwell and the Harkness families. The first victim of the homespun vendetta was a 'possum dog belonging to Bill Harkness. The Harkness family evened up this dire loss by laying out the chief of the Folwell clan. The Folwells were prompt at repartee. They oiled up their squirrel rifles and made it feasible for Bill Harkness to follow his dog to a land where the 'possums come down when treed without the stroke of an ax.

The feud flourished for forty years. Harknesses were shot at the plough, through their lamp-lit cabin windows, coming from camp-meetings, asleep, in duello, sober and otherwise, singly and in family groups, prepared and unprepared. Folwells had the branches of their family tree lopped off in similar ways, as the traditions of their country prescribed and authorized.

By and by the pruning left but a single member of each family. And then Cal Harkness, probably reasoning that further pursuance of the controversy would give a too-decided personal flavor to the feud, suddenly disappeared from the relieved Cumberlands, baulking the avenging hand of Sam, the ultimate opposing Folwell.

A year afterward Sam Folwell learned that his hereditary,

unsuppressed enemy was living in New York City. Sam turned over the big iron wash-pot in the yard, scraped off some of the soot, which he mixed with lard and shined his boots with the compound. He put on his store clothes of butternut-dyed black, a white shirt and collar, and packed a carpet-sack with Spartan *lingerie*. He took his squirrel rifle from its hooks, but put it back again with a sigh. However ethical and plausible the habit might be in the Cumberlands, perhaps New York would not swallow his pose of hunting squirrels among the skyscrapers along Broadway. An ancient but reliable Colt's revolver that he resurrected from a bureau drawer seemed to proclaim itself the pink of weapons for metropolitan adventure and vengeance. This and a hunting-knife in a leather sheath, Sam packed in the carpet-sack. As he started, muleback, for the lowland railroad station the last Folwell turned in his saddle and looked grimly at the little cluster of white-pine slabs in the clump of cedars that marked the Folwell burying-ground.

Sam Folwell arrived in New York in the night. Still moving and living in the free circles of nature, he did not perceive the formidable, pitiless, restless, fierce angles of the great city waiting in the dark to close about the rotundity of his heart and brain and mould him to the form of its millions of re-shaped victims. A cabby picked him out of the whirl, as Sam himself had often picked a nut from a bed of wind-tossed autumn leaves, and whisked him away to a hotel commensurate to his boots and carpet-sack.

On the next morning the last of the Folwells made his sortie into the city that sheltered the last Harkness. The Colt was thrust beneath his coat and secured by a narrow leather belt; the hunting-knife hung between his shoulder-blades, with the haft an inch below his coat collar. He knew this much —that Cal Harkness drove an express wagon somewhere in that town, and that he, Sam Folwell, had come to kill him.

And as he stepped upon the sidewalk the red came into his eye and the feud-hate into his heart.

The clamor of the central avenues drew him thitherward. He had half expected to see Cal coming down the street in his shirt-sleeves with a jug and a whip in his hand, just as he would have seen him in Frankfort or Laurel City. But an hour went by and Cal did not appear. Perhaps he was waiting in ambush, to shoot him from a door or a window. Sam kept a sharp eye on doors and windows for a while.

About noon the city tired of playing with its mouse and suddenly squeezed him with its straight lines.

Sam Folwell stood where two great, rectangular arteries of the city cross. He looked four ways, and saw the world hurled from its orbit and reduced by spirit level and tape to an edged and cornered plane. All life moved on tracks, in grooves, according to system, within boundaries, by rote. The root of life was the cube root; the measure of existence was square measure. People streamed by in straight rows; the horrible din and crash stupefied him.

Sam leaned against the sharp corner of a stone building. Those faces passed him by thousands, and none of them were turned toward him. A sudden foolish fear that he had died and was a spirit, and that they could not see him, seized him. And then the city smote him with loneliness.

A fat man dropped out of the stream and stood a few feet distant, waiting for his car. Sam crept to his side and shouted above the tumult into his ear:

"The Rankinses' hogs weighed more'n ourn a whole passel, but the mash in thar neighborhood was a fine chance better than what it was down——"

The fat man moved away unostentatiously, and bought roasted chestnuts to cover his alarm.

Sam felt the need of a drop of mountain dew. Across the street men passed in and out through swinging doors. Brief glimpses could be had of a glistening bar and its bedeckings. The feudist crossed and essayed to enter. Again had Art eliminated the familiar circle. Sam's hand found no door-knob—it slid, in vain, over a rectangular brass plate and polished oak with nothing even so large as a pin's head upon which his fingers might close.

Abashed, reddened, heartbroken, he walked away from the bootless door and sat upon a step. A locust club tickled him in the ribs.

"Take a walk for yourself," said the policeman. "You've been loafing around here long enough."

At the next corner a shrill whistle sounded in Sam's ear. He wheeled around and saw a black-browed villain scowling at him over peanuts heaped on a steaming machine. He started across the street. An immense engine, running without mules, with the voice of a bull and the smell of a smoky lamp, whizzed past, grazing his knee. A cab-driver bumped him with a hub and explained to him that kind words were invented to be used on other occasions. A motorman clanged his bell wildly and, for once in his life, corroborated a cab-driver. A large lady in a changeable silk waist dug an elbow into his back, and a newsy pensively pelted him with banana rinds, murmuring, "I hates to do it—but if anybody seen me let it pass!"

Cal Harkness, his day's work over and his express wagon stabled, turned the sharp edge of the building that, by the cheek of architects, is modelled upon a safety razor. Out of the mass of hurrying people his eye picked up, three yards away, the surviving bloody and implacable foe of his kith and kin.

He stopped short and wavered for a moment, being unarmed and sharply surprised. But the keen mountaineer's eye of Sam Folwell had picked him out.

There was a sudden spring, a ripple in the stream of passers-by and the sound of Sam's voice crying:

"Howdy, Cal! I'm durned glad to see ye."

And in the angles of Broadway, Fifth Avenue, and Twenty-third Street the Cumberland feudists shook hands.

Transients in Arcadia

THERE IS A HOTEL on Broadway that has escaped discovery by the summer-resort promoters. It is deep and wide and cool. Its rooms are finished in dark oak of a low temperature. Home-made breezes and deep-green shrubbery give it the delights without the inconveniences of the Adirondacks. One can mount its broad staircases or glide dreamily upward in its aërial elevators, attended by guides in brass buttons, with a serene joy that Alpine climbers have never attained. There is a chef in its kitchen who will prepare for you brook trout better than the White Mountains ever served, sea food that would turn Old Point Comfort—"by Gad, sah!"—green with envy, and Maine venison that would melt the official heart of the game warden.

A few have found out this oasis in the July desert of Manhattan. During that month you will see the hotel's reduced array of guests scattered luxuriously about in the cool twilight of its lofty dining-room, gazing at one another across the snowy waste of unoccupied tables, silently congratulatory.

Superfluous, watchful, pneumatically moving waiters hover near, supplying every want before it is expressed. The temperature is perpetual April. The ceiling is painted in water colors to counterfeit a summer sky across which delicate clouds drift and do not vanish as those of nature do to our regret.

The pleasing, distant roar of Broadway is transformed in the imagination of the happy guests to the noise of a waterfall filling the woods with its restful sound. At every strange footstep the guests turn an anxious ear, fearful lest their retreat be discovered and invaded by the restless pleasure-seekers who are forever hounding Nature to her deepest lairs.

Thus in the depopulated caravansary the little band of connoisseurs jealously hide themselves during the heated season, enjoying to the uttermost the delights of mountain and sea-shore that art and skill have gathered and served to them.

In this July came to the hotel one whose card that she sent to the clerk for her name to be registered read "Mme. Héloise D'Arcy Beaumont."

Madame Beaumont was a guest such as the Hotel Lotus loved. She possessed the fine air of the élite, tempered and sweetened by a cordial graciousness that made the hotel employés her slaves. Bell-boys fought for the honor of answering her ring; the clerks, but for the question of ownership, would have deeded to her the hotel and its contents; the other guests regarded her as the final touch of feminine exclusive-ness and beauty that rendered the entourage perfect.

This super-excellent guest rarely left the hotel. Her habits were consonant with the customs of the discriminating patrons of the Hotel Lotus. To enjoy that delectable hostelry one must forego the city as though it were leagues away. By night a brief excursion to the nearby roofs is in order; but during the torrid day one remains in the umbrageous fast-nesses of the Lotus as a trout hangs poised in the pellucid sanctuaries of his favorite pool.

Though alone in the Hotel Lotus, Madame Beaumont preserved the state of a queen whose loneliness was of position only. She breakfasted at ten, a cool, sweet, leisurely, delicate being who glowed softly in the dimness like a jasmine flower in the dusk.

But at dinner was Madame's glory at its height. She wore a gown as beautiful and immaterial as the mist from an unseen cataract in a mountain gorge. The nomenclature of this gown is beyond the guess of the scribe. Always pale-red roses reposed against its lace-garnished front. It was a gown that the head-waiter viewed with respect and met at the door. You thought of Paris when you saw it, and maybe of mysterious countesses, and certainly of Versailles and rapiers and Mrs. Fiske and rouge-et-noir. There was an untraceable rumor in the Hotel Lotus that Madame was a cosmopolite, and that she was pulling with her slender white hands certain strings between the nations in the favor of Russia. Being a citizeness of the world's smoothest roads it was small wonder that she was quick to recognize in the refined purlieus of the Hotel Lotus the most desirable spot in America for a restful sojourn during the heat of midsummer.

On the third day of Madame Beaumont's residence in the hotel a young man entered and registered himself as a guest. His clothing—to speak of his points in approved order—was quietly in the mode; his features good and regular; his expression that of a poised and sophisticated man of the world. He informed the clerk that he would remain three or four days, inquired concerning the sailing of European steamships, and sank into the blissful inanition of the nonpareil hotel with the contented air of a traveller in his favorite inn.

The young man—not to question the veracity of the register—was Harold Farrington. He drifted into the exclusive and calm current of life in the Lotus so tactfully and silently that not a ripple alarmed his fellow-seekers after rest. He ate in the Lotus and of its patronym, and was lulled into blissful peace with the other fortunate mariners. In one day he acquired his table and his waiter and the fear lest the panting chasers after repose that kept Broadway warm should pounce upon and destroy this contiguous but covert haven.

After dinner on the next day after the arrival of Harold Farrington Madame Beaumont dropped her handkerchief in passing out. Mr. Farrington recovered and returned it without the effusiveness of a seeker after acquaintance.

Perhaps there was a mystic freemasonry between the discriminating guests of the Lotus. Perhaps they were drawn one to another by the fact of their common good fortune in discovering the acme of summer resorts in a Broadway hotel. Words delicate in courtesy and tentative in departure from formality passed between the two. And, as if in the expedient atmosphere of a real summer resort, an acquaintance grew, flowered and fructified on the spot as does the mystic plant of the conjuror. For a few moments they stood on a balcony upon which the corridor ended, and tossed the feathery ball of conversation.

"One tires of the old resorts," said Madame Beaumont, with a faint but sweet smile. "What is the use to fly to the mountains or the seashore to escape noise and dust when the very people that make both follow us there?"

"Even on the ocean," remarked Farrington sadly, "the Philistines be upon you. The most exclusive steamers are getting to be scarcely more than ferry boats. Heaven help us when the summer resorter discovers that the Lotus is further away from Broadway than Thousand Islands or Mackinac."

"I hope our secret will be safe for a week, anyhow," said Madame, with a sigh and a smile. "I do not know where I would go if they should descend upon the dear Lotus. I know of but one place so delightful in summer, and that is the castle of Count Polinski, in the Ural Mountains."

"I hear that Baden-Baden and Cannes are almost deserted this season," said Farrington. "Year by year the old resorts fall in disrepute. Perhaps many others, like ourselves, are seeking out the quiet nooks that are overlooked by the majority."

"I promise myself three days more of this delicious rest," said Madame Beaumont. "On Monday the *Cedric* sails."

Harold Farrington's eyes proclaimed his regret. "I too must leave on Monday," he said, "but I do not go abroad."

Madame Beaumont shrugged one round shoulder in a foreign gesture.

"One cannot hide here forever, charming though it may be. The château has been in preparation for me longer than a month. Those house parties that one must give—what a nuisance! But I shall never forget my week in the Hotel Lotus."

"Nor shall I," said Farrington in a low voice, "and I shall never *forgive* the *Cedric*."

On Sunday evening, three days afterward, the two sat at a little table on the same balcony. A discreet waiter brought ices and small glasses of claret cup.

Madame Beaumont wore the same beautiful evening gown that she had worn each day at dinner. She seemed thoughtful. Near her hand on the table lay a small chatelaine purse. After she had eaten her ice she opened the purse and took out a one-dollar bill.

"Mr. Farrington," she said, with the smile that had won the Hotel Lotus, "I want to tell you something. I'm going to leave before breakfast in the morning, because I've got to go back to my work. I'm behind the hosiery counter at Casey's Mammoth Store, and my vacation's up at eight o'clock tomorrow. That paper dollar is the last cent I'll see till I draw my eight dollars salary next Saturday night. You're a real gentleman, and you've been good to me, and I wanted to tell you before I went.

"I've been saving up out of my wages for a year just for this vacation. I wanted to spend one week like a lady if I never do another one. I wanted to get up when I please instead of having to crawl out at seven every morning; and I wanted to live on the best and be waited on and ring bells for things just like rich folks do. Now I've done it, and I've had the happiest time I ever expect to have in my life. I'm going back to my work and my little hall bedroom satisfied for another year. I wanted to tell you about it, Mr. Farrington, because I—I thought you kind of liked me, and I—I liked you. But, oh, I couldn't help deceiving you up till now, for it was all just like a fairy tale to me. So I talked about Europe and the things I've read about in other countries, and made you think I was a great lady.

"This dress I've got on—it's the only one I have that's fit to wear—I bought from O'Dowd & Levinsky on the instalment plan.

"Seventy-five dollars is the price, and it was made to measure. I paid $10 down, and they're to collect $1 a week till it's paid for. That'll be about all I have to say, Mr. Farrington, except that my name is Mamie Siviter instead of Madame Beaumont, and I thank you for your attentions. This dollar will pay the instalment due on the dress tomorrow. I guess I'll go up to my room now."

Harold Farrington listened to the recital of the Lotus's loveliest guest with an impassive countenance. When she had concluded he drew a small book like a checkbook from his coat pocket. He wrote upon a blank form in this with a stub of pencil, tore out the leaf, tossed it over to his companion and took up the paper dollar.

"I've got to go to work, too, in the morning," he said, "and I might as well begin now. There's a receipt for the dollar instalment. I've been a collector for O'Dowd & Levinsky for three years. Funny, ain't it, that you and me both had the same idea about spending our vacation? I've always wanted to put up at a swell hotel, and I saved up out of my twenty per, and did it. Say, Mame, how about a trip to Coney Saturday night on the boat—what?"

The face of the pseudo Madame Héloise D'Arcy Beaumont beamed.

"Oh, you bet I'll go, Mr. Farrington. The store closes at twelve on Saturdays. I guess Coney'll be all right even if we did spend a week with the swells."

Below the balcony the sweltering city growled and buzzed in the July night. Inside the Hotel Lotus the tempered, cool shadows reigned, and the solicitous waiter single-footed near the low windows, ready at a nod to serve Madame and her escort.

At the door of the elevator Farrington took his leave, and Madame Beaumont made her last ascent. But before they reached the noiseless cage he said: "Just forget that 'Harold Farrington,' will you?—McManus is the name—James McManus. Some call me Jimmy."

"Good-night, Jimmy," said Madame.

The Trimmed Lamp

OF COURSE there are two sides to the question. Let us look at the other. We often hear "shop-girls" spoken of. No such persons exist. There are girls who work in shops. They make their living that way. But why turn their occupation into an adjective? Let us be fair. We do not refer to the girls who live on Fifth Avenue as "marriage-girls."

Lou and Nancy were chums. They came to the big city to find work because there was not enough to eat at their homes to go around. Nancy was nineteen; Lou was twenty. Both were pretty, active country girls who had no ambition to go on the stage.

The little cherub that sits up aloft guided them to a cheap and respectable boarding-house. Both found positions and became wage-earners. They remained chums. It is at the end of six months that I would beg you to step forward and be introduced to them. Meddlesome Reader: My Lady Friends, Miss Nancy and Miss Lou. While you are shaking hands please take notice—cautiously—of their attire. Yes, cautiously; for they are as quick to resent a stare as a lady in a box at the horse show is.

Lou is a piece-work ironer in a hand laundry. She is clothed in a badly fitting purple dress, and her hat plume is four inches too long; but her ermine muff and scarf cost $25, and its fellow beasts will be ticketed in the windows at $7.98 before the season is over. Her cheeks are pink, and her light blue eyes bright. Contentment radiates from her.

Nancy you would call a shop-girl—because you have the habit. There is no type; but a perverse generation is always seeking a type; so this is what the type should be. She has the high-ratted pompadour and the exaggerated straight-front. Her skirt is shoddy, but has the correct flare. No furs protect her against the bitter spring air, but she wears her short broadcloth jacket as jauntily as though it were Persian lamb! On her face and in her eyes, remorseless type-seeker, is the typical shop-girl expression. It is a look of silent but contemptuous revolt against cheated womanhood; of sad prophecy of the vengeance to come. When she laughs her loudest the look is still there. The same look can be seen in the eyes of Russian peasants; and those of us left will see it some day on Gabriel's face when he comes to blow us up. It is a look that should wither and abash man; but he has been known to smirk at it and offer flowers—with a string tied to them.

Now lift your hat and come away, while you receive Lou's

cheery "See you again," and the sardonic, sweet smile of Nancy that seems, somehow, to miss you and go fluttering like a white moth up over the housetops to the stars.

The two waited on the corner for Dan. Dan was Lou's steady company. Faithful? Well, he was on hand when Mary would have had to hire a dozen subpœna servers to find her lamb.

"Ain't you cold, Nancy?" said Lou. "Say, what a chump you are for working in that old store for $8 a week! I made $18.50 last week. Of course ironing ain't as swell work as selling lace behind a counter, but it pays. None of us ironers make less than $10. And I don't know that it's any less respectful work, either."

"You can have it," said Nancy, with uplifted nose. "I'll take my eight a week and hall bedroom. I like to be among nice things and swell people. And look what a chance I've got! Why, one of our glove girls married a Pittsburgh—a steel maker, or blacksmith or something—the other day worth a million dollars. I'll catch a swell myself some time. I ain't bragging on my looks or anything; but I'll take my chances where there's big prizes offered. What show would a girl have in a laundry?"

"Why, that's where I met Dan," said Lou, triumphantly. "He came in for his Sunday shirt and collars and saw me at the first board, ironing. We all try to get to work at the first board. Ella Maginnis was sick that day, and I had her place. He said he noticed my arms first, how round and white they was. I had my sleeves rolled up. Some nice fellows come into laundries. You can tell 'em by their bringing their clothes in suit cases, and turning in the door sharp and sudden."

"How can you wear a waist like that, Lou?" said Nancy, gazing down at the offending article with sweet scorn in her heavy-lidded eyes. "It shows fierce taste."

"This waist?" said Lou, with wide-eyed indignation. "Why,

I paid $16 for this waist. It's worth twenty-five. A woman left it to be laundered, and never called for it. The boss sold it to me. It's got yards and yards of hand embroidery on it. Better talk about that ugly, plain thing you've got on."

"This ugly, plain thing," said Nancy, calmly, "was copied from one that Mrs. Van Alstyne Fisher was wearing. The girls say her bill in the store last year was $12,000. I made mine, myself. It cost me $1.50. Ten feet away you couldn't tell it from hers."

"Oh, well," said Lou, good-naturedly, "if you want to starve and put on airs, go ahead. But I'll take my job and good wages; and after hours give me something as fancy and attractive to wear as I am able to buy."

But just then Dan came—a serious young man with a ready-made necktie, who had escaped the city's brand of frivolity—an electrician earning $30 per week who looked upon Lou with the sad eyes of Romeo, and thought her embroidered waist a web in which any fly should delight to be caught.

"My friend, Mr. Owens—shake hands with Miss Danforth," said Lou.

"I'm mighty glad to know you, Miss Danforth," said Dan, with outstretched hand. "I've heard Lou speak of you so often."

"Thanks," said Nancy, touching his fingers with the tips of her cool ones, "I've heard her mention you—a few times."

Lou giggled.

"Did you get that handshake from Mrs. Van Alstyne Fisher, Nance?" she asked.

"If I did, you can feel safe in copying it," said Nancy.

"Oh, I couldn't use it at all. It's too stylish for me. It's intended to set off diamond rings, that high shake is. Wait till I get a few and then I'll try it."

"Learn it first," said Nancy, wisely, "and you'll be more likely to get the rings."

"Now, to settle this argument," said Dan, with his ready, cheerful smile, "let me make a proposition. As I can't take both of you up to Tiffany's and do the right thing, what do you say to a little vaudeville? I've got the tickets. How about looking at stage diamonds since we can't shake hands with the real sparklers?"

The faithful squire took his place close to the curb; Lou next, a little peacocky in her bright and pretty clothes; Nancy on the inside, slender, and soberly clothed as the sparrow, but with the true Van Alstyne Fisher walk—thus they set out for their evening's moderate diversion.

I do not suppose that many look upon a great department store as an educational institution. But the one in which Nancy worked was something like that to her. She was surrounded by beautiful things that breathed of taste and refinement. If you live in an atmosphere of luxury, luxury is yours whether your money pays for it, or another's.

The people she served were mostly women whose dress, manners, and position in the social world were quoted as criterions. From them Nancy began to take toll—the best from each according to her view.

From one she would copy and practise a gesture, from another an eloquent lifting of an eyebrow, from others, a manner of walking, of carrying a purse, of smiling, of greeting a friend, of addressing "inferiors in station." From her best beloved model, Mrs. Van Alstyne Fisher, she made requisition for that excellent thing, a soft, low voice as clear as silver and as perfect in articulation as the notes of a thrush. Suffused in the aura of this high social refinement and good breeding, it was impossible for her to escape a deeper effect of it. As good habits are said to be better than good principles, so, perhaps, good manners are better than good habits. The teachings of your parents may not keep alive your New England conscience; but if you sit on a straight-back chair and repeat the words "prisms and pilgrims" forty times the devil will flee from you. And when Nancy spoke in the Van Alstyne Fisher tones she felt the thrill of *noblesse oblige* to her very bones.

There was another source of learning in the great departmental school. Whenever you see three or four shop-girls gather in a bunch and jingle their wire bracelets as an accompaniment to apparently frivolous conversation, do not think that they are there for the purpose of criticizing the way Ethel does her back hair. The meeting may lack the dignity of the deliberative bodies of man; but it has all the importance of the occasion on which Eve and her first daughter first put their heads together to make Adam understand his proper place in the household. It is Woman's Conference for Common Defense and Exchange of Strategical Theories of Attack and Repulse upon and against the World, which is a Stage, and Man, its Audience who Persists in Throwing Bouquets Thereupon. Woman, the most helpless of the young of any animal—with the fawn's grace but without its fleetness; with the bird's beauty but without its power of flight; with the honey-bee's burden of sweetness but without its—— Oh, let's drop that simile—some of us may have been stung.

During this council of war they pass weapons one to another, and exchange stratagems that each has devised and formulated out of the tactics of life.

"I says to 'im," says Sadie, "ain't you the fresh thing! Who do you suppose I am, to be addressing such a remark to me? And what do you think he says back to me?"

The heads, brown, black, flaxen, red, and yellow bob together; the answer is given; and the parry to the thrust is decided upon, to be used by each thereafter in passages-at-arms with the common enemy, man.

Thus Nancy learned the art of defense; and to women successful defense means victory.

The curriculum of a department store is a wide one. Perhaps no other college could have fitted her as well for her life's ambition—the drawing of a matrimonial prize.

Her station in the store was a favored one. The music room was near enough for her to hear and become familiar with the works of the best composers—at least to acquire the familiarity that passed for appreciation in the social world in which she was vaguely trying to set a tentative and aspiring foot. She absorbed the educating influence of art wares, of costly and dainty fabrics, of adornments that are almost culture to women.

The other girls soon became aware of Nancy's ambition. "Here comes your millionaire, Nancy," they would call to her whenever any man who looked the rôle approached her counter. It got to be a habit of men, who were hanging about while their women folk were shopping, to stroll over to the handkerchief counter and dawdle over the cambric squares. Nancy's imitation high-bred air and genuine dainty beauty was what attracted. Many men thus came to display their graces before her. Some of them may have been millionaires; others were certainly no more than their sedulous apes. Nancy learned to discriminate. There was a window at the end of the handkerchief counter; and she could see the rows of vehicles waiting for the shoppers in the street below. She looked and perceived that automobiles differ as well as do their owners.

Once a fascinating gentleman bought four dozen handkerchiefs, and wooed her across the counter with a King Cophetua air. When he had gone one of the girls said:

"What's wrong, Nance, that you didn't warm up to that fellow? He looks the swell article, all right, to me."

"Him?" said Nancy, with her coolest, sweetest, most impersonal, Van Alstyne Fisher smile; "not for mine. I saw him drive up outside. A 12 H. P. machine and an Irish chauffeur! And you saw what kind of handkerchiefs he bought— silk! And he's got dactylis on him. Give me the real thing or nothing, if you please."

Two of the most "refined" women in the store—a forelady and a cashier—had a few "swell gentlemen friends" with whom they now and then dined. Once they included Nancy in an invitation. The dinner took place in a spectacular café whose tables are engaged for New Year's Eve a year in advance. There were two "gentlemen friends"—one without any hair on his head—high living ungrew it; and we can prove it —the other a young man whose worth and sophistication he impressed upon you in two convincing ways—he swore that all the wine was corked; and he wore diamond cuff buttons. This young man perceived irresistible excellencies in Nancy. His taste ran to shop-girls; and here was one that added the voice and manners of his high social world to the franker charms of her own caste. So, on the following day, he appeared in the store and made her a serious proposal of marriage over a box of hemstitched, grass-bleached Irish linens. Nancy declined. A brown pompadour ten feet away had been using her eyes and ears. When the rejected suitor had gone she heaped carboys of upbraidings and horror upon Nancy's head.

"What a terrible little fool you are! That fellow's a millionaire—he's a nephew of old Van Skittles himself. And he was talking on the level, too. Have you gone crazy, Nance?"

"Have I?" said Nancy. "I didn't take him, did I? He isn't a millionaire so hard that you could notice it, anyhow. His family only allows him $20,000 a year to spend. The bald-headed fellow was guying him about it the other night at supper."

The brown pompadour came nearer and narrowed her eyes.

"Say, what do you want?" she inquired, in a voice hoarse for lack of chewing-gum. "Ain't that enough for you? Do you want to be a Mormon, and marry Rockefeller and Gladstone Dowie and the King of Spain and the whole bunch? Ain't $20,000 a year good enough for you?"

Nancy flushed a little under the level gaze of the black, shallow eyes.

"It wasn't altogether the money, Carrie," she explained. "His friend caught him in a rank lie the other night at dinner. It was about some girl he said he hadn't been to the theater with. Well, I can't stand a liar. Put everything together—I don't like him; and that settles it. When I sell out it's not going to be on any bargain day. I've got to have something that sits up in a chair like a man, anyhow. Yes, I'm looking out for a catch; but it's got to be able to do something more than make a noise like a toy bank."

"The physiopathic ward for yours!" said the brown pompadour, walking away.

These high ideas, if not ideals—Nancy continued to cultivate on $8 per week. She bivouacked on the trail of the great unknown "catch" eating her dry bread and tightening her belt day by day. On her face was the faint, soldierly, sweet, grim smile of the preordained man-hunter. The store was her forest; and many times she raised her rifle at game that seemed broad-antlered and big; but always some deep unerring instinct—perhaps of the huntress, perhaps of the woman —made her hold her fire and take up the trail again.

Lou flourished in the laundry. Out of her $18.50 per week she paid $6 for her room and board. The rest went mainly for clothes. Her opportunities for bettering her taste and manners were few compared with Nancy's. In the steaming laundry there was nothing but work, work and her thoughts of the evening pleasures to come. Many costly and showy fabrics passed under her iron; and it may be that her growing fondness for dress was thus transmitted to her through the conducting metal.

When the day's work was over Dan awaited her outside, her faithful shadow in whatever light she stood.

Sometimes he cast an honest and troubled glance at Lou's clothes that increased in conspicuity rather than in style; but this was no disloyalty; he deprecated the attention they called to her in the streets.

And Lou was no less faithful to her chum. There was a law that Nancy should go with them on whatsoever outings they might take. Dan bore the extra burden heartily and in good cheer. It might be said that Lou furnished the color, Nancy the tone, and Dan the weight of the distraction-seeking trio. The escort, in his neat but obviously ready-made suit, his ready-made tie and unfailing, genial, ready-made wit never startled or clashed. He was of that good kind that you are likely to forget while they are present, but remember distinctly after they are gone.

To Nancy's superior taste the flavor of these ready-made pleasures was sometimes a little bitter: but she was young; and youth is a gourmand, when it cannot be a gourmet.

"Dan is always wanting me to marry him right away," Lou told her once. "But why should I? I'm independent. I can do as I please with the money I earn; and he never would agree for me to keep on working afterward. And say, Nance, what do you want to stick to that old store for, and half starve and half dress yourself? I could get you a place in the laundry right now if you'd come. It seems to me that you could afford to be a little less stuck-up if you could make a good deal more money."

"I don't think I'm stuck-up, Lou," said Nancy, "but I'd rather live on half rations and stay where I am. I suppose I've got the habit. It's the chance that I want. I don't expect to be always behind a counter. I'm learning something new every day. I'm right up against refined and rich people all the time—even if I do only wait on them; and I'm not missing any pointers that I see passing around."

"Caught your millionaire yet?" asked Lou with her teasing laugh.

"I haven't selected one yet," answered Nancy. "I've been looking them over."

"Goodness! the idea of picking over 'em! Don't you ever let one get by you, Nance—even if he's a few dollars shy. But of course you're joking—millionaires don't think about working girls like us."

"It might be better for them if they did," said Nancy, with cool wisdom. "Some of us could teach them how to take care of their money."

"If one was to speak to me," laughed Lou, "I know I'd have a duck-fit."

"That's because you don't know any. The only difference between swells and other people is you have to watch 'em closer. Don't you think that red silk lining is just a little bit too bright for that coat, Lou?"

Lou looked at the plain, dull olive jacket of her friend.

"Well, no, I don't—but it may seem so beside that faded-looking thing you've got on."

"This jacket," said Nancy, complacently, "has exactly the cut and fit of one that Mrs. Van Alstyne Fisher was wearing the other day. The material cost me $3.98. I suppose hers cost about $100 more."

"Oh, well," said Lou, lightly, "it don't strike me as millionaire bait. Shouldn't wonder if I catch one before you do, anyway."

Truly it would have taken a philosopher to decide upon the values of the theories held by the two friends. Lou, lacking that certain pride and fastidiousness that keeps stores and desks filled with girls working for the barest living, thumped away gaily with her iron in the noisy and stifling laundry. Her wages supported her even beyond the point of comfort; so that her dress profited until sometimes she cast a sidelong glance of impatience at the neat but inelegant apparel of Dan —Dan the constant, the immutable, the undeviating.

As for Nancy, her case was one of tens of thousands. Silk and jewels and laces and ornaments and the perfume and music of the fine world of good-breeding and taste—these were made for woman; they are her equitable portion. Let her keep near them if they are a part of life to her, and if she will. She is no traitor to herself, as Esau was; for she keeps her birthright and the pottage she earns is often very scant.

In this atmosphere Nancy belonged; and she throve in it and ate her frugal meals and schemed over her cheap dresses with a determined and contented mind. She already knew woman; and she was studying man, the animal, both as to his habits and eligibility. Some day she would bring down the game that she wanted; but she promised herself it would be what seemed to her the biggest and the best, and nothing smaller.

Thus she kept her lamp trimmed and burning to receive the bridegroom when he should come.

But another lesson she learned, perhaps unconsciously. Her standard of values began to shift and change. Sometimes the dollar-mark grew blurred in her mind's eye, and shaped itself into letters that spelled such words as "truth" and "honor" and now and then just "kindness." Let us make a likeness of one who hunts the moose or elk in some mighty wood. He sees a little dell, mossy and embowered, where a rill trickles, babbling to him of rest and comfort. At these times the spear of Nimrod himself grows blunt.

So, Nancy wondered sometimes if Persian lamb was always quoted at its market value by the hearts that it covered.

One Thursday evening Nancy left the store and turned across Sixth Avenue westward to the laundry. She was expected to go with Lou and Dan to a musical comedy.

Dan was just coming out of the laundry when she arrived. There was a queer, strained look on his face.

"I thought I would drop around to see if they had heard from her," he said.

"Heard from who?" asked Nancy. "Isn't Lou there?"

"I thought you knew," said Dan. "She hasn't been here or at the house where she lived since Monday. She moved all her things from there. She told one of the girls in the laundry she might be going to Europe."

"Hasn't anybody seen her anywhere?" asked Nancy.

Dan looked at her with his jaws set grimly, and a steely gleam in his steady gray eyes.

"They told me in the laundry," he said, harshly, "that they saw her pass yesterday—in an automobile. With one of the millionaires, I suppose, that you and Lou were forever busying your brains about."

For the first time Nancy quailed before a man. She laid her hand that trembled slightly on Dan's sleeve.

"You've no right to say such a thing to me, Dan—as if I had anything to do with it!"

"I didn't mean it that way," said Dan, softening. He fumbled in his vest pocket.

"I've got the tickets for the show to-night," he said, with a gallant show of lightness. "If you——"

Nancy admired pluck whenever she saw it.

"I'll go with you, Dan," she said.

Three months went by before Nancy saw Lou again.

At twilight one evening the shop-girl was hurrying home along the border of a little quiet park. She heard her name called, and wheeled about in time to catch Lou rushing into her arms.

After the first embrace they drew their heads back as serpents do, ready to attack or to charm, with a thousand questions trembling on their swift tongues. And then Nancy noticed that prosperity had descended upon Lou, manifesting itself in costly furs, flashing gems, and creations of the tailor's art.

"You little fool!" cried Lou, loudly and affectionately. "I see you are still working in that store, and as shabby as ever. And how about that big catch you were going to make—nothing doing yet, I suppose?"

And then Lou looked, and saw that something better than prosperity had descended upon Nancy—something that shone brighter than gems in her eyes and redder than a rose in her cheeks, and that danced like electricity anxious to be loosed from the tip of her tongue.

"Yes, I'm still in the store," said Nancy, "but I'm going to leave it next week. I've made my catch—the biggest catch in the world. You won't mind now, Lou, will you?—I'm going to be married to Dan—to Dan!—he's my Dan now—why, Lou!"

Around the corner of the park strolled one of those new-crop, smooth-faced young policemen that are making the force more endurable—at least to the eye. He saw a woman with an expensive fur coat and diamond-ringed hands crouching down against the iron fence of the park sobbing turbulently, while a slender, plainly dressed working girl leaned close, trying to console her. But the Gibsonian cop, being of the new order, passed on, pretending not to notice, for he was wise enough to know that these matters are beyond help so far as the power he represents is concerned, though he rap the pavement with his nightstick till the sound goes up to the furthermost stars.

The Pendulum

"EIGHTY-FIRST STREET—let 'em out, please," yelled the shepherd in blue.

A flock of citizen sheep scrambled out and another flock scrambled aboard. Ding-ding! The cattle cars of the Manhattan Elevated rattled away, and John Perkins drifted down the stairway of the station with the released flock.

John walked slowly toward his flat. Slowly, because in the lexicon of his daily life there was no such word as "perhaps." There are no surprises awaiting a man who has been married two years and lives in a flat. As he walked John Perkins prophesied to himself with gloomy and downtrodden cynicism the foregone conclusions of the monotonous day.

Katy would meet him at the door with a kiss flavored with cold cream and butter-scotch. He would remove his coat, sit upon a macadamized lounge and read, in the evening paper, of Russians and Japs slaughtered by the deadly linotype. For dinner there would be pot roast, a salad flavored with a dressing warranted not to crack or injure the leather, stewed rhubarb and the bottle of strawberry marmalade blushing at the certificate of chemical purity on its label. After dinner Katy would show him the new patch in her crazy quilt that the iceman had cut for her off the end of his four-in-hand. At half-past seven they would spread newspapers over the furniture to catch the pieces of plastering that fell when the fat man in the flat overhead began to take his physical culture exercises. Exactly at eight Hickey & Mooney, of the vaudeville team (unbooked) in the flat across the hall, would yield to the gentle influence of delirium tremens and begin to overturn chairs under the delusion that Hammerstein was pursuing them with a five-hundred-dollar-a-week contract. Then the gent at the window across the air-shaft would get out his flute; the nightly gas leak would steal forth to frolic in the highways; the dumb-waiter would slip off its trolley; the janitor would drive Mrs. Zanowitski's five children once more across the Yalu; the lady with the champagne shoes and the Skye terrier would trip downstairs and paste her Thursday name over her bell and letter-box—and the evening routine of the Frogmore flats would be under way.

John Perkins knew these things would happen. And he knew that at a quarter past eight he would summon his nerve and reach for his hat, and that his wife would deliver this speech in a querulous tone:

"Now, where are you going, I'd like to know, John Perkins?"

"Thought I'd drop up to McCloskey's," he would answer, "and play a game or two of pool with the fellows."

Of late such had been John Perkins's habit. At ten or eleven he would return. Sometimes Katy would be asleep; sometimes waiting up, ready to melt in the crucible of her ire a little more gold plating from the wrought steel chains of matrimony. For these things Cupid will have to answer when he stands at the bar of justice with his victims from the Frogmore flats.

To-night John Perkins encountered a tremendous upheaval of the commonplace when he reached his door. No Katy was there with her affectionate, confectionate kiss. The three rooms seemed in portentous disorder. All about lay her things in confusion. Shoes in the middle of the floor, curling tongs, hair bows, kimonos, powder box, jumbled together on dresser and chairs—this was not Katy's way. With a sinking heart John saw the comb with a curling cloud of her brown hair among its teeth. Some unusual hurry and perturbation must have possessed her, for she always carefully placed these combings in the little blue vase on the mantel to be some day formed into the coveted feminine "rat."

Hanging conspicuously to the gas jet by a string was a folded paper. John seized it. It was a note from his wife running thus:

DEAR JOHN:

I just had a telegram saying mother is very sick. I am going to take the 4:30 train. Brother Sam is going to meet me at the depot there. There is cold mutton in the icebox. I hope it isn't her quinzy again. Pay the milkman 50 cents. She had it bad last spring. Don't forget to write to the company about the gas meter, and your good socks are in the top drawer. I will write to-morrow.

Hastily,
KATY.

Never during their two years of matrimony had he and Katy been separated for a night. John read the note over and over in a dumbfounded way. Here was a break in a routine that had never varied, and it left him dazed.

There on the back of a chair hung, pathetically empty and formless, the red wrapper with black dots that she always wore while getting the meals. Her week-day clothes had been tossed here and there in her haste. A little paper bag of her favorite butter-scotch lay with its string yet unwound. A daily paper sprawled on the floor, gaping rectangularly where a railroad time-table had been clipped from it. Everything in the room spoke of a loss, of an essence gone, of its soul and life departed. John Perkins stood among the dead remains with a queer feeling of desolation in his heart.

He began to set the rooms tidy as well as he could. When he touched her clothes a thrill of something like terror went through him. He had never thought what existence would be without Katy. She had become so thoroughly annealed into his life that she was like the air he breathed—necessary but scarcely noticed. Now, without warning, she was gone, vanished, as completely absent as if she had never existed. Of course it would be only for a few days, or at most a week or two, but it seemed to him as if the very hand of death had pointed a finger at his secure and uneventful home.

John dragged the cold mutton from the icebox, made coffee, and sat down to a lonely meal face to face with the strawberry marmalade's shameless certificate of purity. Bright among withdrawn blessings now appeared to him the ghosts of pot roasts and the salad with tan polish dressing. His home was dismantled. A quinzied mother-in-law had knocked his lares and penates sky-high. After his solitary meal John sat at a front window.

He did not care to smoke. Outside the city roared to him to come join in its dance of folly and pleasure. The night was his. He might go forth unquestioned and thrum the strings of jollity as free as any gay bachelor there. He might carouse and wander and have his fling until dawn if he liked; and there would be no wrathful Katy waiting for him, bearing the chalice that held the dregs of his joy. He might play pool at McCloskey's with his roistering friends until Aurora dimmed the electric bulbs if he chose. The hymeneal strings that had curbed him always when the Frogmore flats had palled upon him were loosened. Katy was gone.

John Perkins was not accustomed to analyzing his emotions. But as he sat in his Katy-bereft 10 x 12 parlor he hit unerringly upon the keynote of his discomfort. He knew now that Katy was necessary to his happiness. His feeling for her, lulled into unconsciousness by the dull round of domesticity, had been sharply stirred by the loss of her presence. Has it not been dinned into us by proverb and sermon and fable that we never prize the music till the sweet-voiced bird has flown—or in other no less florid and true utterances?

"I'm a double-dyed dub," mused John Perkins, "the way I've been treating Katy. Off every night playing pool and bumming with the boys instead of staying home with her. The poor girl here all alone with nothing to amuse her, and me acting that way! John Perkins, you're the worst kind of a shine. I'm going to make it up for the little girl. I'll take her out and let her see some amusement. And I'll cut out the McCloskey gang right from this minute."

Yes, there was the city roaring outside for John Perkins to come dance in the train of Momus. And at McCloskey's the boys were knocking the balls idly into the pockets against the hour for the nightly game. But no primrose way nor clicking cue could woo the remorseful soul of Perkins the bereft. The thing that was his, lightly held and half scorned, had been taken away from him, and he wanted it. Backward to a certain man named Adam, whom the cherubim bounced from the orchard, could Perkins, the remorseful, trace his descent.

Near the right hand of John Perkins stood a chair. On the back of it stood Katy's blue shirtwaist. It still retained something of her contour. Midway of the sleeves were fine, individual wrinkles made by the movements of her arms in working for his comfort and pleasure. A delicate but impelling odor of bluebells came from it. John took it and looked long and soberly at the unresponsive grenadine. Katy had never been unresponsive. Tears:—yes, tears—came into John Perkins's eyes. When she came back things would be different. He would make up for all his neglect. What was life without her?

The door opened. Katy walked in carrying a little hand satchel. John stared at her stupidly.

"My! I'm glad to get back," said Katy. "Ma wasn't sick to amount to anything. Sam was at the depot, and said she just had a little spell, and got all right soon after they telegraphed. So I took the next train back. I'm just dying for a cup of coffee."

Nobody heard the click and rattle of the cogwheels as the

third-floor-front of the Frogmore flats buzzed its machinery back into the Order of Things. A band slipped, a spring was touched, the gear was adjusted and the wheels revolved in their old orbit.

John Perkins looked at the clock. It was 8.15. He reached for his hat and walked to the door.

"Now, where are you going, I'd like to know, John Perkins?" asked Katy, in a querulous tone.

"Thought I'd drop up to McCloskey's," said John, "and play a game or two of pool with the fellows."

Two Thanksgiving Day Gentlemen

THERE is one day that is ours. There is one day when all we Americans who are not self-made go back to the old home to eat saleratus biscuits and marvel how much nearer to the porch the old pump looks than it used to. Bless the day. President Roosevelt gives it to us. We hear some talk of the Puritans, but don't just remember who they were. Bet we can lick 'em, anyhow, if they try to land again. Plymouth Rocks? Well, that sounds more familiar. Lots of us have had to come down to hens since the Turkey Trust got its work in. But somebody in Washington is leaking out advance information to 'em about these Thanksgiving proclamations.

The big city east of the cranberry bogs has made Thanksgiving Day an institution. The last Thursday in November is the only day in the year on which it recognizes the part of America lying across the ferries. It is the one day that is purely American. Yes, a day of celebration, exclusively American.

And now for the story which is to prove to you that we have traditions on this side of the ocean that are becoming

older at a much rapider rate than those of England are—
thanks to our git-up and enterprise.

Stuffy Pete took his seat on the third bench to the right as
you enter Union Square from the east, at the walk opposite
the fountain. Every Thanksgiving Day for nine years he had
taken his seat there promptly at 1 o'clock. For every time he
had done so things had happened to him—Charles Dickensy
things that swelled his waistcoat above his heart, and equally
on the other side.

But to-day Stuffy Pete's appearance at the annual trysting
place seemed to have been rather the result of habit than of
the yearly hunger which, as the philanthropists seem to think,
afflicts the poor at such extended intervals.

Certainly Pete was not hungry. He had just come from a
feast that had left him of his powers barely those of respira-
tion and locomotion. His eyes were like two pale gooseberries
firmly imbedded in a swollen and gravy-smeared mask of
putty. His breath came in short wheezes; a senatorial roll of
adipose tissue denied a fashionable set to his upturned coat
collar. Buttons that had been sewed upon his clothes by kind
Salvation fingers a week before flew like pop-corn, strewing
the earth around him. Ragged he was, with a split shirt front
open to the wishbone; but the November breeze, carrying fine
snowflakes, brought him only a grateful coolness. For Stuffy
Pete was overcharged with the caloric produced by a super-
bountiful dinner, beginning with oysters and ending with
plum pudding, and including (it seemed to him) all the roast
turkey and baked potatoes and chicken salad and squash pie
and ice cream in the world. Wherefore he sat, gorged, and
gazed upon the world with after-dinner contempt.

The meal had been an unexpected one. He was passing a
red brick mansion near the beginning of Fifth Avenue, in
which lived two old ladies of ancient family and a reverence
for traditions. They even denied the existence of New York,

and believed that Thanksgiving Day was declared solely for Washington Square. One of their traditional habits was to station a servant at the postern gate with orders to admit the first hungry wayfarer that came along after the hour of noon had struck, and banquet him to a finish. Stuffy Pete happened to pass by on his way to the park, and the seneschals gathered him in and upheld the custom of the castle.

After Stuffy Pete had gazed straight before him for ten minutes he was conscious of a desire for a more varied field of vision. With a tremendous effort he moved his head slowly to the left. And then his eyes bulged out fearfully, and his breath ceased, and the rough-shod ends of his short legs wriggled and rustled on the gravel.

For the Old Gentleman was coming across Fourth Avenue toward his bench.

Every Thanksgiving Day for nine years the Old Gentleman had come there and found Stuffy Pete on his bench. That was a thing that the Old Gentleman was trying to make a tradition of. Every Thanksgiving Day for nine years he had found Stuffy there, and had led him to a restaurant and watched him eat a big dinner. They do those things in England unconsciously. But this is a young country, and nine years is not so bad. The Old Gentleman was a stanch American patriot, and considered himself a pioneer in American tradition. In order to become picturesque we must keep on doing one thing for a long time without ever letting it get away from us. Something like collecting the weekly dimes in industrial insurance. Or cleaning the streets.

The Old Gentleman moved, straight and stately, toward the Institution that he was rearing. Truly, the annual feeding of Stuffy Pete was nothing national in its character, such as the Magna Charta or jam for breakfast was in England. But it was a step. It was almost feudal. It showed, at least, that a Custom was not impossible to New Y—ahem!—America.

The Old Gentleman was thin and tall and sixty. He was dressed all in black, and wore the old-fashioned kind of glasses that won't stay on your nose. His hair was whiter and thinner than it had been last year, and he seemed to make more use of his big, knobby cane with the crooked handle.

As his established benefactor came up Stuffy wheezed and shuddered like some woman's over-fat pug when a street dog bristles up at him. He would have flown, but all the skill of Santos-Dumont could not have separated him from his bench. Well had the myrmidons of the two old ladies done their work.

"Good morning," said the Old Gentleman. "I am glad to perceive that the vicissitudes of another year have spared you to move in health about the beautiful world. For that blessing alone this day of thanksgiving is well proclaimed to each of us. If you will come with me, my man, I will provide you with a dinner that should make your physical being accord with the mental."

That is what the Old Gentleman said every time. Every Thanksgiving Day for nine years. The words themselves almost formed an Institution. Nothing could be compared with them except the Declaration of Independence. Always before they had been music in Stuffy's ears. But now he looked up at the Old Gentleman's face with tearful agony in his own. The fine snow almost sizzled when it fell upon his perspiring brow. But the Old Gentleman shivered a little and turned his back to the wind.

Stuffy had always wondered why the Old Gentleman spoke his speech rather sadly. He did not know that it was because he was wishing every time that he had a son to succeed him. A son who would come there after he was gone— a son who would stand proud and strong before some subsequent Stuffy, and say: "In memory of my father." Then it would be an Institution.

But the Old Gentleman had no relatives. He lived in rented rooms in one of the decayed old family brownstone mansions in one of the quiet streets east of the park. In the winter he raised fuchsias in a little conservatory the size of a steamer trunk. In the spring he walked in the Easter parade. In the summer he lived at a farmhouse in the New Jersey hills, and sat in a wicker armchair, speaking of a butterfly, the ornithoptera amphrisius, that he hoped to find some day. In the autumn he fed Stuffy a dinner. These were the Old Gentleman's occupations.

Stuffy Pete looked up at him for a half minute, stewing and helpless in his own self-pity. The Old Gentleman's eyes were bright with the giving-pleasure. His face was getting more lined each year, but his little black necktie was in as jaunty a bow as ever, and his linen was beautiful and white, and his gray mustache was curled gracefully at the ends. And then Stuffy made a noise that sounded like peas bubbling in a pot. Speech was intended; and as the Old Gentleman had heard the sounds nine times before, he rightly construed them into Stuffy's old formula of acceptance.

"Thankee, sir. I'll go with ye, and much obliged. I'm very hungry, sir."

The coma of repletion had not prevented from entering Stuffy's mind the conviction that he was the basis of an Institution. His Thanksgiving appetite was not his own; it belonged by all the sacred rights of established custom, if not by the actual Statute of Limitations, to this kind old gentleman who had preëmpted it. True, America is free; but in order to establish tradition some one must be a repetend—a repeating decimal. The heroes are not all heroes of steel and gold. See one here that wielded only weapons of iron, badly silvered, and tin.

The Old Gentleman led his annual protégé southward to

the restaurant, and to the table where the feast had always occurred. They were recognized.

"Here comes de old guy," said a waiter, "dat blows dat same bum to a meal every Thanksgiving."

The Old Gentleman sat across the table glowing like a smoked pearl at his corner-stone of future ancient Tradition. The waiters heaped the table with holiday food—and Stuffy, with a sigh that was mistaken for hunger's expression, raised knife and fork and carved for himself a crown of imperishable bay.

No more valiant hero ever fought his way through the ranks of an enemy. Turkey, chops, soups, vegetables, pies, disappeared before him as fast as they could be served. Gorged nearly to the uttermost when he entered the restaurant, the smell of food had almost caused him to lose his honor as a gentleman, but he rallied like a true knight. He saw the look of beneficent happiness on the Old Gentleman's face—a happier look than even the fuchsias and the ornithoptera amphrisius had ever brought to it—and he had not the heart to see it wane.

In an hour Stuffy leaned back with a battle won.

"Thankee kindly, sir," he puffed like a leaky steam pipe; "thankee kindly for a hearty meal."

Then he arose heavily with glazed eyes and started toward the kitchen. A waiter turned him about like a top, and pointed him toward the door. The Old Gentleman carefully counted out $1.30 in silver change, leaving three nickels for the waiter.

They parted as they did each year at the door, the Old Gentleman going south, Stuffy north.

Around the first corner Stuffy turned, and stood for one minute. Then he seemed to puff out his rags as an owl puffs out his feathers, and fell to the sidewalk like a sunstricken horse.

When the ambulance came the young surgeon and the

driver cursed softly at his weight. There was no smell of whiskey to justify a transfer to the patrol wagon, so Stuffy and his two dinners went to the hospital. There they stretched him on a bed and began to test him for strange diseases, with the hope of getting a chance at some problem with the bare steel.

And lo! an hour later another ambulance brought the Old Gentleman. And they laid him on another bed and spoke of appendicitis, for he looked good for the bill.

But pretty soon one of the young doctors met one of the young nurses whose eyes he liked, and stopped to chat with her about the cases.

"That nice old gentleman over there, now," he said, "you wouldn't think that was a case of almost starvation. Proud old family, I guess. He told me he hadn't eaten a thing for three days."

The Making of a New Yorker

BESIDES MANY THINGS, Raggles was a poet. He was called a tramp; but that was only an elliptical way of saying that he was a philosopher, an artist, a traveller, a naturalist, and a discoverer. But most of all he was a poet. In all his life he never wrote a line of verse; he lived his poetry. His Odyssey would have been a Limerick, had it been written. But, to linger with the primary proposition, Raggles was a poet.

Raggles's specialty, had he been driven to ink and paper, would have been sonnets to the cities. He studied cities as women study their reflections in mirrors; as children study the glue and sawdust of a dislocated doll; as the men who write about wild animals study the cages in the zoo. A city to Raggles was not merely a pile of bricks and mortar, peopled by a certain number of inhabitants; it was a thing with soul characteristic and distinct; an individual conglomeration of life, with its own peculiar essence, flavor, and feeling. Two thousand miles to the north and south, east and west, Raggles wandered in poetic fervor, taking the cities to his breast. He footed it on dusty roads, or sped magnificently in freight cars, counting time as of no account. And when he had found the heart of a city and listened to its secret confession, he strayed on, restless, to another. Fickle Raggles!—but perhaps he had not met the civic corporation that could engage and hold his critical fancy.

Through the ancient poets we have learned that the cities are feminine. So they were to poet Raggles; and his mind carried a concrete and clear conception of the figure that symbolized and typified each one that he had wooed.

Chicago seemed to swoop down upon him with a breezy suggestion of Mrs. Partington, plumes and patchouli, and to disturb his rest with a soaring and beautiful song of future promise. But Raggles would awake to a sense of shivering cold and a haunting impression of ideals lost in a depressing aura of potato salad and fish.

Thus Chicago affected him. Perhaps there is a vagueness and inaccuracy in the description; but that is Raggles's fault. He should have recorded his sensations in magazine poems.

Pittsburgh impressed him as the play of "Othello" performed in the Russian language in a railroad station by Dockstader's minstrels. A royal and generous lady this Pittsburgh, though—homely, hearty, with flushed face, washing the dishes in a silk dress and white kid slippers, and bidding Raggles sit before the roaring fireplace and drink champagne with his pigs' feet and fried potatoes.

New Orleans had simply gazed down upon him from a balcony. He could see her pensive, starry eyes and catch the flutter of her fan, and that was all. Only once he came face to face with her. It was at dawn, when she was flushing the red bricks of the banquette with a pail of water. She laughed and hummed a chansonette and filled Raggles's shoes with ice-cold water. Allons!

Boston construed herself to the poetic Raggles in an erratic and singular way. It seemed to him that he had drunk cold tea and that the city was a white, cold cloth that had been bound tightly around his brow to spur him to some unknown but tremendous mental effort. And, after all, he came to shovel snow for a livelihood; and the cloth, becoming wet, tightened its knots and could not be removed.

Indefinite and unintelligible ideas, you will say; but your disapprobation should be tempered with gratitude, for these are poets' fancies—and suppose you had come upon them in verse!

One day Raggles came and laid siege to the heart of the great city of Manhattan. She was the greatest of all; and he wanted to learn her note in the scale; to taste and appraise and classify and solve and label her and arrange her with the other cities that had given him up the secret of their individuality. And here we cease to be Raggles's translator and become his chronicler.

Raggles landed from a ferry-boat one morning and walked into the core of the town with the blasé air of a cosmopolite. He was dressed with care to play the rôle of an "unidentified man." No country, race, class, clique, union, party clan, or bowling association could have claimed him. His clothing, which had been donated to him piece-meal by citizens of different height, but same number of inches around the heart, was not yet as uncomfortable to his figure as those specimens of raiment, self-measured, that are railroaded to you by transcontinental tailors with a suit case, suspenders, silk handkerchief and pearl studs as a bonus. Without money—as a poet should be—but with the ardor of an astronomer discovering a new star in the chorus of the milky way, or a man who has seen ink suddenly flow from his fountain pen, Raggles wandered into the great city.

Late in the afternoon he drew out of the roar and commotion with a look of dumb terror on his countenance. He was defeated, puzzled, discomfited, frightened. Other cities had been to him as long primer to read; as country maidens quickly to fathom; as send-price-of-subscription-with-answer rebuses to solve; as oyster cocktails to swallow; but here was one as cold, glittering, serene, impossible as a four-carat diamond in a window to a lover outside fingering damply in his pocket his ribbon-counter salary.

The greetings of the other cities he had known—their homespun kindliness, their human gamut of rough charity, friendly curses, garrulous curiosity, and easily estimated credulity or indifference. This city of Manhattan gave him no clue; it was walled against him. Like a river of adamant it flowed past him in the streets. Never an eye was turned upon him; no voice spoke to him. His heart yearned for the clap of Pittsburgh's sooty hand on his shoulder; for Chicago's menacing but social yawp in his ear; for the pale and eleemosynary stare through the Bostonian eyeglass—even for the precipitate but unmalicious boot-toe of Louisville or St. Louis.

On Broadway Raggles, successful suitor of many cities, stood, bashful, like any country swain. For the first time he experienced the poignant humiliation of being ignored. And when he tried to reduce this brilliant, swiftly changing, ice-cold city to a formula he failed utterly. Poet though he was, it offered him no color similes, no points of comparison, no flaw in its polished facets, no handle by which he could hold it up and view its shape and structure, as he familiarly and often contemptuously had done with other towns. The houses were interminable ramparts loopholed for defence; the people were bright but bloodless spectres passing in sinister and selfish array.

The thing that weighed heaviest on Raggles's soul and clogged his poet's fancy was the spirit of absolute egotism that seemed to saturate the people as toys are saturated with paint. Each one that he considered appeared a monster of abominable and insolent conceit. Humanity was gone from them; they were toddling idols of stone and varnish, worshipping themselves and greedy for though oblivious of worship from their fellow graven images. Frozen, cruel, implacable, impervious, cut to an identical pattern, they hurried on their ways like statues brought by some miracle to motion, while soul and feeling lay unaroused in the reluctant marble.

Gradually Raggles became conscious of certain types. One was an elderly gentleman with a snow-white, short beard, pink, unwrinkled face, and stony, sharp blue eyes, attired in the fashion of a gilded youth, who seemed to personify the city's wealth, ripeness and frigid unconcern. Another type was a woman, tall, beautiful, clear as a steel engraving, goddesslike, calm, clothed like the princesses of old, with eyes as coldly blue as the reflection of sunlight on a glacier. And another was a by-product of this town of marionettes—a broad, swaggering, grim, threateningly sedate fellow, with a jowl as large as a harvested wheat field, the complexion of a baptized infant, and the knuckles of a prize-fighter. This type leaned against cigar signs and viewed the world with frappéd contumely.

A poet is a sensitive creature, and Raggles soon shriveled in the bleak embrace of the undecipherable. The chill, sphinx-like, ironical, illegible, unnatural, ruthless expression of the city left him downcast and bewildered. Had it no heart? Better the woodpile, the scolding of vinegar-faced housewives at back doors, the kindly spleen of bartenders behind provincial free-lunch counters, the amiable truculence of rural constables, the kicks, arrests, and happy-go-lucky chances of the other vulgar, loud, crude cities than this freezing heartlessness.

Raggles summoned his courage and sought alms from the populace. Unheeding, regardless, they passed on without the wink of an eyelash to testify that they were conscious of his existence. And then he said to himself that this fair but pitiless city of Manhattan was without a soul; that its inhabitants were mannikins moved by wires and springs, and that he was alone in a great wilderness.

Raggles started to cross the street. There was a blast, a roar, a hissing and a crash as something struck him and hurled him over and over six yards from where he had been. As he was coming down like the stick of a rocket the earth and all the cities thereof turned to a fractured dream.

Raggles opened his eyes. First an odor made itself known to him—an odor of the earliest spring flowers of Paradise. And then a hand soft as a falling petal touched his brow. Bending over him was the woman clothed like the princess of old, with blue eyes, now soft and humid with human sympathy. Under his head on the pavement were silks and furs. With Raggles's hat in his hand and with his face pinker than ever from a vehement outburst of oratory against reckless driving, stood the elderly gentleman who personified the city's wealth and ripeness. From a near-by café hurried the by-product with the vast jowl and baby complexion, bearing a glass full of crimson fluid that suggested delightful possibilities.

"Drink dis, sport," said the by-product, holding the glass to Raggles's lips.

Hundreds of people huddled around in a moment, their faces wearing the deepest concern. Two flattering and gorgeous policemen got into the circle and pressed back the overplus of Samaritans. An old lady in a black shawl spoke loudly of camphor; a newsboy slipped one of his papers beneath Raggles's elbow, where it lay on the muddy pavement. A brisk young man with a notebook was asking for names.

A bell clanged importantly, and the ambulance cleaned a lane through the crowd. A cool surgeon slipped into the midst of affairs.

"How do you feel, old man?" asked the surgeon, stooping easily to his task. The princess of silks and satins wiped a red drop or two from Raggles's brow with a fragrant cobweb.

"Me?" said Raggles, with a seraphic smile. "I feel fine."

He had found the heart of his new city.

In three days they let him leave his cot for the convalescent ward in the hospital. He had been in there an hour when the attendants heard sounds of conflict. Upon investigation they found that Raggles had assaulted and damaged a brother convalescent—a glowering transient whom a freight train collision had sent in to be patched up.

"What's all this about?" inquired the head nurse.

"He was runnin' down me town," said Raggles.

"What town?" asked the nurse.

"Noo York," said Raggles.

The Lost Blend

SINCE the bar has been blessed by the clergy, and cocktails open the dinners of the elect, one may speak of the saloon. Teetotalers need not listen, if they choose; there is always the slot restaurant, where a dime dropped into the cold bouillon aperture will bring forth a dry Martini.

Con Lantry worked on the sober side of the bar in Kenealy's café. You and I stood, one-legged like geese, on the other side and went into voluntary liquidation with our week's wages. Opposite danced Con, clean, temperate, clear-headed, polite, white-jacketed, punctual, trustworthy, young, responsible, and took our money.

The saloon (whether blessed or cursed) stood in one of those little "places" which are parallelograms instead of streets, and inhabited by laundries, decayed Knickerbocker families and Bohemians who have nothing to do with either.

Over the café lived Kenealy and his family. His daughter Katherine had eyes of dark Irish—but why should you be told? Be content with your Geraldine or your Eliza Ann. For Con dreamed of her; and when she called softly at the foot of the back stairs for the pitcher of beer for dinner, his heart went up and down like a milk punch in the shaker. Orderly and fit are the rules of Romance; and if you hurl the last shilling of your fortune upon the bar for whiskey, the bartender shall take it, and marry his boss's daughter, and good will grow out of it.

But not so Con. For in the presence of woman he was tongue-tied and scarlet. He who would quell with his eye the sonorous youth whom the claret punch made loquacious, or smash with lemon squeezer the obstreperous, or hurl gutterward the cantankerous without a wrinkle coming to his white lawn tie, when he stood before a woman he was voiceless, incoherent, stuttering, buried beneath a hot avalanche of bashfulness and misery. What then was he before Katherine? A trembler, with no word to say for himself, a stone without blarney, the dumbest lover that ever babbled of the weather in the presence of his divinity.

There came to Kenealy's two sunburned men, Riley and McQuirk. They had conference with Kenealy; and then they took possession of a back room which they filled with bottles and siphons and jugs and druggist's measuring glasses. All the appurtenances and liquids of a saloon were there, but they dispensed no drinks. All day long the two sweltered in there, pouring and mixing unknown brews and decoctions from the liquors in their store. Riley had the education, and he figured on reams of paper, reducing gallons to ounces and quarts to fluid drams. McQuirk, a morose man with a red eye, dashed each unsuccessful completed mixture into the waste pipe with curses gentle, husky and deep. They labored heavily and untiringly to achieve some mysterious solution like two alchemists striving to resolve gold from the elements.

Into this back room one evening when his watch was done sauntered Con. His professional curiosity had been stirred by these occult bartenders at whose bar none drank, and who daily drew upon Kenealy's store of liquors to follow their consuming and fruitless experiments.

Down the back stairs came Katherine with her smile like sunrise on Gweebarra Bay.

"Good evening, Mr. Lantry," says she. "And what is the news to-day, if you please?"

"It looks like r-rain," stammered the shy one, backing to the wall.

"It couldn't do better," said Katherine. "I'm thinking there's nothing the worse off for a little water." In the back room Riley and McQuirk toiled like bearded witches over their strange compounds. From fifty bottles they drew liquids carefully measured after Riley's figures, and shook the whole together in a great glass vessel. Then McQuirk would dash it out, with gloomy profanity, and they would begin again.

"Sit down," said Riley to Con, "and I'll tell you.

"Last summer me and Tim concludes that an American bar in this nation of Nicaragua would pay. There was a town on the coast where there's nothing to eat but quinine and nothing to drink but rum. The natives and foreigners lay down with chills and get up with fevers; and a good mixed drink is nature's remedy for all such tropical inconveniences.

"So we lays in a fine stock of wet goods in New York, and bar fixtures and glassware, and we sails for that Santa Palma town on a lime steamer. On the way me and Tim sees flying fish and play seven-up with the captain and steward, and already begins to feel like the high-ball kings of the tropics of Capricorn.

"When we gets in five hours of the country that we was going to introduce to long drinks and short change the captain calls us over to the starboard binnacle and recollects a few things.

"'I forgot to tell you, boys,' says he, 'that Nicaragua slapped an import duty of 48 per cent. ad valorem on all bottled goods last month. The President took a bottle of Cincinnati hair tonic by mistake for tabasco sauce, and he's getting even. Barrelled goods is free.'

"'Sorry you didn't mention it sooner,' says we. And we bought two forty-two gallon casks from the captain, and opened every bottle we had and dumped the stuff altogether in the casks. That 48 per cent. would have ruined us; so we took the chances on making that $1,200 cocktail rather than throw the stuff away.

"Well, when we landed we tapped one of the barrels. The mixture was something heartrending. It was the color of a plate of Bowery pea soup, and it tasted like one of those coffee substitutes your aunt makes you take for the heart trouble you get by picking losers. We gave a nigger four fingers of it to try it, and he lay under a cocoanut tree three days beating the sand with his heels and refused to sign a testimonial.

"But the other barrel! Say, bartender, did you ever put on a straw hat with a yellow band around it and go up in a balloon with a pretty girl with $8,000,000 in your pocket all at the same time? That's what thirty drops of it would make you feel like. With two fingers of it inside you you would bury your face in your hands and cry because there wasn't anything more worth while around for you to lick than little Jim Jeffries. Yes, sir, that stuff in that second barrel was distilled elixir of battle, money and high life. It was the color of gold and as clear as glass, and it shone after dark like the sunshine was still in it. A thousand years from now you'll get a drink like that across the bar.

"Well, we started up business with that one line of drinks, and it was enough. The piebald gentry of that country stuck to it like a hive of bees. If that barrel had lasted that country would have become the greatest on earth. When we opened up of mornings we had a line of generals and colonels and ex-presidents and revolutionists a block long waiting to be served. We started in at 50 cents silver a drink. The last ten gallons went easy at $5 a gulp. It was wonderful stuff. It gave a man courage and ambition and nerve to do anything; at the same time he didn't care whether his money was tainted or fresh from the Ice Trust. When that barrel was half gone Nicaragua had repudiated the National debt, removed the duty on cigarettes and was about to declare war on the United States and England.

" 'Twas by accident we discovered this king of drinks, and 'twill be by good luck if we strike it again. For ten months we've been trying. Small lots at a time, we've mixed barrels of all the harmful ingredients known to the profession of drinking. Ye could have stocked ten bars with the whiskies, brandies, cordials, bitters, gins and wines me and Tim have wasted. A glorious drink like that to be denied the world! 'Tis a sorrow and a loss of money. The United States as a nation would welcome a drink of that sort, and pay for it."

All the while McQuirk had been carefully measuring and pouring together small quantities of various spirits, as Riley called them, from his latest pencilled prescription. The completed mixture was of a vile, mottled chocolate color. Mc-

Quirk tasted it, and hurled it, with appropriate epithets, into the waste sink.

" 'Tis a strange story, even if true," said Con. "I'll be going now along to my supper."

"Take a drink," said Riley. "We've all kinds except the lost blend."

"I never drink," said Con, "anything stronger than water. I am just after meeting Miss Katherine by the stairs. She said a true word, 'There's not anything,' says she, 'but is better off for a little water.' "

When Con had left them Riley almost felled McQuirk by a blow on the back.

"Did ye hear that?" he shouted. "Two fools are we. The six dozen bottles of 'pollinaris we had on the ship—ye opened them yourself—which barrel did ye pour them in—which barrel, ye mudhead?"

"I mind," said McQuirk, slowly, " 'twas in the second barrel we opened. I mind the blue piece of paper pasted on the side of it."

"We've got it now," cried Riley. " 'Twas that we lacked. 'Tis the water that does the trick. Everything else we had right. Hurry, man, and get two bottles of 'pollinaris from the bar, while I figure out the proportionments with me pencil."

An hour later Con strolled down the sidewalk toward Kenealy's café. Thus faithful employees haunt, during their recreation hours, the vicinity where they labor, drawn by some mysterious attraction.

A police patrol wagon stood at the side door. Three able cops were half carrying, half hustling Riley and McQuirk up its rear steps. The eyes and faces of each bore the bruises and cuts of sanguinary and assiduous conflict. Yet they whooped with strange joy, and directed upon the police the feeble remnants of their pugnacious madness.

"Began fighting each other in the back room," explained

Kenealy to Con. "And singing! That was worse. Smashed everything pretty much up. But they're good men. They'll pay for everything. Trying to invent some new kind of cocktail, they was. I'll see they come out all right in the morning."

Con sauntered into the back room to view the battlefield. As he went through the hall Katherine was just coming down the stairs.

"Good evening again, Mr. Lantry," said she. "And is there no news from the weather yet?"

"Still threatens r-rain," said Con, slipping past with red in his smooth, pale cheek.

Riley and McQuirk had indeed waged a great and friendly battle. Broken bottles and glasses were everywhere. The room was full of alcohol fumes; the floor was variegated with spirituous puddles.

On the table stood a 32-ounce glass, graduated measure. In the bottom of it were two tablespoonfuls of liquid—a bright golden liquid that seemed to hold the sunshine a prisoner in its auriferous depths.

Con smelled it. He tasted it. He drank it.

As he returned through the hall Katherine was just going up the stairs.

"No news yet, Mr. Lantry?" she asked with her teasing laugh.

Con lifted her clear from the floor and held her there.

"The news is," he said, "that we're to be married."

"Put me down, sir!" she cried indignantly, "or I will——
Oh, Con, oh, wherever did you get the nerve to say it?"

A Harlem Tragedy

HARLEM.

Mrs. Fink had dropped into Mrs. Cassidy's flat one flight below.

"Ain't it a beaut?" said Mrs. Cassidy.

She turned her face proudly for her friend Mrs. Fink to see. One eye was nearly closed, with a great, greenish-purple bruise around it. Her lip was cut and bleeding a little and there were red finger-marks on each side of her neck.

"My husband wouldn't ever think of doing that to me," said Mrs. Fink, concealing her envy.

"I wouldn't have a man," declared Mrs. Cassidy, "that didn't beat me up at least once a week. Shows he thinks something of you. Say! but that last dose Jack gave me wasn't no homeopathic one. I can see stars yet. But he'll be the sweetest man in town for the rest of the week to make up for it. This eye is good for theater tickets and a silk shirt waist at the very least."

"I should hope," said Mrs. Fink, assuming complacency, "that Mr. Fink is too much of a gentleman ever to raise his hand against me."

"Oh, go on, Maggie!" said Mrs. Cassidy, laughing and applying witch hazel, "you're only jealous. Your old man is too frappéd and slow to ever give you a punch. He just sits down and practises physical culture with a newspaper when he comes home—now ain't that the truth?"

"Mr. Fink certainly peruses of the papers when he comes home," acknowledged Mrs. Fink, with a toss of her head; "but he certainly don't ever make no Steve O'Donnell out of me just to amuse himself—that's a sure thing."

Mrs. Cassidy laughed the contented laugh of the guarded
and happy matron. With the air of Cornelia exhibiting her
jewels, she drew down the collar of her kimono and revealed
another treasured bruise, maroon-colored, edged with olive
and orange—a bruise now nearly well, but still to memory
dear.

Mrs. Fink capitulated. The formal light in her eye softened
to envious admiration. She and Mrs. Cassidy had been chums
in the downtown paper-box factory before they had married,
one year before. Now she and her man occupied the flat
above Mame and her man. Therefore she could not put on
airs with Mame.

"Don't it hurt when he soaks you?" asked Mrs. Fink,
curiously.

"Hurt!"—Mrs. Cassidy gave a soprano scream of delight.
"Well, say—did you ever have a brick house fall on you?—
well, that's just the way it feels—just like when they're digging
you out of the ruins. Jack's got a left that spells two matinées
and a new pair of Oxfords—and his right!—well, it takes a
trip to Coney and six pairs of open-work silk lisle threads to
make that good."

"But what does he beat you for?" inquired Mrs. Fink, with
wide-open eyes.

"Silly!" said Mrs. Cassidy, indulgently. "Why, because he's
full. It's generally on Saturday nights."

"But what cause do you give him?" persisted the seeker
after knowledge.

"Why, didn't I marry him? Jack comes in tanked up; and
I'm here, ain't I? Who else has he got a right to beat? I'd
just like to catch him once beating anybody else! Sometimes
it's because supper ain't ready; and sometimes it's because it
is. Jack ain't particular about causes. He just lushes till he
remembers he's married, and then he makes for home and
does me up. Saturday nights I just move the furniture with

sharp corners out of the way, so I won't cut my head when
he gets his work in. He's got a left swing that jars you! Sometimes I take the count in the first round; but when I feel like
having a good time during the week or want some new rags
I come up again for more punishment. That's what I done
last night. Jack knows I've been wanting a black silk waist for
a month, and I didn't think just one black eye would bring it.
Tell you what, Mag, I'll bet you the ice cream he brings it
to-night."

Mrs. Fink was thinking deeply.

"My Mart," she said, "never hit me a lick in his life. It's
just like you said, Mame; he comes in grouchy and ain't got
a word to say. He never takes me out anywhere. He's a chair-
warmer at home for fair. He buys me things, but he looks so
glum about it that I never appreciate 'em."

Mrs. Cassidy slipped an arm around her chum.

"You poor thing!" she said. "But everybody can't have a
husband like Jack. Marriage wouldn't be no failure if they was
all like him. These discontented wives you hear about—what
they need is a man to come home and kick their slats in once
a week, and then make it up in kisses, and chocolate creams.
That'd give 'em some interest in life. What I want is a master-
ful man that slugs you when he's jagged and hugs you when
he ain't jagged. Preserve me from the man that ain't got the
sand to do neither!"

Mrs. Fink sighed.

The hallways were suddenly filled with sound. The door
flew open at the kick of Mr. Cassidy. His arms were occupied
with bundles. Mame flew and hung about his neck. Her
sound eye sparkled with the love light that shines in the eye
of the Maori maid when she recovers consciousness in the
hut of the wooer who has stunned and dragged her there.

"Hello, old girl!" shouted Mr. Cassidy. He shed his bundles
and lifted her off her feet in a mighty hug. "I got tickets for

Barnum & Bailey's, and if you'll bust the string of one of them bundles I guess you'll find that silk waist—why, good evening, Mrs. Fink—I didn't see you at first. How's old Mart coming along?"

"He's very well, Mr. Cassidy—thanks," said Mrs. Fink. "I must be going along up now. Mart'll be home for supper soon. I'll bring you down the pattern you wanted to-morrow, Mame."

Mrs. Fink went up to her flat and had a little cry. It was a meaningless cry, the kind of cry that only a woman knows about, a cry from no particular cause, altogether an absurd cry; the most transient and the most hopeless cry in the repertory of grief. Why had Martin never thrashed her? He was as big and strong as Jack Cassidy. Did he not care for her at all? He never quarrelled; he came home and lounged about silent, glum, idle. He was a fairly good provider, but he ignored the spices of life.

Mrs. Fink's ship of dreams was becalmed. Her captain ranged between plum duff and his hammock. If only he would shiver his timbers or stamp his foot on the quarter-deck now and then! And she had thought to sail so merrily, touching at ports in the Delectable Isles! But now, to vary the figure, she was ready to throw up the sponge, tired out, without a scratch to show for all those tame rounds with her sparring partner. For one moment she almost hated Mame—Mame, with her cuts and bruises, her salve of presents and kisses; her stormy voyage with her fighting, brutal, loving mate.

Mr. Fink came home at 7. He was permeated with the curse of domesticity. Beyond the portals of his cozy home he cared not to roam, to roam. He was the man who had caught the street car, the anaconda that had swallowed its prey, the tree that lay as it had fallen.

"Like the supper, Mart?" asked Mrs. Fink, who had striven over it.

"M-m-m-yep," grunted Mr. Fink.

After supper he gathered his newspapers to read. He sat in his stocking feet.

Arise, some new Dante, and sing me the befitting corner of perdition for the man who sitteth in the house in his stock-inged feet. Sisters in Patience who by reason of ties or duty have endured it in silk, yarn cotton, lisle thread or woollen —does not the new canto belong?

The next day was Labor Day. The occupations of Mr. Cassidy and Mr. Fink ceased for one passage of the sun. Labor, triumphant, would parade and otherwise disport itself.

Mrs. Fink took Mrs. Cassidy's pattern down early. Mame had on her new silk waist. Even her damaged eye managed to emit a holiday gleam. Jack was fruitfully penitent, and there was a hilarious scheme for the day afoot, with parks and picnics and Pilsener in it.

A rising, indignant jealousy seized Mrs. Fink as she returned to her flat above. Oh, happy Mame, with her bruises and her quick-following balm! But was Mame to have a monopoly of happiness? Surely Martin Fink was as good a man as Jack Cassidy. Was his wife to go always unbelabored and uncaressed? A sudden, brilliant breathless idea came to Mrs. Fink. She would show Mame that there were husbands as able to use their fists and perhaps to be as tender afterward as any Jack.

The holiday promised to be a nominal one with the Finks. Mrs. Fink had the stationary washtubs in the kitchen filled with a two-weeks' wash that had been soaking overnight. Mr. Fink sat in his stockinged feet reading a newspaper. Thus Labor Day presaged to speed.

Jealousy surged high in Mrs. Fink's heart and higher still surged an audacious resolve. If her man would not strike her —if he would not so far prove his manhood, his prerogative and his interest in conjugal affairs, he must be prompted to do his duty.

Mr. Fink lit his pipe and peacefully rubbed an ankle with a stockinged toe. He reposed in the state of matrimony like a lump of unblended suet in a pudding. This was his level Elysium—to sit at ease vicariously girdling the world in print amid the wifely splashing of suds and the agreeable smells of breakfast dishes departed and dinner ones to come. Many ideas were far from his mind; but the furthest one was the thought of beating his wife.

Mrs. Fink turned on the hot water and set the washboards in the suds. Up from the flat below came the gay laugh of Mrs. Cassidy. It sounded like a taunt, a flaunting of her own happiness in the face of the unslugged bride above. Now was Mrs. Fink's time.

Suddenly she turned like a fury upon the man reading.

"You lazy loafer!" she cried, "must I work my arms off washing and toiling for the ugly likes of you? Are you a man or are you a kitchen hound?"

Mr. Fink dropped his paper, motionless from surprise. She feared that he would not strike—that the provocation had been insufficient. She leaped at him and struck him fiercely in the face with her clenched hand. In that instant she felt a thrill of love for him such as she had not felt for many a day. Rise up, Martin Fink, and come into your kingdom! Oh, she must feel the weight of his hand now—just to show that he cared—just to show that he cared!

Mr. Fink sprang to his feet—Maggie caught him again on the jaw with a wide swing of her other hand. She closed her eyes in that fearful, blissful moment before his blow should come—she whispered his name to herself—she leaned to the expected shock, hungry for it.

In the flat below Mr. Cassidy, with a shamed and contrite face, was powdering Mame's eye in preparation for their junket. From the flat above came the sound of a woman's voice, high-raised, a bumping, a stumbling and a shuffling, a chair overturned—unmistakable sounds of domestic conflict.

"Mart and Mag scrapping?" postulated Mr. Cassidy. "Didn't know they ever indulged. Shall I trot up and see if they need a sponge holder?"

One of Mrs. Cassidy's eyes sparkled like a diamond. The other twinkled at least like paste.

"Oh, oh," she said, softly and without apparent meaning in the feminine ejaculatory manner. "I wonder if—wonder if! Wait, Jack, till I go up and see."

Up the stairs she sped. As her foot struck the hallway above out from the kitchen door of her flat wildly flounced Mrs. Fink.

"Oh, Maggie," cried Mrs. Cassidy, in a delighted whisper; "did he? Oh, did he?"

Mrs. Fink ran and laid her face upon her chum's shoulder and sobbed hopelessly.

Mrs. Cassidy took Maggie's face between her hands and lifted it gently. Tear-stained it was, flushing and paling, but its velvety, pink-and-white, becomingly freckled surface was unscratched, unbruised, unmarred by the recreant fist of Mr. Fink.

"Tell me, Maggie," pleaded Mame, "or I'll go in there and find out. What was it? Did he hurt you—what did he do?"

Mrs. Fink's face went down again despairingly on the bosom of her friend.

"For God's sake don't open that door, Mame," she sobbed. "And don't ever tell nobody—keep it under your hat. He—he never touched me, and—he's—oh, Gawd—he's washin' the clothes—he's washin' the clothes!"

A Midsummer Knight's Dream

"The knights are dead;
Their swords are rust.
Except a few who have to hust-
Le all the time
To raise the dust."

DEAR READER: It was summertime. The sun glared down upon the city with pitiless ferocity. It is difficult for the sun to be ferocious and exhibit compunction simultaneously. The heat was—oh, bother thermometers!—who cares for standard measures, anyhow? It was so hot that——

The roof gardens put on so many extra waiters that you could hope to get your gin fizz now—as soon as all the other people got theirs. The hospitals were putting in extra cots for bystanders. For when little woolly dogs loll their tongues out and say "woof, woof!" at the fleas that bite 'em, and nervous old black bombazine ladies screech "Mad dog!" and policemen begin to shoot, somebody is going to get hurt. The man from Pompton, N. J., who always wears an overcoat in July, had turned up in a Broadway hotel drinking hot Scotches and enjoying his annual ray from the calcium. Philanthropists were petitioning the Legislature to pass a bill requiring builders to make tenement fire-escapes more commodious, so that families might die all together of the heat instead of one or two at a time. So many men were telling you about the number of baths they took each day that you wondered how they got along after the real lessee of the apartment came back to town and thanked 'em for taking such good care of it. The young man who called loudly for cold beef and beer in the restaurant, protesting that roast pullet and Burgundy was really too heavy for such weather, blushed when he met your eye, for you had heard him all winter calling, in modest tones, for the same ascetic viands. Soup, pocketbooks, shirt waists, actors, and baseball excuses grew thinner. Yes, it was summertime.

A man stood at Thirty-fourth Street waiting for a downtown car. A man of forty, gray-haired, pink-faced, keen, nervous, plainly dressed, with a harassed look around the eyes. He wiped his forehead and laughed loudly when a fat man with an outing look stopped and spoke with him.

"No, siree," he shouted with defiance and scorn. "None of your old mosquito-haunted swamps and skyscraper mountains without elevators for me. When I want to get away from hot weather I know how to do it. New York, sir, is the finest summer resort in the country. Keep in the shade and watch your diet, and don't get too far away from an electric fan. Talk about your Adirondacks and your Catskills! There's more solid comfort in the borough of Manhattan than in all the rest of the country together. No, siree! No tramping up perpendicular cliffs and being waked up at 4 in the morning by a million flies, and eating canned goods straight from the city for me. Little old New York will take a few select summer boarders; comforts and conveniences of home—that's the ad. that I answer every time."

"You need a vacation," said the fat man, looking closely at the other. "You haven't been away from town in years. Better come with me for two weeks, anyhow. The trout in the Beaverkill are jumping at anything now that looks like a fly. Harding writes me that he landed a three-pound brown last week."

"Nonsense!" cried the other man. "Go ahead, if you like, and boggle around in rubber boots wearing yourself out trying to catch fish. When I want one I go to a cool restaurant and order it. I laugh at you fellows whenever I think of you hustling around in the heat in the country thinking you are having a good time. For me Father Knickerbocker's little improved farm with the big shady lane running through the middle of it."

The fat man sighed over his friend and went his way. The man who thought New York was the greatest summer resort in the country boarded a car and went buzzing down to his office. On the way he threw away his newspaper and looked up at a ragged patch of sky above the housetops.

"Three pounds!" he muttered, absently. "And Harding isn't a liar. I believe, if I could—but it's impossible—they've got to have another month—another month at least."

In his office the upholder of urban midsummer joys dived, head foremost, into the swimming pool of business. Adkins, his clerk, came and added a spray of letters, memoranda and telegrams.

At 5 o'clock in the afternoon the busy man leaned back in his office chair, put his feet on the desk and mused aloud:

"I wonder what kind of bait Harding used."

. . . .

She was all in white that day; and thereby Compton lost a bet to Gaines. Compton had wagered she would wear light blue, for she knew that was his favorite color, and Compton was a millionaire's son, and that almost laid him open to the charge of betting on a sure thing. But white was her choice, and Gaines held up his head with twenty-five's lordly air.

The little summer hotel in the mountains had a lively crowd that year. There were two or three young college men and a couple of artists and a young naval officer on one side. On the other there were enough beauties among the young ladies for the correspondent of a society paper to refer to them as a "bevy." But the moon among the stars was Mary Sewell. Each one of the young men greatly desired to arrange matters so that he could pay her millinery bills, and fix the furnace, and have her do away with the "Sewell" part of her name forever. Those who could stay only a week or two went away hinting at pistols and blighted hearts. But Compton stayed like the mountains themselves, for he could afford it. And Gaines stayed because he was a fighter and wasn't afraid of millionaires' sons, and—well, he adored the country.

"What do you think, Miss Mary?" he said once. "I knew a duffer in New York who claimed to like it in the summertime. Said you could keep cooler there than you could in the woods. Wasn't he an awful silly? I don't think I could breathe on Broadway after the 1st of June."

"Mamma was thinking of going back week after next," said Miss Mary with a lovely frown.

"But when you think of it," said Gaines, "there are lots of jolly places in town in the summer. The roof gardens, you know, and the—er—the roof gardens."

Deepest blue was the lake that day—the day when they had the mock tournament, and the men rode clumsy farm horses around in a glade in the woods and caught curtain rings on the end of a lance. Such fun!

Cool and dry as the finest wine came the breath of the shadowed forest. The valley below was a vision seen through an opal haze. A white mist from hidden falls blurred the green of a hand's breadth of tree tops halfway down the gorge. Youth made merry hand-in-hand with young summer. Nothing on Broadway like that.

The villagers gathered to see the city folks pursue their mad drollery. The woods rang with the laughter of pixies and naiads and sprites. Gaines caught most of the rings. His was the privilege to crown the queen of the tournament. He was the conquering knight—as far as the rings went. On his arm he wore a white scarf. Compton wore light blue. She had declared her preference for blue, but she wore white that day.

Gaines looked about for the queen to crown her. He heard

her merry laugh, as if from the clouds. She had slipped away and climbed Chimney Rock, a little granite bluff, and stood there, a white fairy among the laurels, fifty feet above their heads.

Instantly he and Compton accepted the implied challenge. The bluff was easily mounted at the rear, but the front offered small hold to hand or foot. Each man quickly selected his route and began to climb. A crevice, a bush, a slight projection, a vine or tree branch—all of these were aids that counted in the race. It was all foolery—there was no stake; but there was youth in it, cross reader, and light hearts, and something else that Miss Clay writes so charmingly about.

Gaines gave a great tug at the root of a laurel and pulled himself to Miss Mary's feet. On his arm he carried the wreath of roses; and while the villagers and summer boarders screamed and applauded below he placed it on the queen's brow.

"You are a gallant knight," said Miss Mary.

"If I could be your true knight always," began Gaines, but Miss Mary laughed him dumb, for Compton scrambled over the edge of the rock one minute behind time.

What a twilight that was when they drove back to the hotel! The opal of the valley turned slowly to purple, the dark woods framed the lake as a mirror, the tonic air stirred the very soul in one. The first pale stars came out over the mountain tops where yet a faint glow of——

.   .   .   .   .

"I beg your pardon, Mr. Gaines," said Adkins.

The man who believed New York to be the finest summer resort in the world opened his eyes and kicked over the mucilage bottle on his desk.

"I—I believe I was asleep," he said.

"It's the heat," said Adkins. "It's something awful in the city these——"

"Nonsense!" said the other. "The city beats the country ten to one in summer. Fools go out tramping in muddy brooks and wear themselves out trying to catch little fish as long as your finger. Stay in town and keep comfortable—that's my idea."

"Some letters just came," said Adkins. "I thought you might like to glance at them before you go."

Let us look over his shoulder and read just a few lines of one of them:

MY DEAR, DEAR HUSBAND: Just received your letter ordering us to stay another month. . . . Rita's cough is almost gone. . . . Johnny has simply gone wild like a little Indian. . . . Will be the making of both children . . . work so hard, and I know that your business can hardly afford to keep us here so long . . . best man that ever . . . you always pretend that you like the city in summer . . . trout fishing that you used to be so fond of . . . and all to keep us well and happy . . . come to you if it were not doing the babies so much good. . . . I stood last evening on Chimney Rock in exactly the same spot where I was when you put the wreath of roses on my head . . . through all the world . . . when you said you would be my true knight . . . fifteen years ago, dear, just think! . . . have always been that to me . . . ever and ever,

MARY.

The man who said he thought New York the finest summer resort in the country dropped into a café on his way home and had a glass of beer under an electric fan.

"Wonder what kind of a fly old Harding used," he said to himself.

The Last Leaf

IN A LITTLE DISTRICT west of Washington Square the streets have run crazy and broken themselves into small strips called "places." These "places" make strange angles and curves. One street crosses itself a time or two. An artist once discovered a valuable possibility in this street. Suppose a collector with a bill for paints, paper and canvas should, in traversing this route, suddenly meet himself coming back, without a cent having been paid on account!

So, to quaint old Greenwich Village the art people soon came prowling, hunting for north windows and eighteenth-century gables and Dutch attics and low rents. Then they imported some pewter mugs and a chafing dish or two from Sixth Avenue, and became a "colony."

At the top of a squatty, three-story brick Sue and Johnsy had their studio. "Johnsy" was familiar for Joanna. One was from Maine; the other from California. They had met at the *table d'hôte* of an Eighth Street "Delmonico's," and found their tastes in art, chicory salad and bishop sleeves so congenial that the joint studio resulted.

That was in May. In November a cold, unseen stranger, whom the doctors called Pneumonia, stalked about the colony, touching one here and there with his icy fingers. Over on the east side this ravager strode boldly, smiting his victims by scores, but his feet trod slowly through the maze of the narrow and moss-grown "places."

Mr. Pneumonia was not what you would call a chivalric old gentleman. A mite of a little woman with blood thinned by California zephyrs was hardly fair game for the red-fisted, short-breathed old duffer. But Johnsy he smote; and she lay, scarcely moving, on her painted iron bedstead, looking through the small Dutch window-panes at the blank side of the next brick house.

One morning the busy doctor invited Sue into the hallway with a shaggy, gray eyebrow.

"She has one chance in—let us say, ten," he said, as he shook down the mercury in his clinical thermometer. "And that chance is for her to want to live. This way people have of lining-up on the side of the undertaker makes the entire pharmacopœia look silly. Your little lady has made up her mind that she's not going to get well. Has she anything on her mind?"

"She—she wanted to paint the Bay of Naples some day," said Sue.

"Paint?—bosh! Has she anything on her mind worth thinking about twice—a man for instance?"

"A man?" said Sue, with a jew's-harp twang in her voice. "Is a man worth—but, no, doctor; there is nothing of the kind."

"Well, it is the weakness, then," said the doctor. "I will do all that science, so far as it may filter through my efforts, can accomplish. But whenever my patient begins to count the carriages in her funeral procession I subtract 50 per cent. from the curative power of medicines. If you will get her to ask one question about the new winter styles in cloak sleeves I will promise you a one-in-five chance for her, instead of one in ten."

After the doctor had gone Sue went into the workroom and cried a Japanese napkin to a pulp. Then she swaggered into Johnsy's room with her drawing board, whistling ragtime.

Johnsy lay, scarcely making a ripple under the bedclothes, with her face toward the window. Sue stopped whistling, thinking she was asleep.

She arranged her board and began a pen-and-ink drawing to illustrate a magazine story. Young artists must pave their way to Art by drawing pictures for magazine stories that young authors write to pave their way to Literature.

As Sue was sketching a pair of elegant horseshow riding trousers and a monocle on the figure of the hero, an Idaho cowboy, she heard a low sound, several times repeated. She went quickly to the bedside.

Johnsy's eyes were open wide. She was looking out the window and counting—counting backward.

"Twelve," she said, and a little later "eleven"; and then "ten," and "nine"; and then "eight" and "seven," almost together.

Sue looked solicitously out of the window. What was there to count? There was only a bare, dreary yard to be seen, and the blank side of the brick house twenty feet away. An old, old ivy vine, gnarled and decayed at the roots, climbed half way up the brick wall. The cold breath of autumn had stricken its leaves from the vine until its skeleton branches clung, almost bare, to the crumbling bricks.

"What is it, dear?" asked Sue.

"Six," said Johnsy, in almost a whisper. "They're falling faster now. Three days ago there were almost a hundred. It made my head ache to count them. But now it's easy. There goes another one. There are only five left now."

"Five what, dear? Tell your Sudie."

"Leaves. On the ivy vine. When the last one falls I must go, too. I've known that for three days. Didn't the doctor tell you?"

"Oh, I never heard of such nonsense," complained Sue, with magnificent scorn. "What have old ivy leaves to do with your getting well? And you used to love that vine so, you naughty girl. Don't be a goosey. Why, the doctor told me this morning that your chances for getting well real soon were— let's see exactly what he said—he said the chances were ten to one! Why, that's almost as good a chance as we have in

New York when we ride on the street cars or walk past a new building. Try to take some broth now, and let Sudie go back to her drawing, so she can sell the editor man with it, and buy port wine for her sick child, and pork chops for her greedy self."

"You needn't get any more wine," said Johnsy, keeping her eyes fixed out the window. "There goes another. No, I don't want any broth. That leaves just four. I want to see the last one fall before it gets dark. Then I'll go, too."

"Johnsy, dear," said Sue, bending over her, "will you promise me to keep your eyes closed, and not look out the window until I am done working? I must hand those drawings in by to-morrow. I need the light, or I would draw the shade down."

"Couldn't you draw in the other room?" asked Johnsy, coldly.

"I'd rather be here by you," said Sue. "Besides, I don't want you to keep looking at those silly ivy leaves."

"Tell me as soon as you have finished," said Johnsy, closing her eyes, and lying white and still as a fallen statue, "because I want to see the last one fall. I'm tired of waiting. I'm tired of thinking. I want to turn loose my hold on everything, and go sailing down, down, just like one of those poor, tired leaves."

"Try to sleep," said Sue. "I must call Behrman up to be my model for the old hermit miner. I'll not be gone a minute. Don't try to move 'til I come back."

Old Behrman was a painter who lived on the ground floor beneath them. He was past sixty and had a Michael Angelo's Moses beard curling down from the head of a satyr along the body of an imp. Behrman was a failure in art. Forty years he had wielded the brush without getting near enough to touch the hem of his Mistress's robe. He had been always about to paint a masterpiece, but had never yet begun it. For several years he had painted nothing except now and then a daub in the line of commerce or advertising. He earned a little by serving as a model to those young artists in the colony who could not pay the price of a professional. He drank gin to excess, and still talked of his coming masterpiece. For the rest he was a fierce little old man, who scoffed terribly at softness in any one, and who regarded himself as especial mastiff-in-waiting to protect the two young artists in the studio above.

Sue found Behrman smelling strongly of juniper berries in his dimly lighted den below. In one corner was a blank canvas on an easel that had been waiting there for twenty-five years to receive the first line of the masterpiece. She told him of Johnsy's fancy, and how she feared she would, indeed, light and fragile as a leaf herself, float away, when her slight hold upon the world grew weaker.

Old Behrman, with his red eyes plainly streaming, shouted his contempt and derision for such idiotic imaginings.

"Vass!" he cried. "Is dere people in de world mit der foolishness to die because leafs dey drop off from a confounded vine? I haf not heard of such a thing. No, I will not bose as a model for your fool hermit-dunderhead. Vy do you allow dot silly pusiness to come in der brain of her? Ach, dot poor leetle Miss Yohnsy."

"She is very ill and weak," said Sue, "and the fever has left her mind morbid and full of strange fancies. Very well, Mr. Behrman, if you do not care to pose for me, you needn't. But I think you are a horrid old—old flibbertigibbet."

"You are just like a woman!" yelled Behrman. "Who said I will not bose? Go on. I come mit you. For half an hour I haf peen trying to say dot I am ready to bose. Gott! dis is not any blace in which one so goot as Miss Yohnsy shall lie sick. Some day I vill baint a masterpiece, and ve shall all go away. Gott! yes."

Johnsy was sleeping when they went upstairs. Sue pulled the shade down to the window-sill, and motioned Behrman into the other room. In there they peered out the window fearfully at the ivy vine. Then they looked at each other for a moment without speaking. A persistent, cold rain was falling, mingled with snow. Behrman, in his old blue shirt, took his seat as the hermit miner on an upturned kettle for a rock.

When Sue awoke from an hour's sleep the next morning she found Johnsy with dull, wide-open eyes staring at the drawn green shade.

"Pull it up; I want to see," she ordered, in a whisper.

Wearily Sue obeyed.

But, lo! after the beating rain and fierce gusts of wind that had endured through the livelong night, there yet stood out against the brick wall one ivy leaf. It was the last on the vine. Still dark green near its stem, but with its serrated edges tinted with the yellow of dissolution and decay, it hung bravely from a branch some twenty feet above the ground.

"It is the last one," said Johnsy. "I thought it would surely fall during the night. I heard the wind. It will fall to-day, and I shall die at the same time."

"Dear, dear!" said Sue, leaning her worn face down to the pillow, "think of me, if you won't think of yourself. What would I do?"

But Johnsy did not answer. The lonesomest thing in all the world is a soul when it is making ready to go on its mysterious, far journey. The fancy seemed to possess her more strongly as one by one the ties that bound her to friendship and to earth were loosed.

The day wore away, and even through the twilight they could see the lone ivy leaf clinging to its stem against the wall. And then, with the coming of the night the north wind was again loosed, while the rain still beat against the windows and pattered down from the low Dutch eaves.

When it was light enough Johnsy, the merciless, commanded that the shade be raised.

The ivy leaf was still there.

Johnsy lay for a long time looking at it. And then she called to Sue, who was stirring her chicken broth over the gas stove.

"I've been a bad girl, Sudie," said Johnsy. "Something has made that last leaf stay there to show me how wicked I was. It is a sin to want to die. You may bring me a little broth now, and some milk with a little port in it, and—no; bring me a hand-mirror first, and then pack some pillows about me, and I will sit up and watch you cook."

An hour later she said:

"Sudie, some day I hope to paint the Bay of Naples."

The doctor came in the afternoon, and Sue had an excuse to go into the hallway as he left.

"Even chances," said the doctor, taking Sue's thin, shaking hand in his. "With good nursing you'll win. And now I must see another case I have downstairs. Behrman, his name is— some kind of an artist, I believe. Pneumonia, too. He is an old, weak man, and the attack is acute. There is no hope for him; but he goes to the hospital to-day to be made more comfortable."

The next day the doctor said to Sue: "She's out of danger. You've won. Nutrition and care now—that's all."

And that afternoon Sue came to the bed where Johnsy lay, contentedly knitting a very blue and very useless woollen shoulder scarf, and put one arm around her, pillows and all.

"I have something to tell you, white mouse," she said. "Mr. Behrman died of pneumonia to-day in the hospital. He was ill only two days. The janitor found him on the morning of the first day in his room downstairs helpless with pain. His shoes and clothing were wet through and icy cold. They couldn't imagine where he had been on such a dreadful night. And then they found a lantern, still lighted, and a ladder that had been dragged from its place, and some scattered brushes, and a palette with green and yellow colors mixed on it, and

—look out the window, dear, at the last ivy leaf on the wall.
Didn't you wonder why it never fluttered or moved when
the wind blew? Ah, darling, it's Behrman's masterpiece—he
painted it there the night that the last leaf fell."

The Count and the Wedding Guest

ONE EVENING when Andy Donovan went to dinner at his Second Avenue boarding-house, Mrs. Scott introduced him to a
new boarder, a young lady, Miss Conway. Miss Conway was
small and unobtrusive. She wore a plain, snuffy-brown dress,
and bestowed her interest, which seemed languid, upon her
plate. She lifted her diffident eyelids and shot one perspicu-
ous, judicial glance at Mr. Donovan, politely murmured his
name, and returned to her mutton. Mr. Donovan bowed with
the grace and beaming smile that were rapidly winning for
him social, business and political advancement, and erased
the snuffy-brown one from the tablets of his consideration.

Two weeks later Andy was sitting on the front steps enjoying his cigar. There was a soft rustle behind and above him
and Andy turned his head—and had his head turned.

Just coming out of the door was Miss Conway. She wore
a night-black dress of *crêpe de—crêpe de—*oh, this thin black
goods. Her hat was black, and from it drooped and fluttered
an ebon veil, filmy as a spider's web. She stood on the top
step and drew on black silk gloves. Not a speck of white or
a spot of color about her dress anywhere. Her rich golden hair
was drawn, with scarcely a ripple, into a shining, smooth knot
low on her neck. Her face was plain rather than pretty, but
it was now illuminated and made almost beautiful by her
large gray eyes that gazed above the houses across the street

into the sky with an expression of the most appealing sadness and melancholy.

Gather the idea, girls—all black, you know, with the preference for *crêpe de*—oh, *crêpe de Chine*—that's it. All black, and that sad, faraway look, and the hair shining under the black veil (you have to be a blonde, of course), and try to look as if, although your young life had been blighted just as it was about to give a hop-skip-and-a-jump over the threshold of life, a walk in the park might do you good, and be sure to happen out the door at the right moment, and—oh, it'll fetch 'em every time. But it's fierce, now, how cynical I am, ain't it?—to talk about mourning costumes this way.

Mr. Donovan suddenly reinscribed Miss Conway upon the tablets of his consideration. He threw away the remaining inch and a quarter of his cigar, that would have been good for eight minutes yet, and quickly shifted his center of gravity to his low-cut patent leathers.

"It's a fine, clear evening, Miss Conway," he said; and if the Weather Bureau could have heard the confident emphasis of his tones it would have hoisted the square white signal, and nailed it to the mast.

"To them that has the heart to enjoy it, it is, Mr. Donovan," said Miss Conway, with a sigh.

Mr. Donovan, in his heart, cursed fair weather. Heartless weather! It should hail and blow and snow to be consonant with the mood of Miss Conway.

"I hope none of your relatives—I hope you haven't sustained a loss?" ventured Mr. Donovan.

"Death has claimed," said Miss Conway, hesitating—"not a relative, but one who—but I will not intrude my grief upon you, Mr. Donovan."

"Intrude?" protested Mr. Donovan. "Why, say, Miss Conway, I'd be delighted, that is, I'd be sorry—I mean I'm sure nobody could sympathize with you truer than I would."

Miss Conway smiled a little smile. And oh, it was sadder than her expression in repose.

"'Laugh, and the world laughs with you; weep, and they give you the laugh,'" she quoted. "I have learned that, Mr. Donovan. I have no friends or acquaintances in this city. But you have been kind to me. I appreciate it highly."

He had passed her the pepper twice at the table.

"It's tough to be alone in New York—that's a cinch," said Mr. Donovan. "But, say—whenever this little old town does loosen up and get friendly it goes the limit. Say you took a little stroll in the park, Miss Conway—don't you think it might chase away some of your mullygrubs? And if you'd allow me——"

"Thanks, Mr. Donovan. I'd be pleased to accept of your escort if you think the company of one whose heart is filled with gloom could be anyways agreeable to you."

Through the open gates of the iron-railed, old, downtown park, where the elect once took the air, they strolled, and found a quiet bench.

There is this difference between the grief of youth and that of old age; youth's burden is lightened by as much of it as another shares; old age may give and give, but the sorrow remains the same.

"He was my fiancé," confided Miss Conway, at the end of an hour. "We were going to be married next spring. I don't want you to think that I am stringing you, Mr. Donovan, but he was a real Count. He had an estate and a castle in Italy. Count Fernando Mazzini was his name. I never saw the beat of him for elegance. Papa objected, of course, and once we eloped, but Papa overtook us, and took us back. I thought sure Papa and Fernando would fight a duel. Papa has a livery business—in P'kipsee, you know.

"Finally, Papa came 'round, all right, and said we might be married next spring. Fernando showed him proofs of his title and wealth, and then went over to Italy to get the castle fixed up for us. Papa's very proud and, when Fernando wanted to give me several thousand dollars for my trousseau he called him down something awful. He wouldn't even let me take a ring or any presents from him. And when Fernando sailed I came to the city and got a position as cashier in a candy store.

"Three days ago I got a letter from Italy, forwarded from P'kipsee, saying that Fernando had been killed in a gondola accident.

"That is why I am in mourning. My heart, Mr. Donovan, will remain forever in his grave. I guess I am poor company, Mr. Donovan, but I cannot take any interest in no one. I should not care to keep you from gayety and your friends who can smile and entertain you. Perhaps you would prefer to walk back to the house?"

Now, girls, if you want to observe a young man hustle out after a pick and shovel, just tell him that your heart is in some other fellow's grave. Young men are grave-robbers by nature. Ask any widow. Something must be done to restore that missing organ to weeping angels in *crêpe de Chine*. Dead men certainly get the worst of it from all sides.

"I'm awful sorry," said Mr. Donovan, gently. "No, we won't walk back to the house just yet. And don't say you haven't no friends in this city, Miss Conway. I'm awful sorry, and I want you to believe I'm your friend, and that I'm awful sorry."

"I've got his picture here in my locket," said Miss Conway, after wiping her eyes with her handkerchief. "I never showed it to anybody; but I will to you, Mr. Donovan, because I believe you to be a true friend."

Mr. Donovan gazed long and with much interest at the photograph in the locket that Miss Conway opened for him. The face of Count Mazzini was one to command interest. It was a smooth, intelligent, bright, almost a handsome face—

the face of a strong, cheerful man who might well be a leader among his fellows.

"I have a larger one, framed, in my room," said Miss Conway. "When we return I will show you that. They are all I have to remind me of Fernando. But he ever will be present in my heart, that's a sure thing."

A subtle task confronted Mr. Donovan—that of supplanting the unfortunate Count in the heart of Miss Conway. This his admiration for her determined him to do. But the magnitude of the undertaking did not seem to weigh upon his spirits. The sympathetic but cheerful friend was the rôle he essayed; and he played it so successfully that the next half-hour found them conversing pensively across two plates of ice-cream, though yet there was no diminution of the sadness in Miss Conway's large gray eyes.

Before they parted in the hall that evening she ran upstairs and brought down the framed photograph wrapped lovingly in a white silk scarf. Mr. Donovan surveyed it with inscrutable eyes.

"He gave me this the night he left for Italy," said Miss Conway. "I had the one for the locket made from this."

"A fine-looking man," said Mr. Donovan, heartily. "How would it suit you, Miss Conway, to give me the pleasure of your company to Coney next Sunday afternoon?"

A month later they announced their engagement to Mrs. Scott and the other boarders. Miss Conway continued to wear black.

A week after the announcement the two sat on the same bench in the downtown park, while the fluttering leaves of the trees made a dim kinetoscopic picture of them in the moonlight. But Donovan had worn a look of abstracted gloom all day. He was so silent to-night that love's lips could not keep back any longer the question that love's heart propounded.

"What's the matter, Andy, you are so solemn and grouchy to-night?"

"Nothing, Maggie."

"I know better. Can't I tell? You never acted this way before. What is it?"

"It's nothing much, Maggie."

"Yes it is; and I want to know. I'll bet it's some other girl you are thinking about. All right. Why don't you go get her if you want her? Take your arm away, if you please."

"I'll tell you then," said Andy, wisely, "but I guess you won't understand it exactly. You've heard of Mike Sullivan, haven't you? 'Big Mike' Sullivan, everybody calls him."

"No, I haven't," said Maggie. "And I don't want to, if he makes you act like this. Who is he?"

"He's the biggest man in New York," said Andy, almost reverently. "He can about do anything he wants to with Tammany or any other old thing in the political line. He's a mile high and as broad as East River. You say anything against Big Mike, and you'll have a million men on your collarbone in about two seconds. Why, he made a visit over to the old country awhile back, and the kings took to their holes like rabbits.

"Well, Big Mike's a friend of mine. I ain't more than deuce-high in the district as far as influence goes, but Mike's as good a friend to a little man, or a poor man as he is to a big one. I met him to-day on the Bowery, and what do you think he does? Comes up and shakes hands. 'Andy,' says he, 'I've been keeping cases on you. You've been putting in some good licks over on your side of the street, and I'm proud of you. What'll you take to drink?' He takes a cigar and I take a highball. I told him I was going to get married in two weeks. 'Andy,' says he, 'send me an invitation, so I'll keep in mind of it, and I'll come to the wedding.' That's what Big Mike says to me; and he always does what he says.

"You don't understand it, Maggie, but I'd have one of my hands cut off to have Big Mike Sullivan at our wedding. It would be the proudest day of my life. When he goes to a man's wedding, there's a guy being married that's made for life. Now, that's why I'm maybe looking sore to-night."

"Why don't you invite him, then, if he's so much to the mustard?" said Maggie, lightly.

"There's a reason why I can't," said Andy, sadly. "There's a reason why he mustn't be there. Don't ask me what it is, for I can't tell you."

"Oh, I don't care," said Maggie. "It's something about politics, of course. But it's no reason why you can't smile at me."

"Maggie," said Andy, presently, "do you think as much of me as you did of your—as you did of the Count Mazzini?"

He waited a long time, but Maggie did not reply. And then, suddenly she leaned against his shoulder and began to cry— to cry and shake with sobs, holding his arm tightly, and wetting the *crêpe de Chine* with tears.

"There, there, there!" soothed Andy, putting aside his own trouble. "And what is it, now?"

"Andy," sobbed Maggie, "I've lied to you, and you'll never marry me, or love me any more. But I feel that I've got to tell. Andy, there never was so much as the little finger of a count. I never had a beau in my life. But all the other girls had; and they talked about 'em; and that seemed to make the fellows like 'em more. And, Andy, I look swell in black—you know I do. So I went out to a photograph store and bought that picture, and had a little one made for my locket, and made up all that story about the Count and about his being killed, so I could wear black. And nobody can love a liar, and you'll shake me, Andy, and I'll die for shame. Oh, there never was anybody I liked but you—and that's all."

But instead of being pushed away, she found Andy's arm

folding her closer. She looked up and saw his face cleared and smiling.

"Could you—could you forgive me, Andy?"

"Sure," said Andy. "It's all right about that. Back to the cemetery for the Count. You've straightened everything out, Maggie. I was in hopes you would before the wedding-day. Bully girl!"

"Andy," said Maggie, with a somewhat shy smile, after she had been thoroughly assured of forgiveness, "did you believe all that story about the Count?"

"Well, not to any large extent," said Andy, reaching for his cigar case; "because it's Big Mike Sullivan's picture you've got in that locket of yours."

A Municipal Report

The cities are full of pride,
Challenging each to each—
This from her mountainside,
That from her burthened beach.
             R. KIPLING.

Fancy a novel about Chicago or Buffalo, let us say, of Nashville, Tennessee! There are just three big cities in the United States that are "story cities"—New York, of course, New Orleans, and, best of the lot, San Francisco.—FRANK NORRIS.

EAST is East, and West is San Francisco, according to Californians. Californians are a race of people; they are not merely inhabitants of a State. They are the Southerners of the West. Now, Chicagoans are no less loyal to their city; but when you ask them why, they stammer and speak of lake fish and the new Odd Fellows Building. But Californians go into detail.

Of course they have, in the climate, an argument that is good for half an hour while you are thinking of your coal bills and heavy underwear. But as soon as they come to mistake your silence for conviction, madness comes upon them, and they picture the city of the Golden Gate as the Bagdad of the New World. So far, as a matter of opinion, no refutation is necessary. But dear cousins all (from Adam and Eve descended), it is a rash one who will lay his finger on the map and say: "In this town there can be no romance—what could happen here?" Yes, it is a bold and a rash deed to challenge in one sentence, history, romance, and Rand and Mc-Nally.

NASHVILLE.—A city, port of delivery, and the capital of the State of Tennessee, is on the Cumberland River and on the N. C. & St. L. and the L. & N. railroads. This city is regarded as the most important educational centre in the South.

I stepped off the train at 8 P.M. Having searched the thesaurus in vain for adjectives, I must, as a substitution, hie me to comparison in the form of a recipe.

Take of London fog 30 parts; malaria 10 parts; gas leaks 20 parts; dewdrops gathered in a brick yard at sunrise, 25 parts; odor of honeysuckle 15 parts. Mix.

The mixture will give you an approximate conception of a Nashville drizzle. It is not so fragrant as a moth-ball nor as thick as pea-soup; but 'tis enough—'twill serve.

I went to a hotel in a tumbril. It required strong self-suppression for me to keep from climbing to the top of it and giving an imitation of Sidney Carton. The vehicle was drawn by beasts of a bygone era and driven by something dark and emancipated.

I was sleepy and tired, so when I got to the hotel I hurriedly paid it the fifty cents it demanded (with approximate lagniappe, I assure you). I knew its habits; and I did not want to hear it prate about its old "marster" or anything that happened "befo' de wah."

The hotel was one of the kind described as "renovated." That means $20,000 worth of new marble pillars, tiling, electric lights and brass cuspidors in the lobby, and a new L. & N. time table and a lithograph of Lookout Mountain in each one of the great rooms above. The management was without reproach, the attention full of exquisite Southern courtesy, the service as slow as the progress of a snail and as good-humored as Rip Van Winkle. The food was worth traveling a thousand miles for. There is no other hotel in the world where you can get such chicken livers *en brochette*.

At dinner I asked a Negro waiter if there was anything doing in town. He pondered gravely for a minute, and then replied: "Well, boss, I don't really reckon there's anything at all doin' after sundown."

Sundown had been accomplished; it had been drowned in the drizzle long before. So that spectacle was denied me. But I went forth upon the streets in the drizzle to see what might be there.

It is built on undulating grounds; and the streets are lighted by electricity at a cost of $32,470 per annum.

As I left the hotel there was a race riot. Down upon me charged a company of freedmen, or Arabs, or Zulus, armed with—no, I saw with relief that they were not rifles, but whips. And I saw dimly a caravan of black, clumsy vehicles; and at the reassuring shouts, "Kyar you anywhere in the town, boss, fuh fifty cents," I reasoned that I was merely a "fare" instead of a victim.

I walked through long streets, all leading uphill. I wondered how those streets ever came down again. Perhaps they didn't until they were "graded." On a few of the "main streets" I saw lights in stores here and there; saw street cars go by conveying worthy burghers hither and yon; saw people pass engaged in the art of conversation, and heard a burst of semi-lively laughter issuing from a soda-water and ice-cream parlor. The streets other than "main" seemed to have enticed upon their borders houses consecrated to peace and domesticity. In many of them lights shone behind discreetly drawn window shades, in a few pianos tinkled orderly and irreproachable music. There was, indeed, little "doing." I wished I had come before sundown. So I returned to my hotel.

In November, 1864, the Confederate General Hood advanced against Nashville, where he shut up a National force under General Thomas. The latter then sallied forth and defeated the Confederates in a terrible conflict.

All my life I have heard of, admired, and witnessed the fine marksmanship of the South in its peaceful conflicts in the tobacco-chewing regions. But in my hotel a surprise awaited me. There were twelve bright, new, imposing, capacious brass cuspidors in the great lobby, tall enough to be called urns and so wide-mouthed that the crack pitcher of a lady baseball team should have been able to throw a ball into one of them at five paces distant. But, although a terrible battle had raged and was still raging, the enemy had not suffered. Bright, new, imposing, capacious, untouched, they stood. But, shades of Jefferson Brick! the tile floor—the beautiful tile floor! I could not avoid thinking of the battle of Nashville, and trying to draw, as is my foolish habit, some deductions about hereditary marksmanship.

Here I first saw Major (by misplaced courtesy) Wentworth Caswell. I knew him for a type the moment my eyes suffered from the sight of him. A rat has no geographical habitat. My old friend, A. Tennyson, said, as he so well said almost everything:

Prophet, curse me the blabbing lip,
And curse me the British vermin, the rat.

Let us regard the word "British" as interchangeable *ad lib.* A rat is a rat.

This man was hunting about the hotel lobby like a starved dog that had forgotten where he had buried a bone. He had a face of great acreage, red, pulpy, and with a kind of sleepy massiveness like that of Buddha. He possessed one single virtue—he was very smoothly shaven. The mark of the beast is not indelible upon a man until he goes about with a stubble. I think that if he had not used his razor that day I would have repulsed his advances, and the criminal calendar of the world would have been spared the addition of one murder.

I happened to be standing within five feet of a cuspidor when Major Caswell opened fire upon it. I had been observant enough to perceive that the attacking force was using Gatlings instead of squirrel rifles, so I sidestepped so promptly that the major seized the opportunity to apologize to a noncombatant. He had the blabbing lip. In four minutes he had become my friend and had dragged me to the bar.

I desire to interpolate here that I am a Southerner. But I am not one by profession or trade. I eschew the string tie, the slouch hat, the Prince Albert, the number of bales of cotton destroyed by Sherman, and plug chewing. When the orchestra plays "Dixie" I do not cheer. I slide a little lower on the leather-cornered seat and, well, order another Würzburger and wish that Longstreet had—but what's the use?

Major Caswell banged the bar with his fist, and the first gun at Fort Sumter re-echoed. When he fired the last one at Appomattox I began to hope. But then he began on family trees, and demonstrated that Adam was only a third cousin of a collateral branch of the Caswell family. Genealogy disposed of, he took up, to my distaste, his private family matters. He spoke of his wife, traced her descent back to Eve, and profanely denied any possible rumor that she may have had relations in the land of Nod.

By this time I began to suspect that he was trying to obscure by noise the fact that he had ordered the drinks, on the chance that I would be bewildered into paying for them. But when they were down he crashed a silver dollar loudly upon the bar. Then, of course, another serving was obligatory. And when I had paid for that I took leave of him brusquely; for I wanted no more of him. But before I had obtained my release he had prated loudly of an income that his wife received, and showed a handful of silver money.

When I got my key at the desk the clerk said to me courteously: "If that man Caswell has annoyed you, and if you would like to make a complaint, we will have him ejected. He is a nuisance, a loafer, and without any known means of support, although he seems to have some money most the time. But we don't seem to be able to hit upon any means of throwing him out legally."

"Why, no," said I, after some reflection; "I don't see my way clear to making a complaint. But I would like to place myself on record as asserting that I do not care for his company. Your town," I continued, "seems to be a quiet one. What manner of entertainment, adventure, or excitement, have you to offer to the stranger within your gates?"

"Well, sir," said the clerk, "there will be a show here next Thursday. It is—I'll look it up and have the announcement sent up to your room with the ice water. Good-night."

After I went up to my room I looked out the window. It was only about ten o'clock, but I looked upon a silent town. The drizzle continued, spangled with dim lights, as far apart as currants in a cake sold at the Ladies' Exchange.

"A quiet place," I said to myself, as my first shoe struck the ceiling of the occupant of the room beneath mine. "Nothing of the life here that gives color and good variety to the cities in the East and West. Just a good, ordinary, hum-drum, business town."

Nashville occupies a foremost place among the manufacturing centres of the country. It is the fifth boot and shoe market in the United States, the largest candy and cracker manufacturing city in the South, and does an enormous wholesale dry-goods, grocery, and drug business.

I must tell you how I came to be in Nashville, and I assure you the digression brings as much tedium to me as it does to you. I was traveling elsewhere on my own business, but I had a commission from a Northern literary magazine to stop over there and establish a personal connection between the publication and one of its contributors, Azalea Adair.

Adair (there was no clue to the personality except the handwriting) had sent in some essays (lost art!) and poems that had made the editors swear approvingly over their one o'clock luncheon. So they had commissioned me to round up said Adair and corner by contract his or her output at two cents a word before some other publisher offered her ten or twenty.

At nine o'clock the next morning, after my chicken livers *en brochette* (try them if you can find that hotel), I strayed out into the drizzle, which was still on for an unlimited run. At the first corner I came upon Uncle Cæsar. He was a stalwart Negro, older than the pyramids, with gray wool and a face that reminded me of Brutus, and a second afterwards of the late King Cettiwayo. He wore the most remarkable coat that I ever had seen or expect to see. It reached to his ankles and had once been a Confederate gray in color. But rain and sun and age had so variegated it that Joseph's coat, beside it, would have faded to a pale monochrome. I must linger with that coat, for it has to do with the story—the story that is so long in coming, because you can hardly expect anything to happen in Nashville.

Once it must have been the military coat of an officer. The cape of it had vanished, but all adown its front it had been frogged and tasseled magnificently. But now the frogs and tassels were gone. In their stead had been patiently stitched (I surmised by some surviving "black mammy") new frogs made of cunningly twisted common hempen twine. This twine was frayed and disheveled. It must have been added to the coat as a substitute for vanished splendors, with tasteless but painstaking devotion, for it followed faithfully the curves of the long-missing frogs. And, to complete the comedy and pathos of the garment, all its buttons were gone save one. The second button from the top alone remained. The coat was fastened by other twine strings tied through the buttonholes and other holes rudely pierced in the opposite side. There was never such a weird garment so fantastically bedecked and of so many mottled hues. The lone button was the size of a half-dollar, made of yellow horn and sewed on with coarse twine.

This Negro stood by a carriage so old that Ham himself might have started a hack line with it after he left the ark with the two animals hitched to it. As I approached he threw open the door, drew out a feather duster, waved it without using it, and said in deep, rumbling tones:

"Step right in, suh; ain't a speck of dust in it—jus' got back from a funeral, suh."

I inferred that on such gala occasions carriages were given an extra cleaning. I looked up and down the street and perceived that there was little choice among the vehicles for hire that lined the curb. I looked in my memorandum book for the address of Azalea Adair.

"I want to go to 861 Jessamine Street," I said, and was about to step into the hack. But for an instant the thick, long, gorilla-like arm of the Negro barred me. On his massive and saturnine face a look of sudden suspicion and enmity flashed for a moment. Then, with quickly returning conviction, he asked, blandishingly: "What are you gwine there for, boss?"

"What is that to you?" I asked, a little sharply.

"Nothin', suh, jus' nothin'. Only it's a lonesome kind of part of town and few folks ever has business out there. Step right in. The seats is clean—jes' got back from a funeral, suh."

A mile and a half it must have been to our journey's end. I could hear nothing but the fearful rattle of the ancient hack over the uneven brick paving; I could smell nothing but the drizzle, now further flavored with coal smoke and something like a mixture of tar and oleander blossoms. All I could see through the streaming windows were two rows of dim houses.

The city has an area of 10 square miles; 181 miles of streets, of which 137 miles are paved; a system of waterworks that cost $2,000,000, with 77 miles of mains.

Eight-sixty-one Jessamine Street was a decayed mansion. Thirty yards back from the street it stood, outmerged in a splendid grove of trees and untrimmed shrubbery. A row of box bushes overflowed and almost hid the paling fence from sight; the gate was kept closed by a rope noose that encircled the gate post and the first paling of the gate. But when you got inside you saw that 861 was a shell, a shadow, a ghost of former grandeur and excellence. But in the story, I have not yet got inside.

When the hack had ceased from rattling and the weary quadrupeds came to a rest I handed my jehu his fifty cents with an additional quarter, feeling a glow of conscious generosity as I did so. He refused it.

"It's two dollars, suh," he said.

"How's that?" I asked. "I plainly heard you call out at the hotel, 'Fifty cents to any part of the town.'"

"It's two dollars, suh," he repeated obstinately. "It's a long ways from the hotel."

"It is within the city limits and well within them," I argued. "Don't think that you have picked up a greenhorn Yankee. Do you see those hills over there?" I went on, pointing toward the east (I could not see them, myself, for the drizzle); "well, I was born and raised on their other side. You old fool nigger, can't you tell people from other people when you see 'em?"

The grim face of King Cettiwayo softened. "Is you from the South, suh? I reckon it was them shoes of yourn fooled me. They is somethin' sharp in the toes for a Southern gen'l'man to wear."

"Then the charge is fifty cents, I suppose?" said I, inexorably.

His former expression, a mingling of cupidity and hostility, returned, remained ten seconds, and vanished.

"Boss," he said, "fifty cents is right; but I *needs* two dollars, suh; I'm *obleeged* to have two dollars. I ain't *demandin'* it now, suh; after I knows whar you's from; I'm jus' sayin' that I *has* to have two dollars to-night and business is mighty po'."

Peace and confidence settled upon his heavy features. He had been luckier than he had hoped. Instead of having picked up a greenhorn, ignorant of rates, he had come upon an inheritance.

"You confounded old rascal," I said, reaching down to my pocket, "you ought to be turned over to the police."

For the first time I saw him smile. He knew; *he knew*; HE KNEW.

I gave him two one-dollar bills. As I handed them over I noticed that one of them had seen parlous times. Its upper right-hand corner was missing, and it had been torn through in the middle, but joined again. A strip of blue tissue paper, pasted over the split, preserved its negotiability.

Enough of the African bandit for the present: I left him happy, lifted the rope, and opened the creaky gate.

The house, as I said, was a shell. A paint brush had not touched it in twenty years. I could not see why a strong wind should not have bowled it over like a house of cards until I looked again at the trees that hugged it close—the trees that saw the battle of Nashville and still drew their protecting branches around it against storm and enemy and cold.

Azalea Adair, fifty years old, white-haired, a descendant of the cavaliers, as thin and frail as the house she lived in, robed in the cheapest and cleanest dress I ever saw, with an air as simple as a queen's, received me.

The reception room seemed a mile square, because there was nothing in it except some rows of books, on unpainted white-pine bookshelves, a cracked marble-topped table, a rag rug, a hairless horsehair sofa, and two or three chairs. Yes, there was a picture on the wall, a colored crayon drawing of a cluster of pansies. I looked around for the portrait of Andrew Jackson and the pine-cone hanging basket but they were not there.

Azalea Adair and I had conversation, a little of which will be repeated to you. She was a product of the old South, gently nurtured in the sheltered life. Her learning was not broad, but was deep and of splendid originality in its somewhat narrow scope. She had been educated at home, and her knowledge of the world was derived from inference and by inspiration. Of such is the precious, small group of essayists made. While she talked to me I kept brushing my fingers, trying, unconsciously, to rid them guiltily of the absent dust from the half-calf backs of Lamb, Chaucer, Hazlitt, Marcus Aurelius, Montaigne, and Hood. She was exquisite, she was a valuable discovery. Nearly everybody nowadays knows too much—oh, so much too much —of real life.

I could perceive clearly that Azalea Adair was very poor. A house and a dress she had, not much else, I fancied. So, divided between my duty to the magazine and my loyalty to the poets and essayists who fought Thomas in the valley of the Cumberland, I listened to her voice which was like a harpsichord's, and found that I could not speak of contracts. In the presence of the nine Muses and the three Graces one hesitated to lower the topic to two cents. There would have to be another colloquy after I had regained my commercialism. But I spoke of my mission, and three o'clock of the next afternoon was set for the discussion of the business proposition.

"Your town," I said, as I began to make ready to depart (which is the time for smooth generalities), "seems to be a quiet, sedate place. A home town, I should say, where few things out of the ordinary ever happen."

It carries on an extensive trade in stoves and hollow ware with the West and South, and its flouring mills have a daily capacity of more than 2,000 barrels.

Azalea Adair seemed to reflect.

"I have never thought of it that way," she said, with a kind of sincere intensity that seemed to belong to her. "Isn't it in the still, quiet places that things do happen? I fancy that when God began to create the earth on the first Monday morning one could have leaned out one's window and heard the drops of mud splashing from His trowel as He built up the everlasting hills. What did the noisiest project in the world —I mean the building of the tower of Babel—result in finally? A page and a half of Esperanto in the *North American Review.*"

"Of course," said I, platitudinously, "human nature is the same everywhere; but there is more color—er—more drama and movement and—er—romance in some cities than in others."

"On the surface," said Azalea Adair. "I have traveled many times around the world in a golden airship wafted on two wings—print and dreams. I have seen (on one of my imaginary tours) the Sultan of Turkey bowstring with his own hands one of his wives who had uncovered her face in public. I have seen a man in Nashville tear up his theatre tickets because his wife was going out with her face covered—with rice powder. In San Francisco's Chinatown I saw the slave girl Sing Yee dipped slowly, inch by inch, in boiling almond oil to make her swear she would never see her American lover again. She gave in when the boiling oil had reached three inches above her knee. At a euchre party in East Nashville the other night I saw Kitty Morgan cut dead by seven of her schoolmates and lifelong friends because she had married a house painter. The boiling oil was sizzling as high as her heart; but I wish you could have seen the fine little smile that she carried from table to table. Oh, yes, it is a hum-drum town. Just a few miles of red brick houses and mud and stores and lumber yards."

Some one had knocked hollowly at the back of the house. Azalea Adair breathed a soft apology and went to investigate the sound. She came back in three minutes with brightened eyes, a faint flush on her cheeks, and ten years lifted from her shoulders.

"You must have a cup of tea before you go," she said, "and a sugar cake."

She reached and shook a little iron bell. In shuffled a small Negro girl about twelve, barefoot, not very tidy, glowering at me with thumb in mouth and bulging eyes.

Azalea Adair opened a tiny, worn purse and drew out a dollar bill, a dollar bill with the upper right-hand corner missing, torn in two pieces and pasted together again with a strip of blue tissue paper. It was one of those bills I had given the piratical Negro—there was no doubt of it.

"Go up to Mr. Baker's store on the corner, Impy," she said, handing the girl the dollar bill, "and get a quarter of a pound of tea—the kind he always sends me—and ten cents' worth of sugar cakes. Now, hurry. The supply of tea in the house happens to be exhausted," she explained to me.

Impy left by the back way. Before the scrape of her hard, bare feet had died away on the back porch, a wild shriek—I was sure it was hers—filled the hollow house. Then the deep, gruff tones of an angry man's voice mingled with the girl's further squeals and unintelligible words.

Azalea Adair rose without surprise or emotion and disappeared. For two minutes I heard the hoarse rumble of the man's voice; then something like an oath and a slight scuffle, and she returned calmly to her chair.

"This is a roomy house," she said, "and I have a tenant for part of it. I am sorry to have to rescind my invitation to tea. It is impossible to get the kind I always use at the store. Perhaps to-morrow Mr. Baker will be able to supply me."

I was sure that Impy had not had time to leave the house. I inquired concerning street-car lines and took my leave. After I was well on my way I remembered that I had not learned Azalea Adair's name. But to-morrow would do.

That same day I started in on the course of iniquity that this uneventful city forced upon me. I was in the town only two days, but in that time I managed to lie shamelessly by telegraph, and to be an accomplice—after the fact, if that is the correct legal term—to a murder.

As I rounded the corner nearest my hotel the Afrite coachman of the polychromatic, nonpareil coat seized me, swung open the dungeony door of his peripatetic sarcophagus, flirted his feather duster and began his ritual: "Step right in, boss.

Carriage is clean—jus' got back from a funeral. Fifty cents to any——"

And then he knew me and grinned broadly. " 'Scuse me, boss; you is de gen'l'man what rid out with me dis mawnin'. Thank you kindly, suh."

"I am going out to 861 again to-morrow afternoon at three," said I, "and if you will be here, I'll let you drive me. So you know Miss Adair?" I concluded, thinking of my dollar bill.

"I belonged to her father, Judge Adair, suh," he replied.

"I judge that she is pretty poor," I said. "She hasn't much money to speak of, has she?"

For an instant I looked again at the fierce countenance of King Cettiwayo, and then he changed back to an extortionate old Negro hack driver.

"She ain't gwine to starve, suh," he said, slowly. "She has reso'ces, suh; she has reso'ces."

"I shall pay you fifty cents for the trip," said I.

"Dat is puffeckly correct, suh," he answered, humbly. "I jus' *had* to have dat two dollars dis mawnin', boss."

I went to the hotel and lied by electricity. I wired the magazine: "A. Adair holds out for eight cents a word."

The answer that came back was: "Give it to her quick, you duffer."

Just before dinner "Major" Wentworth Caswell bore down upon me with the greetings of a long-lost friend. I have seen few men whom I have so instantaneously hated, and of whom it was so difficult to be rid. I was standing at the bar when he invaded me; therefore I could not wave the white ribbon in his face. I would have paid gladly for the drinks, hoping thereby, to escape another; but he was one of those despicable, roaring, advertising bibbers who must have brass bands and fireworks attend upon every cent that they waste in their follies.

With an air of producing millions he drew two one-dollar

bills from a pocket and dashed one of them upon the bar. I looked once more at the dollar bill with the upper righthand corner missing, torn through the middle, and patched with a strip of blue tissue paper. It was my dollar again. It could have been no other.

I went up to my room. The drizzle and the monotony of a dreary, eventless Southern town had made me tired and listless. I remember that just before I went to bed I mentally disposed of the mysterious dollar bill (which might have formed the clue to a tremendously fine detective story of San Francisco) by saying to myself sleepily: "Seems as if a lot of people here own stock in the Hack-Drivers' Trust. Pays dividends promptly, too. Wonder if——" Then I fell asleep.

King Cettiwayo was at his post the next day, and rattled my bones over the stones out to 861. He was to wait and rattle me back again when I was ready.

Azalea Adair looked paler and cleaner and frailer than she had looked on the day before. After she had signed the contract at eight cents per word she grew still paler and began to slip out of her chair. Without much trouble I managed to get her up on the antediluvian horsehair sofa and then I ran out to the sidewalk and yelled to the coffee-colored Pirate to bring a doctor. With a wisdom that I had not suspected in him, he abandoned his team and struck off up the street afoot, realizing the value of speed. In ten minutes he returned with a grave, gray-haired, and capable man of medicine. In a few words (worth much less than eight cents each) I explained to him my presence in the hollow house of mystery. He bowed with stately understanding, and turned to the old Negro.

"Uncle Cæsar," he said, calmly, "run up to my house and ask Miss Lucy to give you a cream pitcher full of fresh milk and half a tumbler of port wine. And hurry back. Don't drive —run. I want you to get back sometime this week."

It occurred to me that Dr. Merriman also felt a distrust as to the speeding powers of the land-pirate's steeds. After Uncle Cæsar was gone, lumberingly, but swiftly, up the street, the doctor looked me over with great politeness and as much careful calculation until he had decided that I might do.

"It is only a case of insufficient nutrition," he said. "In other words, the result of poverty, pride, and starvation. Mrs. Caswell has many devoted friends who would be glad to aid her, but she will accept nothing except from that old Negro, Uncle Cæsar, who was once owned by her family."

"Mrs. Caswell!" said I, in surprise. And then I looked at the contract and saw that she had signed it "Azalea Adair Caswell."

"I thought she was Miss Adair," I said.

"Married to a drunken, worthless loafer, sir," said the doctor. "It is said that he robs her even of the small sums that her old servant contributes toward her support."

When the milk and wine had been brought the doctor soon revived Azalea Adair. She sat up and talked of the beauty of the autumn leaves that were then in season and their height of color. She referred lightly to her fainting seizure as the outcome of an old palpitation of the heart. Impy fanned her as she lay on the sofa. The doctor was due elsewhere, and I followed him to the door. I told him that it was within my power and intentions to make a reasonable advance of money to Azalea Adair on future contributions to the magazine, and he seemed pleased.

"By the way," he said, "perhaps you would like to know that you have had royalty for a coachman. Old Cæsar's grandfather was a king in Congo. Cæsar himself has royal ways, as you may have observed."

As the doctor was moving off I heard Uncle Cæsar's voice inside: "Did he git bofe of dem two dollars from you, Mis' Zalea?"

"Yes, Cæsar," I heard Azalea Adair answer, weakly. And then I went in and concluded business negotiations with our contributor. I assumed the responsibility of advancing fifty dollars, putting it as a necessary formality in binding our bargain. And then Uncle Cæsar drove me back to the hotel.

Here ends all of the story as far as I can testify as a witness. The rest must be only bare statements of facts.

At about six o'clock I went out for a stroll. Uncle Cæsar was at his corner. He threw open the door of his carriage, flourished his duster, and began his depressing formula: "Step right in, suh. Fifty cents to anywhere in the city—hack's puffickly clean, suh—jus' got back from a funeral——"

And then he recognized me. I think his eyesight was getting bad. His coat had taken on a few more faded shades of color, the twine strings were more frayed and ragged, the last remaining button—the button of yellow horn—was gone. A motley descendant of kings was Uncle Cæsar!

About two hours later I saw an excited crowd besieging the front of the drug store. In a desert where nothing happens this was manna; so I wedged my way inside. On an extemporized couch of empty boxes and chairs was stretched the mortal corporeality of Major Wentworth Caswell. A doctor was testing him for the mortal ingredient. His decision was that it was conspicuous by its absence.

The erstwhile Major had been found dead on a dark street and brought by curious and ennuied citizens to the drug store. The late human being had been engaged in terrific battle—the details showed that. Loafer and reprobate though he had been, he had been also a warrior. But he had lost. His hands were yet clinched so tightly that his fingers would not be opened. The gentle citizens who had known him stood about and searched their vocabularies to find some good words, if it were possible, to speak of him. One kind-looking man said, after much thought: "When 'Cas' was about fo'teen he was one of the best spellers in the school."

While I stood there the fingers of the right hand of "the man that was," which hung down the side of a white pine box, relaxed, and dropped something at my feet. I covered it with one foot quietly, and a little later on I picked it up and pocketed it. I reasoned that in his last struggle his hand must have seized that object unwittingly and held it in a death grip.

At the hotel that night the main topic of conversation, with the possible exceptions of politics and prohibition, was the demise of Major Caswell. I heard one man say to a group of listeners:

"In my opinion, gentlemen, Caswell was murdered by some of these no-account niggers for his money. He had fifty dollars this afternoon which he showed to several gentlemen in the hotel. When he was found the money was not on his person."

I left the city the next morning at nine, and as the train was crossing the bridge over the Cumberland River I took out of my pocket a yellow horn overcoat button the size of a fifty-cent piece, with frayed ends of coarse twine hanging from it, and cast it out of the window into the slow, muddy waters below.

I wonder what's doing in Buffalo!